In an Enemy's Country

Jim Fraiser

In an Enemy's Country
Copyright © 2020 by Jim Fraiser

Cover art by Janie Charbonnet

All rights reserved. No part of this publication may be reproduced, distributed, or transmitted in any form or by any means, including photocopying, recording, or other electronic or mechanical methods, without the prior written permission of the publisher or author, except in the case of brief quotations embodied in critical reviews and certain other noncommercial uses permitted by copyright law.

Although every precaution has been taken to verify the accuracy of the information contained herein, the author and publisher assume no responsibility for any errors or omissions. No liability is assumed for damages that may result from the use of information contained within.

Library of Congress Control Number: 2020924462
ISBN-13: Paperback: 978-1-64749-300-4
         ePub: 978-1-64749-301-1

Printed in the United States of America

GoToPublish LLC
1-888-337-1724
www.gotopublish.com
info@gotopublish.com

PRAISE FOR OTHER BOOKS BY JIM FRAISER

"Fraiser knows how to tell a story, with suspense building throughout…Rich with punchy, whip smart dialogue that rings true, plot twists, sexy dalliances, and over the top action that will keep the reader eagerly turning each page. He has firmly established himself as a major southern writer."

Delta Magazine

"This book can do nothing but add to Jim Fraiser's growing reputation as another Mississippi writer who knows how to tell stories."

Former Mississippi Governor William Winter

"An enjoyable read…gritty realism all the way. Fraiser knows how to tell a compelling story."

Joe Lee, author of *Judgment Day* and *Director's Cut*

"Fraiser's writing conjures up the steamy, often dark ambiance of Mississippi with a rich blend of lush setting, compelling action, and psychological intrigue."

Martin Hegwood, author of *Jackpot Bay* and *Big Easy Backroads*

"Fraiser succeeds in producing suspense and introspection, with clever dialogue providing plenty of depth and humor."

Oxford Eagle

The salty and engaging repartee offers a light-hearted, witty, and penetrating commentary on the protagonist's dilemmas. Fraiser provides a good read with courtroom action, well done dialogue, and a classic final scene…"

Mississippi Libraries Magazine

"Fraiser, a Mississippi novelist and popular historian, has a pleasing prose style, unpretentious and informative, and proves a pretty good scholar to boot."

Mobile Press Register

"Fraiser has assembled an intelligent, enlightening look at one of America's most charming areas."

Publisher's Weekly

By the same Author

Fiction
Shadow Seed
The Delta Factor
Camille
Whiskey with Chaser
Your Love is Wicked and Other Stories

Non-Fiction
M is for Mississippi: An Irreverent Guide to the Magnolia State
Mississippi River Country Tales: A Celebration of 500 Years of Deep South History
For Love of the Game: The Holy Wars of Millsaps College and Mississippi College Football
The Majesty of the Mississippi Delta
The French Quarter of New Orleans
The Majesty of Eastern Mississippi and the Coast
Vanished Mississippi Gulf Coast
The Garden District of New Orleans
The Majesty of Mobile
Historic Architecture of Baton Rouge

For Janie, Luci, Mary Adelyn and Paul, with all my love.

And many thanks to Jason Berry and Charles Wilson for their sage advice and support

Along the journey of our life halfway,
 I found myself in a dark wood;
Wherein the straight road no longer lay.

                                                  Dante

Do good works while it is day… Night is coming.
                                                  John 9:17

PROLOGUE

The tall, angular, shaggy-haired man in a black open collared silk shirt, black designer jeans and dark leather desert shoes eyed the woman seated on the wooden park bench before him.

She lifted the strands of raven-colored hair covering her eyes and forced herself to meet his baleful glare. "What *exactly* do you want with me, this time?" she asked solemnly. "Quit toying with me and tell me what you need me to do."

When he didn't answer, she lowered her eyes, fixing them on her shoe tops. "What must I do?" she asked again, flashing anger for the briefest moment before her eyes shaded into obsidian disks.

"Thanks for coming. I've missed you."

She blinked twice. "I know."

He sat beside her on the bench.

She looked away from him, into the night. Dark grey clouds blotted the purple twilight sky, humidity choked the air. She thought she discerned a trace of magnolia aroma in the heavy air, but the fetid scent of urine the homeless had left in the park smothered the scent.

The clouds hung so low they clipped the tops of the massive live oak that dominated the four block square park. The great oak's ponderous limbs thrust out in every direction, suffocating the smaller pin oaks and magnolias standing at vaguely twisted angles, proof of their life-long struggles for sunlight in the larger tree's shadow.

She wiped beads of sweat from her brow. *How could humidity be this suffocating during December,* she wondered, before reminding herself she now sat in the very heart of tropical Jackson, Mississippi.

Despite the humidity, or perhaps because of it, the tall man's scent, dank, sour, unwashed, except for the recent change of unsullied clothes, assailed her with a vengeance. His breath reeked of something that reminded of carrion. *It's already begun,* she realized with a shudder, feeling a sudden chill in no way connected to the weather.

She waited anxiously for him to speak, burrowing the pointed toes of her shoes into a soft patch of earth below the bench. But he remained silent, distant, peering straight ahead at the two Occupy the Park protesters in the distance, their large pasteboard signs stuck in the ground on stakes beside them, playing checkers on a concrete table beside a dried-up, weather-beaten fountain. Behind these men, across the street from the park, stood a granite replica of an ancient Greek temple with triangular pediment and massive, grey concrete columns. Either a bank or church, she figured, neither of which offered her sanctuary at times like these. She had nothing invested in either.

"If I do this for you, whatever you want me to do...."

"Yes?"

"Will you let me..." She felt his eyes searing irradiated fissures in her cheeks, sensed him inclining his head toward her in a malignant downward arc, his eyes coming level with hers. The fear, the rancid aromas, the heat simmering from his body, and the unexpected humidity stole her breath, choked off her words.

"Let you out of my life forever?" he murmured condescendingly.

She could see his wide, iniquitous grin in her mind's eye, but dared not turn to look. Nothing good would come of his seeing the disgust in her eyes, or of her moving her lips any closer to his.

"Yes," he said in a much kinder tone than she expected. *This was his way of conceding her terms.* At least that's what she hoped, the way a fly hopes the sleeping spider hasn't felt her crashing into his web.

She forced herself to face him. "What do you want me to do?"

Holding her gaze, he gave a barely perceptible smile.

She felt a tightening in her throat, more suffocating than if he had smacked her on the mouth. At least that would have made her feel more alive than his disconcerting, gangrenous smile.

"There's a foul wind blowing in from China, one that should arrive in these parts soon; one that will keep the right people occupied and make our work all the easier to accomplish. He turned to her in time to see her quizzical expression.

"China? Do you mean the virus? What has that to do with…?"

"Never mind. I'll explain later."

"What are you--?"

"Later," he commanded with the confidence of a cat toying with a now three-legged mouse. He turned calmly toward the man on his left. "And what are *you* prepared to do?"

The woman glanced at the thin man. Lurking in the shadows with scraggly mustache and sunken eyes like a cadaver's, he looked like an overcooked radish in his brown polyester shirt, raggedy jeans and tattered work boots.

The gaunt man gave an exasperated look, but spoke in a tone that could never be interpreted as aggressive. "I'm ready to go through with your plan, Ryan. You know that, don't you?"

"But not overly confident of its success?"

Before the other could blurt his usual beggarly response, the man called Ryan said, "Not to worry, my friend. As a modestly popular writer once said, 'the greatest and most powerful revolutions often start very quietly, hidden in the shadows.'"

The woman turned in amazement, wide-eyed and open-mouthed, unable to believe what she had heard. *You've never done anything quietly in your whole damned life*, she thought but didn't say.

"What writer said that?" the thin man asked with more apprehension than curiosity.

"No one of consequence. Until *now*."

CHAPTER ONE

The Christians have a saying—"When God is with you, who can be against you?" Conversely, we lapsed Catholic pagans have a saying of our own—"If the gods grant you lemons, screw the lemonade and find somebody with a flask of smooth Irish whiskey."

I realize that's not much of a philosophy, but when the ball starts rolling downhill, it's not easy to become an Atlas, grasp the world by its handles, paste a besotted grin on your face, and take it like a man. At least not without a reliable stiff drink.

Or so I thought when the tall, beefy man with the Roman nose, thick unkempt hair, silk shirt and narrow horn-rimmed glasses, tinted to camouflage his eyes, sauntered over to my signing table, handed me my book, *Thomas Jefferson and the Good Life*, and said, "Do you think you'll ever write a more substantial book about our third president?"

"Beg pardon?"

"About his views on politics, religion, slavery, and so on? Just sign it, please. No dedication."

I mumbled something like, "I hope so." Then, in response to his obvious disappointment, I said feebly, "I'm sticking to wine, women and song. Nowadays it's not safe to offer an opinion on politics, religion and slavery."

He nodded stiffly, snatched the book off my table with a large paw streaked with veins that seemed powerful enough to wield a Scottish Claymore, and vanished among the crowd.

I say "crowd" only because the tiny signing room in the privately-owned bookstore made five people seem like a crowd. I would have preferred to believe that people were taking cognizance of the need to prepare for the coming Corona virus currently ravaging China and getting used to staying indoors, and not risking their health coming to native son's book signing. But I knew different. No one takes diseases seriously until they come knocking on one's door. Oceans are wide and people are…well, narrow.

And then along came this aggravating fellow--brimming with the very self-confidence that was slipping away from me faster than congressmen take bribes.

And yet, brazen though his comments were, they proved the highlight of my evening's redundant labors.

Much to the reading public's chagrin, I had not chosen as my subject a TV pundit's latest regurgitation of pseudo-liberal or neo-conservative political screed, a celebrity's cocaine-ridden tell all, or the thriller novel with politically correct themes and relatively tame sex scenes of the sort that reduce American housewives to butter.

Well, to hell with it, I say. It wasn't bad for a first effort, even if it wasn't Faulkner, Welty, or even Grisham. The signing tour was more fun than I expected; several of my friends turned out in support in each town, even if they begrudged me the forty-five bucks. Guess I'll be buying the next few rounds at Hal and Mal's bar. I only wish….

"Excuse me, are you John Ferguson?"

I looked up into a pair of lustrous brown eyes and a beguiling smile that froze my brain's neurons in mid-synapse.

Suddenly unable to snatch a witty response from the ether, I uttered, "That's me," brimming with false bravado despite a mouth suddenly as dry as Mississippi pothole in July.

"Hello," she said warmly, extending a slender, elegant hand. "I'm Jenny Shexnayder. Did I miss your signing?"

I stumbled off the bookstore parking lot curb to take her hand. She wore a cotton shirt, designer jeans and brown silk sweater that hugged her perfectly sculpted figure both tightly and modestly at the same time. A lesser man might have crumbled in the face of her good looks, unassuming manner, sonorous voice and ebony-colored shoulder-length hair, but I was far too flummoxed to merely crumble.

Fact was, with one extraordinary exception, I hadn't enjoyed any romantic entanglements with the fair sex since my wife, Beth, died four years earlier. My teenaged daughter and now four-year-old son had become my daily concerns. My Jefferson manuscript, Mayflower lunches with my best buddy, Breeland Jones, and occasional DUI prosecutions on the Natchez Trace had been my only other distractions.

But here she was, a splendid gift from the gods, who, as we all know, help only those who help themselves, and then only rarely and ultimately with a big helping of regret.

Had she asked me to sign a book for her? No, I would certainly have noticed *her*.

"Yes, I'm done," I finally managed despite a tongue suddenly thick as wool. "I didn't see you in there."

"Sorry," she shrugged. "Guess I arrived a little late. I have one of your books, though. Maybe you'll still sign it for me?"

"With pleasure. Would you like to come in, or may I buy you a drink at Fenian's Pub just up the street?"

"I'd like that very much."

She didn't speak again during the first block of our brisk stroll to the pub. That silence drained my confidence like a flame-throwing six-foot-seven relief pitcher taking the hill against a .220 hitter in the ninth. Starving for words with a seemingly endless half-block to go, I risked an attempt at humor. Taking her book in my hand, I held it aloft and said, "Have you read this book? I hear the author is the next Joseph Catalonia."

She peered sideways at me through the darkness (all but one of the block's streetlights had burned out, the only surprise being it was downtown Jackson and one was still working). I imagined she was wondering whether I was bragging, outright lying, failing miserably at small talk, or merely a purveyor of idiotic jokes fit for blockheads at Star Trek conventions or Tea Party rallies.

"Who's Joseph Catalonia?"

"Your guess is as good as mine."

"Oh, that's funny," she said flatly.

She didn't say, "Your wit is as ephemeral as a celebrity marriage," so I took heart and pressed on like the cello player on the Titanic. "Where are you from?"

"You mean before the bookstore?"

"So it's going to be like that, is it?"

"Very likely."

"Good. Thanks. Every writer enjoys following up a poor showing at his hometown book signing with the confidence boost that only an exemplary smart ass of the opposite sex can provide."

"Wonderful! That's just the kind of relationship I was seeking!"

Finnian's Pub was a quaint, red brick two story pub at the corner of Fortification and North Jefferson. Jackson's only Irish bar, it was named for a legendary Irish warrior and famed for its shepherd's pie, scotch eggs, enviable collection of Scotch and Irish whisky, and an open mike in the bar for would be balladeers. In short, Fenians's was the ideal first date option for the bourgeoisie yuppie set.

Consequently, we partook of none of their specialties, ordering a pair of Guinness drafts on the second story balcony, custom made for lovers on warm summer nights crowned by the ubiquitous man in the moon, his cratered face thinly etched with a licentious smile. Of course, we had just met, this was the dead of winter and there was no moon at all, but why should I complain? Complaining, I well knew, only drew the gods' attention, challenging them to do all in their power to make things vastly worse.

"So," she said warmly after sipping her beer, "are you working on another book?"

"No. I'm just now getting over writing this one."

"And when will you get around to it?" "Who knows? Maybe I'll write a legal thriller next time. I'm an assistant U.S. attorney…"

"I know. That's on your book's dust cover."

"…and we happen upon some fascinating stories now and then."

"Why don't you write something of substance about Thomas Jefferson? Or about Jefferson and Adams? Or, better yet, Jefferson versus Hamilton?"

"Actually, you might be interested to know that I never carry ten dollar bills in my wallet so I don't have to look at Hamilton's face."

She wasn't interested at all. "I believe," she said quite seriously, "the Hamilton/Jefferson battle for the American soul still resonates today, far more than any debate over which wines to serve with seafood and what architectural styles to frame on public buildings."

Damn, I thought. *I* wrote the frigging book and she knows more about the subject that I do. What the hell? Don't the gods ever sleep?

****

An hour later I walked her to her older model Buick parked at the bookstore, said goodnight, and left her in front of the restaurant as she insisted. I hit the interstate and wheeled into my gated suburban neighborhood shortly past nine-thirty. Like many Madison neighborhoods, ours was named after the man-made lake planted on its grounds. It was a two-decade old suburb of endlessly repetitively styled houses, all replete with dark red or muted pink brick facades, wide, columned porches, perfectly trimmed lawns stippled with an assortment of silver birch, magnolias, Crepe Myrtles and especially Bradford pears that, left untended, split apart or shed limbs large enough to take down a roof or automobile. Perhaps this is why so many Madison neighborhoods are gated despite our city owning the state's lowest crime rate; we're avoiding the court costs and attorney fees occasioned by having our pear trees maim uninvited guests.

Our town, Madison, is named for our fourth president, and is the quintessential southern small town with more churches than bookstores, capable police and fire departments, and more joie de vivre than you might expect, including a surprisingly well-populated nest of swingers, with several four star restaurants, a multiplex cinema and political infighting of the bumptious variety that never fails to entertain locals and visitors alike. It's the perfect place to live if you prefer conservative politics, abjure crime, appreciate good schools and their-own-business minding-neighbors, can endure the hourly peel of church bells, and prefer freedom from exposure to creative thought and large contingents of people of color.

This was a far cry from my vagabond youth in the Mississippi Delta, where cotton was king and bourbon his queen. There, contact between the races had been as inevitable as it was congenial, and on humid moonstruck evenings I often repaired to a 1930's prohibition-era restaurant to dine in booths on file' gumbo, fried catfish and drinks on the rocks with sun-burnished blondes in short black dresses, and hale fellows very well met after the bottle had gone 'round the table twice.

Suffice it to say, my family and I pretty much keep to ourselves, and very few of our neighbors object.

When my son Will didn't meet me at the back door per usual, I rushed through the darkened house to find him before sleep stole him for the night. My 16-year-old daughter, Anna Grace, met me in the hallway between her room and his and confirmed my greatest fears. "Will's asleep, Dad," she murmured softly. *No bedtime stories and tickle monster embraces for you tonight.*

In the dim light I could barely see the light brown hair cascading over Anna's Grace's shoulders, her newly-turned-almost-woman figure silhouetted by lamplight in the far corner of her room. The twinkle in her eyes that had faded after her mother died had burned brighter by degrees every day she had nurtured her baby brother, and after he had turned two and become, in her words, 'more interesting than a stray cat,' her eyes had, at times, taken on a positively heavenly glow.

I've heard it said that the heart is a resilient little muscle, yet any muscle can atrophy from lack of use. Even so, nothing recharges the soul faster than a toe-headed two-year-old with golden curls, electric-blue eyes and a laugh that makes you believe, if only for a moment, that either God exists or you've somehow gotten the luckiest break in a random and uncaring universe. Maybe even the best break since mother Earth accidentally positioned herself just the right distance from the sun, with a stabilizing moon spinning the needful distance from her, allowing life to flourish on a once comet-pelted molten rock in the back alley of an otherwise unremarkable galaxy.

"Is he in my room or his?" I called after her.

"Dad," she chided from her doorway, "he's four. He can't sleep with you forever."

"You did."

"*I* did not."

"I put you to bed every night of your life after you were 6 months old, read you books, sang you songs, recited you poetry, and told you made-up-on-the-cuff stories for the first ten years of your life."

"Yes, Dad," she groused with faux impatience (or at least I presumed it was faux), "but we did that in *my* bed, and when I fell asleep you got up and went to yours. And you only quit doing it when Mom insisted you quit. Gosh, Dad," she rolled her eyes, ""give it up, will you?"

"So...." I asked, changing the subject. "How's your boyfriend, Mohamed?"

She regarded me as if I had farted in church. "Malik! His name is Malik."

I knew that, of course. But when your sixteen-year-old tenth-grader announces at the dinner table she's dating an Egyptian Muslim, albeit a straight-A-making Egyptian Muslim with an exceptional sense of humor and obvious affection for your daughter, you can't resist poking a little fun. After all, if you get an enormous kick out of baiting the *Christian* fundamentalists now and then, there's no reason to slack up on the ones in the other camp just because they take a shine to your young'un.

But this time Anna didn't appreciate my humor. She suddenly whirled about and closed her door. She didn't' slam it, but the quick exit *sans* goodnight kiss spoke thousands of decibels louder. "Anna Grace?"

Shrugging off her silence to teen angst, I opened Will's door and strained to make him out in the star light shining through his bedroom blinds. His head rested upon his hands rather than his pillow, which had fallen to the floor along with his Avengers-decorated bed sheet.

Maybe it's the blood ties that make all the difference. While standing over Anna Grace's bed after singing her to sleep in years past, I always marveled at how she seemed a spitting image of her mother, the same full lips, lovely hair and button nose. Now I marvel at this sleeping boy, so unrelentingly beautiful, yet nevertheless a mirror image of four-year-old me. Lacking my courser features to be sure, yet somehow offering an undeniable reflection of a youth that had long since passed me by.

The sudden thought, no doubt planted by one of the more puckish gods, that our admiration of our own children is little more than narcissism-*cum*-nursery, almost spoiled the moment.

Almost.

Brushing that thought aside, I lifted his sheets off the floor and lay them softly across his shoulders. After marveling a full minute at the serenity of his unlabored sleep, I backed carefully out of his room, closed the door behind me and shuffled quietly through the darkened living room and switched on the den lights.

Seated in my club chair with a glass of red wine, I asked myself if I shouldn't consider inviting someone else into our lives. Someone besides Malik.

But how would Will react to the presence of a grown woman in his life? He had never known his mother who died shortly after his birth, and I had never brought a date home to meet him.

Why complicate things so? You've only just met a woman, know next to nothing about her except that she's just moved to town from Louisiana, is a substitute school teacher, and occasionally laughs at your better jokes. As Charlie Brown often says in one of Will's books, "Good grief!"

I tasted the wine. It was heaven in a glass-- Volnay from the Burgundy region of France, one of the better discoveries made during my research on the Jefferson book. One of his favorites when traveling the south of France, it's certainly mine now, thanks to reasonably priced, internationally stocked internet wine sales.

So why had an unsettling feeling of dis-ease suddenly descended upon me? Was it the uncertainty of parenting young children without Beth? Was it ongoing guilt over wanting a son so badly that I failed to see the danger to the woman I loved as she struggled to bring him into the world? Or the betrayal of hoping with all my heart to find happiness in the arms of a woman I had only just met?

I didn't know and certainly didn't want to know. That's what wine is for, I told myself, filling my glass again, as if Bacchus held all the answers we benighted mortals needed, if only we could worship deeply enough at his anesthetizing shrine.

CHAPTER TWO

The next morning I wandered into the office with my head down, racked with the thought that I was no longer young enough to drink two glasses of white wine, two draft beers, then a couple more glasses of red wine, with nothing else for dinner but a cheese plate and crackers. A glance at the mountainous stack of files accumulating on my desk since I checked out of the office last Wednesday for my Delta book signing tour sent bile rising in my throat, hastening a sudden trip to the water cooler just outside my office.

I had passed a pleasant evening with an attractive and surprisingly generous woman who neither frowned at my jokes nor scoffed at my rusty attempts at serious conversation. Then I'd come home to two wonderful children and slept in a soft, comfortable adjustable bed. Why wasn't that enough? Why the need for enough alcohol to drown a rat?

And then, as if in answer to my question, I noticed a blue labeled file on the top of the heap with a tab marked "URGENT." Leaning back in my tall, leather chair, I shrugged of the jackhammer in my head and viewed the summary page of my newly assigned case.

A note in U.S. Attorney Jack Ashton's hand, stuck to the first page, read, "Welcome back. Get on this TODAY!!!!"

Before I could read further my desk phone buzzed.

"Hello?"

"John?"

"Yes, Jack?"

"Have you read the file on your desk, dated December 13, that has my note on it?"

"I'm reviewing it now."

"I know it's difficult to come back to reality after a whirlwind book tour through the Mississippi Delta, signing books for all thirteen of your fans, but I need you up to speed on this one right away. You have a preliminary hearing set at nine o'clock Friday before Magistrate Judge Nancy Day. The defense has filed a few motions already."

"What's the rush, Jack? All the paperwork's here," I said, flipping through the slim file. "No prior criminal record, the charge is misdemeanor assault…What's the big deal? The victim somebody known?"

"Take a closer look."

I did. "Oh, the victim's Josh Reed."

"Yes. Josh Reed. The federal marshal in charge of our Chief U.S. District Judge's courtroom. He just happened to be in the clerk's office when this Occupy City Hal// Black Lives Matter white male came in to file a civil rights complaint against the Jackson police for hassling him in Smith Park. The jackass got testy, the clerk called Josh, they had words and this shithead sucker-punched him in the face. They had to scrape him off the floor when Josh and the boys finished with him. We need to button this one down fast so Josh doesn't get slapped with a civil rights complaint next week."

"But it's just a misdemeanor assault case, after all, no weapon no injuries. Hell, Jack, we've got killers, kidnappers, rapists, drug czars and a host of other miscreants worse than this awaiting trial. Why the note and the call?"

He heaved a labored sigh. "You've heard the expression, 'when momma's unhappy, everyone's unhappy'"?

"Sure."

"Well, when Chief Judge Wyngait's marshal is unhappy and complaining like a state government worker asked to do his job, Judge Wyngait's very unhappy. Before long, I'm unhappy, and then…"

"I get the point."

"Check out that file. Make the Chief Judge happy, John."

The defendant's photo graced the first page under Jack's note, and two things were readily apparent about the young man's face. First, but for the dark hair and weasel-thin mustache, he was a dead ringer for the slightly built actor who played the Nazi SS leader in *Inglorious Bastards* and the German bounty hunger in Quentin Tarantino's western flick, *Django*. Second, most people in jailhouse photos looked as if they wanted to be anywhere else, but this fool appeared to be enjoying himself, grinning at the camera like a grown fool, as if he knew a two-ton safe would soon come crashing down on the photographing officer. Very strange.

In every other respect, the report was painfully straightforward. The Jackson police had, according to the defendant (still a John Doe but henceforth known by us as "the ghost"), rousted the Occupy City Hall bums and Black Lives Matter 'revolutionaries' infesting otherwise lovely Smith Park directly behind the Mississippi Governor's Mansion on Amite Street. Of all the protesters, only the Ghost took sufficient umbrage to schlep down to our federal courthouse and demand the necessary papers to file a civil rights complaint against the JPD. When he grew too loud and obnoxious, the clerk sent for Marshal Ashton, who attempted to escort the Ghost out into the mid-day sunshine. Fisticuffs ensued, landing the Ghost in our fine federal facility yesterday, awaiting arrangement on the assault charge. He had eschewed a public defender in favor of hired counsel, who had agreed to postpone the preliminary hearing until Friday to better prepare for it.

The federal probation officer had inserted a Top Priority FBI printout in the file dated December 7, that read-- "Subject claims to be a member of Occupy The Park/Wall Street/City Hall or Black Lives Matter protest. BLM are the groups originally protesting of the murder of a black man, Michael Brown by a white Ferguson, Missouri policeman, but who persist in protesting racism, police brutality, economic inequality, corporate greed and government corruption. Apart from the racial aspect, they appear to be similar to those other protest groups allied for bank reform, defeating Republican politicians, fomenting balanced distribution of wealth, i.e., socialism, and an end to alleged government corruption sponsored by the various states and the federal government. Although those were most active in places like New York City and Boston, some recently appeared in our Smith Park as they have in public places throughout the country.

"Subject has no record of convictions, but fingerprint records indicate he was arrested as a John Doe in New York for blocking the street and causing a disturbance. The charges were dismissed when video evidence from NYPD and protester cell phones indicated that police barricades actually blocked the traffic. It is unknown how long he has been in Mississippi. He was arrested with a pamphlet in his pants pocket that indicated that he may be he may be part of one of the professional protest groups like Crowds on Demand, Antifa or Demand Protest. This appears more likely in that he is Caucasian, has no known political connections, and is not from the South, much less associated in any way with the Jackson, Mississippi area.

"Although his Social Security numbers do not correspond with available matching fingerprints, we have what appears to be a possible photo match between the Subject's New York arrest photo and a much older one of an unidentified member of the United Freedom Front, a 1980's American Marxist organization reputedly involved in numerous bombings of corporate facilities, courthouses and other civil and military federal facilities in Massachusetts and Ohio, and at least one confirmed robbery of a FIDC bank in New York. Although the UFF always called in bomb warnings to avoid casualties, dozens of people were nevertheless injured, no fatalities recorded. They claimed to be protesting U.S involvement in Central America, South African apartheid, and standing armies in America supposedly supported by friendly corporations and funded by federally-insured banks. We're working with the Boston and Deerfield, Ohio federal probation offices to determine if the Subject may be identified as a UFF member surreptitiously photographed by an undercover agent at one of their November 2012 meetings. One of our informants believes the organization may have been reborn in the past decade, various parties having reunited via internet communications. But their use of technology has of late become so sophisticated that they remain one step ahead of us, abandoning meeting locations, web sites, even computer equipment scrubbed clean, hours before we move on their locations.

"Whatever they may be calling themselves now, the members of this terror cell are very well funded; we suspect an international source, possibly from the Middle East or Southeast Asia. In any event, as they have taken no recognizable action in the past six months, they may be planning something significant within the next few months.

"Extreme caution should be used in approaching any suspected members of this cell. Upon first contact, immediately notify the Bureau through its office closest to the reported sighting or incident."

The final item in the file was a notice of representation filed by my good friend, Breeland Jones, with the firm of Hopkins, Reeves and Jones. Breeland hadn't practiced criminal law, or anything other than insurance and toxic tort defense, since shortly after we'd graduated law school two decades ago. I grabbed my cell phone and dialed his number.

After speaking to an endless array of receptionists, secretaries and associates, I finally got him on the line.

"Hello? This is Breeland Jones. To whom am I speaking?"

"Right. As if none of those lackeys told you who was on the line. I've had an easier time getting the governor or my U.S. Senator on the line than getting through to you."

"Oh, hello, John. To what do I owe the pleasure?"

"What gives, Breeland? You so busy you've got no more time for your pal? I thought the tort reform you big firm lawyers so ardently supported had cut down enough of *your* practice that you had time to chat on the phone with your old law school buddy now and then."

"No, John," he said, smooth as the silk in his bow tie. "We're doing just peachy here. What's your urgency? Has government malfeasance and the pending financial cliff resulted in layoffs at our federal building? Do you need a respectable job with our firm? Just email a resume and we'll get back to you after the Rapture."

I couldn't help laughing; Breeland's mild wit, soft voice and eternally pleasant demeanor was such that he could no more render a sincere insult than he could summon the aggression necessary to defend a hardened criminal. What was he up to now?

"How are Will and Anna Grace? Looking forward to Santa Claus, I presume?"

"Thanks for asking, Breeland. They're fine. Anna's in love with a Muslim and Will's already demanding the entire Toys R Us catalogue from Santa. I've got a closet-full of trains, dinosaurs, Avengers books, and toddler friendly board games hidden behind my wardrobe just waiting for him to discover and ruin the holidays for us all."

"And Anna Grace's Christmas list?"

Pause. "Well, now that you mention it, I forgot to ask if she had compiled a list. Guess I better get on the stick, huh?"

"You mean to say you haven't bought her anything yet? What kind of father are you, anyhow?"

"Her mother usually handled that assignment, for obvious reasons. Can you imagine me picking out a teenaged girl's clothes? I try not to think about it, to tell you the truth."

"Clothes, John? Think cash. Teenagers want cash, pal. Trust me on this."

"I suppose you're right. I've had so much on my plate, with the office, the book and the four-year-old. And Anna's not exactly keen on spending quality time with her dad since the new boyfriend showed up. How much time did you spend with your sixteen-year-old daughter back in the dawn of the Industrial Age?"

"Do you remember that court-appointed criminal case you and I handled just out of law school, when the world was young and we were marginally less dull then we are now?"

"Sure. The defendant's first lawyer died the morning of the trial. How could I forget it?" *Now he's getting around to it*, I predicted.

"Do you remember how much time the circuit judge gave us to prepare for that trial?"

"About thirty minutes."

"That's how much time I spent with my teenaged daughter between her first date and her breakup with her boyfriend six months later. Even less since she met the next flame."

"That's what I thought."

"But at least I felt guilty about it."

"What did you do about it?"

"Went to confession."

"What? You're an Episcopalian. Y'all don't do confession."

"Precisely. That's why I went to St. Peter's Catholic Church."

"What?"

"Yes. I had taken my brown bag lunch in Smith Park and on the way back to my office in the bank building I saw the sign advertising confession at the cathedral at noon.

I had seen confession in a million gangster movies and had a pretty good idea how to go about it, so I confessed to ignoring my daughter."

"Did the priest give you absolution?"

"No, I didn't want any. I'm Episcopalian, remember. But I remembered what you had said about how the Irish priests were fun to talk to and they always let you off the hook, making you feel better despite yourself and your multitude of venal sins."

"Breeland.... I don't think I put it exactly that way..."

"But you were right, John. I did feel better about myself, having gotten it off my chest. Played a round of golf that afternoon and shot an 83."

"Really?" I had so forgotten about the Occupy City Hall case at this point, that even his mention of Smith Park didn't resurrect it in my mind.

"Yes, really. You should try it."

"Try what?"

"Go by St. Peters today at noon and confess abandoning your daughter."

"That's a little harsh, don't you think?"

"Then for showing favoritism to your son, at least."

"That's not a sin, is it?"

"How should I know? Like you say, I'm an Episcopalian. We don't believe in sin. In God's name we play; that's our motto. Why don't you come join us at St. James next weekend for our annual Christmas bash and pig roast? We have an ancient music combo that plays your beloved Renaissance music while we quaff beer and gobble roast pig so tender you can gum it without your teeth. And the women are all dressed in such low cut blouses and short skirts that, after a few beers, even your own wife looks good. You don't have to help with the cooking if you don't want to; just come join in for the lust, gluttony and any other Deadly Sins you care to commit. We're the Country Club for Christ, John. We've got a place for you."

"Thanks all the same, Breeland, but I'll stick to fish on Friday and priest-enforced guilt on Sunday."

"Your loss."

"Why didn't you confess to an Episcopal priest? I'm sure they wouldn't mind pinch-hitting now and then. Most of them seem like fine fellows, drinking white wine, enforcing good old fashioned Episcopal rectitude in the parish while favoring the old lady with a good roll in the hay now and then."

"John," he chuckled, "*my* priest is a fine looking woman about thirty years old, with long frizzy blond hair and legs to die for. What's more, she's good friends with my wife, Melody, and I wouldn't confess to her about burping loudly in church, much less lusting after my daughter's college roommates or getting drunk and falling in my neighbor's pool at the neighborhood Christmas party. Even if I believed any of that *was* a sin. Why don't you join us, John? Join the happy team. Besides, you're more pagan than Catholic now, anyway. You've said as much yourself. Have you ever seen anything in the modern world more pagan-looking than our annual goat roast tee shirts?"

"Thanks, but no thanks, Breeland. I may not believe in heaven, hell, or Papal infallibility, but I'll keep dancing with the religion that brung me like every other red-blooded southern lad."

"I don't know, John. Seems like the Baptists and Methodists have more single women per capita than we do. Ever thought about that?"

"No, Breeland, Protestantism just isn't my style."

"Why not?"

I had nothing against them, after all. They're no different from us--fellow travelers to the grave as Dickens so eloquently put it. Like us, they need something to distract them from the fact that we're all born to die, are dying as we sleep, screw and speak, and, more often than not, were born to parents who chose their current means of distraction. Myself, I need more theater, more sensuality in my service. I crave the taste and texture of red wine and unleavened wafers, the emotionally evocative polyphony of Renaissance music, the inspiring Gothic architecture with its flying buttresses, stained glass windows, soaring towers and spires, and last but not least, Christ's semi-nude broken body hanging on the cross that dominates the altar. That's what I require from my sacramental service.

"Okay, Breeland, let me put it this way…Protestants are fine, for the most part, just like Catholics, Anglicans, Hindus, all manner of pagans and agnostics. In short, everyone except an atheist is A-Okay with me, atheists being as heretical as they are ludicrous. But when the more fundamentalist protestant element meet you for the first time and immediately wonder aloud what church you attend, and discover to their horror that you belong to a "cult" like the Episcopal Church, are a pagan, or horror of horrors, a Catholic, you're forced to wonder what else they're thinking while they're looking at you as if you had the face of a gargoyle and the wings to match."

He gave an effected shrug. "What should an upstanding church member say upon meeting you for the first time, John?"

"They should ask, do you drink red or white."

"That's good."

"Actually, I got that one from Beth. My wife was a good half Jew, half Episcopalian, as you know. She related that sentiment on our first date and I knew right way she was the one."

"Indeed she was, buddy. But I think your aversion to Protestantism is more your Delta upbringing showing than anything else. High church or no church, that's the John Ferguson I know. All you Delta guys are snobs."

May be, I wanted to say, but you gotta' love a place where the best fine-dining restaurant is a prohibition-era joint on the wrong side of the tracks; where farmers dressed in cowboy boots and khaki pants, lawyers attired in three-piece suits, and teenagers wearing very little all come together to dine in white-curtained booths, feast on pompano baked in a paper bag and pass a joyously lubricated time."

"The Delta's dying, John. Greenville and Clarksdale look almost abandoned, a Twilight Zone hell for Delta planters."

Sure, but it's still a marvelous region. You don't see African-Americans carjacking whites in downtown Greenwood, nor do you hear white businessmen in Cleveland using the "N" word in family restaurants, as you do here in our antediluvian Capitol City. What is more, there you have restaurants where folks enjoy hot toddies behind white curtains and buzz the waiter when they need more. That slow, gentile pace enjoyed by all Deltans, black and white, greatly improves upon the crime, ubiquitous potholes and occasional racism you see here in Jackson.

"The Delta's dying, bud. And everybody's moving here, just as you did."

"That's right, pal. And when enough of them move here this place will finally have some class. See you at a noon."

CHAPTER THREE

Moments later, my secretary buzzed me before I could catch my breath. "Call holding on line three," she said.

"Who is it?"

"A Ms. Shexnayder."

I took a second to reacquire my bearings. "Put her through, Betty." After a familiar beep, I said, "Hello? Jenny?"

"It's about time," came the welcome voice. "I could have gotten through to President Obama sooner than they patched me through to you."

"How long were you holding?"

"Too long. You busy?"

"I have a job, if that's what you mean."

"Take me on a tour of downtown?"

The night before she had told me she hailed from Covington, Louisiana, had only moved to Jackson two months earlier, and knew nothing about the city. I offered to give her a tour, but she had remained noncommittal throughout the evening, a tactic women often use to perfection, universally known as 'setting the hook.'" She did and I was.

"You've lived here two months and haven't been downtown?"

"Of course I have, silly. Take me on an architectural and historical tour. The Governor's Mansion, places like that. You are aware of such things, aren't you, or do you only write about them if they're located in foreign countries?"

"Do Yankees talk funny? Of course I'm aware of them. It would be a pleasure to heighten your awareness, too. Where are you?"

"Minutes away. I live in the Belhaven neighborhood."

"Where?"

"On Greymont Avenue. I'm renting."

"In the big apartment complex?"

"No, a white ranch house with garage, a small guest house and a pool, a block off Fortification."

I could barely breathe. "You mean 1151 Greymont?"

Silence. "How did you know?"

"I lived in that house years ago."

"What a coincidence."

When I didn't answer, she said, "John?"

"Sorry," I said, shrugging off the river of memories suddenly flooding my consciousness. Memories of Beth, Anna Grace's birth, our years making a family, memories still fresh of the enormous burden of loss. "When would you like your tour?" I asked, hoping my voice hadn't betrayed my thoughts.

"You busy now?"

"Yes, but I'll make time for the woman from Louisiana who's not afraid of Mississippi ghosts."

"Now I'm going to have to beg *your* pardon."

"The house you're renting is haunted. An elderly lady died there decades ago and apparently refuses to give it up. Have you seen her yet?"

"No..."

"You will. I did. And I don't believe in ghosts. Meet me in front of the Governor's Mansion in thirty minutes."

"See you there."

I waited a minute for my heart to stop racing, then reached up on my bookshelf, pulled down a copy of the *WPA Guide to Mississippi*, turned to the chapter on Jackson, and refreshed myself on the city's history and architecture. Satisfied I was ready to offer a worthy tour, I set the book down, opened a drawer, grasped my IPod, donned my earphones, bounded down the stairs from my second story office in the new federal building complex on Court Street, and hoofed it north on Congress Street toward the Governor's Mansion on Capitol Street.

The gods had crafted a perfect day for walking, with a moderately cool 68 degrees, zero humidity, and fluffy white cumulous clouds floating across the sky, shading fortunate mortals from the harshest rays of Sol Invictus. Despite a reasonably warm yet unseasonably humid December thus far, not uncommon here in the near-tropics, weather reports had old man winter scheduled to descend after a thunderstorm front over the weekend.

No time like the present to take in the sights.

Stepping in time with the music, a brisk Courante from Michael Praetorius's *Terpsichore*, I reached Capitol Street and the Governor's Mansion fifteen minutes before the appointed time for our tour, and began making mental notes of the Mansion's Greek Revival elements.

Behind me, a robust voice chimed, "Hey, Ferguson. Haven't seen you in ages!" I turned to find my former law partner, Jerry Harbaugh, known to his friends as "Yardbird," due to his penchant for perching on his back porch with a six pack and bag of potato chips for hours at a time. He was dressed in his perpetual uniform—light brown khaki pants, starched pink cotton shirt with button down collar, Johnson and Murphy shoes, no tie and crisp navy sport jacket. At six feet-two, he stood several inches taller than I, but made up for it by a near-bald pate and a substantial girth.

"How 'bout it Bird? Not in court today, I see?

"Not today, Johnny-boy. Read your article in the State Archives Newsletter last week."

"So? What'd you think?"

"Liked the first part," he grinned, "about Thomas Jefferson reducing taxes, cutting the tariffs, opposing judicial legislation with strict construction of the Constitution…All that good stuff." Then his visage suddenly darkened as if a cloud had settled in the sky above him, choking off Sol's mood-enhancing rays. "But then you say you voted for our former neo-Marxist president! What's wrong with you, boy?"

"I don't know, Jerry. Tell me, what *is* wrong with me?"

He rested his fists confidently on his hips. "You're confused as hell, boy."

"

"John, d'you honestly believe that a socialist Democrat won't run this country into the ground? They ain't for lowering taxes, bub, reducing the debt or limiting the fedr'l guvment."

"Jerry, Thomas Jefferson believed strongly in reducing taxes and the national debt, but he changed his tune when he felt it best for the country."

"What 'chu talking about?" he asked in his best good ole boy patois, genuinely perplexed, as if I were explaining the workings of quarks, black holes or the female mind.

"The sight of blood made Jefferson sick but he sent the Marines to the shores of Tripoli to crush the pirates. He knew the president wasn't authorized by the Constitution to buy real estate, but he made the Louisiana Purchase anyhow."

"I wish we could give parts of it back now. But I'm not following you."

"I'm just saying that, regardless of my views, I voted that way though I disagreed with him about some things, because I thought at the time that was best for my country."

"How the hell could that be?"

I had never made any headway arguing with Jerry, and had no plans to do so today. But I had to get one lick in before changing the subject. "Well, the Democrats got us out of Iran, didn't they?"

He shook his head, feigning (I think) disbelief. "Yeah, but their open door policy on immigration will be the end of America as we know it."

"Whatever happened," I grinned, "to give us your tired, your poor in spirit…?

"Oh, we'll let the foreigner in, John," he groused, "and if they bring that Chinese virus here I've been hearing about, and kill thousands of citizens and wreck our economy, you'll live to regret it, mark my words. But what I'd like to know is why are ya' so fond of the damned Democrat party?

"I'm no fan of either party, Jerry. I'm for law and order, isolationism abroad, low taxes at home and good schools in my hometown. That's why I live in Madison, Jerry. Why don't you come on down and join us in the suburbs, you heah?"

We had waged these battles for years when we shared the narrow grey building at the corner of North State and Capitol Streets, until I had realized the wisdom Ben Franklin espoused when he spoke of the pointlessness of arguing politics with friends and colleagues; you would never change their opinion and who gave you the right to do so, anyhow? Worse, friendships could suffer from resentment over arguments about matters we really knew little about and had even less chance of influencing via the ballot box thanks to a hundred years of Congressional gerrymandering. Losing friends by arguing about politics or religion seemed to me the height of absurdity, if not insanity. Now if the issue was Dodgers versus Giants or Ole Miss versus LSU, well, that was something else entirely.

"Damned good to see you Jerry. Tell your lovely bride Mary Evelyn I said 'Happy Holidays'."

He shook his head again in mock disgust. "What happened to Merry Christmas, Johnny? You afraid of offending *me*? Do I look Jewish or Muslim to you?"

It never ceases to amaze me the way people who are genuinely fond of a friend or colleague nevertheless entirely fail to comprehend what that friend is all about, forgetting to scrub their beliefs clean before hanging them out to dry on their friend's line. Although Jerry and I, like all rational-thinking mortals, cast political correctness out the window during our 'political discussions' and believe that the PC police should be banished to a remote island in the Pacific where they never need fear the vicissitudes of insult or outrage, there are lines everyone should realize they should never cross. At least not on a heavily populated corner of Capitol Street.

Beth was half Jewish, albeit never a practicing Jew in the shadow of her father, the cradle Episcopalian. But her parentage had never stopped Jerry from making anti-Semitic jokes around me, especially during the Middle East unrest and the 9/11 tragedy that ultimately arose from it.

Even so, lashing out at an old friend was not the answer, or at least that's what Beth always tried to teach me. She believed that gentle satire, or humor, when delivered at the right time in the proper manner, usually proved the better approach. Anyhow, it was always more fun skewering blockheads who didn't know satire from sapphire or humor from hubris, than directly insulting them and risking sudden introductions to their fists.

I waited a beat for him to remember about Beth, but when he remained clueless, I simply stood back and gave him an appraising look. "Jesus was a Jew, Bird, same as my Beth. And both of them were very fond of you."

He lowered his head and offered a genuine, surrendering laugh, remembering now where he'd overstepped his bounds. "Okay, Johnny," he said, his cheeks flushed with crimson. "I hear you all the way. Happy Holidays to you and all the little Fergusons."

"And also to you," I said, shaking his hand before he marched briskly down the sidewalk toward Trustmark Bank.

But his comments leading me to think about Beth gave me a pained moment's pause. Often at the most unexpected times, such thoughts took me to a very dark place, one that I had difficulty escaping, even standing on a downtown Jackson street corner.

During such times, my mind's eye ferried me back to a hospital room just a few miles from downtown, where my dying wife Beth struggled valiantly to hold on to an swiftly ebbing life.

"It's not your fault," she whispered, struggling with rapid, shallow breathing. Her usually tanned skin was pale as snow, and when taking her hand I imagined I felt an almost nonexistent pulse. "We made the decision together," she breathed. When she saw the tears welling in my eyes, those I could no longer restrain in her presence, she rasped, "You had no way of knowing their supply of blood was so low."

She'd had a platelet problem that made pregnancy and giving birth dangerous, and the murder-a-day crime rate in Jackson had made dwindling blood supplies a day-to-day issue. And with doctors publically concerning themselves with the ongoing threat to blood supplies caused by the new Covid-19 virus in China, and an inevitable shift of their pandemic to our shores, we had known that, for a variety of reasons, giving birth might well be risky.

But a risk I was willing to take. Having gotten my wish for the first child to be a girl, I now fervently wanted a son. And Beth knew it. After the tests revealed that our child would be a boy, my desire to bring a son into the world only intensified. And now it was time to pay the price for my desires.

"John...."

I rose from my bedside chair, sat beside her, cradled her head gently in my arms, kissed her on the lips, and said, "I love you so much, Beth. I..."

"I love you too, John. I know you'll take good care of Anna Grace. And our boy...."

"Beth..."

"How is Will? Is he..."

"He's sleeping. He's fine. Healthy as can be. He just needs his mother.""John," she managed weakly, her voice fading as hypovolemic shock pressed its deadly course, robbing her body of blood and shutting down her organs. "Love..."

"Beth?" Her voice was now almost imperceptible.

"I'm not afraid....Just sorry I won't be there....To give Will all my love... Yyou...must..."

And with that she was gone.

That was four years ago, and every time I recall that moment it feels more like four seconds ago. Only the blinding brightness of the noonday sun spurred me back to reality. It was then that I noticed one of the ubiquitous downtown beggars standing a few feet from me, watching me closely, as if I were a mere shade, no longer fully present with the living. I snapped out of it, reached in my pocket for some change and handed him all of it. Charity had become a new habit of mine these past four years.

I stretched my back and cast a glance up Capitol Street toward the Governor's Mansion, right into a pair of familiar coffee-colored eyes.

"Well, hello there," I said, feeling appropriately awkward for having completely zoned out on a Capitol Street sidewalk.

Jenny wore a tight black, spandex cycling outfit with a yellow stripe down one side, old running shoes and her head crowned with a yellow scarf. A large pink clip held her long dark hair secure in a ponytail that dangled down her back. She held a touring bike by the handles.

"Who was that?" she asked, gazing after Jerry tromping purposefully down the sidewalk and disappearing into a bank.

As she locked her bike to a street light, I explained that Jerry was an old friend, a former law partner, and, as she may have guessed if she overheard us, slightly conservative in his political outlook.

"Ya think?"

"Yes. A little to the right of John Birch. You heard some of that exchange?"

"Yes. Then you seemed to get lost there for a moment."

I ignored that last part and focused on Jerry. "We practiced law together for five years back in the 1980's. He's a fine lawyer, as honest as they come, and he and his wife, Mary Adelyn, were very good to me when my wife Beth died."

"I see."

I had told her that rather depressing story last night, before she kindly switched the subject back to speculation on Covid 19's reach and the possible justifications for continuing my sideline literary career.

"How long were you here?" I asked sheepishly.

"Long enough."

"Yeah, he's a little conservative, for sure. But he worked hard for our clients, most of them poor whites and blacks, and a smattering of even poorer Choctaws. He never charged any of them more than they could pay. But when a rich prospective client offered us a fat fee if we'd help him bribe a Rankin County judge, Jerry tossed him out of our office before I could figure a way to keep the fee and not offer the bribe."

"Hard to believe."

"Why, because Jerry's not a bleeding heart like the Democrats claim to be? Hell, if they really cared about the poor, wouldn't they give them jobs, a worthwhile education, and some self-respect, not few crumbs as a bribe and a free ride over the financial cliff along with the rest of us?"

"I mean," she corrected me, "it's hard to believe any lawyer could be so charitable, nowadays."

My cheeks suddenly flushed with an embarrassment of twitches. *Don't talk politics with the new romantic interest*, I admonished myself.

"But now that you mentioned it, do you honestly believe the Republicans care about the people?" she asked, sporting a wry grin.

I met her grin with one of my own. "What? Are you a teacher or a socialist? I harbor no love for the Republicans or Democrats, I assure you."

"You sound like a regular little anarchist, ripping both parties the way you do."

Who the hell could blame me, I thought. Tocqueville said that when Jefferson and Hamilton led great political parties, they each had a philosophy designed for the betterment of the country. Since that time, our parties have been small ones, entirely lacking in recognizable philosophies, interested only in winning elections and achieving political gains that keep them in office and the rest of us in the poorhouse. So sure, I'm not fond of either party. How could I be?

"Maybe a little anarchy is what we need right now if that's the only way we can clean house and kick these bastards out of Washington."

"I see," she mused, more pensive than before. "So you admit to being an anarchist?"

"Not hardly. I'm too lazy for anarchy. Besides, they don't hire anarchists in federal prosecutor's offices." I had told her about my job last night, but she had shown little interest in my past, and even less in answering any questions about hers. How we had found anything to discuss for an hour and a half I had no idea.

"I'll bear that in mind," she said with all apparent sincerity. "So..." she purred, suddenly the south Louisiana coquette, "How 'bout my tour?"

I surprised myself and boldly took her by the hand, leading her to the Governor's Mansion's large cast iron front gate. She didn't resist my hand, taking it literally in stride.

"Did you know," I asked, "that Jackson was briefly renamed as Chimneyville, when Cump Sherman, your first LSU president, burned much of it to the ground during the War of Northern Aggression. That was while his Bummers waged terrorist assaults on the populace, raping slave women, murdering children for their mother's silver and gunning down old men in their gardens?"

"Wow, *you* certainly don't take prisoners, do you?"

"Not in Sherman's case. Terrorists who make war on non-combatants don't deserve a break."

"Sherman was a terrorist? How about the slaveholders he was fighting?"

"Robert E. Lee said, "We make war only on armed men; we cannot take revenge for the way our people have suffered without lowering ourselves in the eyes of those abhorred by the atrocities of our enemies.""

"Lee lost. Sherman won. Lee owned slaves and fought to preserve slavery. Sherman and Grant put an end to it."

"I wouldn't expect you to take sides against your LSU president."

"I didn't attend LSU."

"Anyhow, the city of Jackson made a decent recovery after Mr. Lincoln's War. Case in point, you're standing on the loveliest city block in America," I said, beginning her tour by explaining the finer architectural elements of the 1841 Greek Revival style Governor's Mansion, with its lovely semicircular portico supported by four, fluted Corinthian columns. "Those were fashioned after an Athenian monument erected in 334 B.C.," I said. "Just across the street is the ten-story, Gothic-style 1924 Lamar Life Building, Jackson's first 'skyscraper,' replete with crenellated clock tower and gargoyles glaring down from their perches at unsuspecting passersby. To the left you see a granite-columned bank in the monumental Neo-Classical Revival style."

"And that?" she asked, nodding toward the cathedral to the skyscraper's right.

"That's St. Andrews Cathedral."

"Catholic?"

"No, high Episcopalian. Built in 1903, Gothic Revival, or course, *sans* gargoyles, except for a few of the wealthier parishioners. That tower has a belfry, not inhabited by bats, but a few parishioners have bats in their belfries, as we can tell by their penchant for speaking in tongues and voting Republican in local elections and Democrat in the national contests."

When she didn't laugh at my joke, I cleared my throat and guided her to the west corner of the block, where we peered north up North West Street and saw St. Peter's Cathedral. "That's the Catholic church, St. Peter's Cathedral, blessed in 1900. The first Catholic Church was burned by General Grant and his band of Yankee terrorists, who, later as President, was too busy stealing land for the railroads to bother replacing it. This version is Gothic, too, with Carrera marble altars from the same quarry used by Michelangelo."

When I turned to face her, I found her watching me closely. "You're well informed about Mississippi architecture, aren't you," she asked.

"So you're in the dark about your capitol's architecture?"

"I know you can find some great seafood in Baton Rouge, a little political corruption, and that Huey Long was assassinated in that city before he could be elected president. That's about it."

"Impressive."

"No it's not. How do you know so much about Jackson?"

"I picked it up here and there."

"Really?" she asked dryly. "You picked it up? Are you sure you didn't snatch a book off a shelf in your office, maybe the *WPA Guide to Mississippi*, and bone up on a few things before our little tour?"

I blinked; my mouth hung open like the trap door on a worn set of long john underwear. She'd caught me dead to rights showing off with someone who had obviously read the book I had mined as a resource. Recovering somewhat, I mumbled, "Actually yes. That's exactly what I did. How did…"

"Just a guess. I read it a few months before I moved here. Your lecture sounded vaguely familiar."

I ignored the none-to-subtle jibe at my 'lecture.' "Yes, I keep a copy in the office to help answer questions for tourists I happen to meet on the street or during our downtown festivals. And for use in jury arguments when the right situation arises."

"I presume you mean for the history, rather than the architecture?"

"Of course. Even the most highbrow lawyers rarely quote architectural terms to jurors."

"As I recall, Jackson had quite an intriguing history. Tell me about it."

"If I'm not boring you too much with my lectures drawn from a book you've already read."

She gave that coy expression with which women have been charming men since the Garden of Eden. "Pray, continue, counselor. I'm riveted."

Although she smirked when she said it, I thought I detected a growing interest in her eyes, or perhaps that was only wishful thinking on my part. But, I told myself, the fat is in the fire now, and I may as well cook it all the way through.

I led her east down Capitol Street, telling her about the 1840 Greek Revival Old State Capitol on State Street, then stopped in front of a law office at the corner of Capitol and President. "The first state capitol stood here, built in 1890 to house the debates over the proposed 1890 State Constitution," I said.

"I've read something about that convention," she said.

"Yes, it was called to clear up the old laws, manage the railroads, provide for levees in the Mississippi Delta, and disenfranchise blacks with literacy requirements and a poll tax. The present building is owned by a trial lawyer who graces the cover of our phone books and knows far less about realistic-looking toupees than trying cases in federal court."

She took *my* hand this time and offered a pleasing upturned glance that left me weak in the knees. "Now that's what I'm talking about," she said. "Hard core Mississippi history!"

"You like that do you?" I asked. "Then try this on for size." I took her down President Street to Amite and pointed to another law office on the northwest corner. "Long ago on that property stood the home of one Judge Brame, a Georgian Colonial mansion with fluted columns and an impressive square portico. Legislators slipped out of the Old Capitol to climb through a trap door and enjoy clandestine afternoon delights with their lady friends, prostitutes and each other's wives."

"You don't say?"

"Well, the WPA Guide says so, and I don't believe its esteemed author, Eudora Welty, would lie about something like that. The present building is also owned by a famous trial lawyer, but we haven't heard much from him since he pled guilty to conspiring to bribe a circuit judge last year."

"You mean that's the office of…"

"Yes."

"The book? The forthcoming movie?"

"Correct. Mr. Faulkner said, 'the past is never dead, it's never even past.' And like the past, corruption never dies, once it takes hold of a person or a place."

"Spoken like a prosecutor. But thanks for the tip, though I'm neither politician nor lawyer."

"But you do live in a house with a ghost," I said, unthinkingly, referring to the ghost of the elderly lady who had died in the house before Beth and I purchased it. "The past is with you, whether you believe it or not."

"Your past, too, apparently."

"Yes," I said, suddenly as somber as I had been giddy a moment before. This time, I shoved those thoughts of my wife's death aside. "But enough of ghosts."

Recognizing my change in mood, and probably intuiting the reason for it, she smoothly changed the subject. "When was Jackson founded?"

Her eyes sparkled with such apparent interest that I began to wonder if she had any professional acting experience. Not that clever, attractive women like Jenny needed it to induce guys like me to tell them whatever they wanted or didn't really want to hear.

"In 1821. General Thomas Hinds, Mississippi's hero of the Battle of New Orleans, helped the legislature take advantage of some land stolen…I mean gained by treaty with the Choctaws at gunpoint, near the state's geographical center. Hinds chose a spot near LeFleur's Bluff, located on a river but high enough not to flood. The Legislature named the city after Andrew Jackson, the recognized hero of the Battle of New Orleans, and the county after Hinds. They laid out the city on a checkerboard plan President Jefferson had suggested several years earlier."

"Hmm. The Battle of New Orleans… How do you know so much about that? I couldn't tell you a thing about it and I lived in Louisiana for years."

"That's certainly par for course. One of the most significant battles waged on American soil where a rag tag group of Tennessee riflemen, Mississippi Dragoons, one of whom was my great, great grandfather, Sgt. John Ferguson, renegade piratical terrorists, Choctaw Indians and U.S. Regulars took on the world's greatest fighting force and blasted them off the continental shelf. And almost no one could give you book or verse."

She asked me another question so softly I didn't hear it.

"What's that?" I asked.

"Perhaps you could hear me better if your music wasn't so loud."

"My what? Oh…" I had become so accustomed to wearing my headphones while taking my lunchtime strolls that I no longer noticed wearing them when my friends accosted me on the street. Although I had done it for years, they usually assumed it to be just another quirky habit I had acquired after my wife's passing. But some people, mostly acquaintances who didn't know me well, thought me rude for not turning off the music and according them my complete attention. But 16th Century music was not of the loud variety, and I could hear what they were saying perfectly well. I told *her* so, and she seemed copacetic with the explanation.

"Sure," she said. "But if I can hear it too, it's probably loud enough to hurt your ear drums over time."

"You're right, of course," I said, turning off my IPhone and stuffing it inside my pants pocket. It didn't really matter whether I had it on or not; the music was always playing inside my head.

"You're a big Renaissance music fan?" she asked, more polite than curious, or so I felt at the time.

"I'm afraid so," I shrugged. "I find I can't do without it unless I have something else to focus on. I always listen on walks, standing in line at the grocery store, or during political speeches I'm forced to attend. It's part and parcel of my adult ADHD personality."

"Why not classical or baroque?"

"Baroque's fine for weddings feted with a crackerjack organist and a capable trumpet player. But classical music, like analytical philosophy, is too dull, too emotionless, and far too complicated for me to understand, much less appreciate. You can keep Kant and Beethoven, Spinoza and Mozart; give me something livelier, like Pascal and Josquin de Prez, or Voltaire and Michael Praetorius. It's like my other favorite-R&B or Soul to my generation-- sometimes spiritual, other times sensual, but always resonating with an emotional punch the other musical forms can't match. Of course they don't play Josquin in many Delta juke joints…"

She laughed and regarded me with a critical eye. "You're bundle of contradictions," she finally said.

"How do you mean?"

"You hate the Republicans but lambaste the Democrats. You write about the Founders, our first political philosophers, but only about their love of wine, food and architecture. You have a barely detectable air of sadness about you, yet you listen to happy Renaissance dances and Christmas songs on your IPod every day."

"You disapprove?"

"No. It's just…"

"What?" Had I said something wrong, I wondered. Everything was going so well until…. Damn my luck for running into Jerry just as she arrived. Did I come across as a jackass? Too opinionated? A sad sack of indeterminate cause? A Renaissance music geek? As it turned out, her objection proved something else entirely.

"It's such a pleasure to hear you talk passionately about the things you love—history, architecture, politics, music, but then…"

"Then…what?"

"At times you come across as so….so…"

"What?"

"Unseasoned, maybe?"

We stood for a while, pondering the other's words. What the hell did she mean by 'unseasoned', and imposing her past on me? And why couldn't I keep my damned mouth shut when circumstances involving religion, politics or romance demanded it?

We strolled west on Amite Street until we reached the rear of the Governor's Mansion where I led her across the street for a stroll through lovely Smith Park, a green square built in 1822 with towering oaks, two dried up fountains, an impressive array of magnolias and live oaks, an open air theater and a National Historic Register listing.

St. Peter's Cathedral cast a long shadow over us, giving full vent to the gentle breeze flitting through our hair, heightening our pleasure in the sunlight dappling through a gargantuan live oak's branches. The park's great oak sentinels, denuded of their greenery, gave silent testimony that winter was coming, even to the tropics. An elderly woman ambled slowly past one of the fountains toward the far side of the park; several romantically-inclined couples adorned the wood benches scattered across the lawn.

I ached to follow their example with this splendid Louisiana woman beside me, but I hadn't the courage to suggest it. Instead I casually mentioned I was working on a case that arose from events begun in the park. However, the park was now devoid of the protesters who sparked the controversy, thus ripe for romantic couples stealing a kiss during lunch.

She asked me a few perfunctory questions about my case, then we didn't speak for the next few minutes. But it wasn't an awkward silence; more a peaceful one, the kind that made me feel okay about our second encounter.

Did we actually have a budding relationship on our hands? I wondered. Or at least a chance at one? I didn't know. But for a reason that wasn't entirely clear to me, I actually did care. For the first time in four years, I really did care. Maybe that was something. If she'd see me again, that would be something else.

She had to meet a friend for lunch, and I could see by the Trustmark Bank clock it was time to head toward the Mayflower several blocks west on Capitol Street to meet Breeland Jones for lunch. I escorted her to her bike and watched her un-attach it from the light pole. As she bent down to unlock it, I noticed for the first time that her hips, fully revealed in her spandex pants, were as alluring in the daylight as her eyes had been the night before.

"See you again?" I asked.

"If you want."

"How will I get in touch with you?"

"Don't worry," she said mounting her bike. "I'll phone you. I've got your number."

That's probably more true than you realize, I thought as she pedaled east on Capitol Street, darting in and out of traffic like a teenager navigating the streets of New York or Paris. Sure, I thought, she's about thirty-five going on nineteen and I'm immature. There's just no wining with women, I told myself as I quickened my pace in the other direction, hoping not to offend Breeland by arriving late for lunch.

CHAPTER FOUR

I arrived at the Mayflower in time to stand in line on the sidewalk with Breeland. Quite popular with the noon-time lunch crowd despite Jackson's decade-long downtown decline, the seventy-five-year-old café greeted patrons with a large, art deco-style neon sign hanging over a projecting corner in the old New Orleans style of a Tujague's or Mandina's. The interior reminded of better times with black-and-white tile floors, tables and booths, and a long lunch counter in the back with vinyl spinning stools. Old photographs of turn-of-the century Jackson and posters of the Beatles and Rolling Stones helped carry the retro theme. Their seafood, especially the gumbo and Redfish Jane (topped with crabmeat) went down easy, especially with the modest prices and brown bag liquor-and-wine policy.

But the plate lunches reigned supreme at high noon, with fried eggplant, creamed corn, the surprisingly tasty mystery fish (Tilapia we hoped), and salad enlivened with the estimable joint's very own comeback salad dressing that made salad eaters out of guys whose forebears hadn't stood upright until three generations before.

Breeland seemed even more ebullient than earlier on the phone. "So," he beamed irritatingly, "did you take my advice and drop by St. Peters for confession on the way here?"

Though I hated to dampen his high spirits, I decided it was time to broach his injudicious foray into criminal law. "Speaking of confession, Breeland, were you going to tell me you were handling an arraignment Friday or were you planning on taking me by surprise like Stonewall Jackson took Hooker at Chancellorsville?"

As if he had been expecting my question, he calmly replied, "I didn't know if we should discuss the case socially or not. I've never handled a criminal case in federal court before."

"Yes, Breeland, it's called 'discovery,' whether by handing over documents at the office or shooting the breeze at lunch. But now that you mention it, what the hell are you doing handling a case with no experience in federal criminal law? Has the economy sunk so far and brought you so low as to take money out of shysters' pockets by handling criminal cases? Aren't you afraid of handling them as Packenham handled tactics during the Battle of New Orleans? They packed his bullet ridden corpse in an oversized pickle jar of rum and shipped him back to Britain, saying he traveled in good spirits."

"You should have been an actor, John, with your sense of the melodramatic. You won't believe this, but my client insisted upon hiring me. He sought me out and wouldn't take no for an answer."

"Sought you out? He was in jail."

"He sent somebody with the money. This tall, laconic fellow sat in my office lobby for three hours waiting to see me, then paid a $10,000 cash retainer on the spot, and signed a contract to pay $10,000 more before trial, and another $10,000 on appeal should that need should arise."

When I managed to speak, I said, "Did either of them know you're a civil attorney who hasn't tried a criminal case in twenty years, and never one in federal court?"

"I told him that," he said, shuffling toward an open table. "Told him I only tried one--our dead lawyer case, years earlier. He said, 'well you won the only one you tried, didn't you?' I said, 'I just got lucky there,' but he didn't care. He handed me a briefcase full of hundreds, several documents relevant to this case, and told me to keep the briefcase, the client was waiting for me at the jail, and he'd see me at the hearing."

"Who? Who would see you at the hearing? And what's your client's name," I asked, sliding into a booth across from him.

Breeland seemed a little confused for a second, going so far as to actually scratch his head full of straight blond hair. His light blue eyes darkened as he struggled with my question. "I...I can't remember. The fellow gave me a name, but I've forgotten it. My client never told me his name. I.... Do you think I'm way in over my head?"

At six foot, two, about 185 pounds, with bean poles for legs and a placid expression pasted on his face worthy of an insurance defense attorney, Breeland reminded of a stork standing guard on a millionaire's lawn. I couldn't imagine him speaking to a criminal in the jail, much less defending one in federal court.

Not that he wasn't a fine lawyer. Years ago, after he had left our office sharing arrangement and joined his law firm, he defended a homeowner in a lawsuit filed by my contractor client, and whipped me so badly we never spoke of it since. We aped Cornwallis and Washington after the surrender at Yorktown; just as Cornwallis was so humiliated he sent a subordinate to give Washington his sword, I sent a clerk to Breeland's office with the final order, and let Breeland take the signed order to the judge by himself.

But that was civil law in state court, and this was another can of worms entirely. I had no desire to see a good friend suffer my fate from years past, much less be the instrument of *his* humiliation. Now that Breeland had taken a sizeable retainer, Judge Day would never release him from the case. So I decided to soften the blow as much as possible.

"I don't have to tell you what a good lawyer you are, Breeland. And I'll hand over your discovery materials as soon as I can. It would help if I knew your client's name, so I could tell you if he has a criminal record, but it's obvious he's told you not to reveal it, so I'll just answer your question and say that even a good lawyer like you can't make chicken salad out of chickenshit."

"Is that what you think of our menu?" asked our waitress, who had sidled up to our booth just in time to catch the tail end of our conversation. She was our Mayflower favorite, about 28 or 30, tall, blonde as Breeland, possessed of an ideal personality for her profession.

"How you doin', fellahs?" asked a heavy-set, bearded black man behind her.

"Doing great, Frank. And you?"

"Never better," he said, his bald head shimmering with the Mayflower's neon ambiance, a long white linen napkin draped over his muscular arm. "What you boys want to drink?"

We both wanted unsweet tea with lemon.

"Coming right up," Frank said, whizzing by our booth toward the pitchers of tea resting midway on the counter.

The waitress leaned over our table. "So, what'll you guys have today?"

"Your phone number," I said, never lifting my eyes from the menu, "and the mystery fish, fried eggplant, green beans and a salad."

"I'll have the roast beef, and surprise me with the vegetables," Breeland offered.

"Got it," she said. "And I gave you my phone number last year, John," she chided playfully, "and you never called."

"I lost it. Breeland took me drinking later than evening and I never saw it again. That's why I'm asking you for it now."

"Missed your chance," she said, striding away holding her ring finger aloft to display the new diamond that sparkled wickedly in the restaurant's multitude of mirrors and neon lights.

"Speaking of discovery…" Breeland began.

"What's that?" I asked, watching the waitress and all her spectacular moving parts disappear into the kitchen like Selene, goddess of the moon, dissolving into a vaporous mist. "We were speaking of discovery?"

"Yes. Do you have any witness statements I need to see?"

"I do."

"Well? May I have them?"

"Sure, Breeland. Four days before the trial. That's what the discovery rules provide in federal court. But I can tell you without fear of contradiction that the federal marshal your client sucker-punched will be in attendance."

"I see."

"Do you?" I asked grimly. "Do you even know the first rule about trying a case in federal criminal court? I'm worried about you, partner. These Occupy the Park or City Hall protesters are either deluded or dangerous, and I'm not sure which. Either way, they're not going to be happy when I convict one of their own. And they'll blame you, not me, for the result. They can't file a bar complaint for incompetence against me since I'm not their attorney. Damn, buddy, I wish you could give that money back."

"I do, too. But my wife's already spent it."

"Already?"

"In her mind she has. That's all that matters."

"The point is—"

"What's the matter, John? You think your Yankee government is perfect? That black lives don't matter?"

I succeeded, with great effort, in keeping it friendly. Mostly. "Oh for God's sake Breeland. Your client cares about as much for justice as did Billy the Kid, and as much about black lives as did Adolph Hitler. He was a hired Antifa protester with a history of fomenting bedlam for fun and profit. Are you really that daft, or are you incapable of seeing any farther than the nose on your face?"

"I can see the moon. How far is that?"

"Here you go, fellahs," Frank said, handing us our tea glasses before humming off to greet a favorite lady customer.

Changing the subject, Breeland said, "By the way, I couldn't help noticing your renewed interest in our waitress. Anything happening on the romantic front I should know about?"

I stared at him blankly. What brought that on, I wondered? Had he seen me walking with Jenny earlier? "Why, no, Breeland. Nothing at all. Why do you ask?"

"Oh, I don't know. You know how Jackson women are, always looking for love at Christmas time. I thought maybe you had in mind striking while the Christmas lights were hot."

I hoped he hadn't seen me wince. I turned my head to hide it from him, but he was surely right about one thing; anyone facing the prospect of spending Christmas alone had a desperate holiday in store. Certainly no one more than myself these past few years.

And just like that, I was no longer present at my table in the Mayflower, but thinking about my life that was and could have still been, had not fate removed the finest person I had ever known from the world. And romantic songs notwithstanding, it had been a truly wonderful time.

Christmas with Beth and Anna Grace had always been our most joyous time of year. Though Orange Beach in summer, Ole Miss's oak-shaded-grove in fall, and New Orleans Mardi Gras in the spring rated a close second, third and fourth, nothing topped Jesus's birthday for a month of unadulterated family fun and seasonal anticipation.

In my mind's eye I suddenly saw our last Christmas together five years ago. Beth was pregnant, Anna Grace giddy about the smartly wrapped presents nestled under our red, gold and purple trimmed Frasier Fir.

On Christmas Day, our last in the Greymont house, we entertained both our mothers, all our siblings, our maid, and two of our divorced friends, and enjoyed a spectacular holiday feast. After we laid a sleeping Anna Grace's Santa deliveries under the tree and filled her stocking over the fire place, we bid everyone goodnight and hopped under the covers for a "long winter's night."

As we had done during her pregnancy with Anna Grace, I lifted Beth's nightshirt and I placed my ear against her swollen belly, listening intently for baby sounds. Then I moved my lips near her navel and wished Will a Merry Christmas, recited a poem I had written in his honor, and sang a verse of *Away in a Manger*, imagining as daddies-to-be-do, that he would come into the world recalling at least the first two verses. Then Beth kissed me as she hadn't in several years.

"I love you," she said.

"Not as much as I love you," I replied earnestly.

But that had proved, if not a lie, then certainly an overstatement. The time soon came when I had to make a choice, one that a doctor had earlier suggested I might need to make if we continued with the pregnancy.

Then her doctor brought that reality home with a vengeance just before he wheeled Beth into the delivery room to deliver Will. "We thought we had enough blood on hand," he said somberly, "in case your wife started bleeding. We had the usual killings and a big accident involving several cars and a bus last night, and our platelet supply is lower than we realized. But," he murmured reassuringly, placing his bony hand on my shoulder, "we're going to do our best. However, in the event that it comes to that, which one would you have me save if I must make the choice?"

I became a very serious Catholic that night, make no mistake. No one laughs at God in a hospital, they say, and for once "they" were right. The bleeding problem had reared its ugly head with Anna Grace twelve years earlier, but resurfaced when she became pregnant with Will.

Neither of us would hear of ending the pregnancy, no matter the risk to Beth. Would I have felt the same way, I wondered ever since, if it had been my life hanging in the balance?

A month before delivering Will, upon observing me digging in my heels on that issue and aware of her faltering courage as the condition worsened, our doctor had said, "I'm sure there's nothing to be worried about. She'll have the best emergency medical care in the world here at the university hospital."

And we believed him. I because I wanted to, and she because she knew I wanted her to. The difference was that she was being courageous and I merely selfish. I wanted a son, and already knew her healthy child would be a boy. My little girl was growing up and I needed another shot at paradise. We--

"John?"

I looked up from my glass of tea at Breeland's befuddled expression. "Yes?"

"You kinda drifted off, there, buddy?"

"Sorry."

"What about that woman in your neighborhood? The one you brought to the Christmas party at my office. You still seeing her?"

"No."

"Why not?"

"I knocked on her door one day, and she told me it was over. I said, 'that's fine, but do you mind telling me why?' She told me it was just time for the relationship to end."

"She was a real looker. Were you devastated?"

"If anything I was devastated about not being devastated."

"In other words, you met somebody else, too."

"Maybe…"

"Do you think this mystery woman might be a… prospect?"

I considered for a moment. "I don't know, Breeland. I've never thought anyone could take Beth's place. I'm not sure the woman exists who can replace her."

"No one's replacing her, John. Only succeeding her. And I say it's high time you found the successor."

"I don't know, pal. I just don't know about that," I said, hunching my shoulders in what must have seemed an unqualified demonstration of resignation. "But one thing I do know is that if you represent this protester in court next week I'm going to send you away reamed, steamed and dry cleaned."

He smiled broadly as he savored a final taste of eggplant. "I intend to win my first criminal case in twenty years, and I'm prepared to put my money where my mouth is."

"Is that so?"

"It is. Loser buys the beer. Deal?"

"Breeland," I said, with as much seriousness as I could muster under the circumstances, "this is not like one of our weekend golf matches, where the only thing we risk is the chance of eating a little crow or buying the drinks. They don't say 'making a federal case out of it' for nothing. Your client, and the people he hangs out with, may be dangerous. He did assault a federal marshal, after all."

"This is not Dodge City," he said like a traffic cop scolding a jaywalker, "and my client didn't gun down Matt Dillon. He just defended himself from an abusive government functionary who interfered with his ability to exercise his right to take another government functionary to task for interfering with his right to engage in freedom of speech."

"Yes, and he did it with enough violence to insure that he will now get to exercise his second greatest right as a free citizen, his right to a trial by jury."

"To the Founders," he said, raising his glass of tea.

"You just don't get it," I groaned, shaking my head, pointedly refusing to join his toast. "If your client doesn't like the way his preliminary hearing goes, to say nothing of his jury trial, he may file a bar complaint against you for taking a case far outside your expertise. You don't know a thing about this guy, or what he may be capable of. Do you have any information on his background, his associates, and his prior record? His name, even? Anything at all?"

Breeland waived me off, nodding 'no' while ecstatically chewing another eggplant morsel. "Four days before trial, John. I'll tell you four days before trial. Or aren't you familiar with the discovery rules in federal court?"

I looked at him with studied disbelief.

"I learn fast, don't I?" he grinned.

CHAPTER FIVE

The dark-haired black man with thick, tinted glasses and a surprisingly elegant bearing despite his blood-stained sweat shirt and blue jeans, sat beside the younger, shorter, stockier white man with close-cropped prematurely grey hair, in the rear of the old green Buick. A glance outside the rear window revealed that the digging continued as it had since they jerked the old man's body from the trunk and laid it on the ground in a secluded area of the rural garbage dump in south Jackson.

"Can you believe," said the white man, wiping sweat from his neck, "it's so hot down here in December? Hell, Africa was cooler than this in the winter."

"Doesn't seem to bother *him*, does it? Still digging without a break, and won't stop 'till it's done."

"Why'd he want the old man dead, anyhow?"

"You shot a man and don't know why?"

"He ordered it. You don't disobey him any more than I do."

"Well….If you're truly interested…"

"I'm not."

"…he witnessed the courthouse scrap with the marshal. Before that, he saw the incident in the park that put our plan into action. Would have made an inconvenient witness in either case."

"His tough luck."

"Not much of an epitaph," said the black man, staring straight ahead through the Buick's front window, "for a man killed for being in the wrong place at the wrong time."

"Excuse me, Aziz, but since when did you get teary-eyed over collateral damage?"

The man called Aziz turned to face his companion. He had long since grown accustomed to Gitt's wild-eyed visage that reminded him of two fireflies dancing side-by-side, more or less, in the night. Although most people maintained their distance from the strange little man, Aziz feared no man apart from the one digging a grave several yards behind the Buick. Still, he had no intention of insulting Gitt, who handled all their wet work that didn't involve explosives.

"I'd have slashed the old man's throat myself if *he* had given the order," Aziz said. "Cracker didn't mean anything to me. None of them do. Present company excluded, of course."

The white man averted his eyes from Aziz's, glancing back through the rear windshield to see if the burial detail was nearing completion. He wanted to make a witty reply, but decided against it. They only worked together; they weren't there to massage each other's egos. Gitt only sought to leave the garbage dump-turned burial ground and get on with the business at hand.

"Okay," the tall man shouted behind them. "That's done. Let's move." He tossed the shovel and his gloves into a pile of large black garbage bags surrounded by broken furniture, crushed soda cans and rotten food of a limitless variety, then deposited himself in the driver's seat. "It's long past time to go see a man about a horse."

"You mean 'horse's ass' don't you?"

"Why Gitts," the tall man snorted as he slammed down the accelerator and spun the car around a bend, onto the dirt road that led to the garbage dump's main gate. "You shouldn't disparage people you hardly know. They might surprise you, after all."

"You sure you didn't get sunstroke from digging that hole back there?"

"Not at all. Rather enjoyed it. We need more exercise, now and then. You especially, Gitts. You could use a few passes around the track."

"You know I don't like it when you call me that."

The tall man peered menacingly into the rearview mirror. "So?"

"Nothing. I'm just saying it's Gitt, not Gitts."

"So you say, Gitts. So you keep saying. Anyhow, I think this prosecutorial prospect has more potential than you realize. And I believe I know precisely how to tap it."

"And if you're wrong, Ryan?" Aziz asked.

The driver glanced out his window at the garbage dump they were leaving, then fixed his eyes on the paved road ahead. "There's plenty of room left in this dump, isn't there?"

"Amen," the black man agreed.

"What do you say Gitts?" Ryan grinned. "Plenty of room, eh?"

The man calling himself Gitt chose not to answer. It's not wise, he mused, poking a Grizzly bear with a stick whether it was smiling or not.

CHAPTER SIX

I wrapped up my work day by sending queries to the F.B.I., DEA and Massachusetts, Ohio and New York highway patrols seeking information on the identity of the Ghost and his confederates among the Occupy the Park/Antifa crowd. Then headed north on I-55 and picked up Anna Grace at her school a mere five minutes from our home.

She seemed distant during the ride home, barely responding to my questions about her school day or weekend plans.

"See your friends today?" I asked tentatively.

"Yep."

"How was the history test?"

"Okay."

"Just okay? You know it would be humiliating for us both if you made anything less than an A in history with a published amateur historian for a father."

"My teacher read your book."

"And?"

"And what?"

"Did he like it?"

"Yes, *she* liked it."

"Uhmm, good. How's school going?"

"Not good."

"Why?"

"Got in an argument with my teacher," she mumbled blandly, as if relating swatting a fly during lunch.

"What about?"

She took a long glance out the window, purposefully avoiding my gaze. "She told us that the virus in China was killing thousands every day, and it was just a matter of time before it came to America."

"So? It's just the flu," I said, knowing nothing more about it than that, but hoping to sound as nonchalant as possible in the face of my daughter's apparent concern. I needn't have bothered, as it turned out.

"I said, if it's going to kill us all, why should we worry about studying? So she said, 'you had better learn your algebra problems by tomorrow or you'll wish you had the plague.' So I asked if she knew of the answers to the problems, and she said, 'yes.' Then I asked, 'why are you asking us?' Big fireworks after that."

This she related as emotionless as a Darwinian scientist at a Southern Baptist revival.

What's wrong with this picture, I wondered. Anna Grace usually enjoyed chatting during rides home from school. Except for bad days, which had been more frequent of late, when she had little or nothing to say. Or nothing that wasn't darker than a down on his luck comedian's jokes. Otherwise, she enjoyed regaling me with tales of lunchroom tiffs, boyfriend sightings and her witty but non-punishable comments in class.

Not so today.

Had she recently been shutting herself in her room after school, I pondered, coming out only for dinner? Playing with Will only in her room and not in the den, as she had for the past several years? I couldn't say for sure. And that was a real shame, I admitted to myself.

We simply weren't communicating as we had before. Had I done something wrong? I couldn't remember anything spectacular. Had I been paying too much attention to Will? Sure, but he was paying a lot more attention to me than she had since she turned fourteen.

I had taken them to Disneyland, a Dodger game and Universal Studios in Los Angeles this past October. We'd all had a great time; perhaps not quite as much as Anna Grace, her mother and I had enjoyed at Disneyworld six years earlier, but it sure as hell beat another weekend in Madison with nothing new on at the cinema and the crosstown Braves' triple-A ball club out of town.

Sure, she got a little bored at the Dodgers game, even though my Bums completed a thrilling sweep of the hated Giants. But she opened up at the hotel room afterwards, admitting she had a new boyfriend named Malik. I had taken this as a good sign, since she hadn't made many new girl friends at her new school in Madison. Instead, she had acquired a coterie of male buddies in the band and on the debate team, none of whom had previously summoned the courage to ask this beautiful, blossoming young woman for a date.

Middle School can be tough for the new teenaged girl in town, especially at the age where many of the girls are meaner than prison guards at Angola. This often prompts the new girl to seek companionship of the uncomplicated male variety, opening up an entirely different cans of worms for dad.

But I never worried about Malik or any of her other buddies as potential love interests. They were the smartest kids in school, and all very respectful and well-behaved. An international crowd to be sure: a Jew, an Asian (Chinese, I think), an Indian, one black kid and one WASP. And one Egyptian Muslim named Malik. All of them had one more thing in common until Malik made his move—not the slightest hope of snaring a flesh and blood girlfriend.

Anna Grace had a solitary existence in common with them since we moved her to Madison and away from her best friend at absurdly expensive St. Andrews Episcopal junior high school in Jackson. She and her girlfriend had since drifted apart and my baby floundered as the new kid in school with nary a femme buddy to her name.

To say that she hadn't exactly blended in with the new high school crowd was an understatement. This happened partly because of her liberal beliefs (inherited from her mother, not me), her penchant for aggressively speaking her mind (that one's on me) about issues such as gay marriage, civil rights, and recently, thanks to Malik, how Mohammed should be ranked alongside Jesus and Isaiah in the prophet hall of fame. She had gone from popular at private school to pariah in public school in the space of a few weeks, with the result that she had settled comfortably in with her male amigos from the International House of Pan-flakes.

I had invited her friends to our July the 4th party last year to verify they were as clean cut as advertised. They were, it turned out, and far more than that. A finer group of boys I had never met, and felt proud she had chosen so well.

I had phoned each boy and invited him to the party, seizing my first opportunity to converse with Malik. Anna Grace had told me about his great sense of humor in the face of suspicion and even abuse, especially after the 9/11 tragedy and the Iraq and Afghanistan conflicts. So when he answered the phone, I said, "I know you're probably foresworn to destroy the United States, but would you like to come to our July the 4th party?"

"Sure," he laughed. "The girls will be wearing hijabs, right?"

I liked him immediately, but hadn't known they'd begun 'dating' shortly after that party until she 'fessed up during our October LA sojourn.

Teenagers....What are you going to do?

Unable to stomach another second of her silence, I blurted, "How's your boyfriend, Mohammed?"

"It's Malik!" she grumbled, clearly not in the mood for our usual smarmy banter.

I decided to give her some space, a tactic Beth had warned would become *de rigueur* after teenaged angst reared its ugly head. At any rate, arguing with a teenaged girl, or any woman you're related to, really, is tantamount to King Canute commanding the sea to recede. Better to let it ride, even though at times, it rides like a blind race horse over a cliff.

We drove through our neighborhood in silence.

By contrast, Will greeted me at our back door, squealing, "Daddy, Daddy," and leaping into my arms. Anna Grace shoved her way around us and made a beeline for her room.

Our nanny, a reserved, soft-spoken Romanian woman named Marianna, fixed us a dinner of turkey sandwiches, strawberries and asparagus before kissing Will goodbye and driving to her apartment in Ridgeland five miles away. I confiscated Anna's cell phone and set her to work on Algebra in the dining room. Will and I fired plastic Angry Birds from pint-sized catapults at small green pig heads perched on forts constructed of stacked plastic blocks.

Two hours of play and an episode of *Wild Kratts* later, I bathed Will and stood him on a bathroom chair to brush his teeth.

"Dad," he asked innocently, "I like Marianna. Was mommy as fun as she is?"

"More fun, believe me. You should have seen her with Anna Grace on the Matterhorn ride at Disneyworld. Now why don't you put on your pajamas so we can read our books and sing some songs."

With his head nestled on my shoulder I read him several of Jack Prelusky's rhyming dinosaur books, then spun a long story about a time machine visit to the dinosaur age, riding on Triceratops' backs, dodging the elephantine feet of long necked Siesmasauruses, and hiding from T-Rexes in a prehistoric forest.

When he finally drifted off, I carefully slipped my arm from underneath his neck and padded silently out of his room.

I seated myself in the den with a can of ark Chocolate Piroulines and glass of red Burgundy wine beside me, where an unexpected sense of loneliness hit me like an NFL linebacker on steroids.

As Tennessee Williams well knew, the solitary soul has little resort but to the kindness of strangers. Strangers like the high school bus driver who agreed to use our neighborhood gate code, against school rules, to weave his way to our doorstep and collect Anna Grace at 6:30 AM so I could stay home with my slumbering four-year-old until his nanny arrived at 7:30. Or the neighbor two doors down, a gay nurse, Wyatt, who lived alone and usually worked nights, yet never failed answer my call to tend Will and assure me that my boy wasn't dying from fever, cough or the common cold.

But there was one stranger I came to depend upon the most: my cross-street neighbor, Lindsey. She was a twenty-nine-year old lawyer for a Ridgeland insurance defense firm whom I had never met my first year in the neighborhood. Like Wyatt, she never attended those feisty neighborhood parties celebrating reconstituted pagan festivals such as Mardi Gras, St. Patrick's Day, Halloween and Christmas.

Then one day she knocked on our door, ostensibly the good neighbor checking on me and the kids, undoubtedly in light of my presumed inability to properly care for my kids during my recently enforced widowhood. Funny, I thought, she hardly seemed the motherly type. And she wasn't, I soon discovered. She made idle conversation as I cooked supper for the kids and changed Will's diapers, then, shortly after the nanny arrived to spell me for a few hours, invited me over for a drink.

She sat me on her brown leather couch, tuned in Netflix on her large flat screen TV, lit the fireplace, and poured two glasses of white wine. That she happened to open a bottle of Chambertin seemed quite the coincidence until I noticed that she often spoke with Wyatt on her front porch, and I had ordered him a bottle of that smooth Burgundy white in thanks for his help with Will.

So the very next Saturday after that first evening when my palsied social skills prevented me from taking the hint, she phoned and asked me to help her fix her clogged sink drain. Here's the reason she was so neighborly I told myself on the way to her door.

I had turned Will over to Anna Grace, grabbed a wrench and a hammer (in case things got desperate) and rang Lindsey's doorbell. She met me at the door *au natural*, brazenly gracing her doorway until my stunned surprise turned to a realization of the possibilities that lay ahead.

Needless to say, Wyatt rounded a corner just as she answered the door, so he got an eyeful of her too. She grinned broadly as he gave a thumbs-up gesture driving by her house.

Once inside, the front door closed behind me, an unexpected terror seized me by the throat. I hadn't been with a woman in two years and didn't know a thing about this one. What should I do? How should I go about it?

I had dated around at Ole Miss and later in Jackson before meeting Beth, and well knew every woman was different where her sexual preferences were concerned. What if I couldn't satisfy her? Would she like oral sex? Would she throw my back out with outlandish sexual positions?

No doubt recognizing my plight, she pinned me to the door, cupped her hands on the back of my head, pressed herself against me, and kissed me on the mouth. Somehow, in that wondrous moment, all those fears and anxieties vanished like the proverbial mist. Life took its course, as it has always done between prospective lovers, despite the gods' best efforts to befuddle us whenever they can.

The affair lasted for about a year.

She was on the partner track, she later explained, and had no time for serious 'relationships.' She figured correctly that I was suffering from a need I had buried on behalf of my children after discovering the terrific depth of commitment single parenthood required. She may have intuited my feelings of self-recrimination harbored since Beth's death in childbirth. Most importantly, she was as horny as I and lived right across the street.

We were perfectly suited as lovers; she needed me as I needed her, about two or three times a week.

The affair lasted longer than either of us expected, until she made partner and her priorities swiftly changed. Two months later she moved away and I never saw her again. Once again the gods had left me awaiting their next benevolent offering of the imponderable kindness of strangers.

Was Jenny to be that offering? Had we anything to offer each other by way of a meaningful relationship? Better sex than masturbation? Heartfelt affection or intellectual compatibility? An actual date at a restaurant?

I flicked on the den TV. As usual, when I most needed a worthwhile distraction, nothing but network drivel and worn out cable reruns ruled the airwaves. Worse, while flipping channels too slowly I inadvertently witnessed a few seconds of a reality show, then heard a talk show host declare Miley Cyrus one of the year's most influential people.

Worse still, the Democrat Nightly News criticized the president for taking the Corona Virus too lightly, hoping to gain an edge in the forthcoming presidential election. I didn't bother to check Fox News to see how the president had most recently achieved the right to sainthood, as the forfeiting of virtue by the American Fourth Estate always made me nauseous with more than a few minutes exposure.

Hell, even the History Channel had given in and resorted to the same ludicrosities the other networks fobbed off on us as reality. If that hadn't heralded the coming end of our civilization, it certainly contributed to the sterilized imaginations and feeble wills of my fellow countrymen. When many Americans take a break from their unlimited scramble for wealth and power, a pursuit substituted for their forebears' devotion to duty, integrity and sacrifice, they turn not to books or even thought-provoking cinema, but to television programs designed to distract them from their exponentially growing tax burden and ever-shrinking liberties. The circus, if you will, to go along with their government dole bread.

In protest, I drew a volume of Plutarch from my den bookshelf—the one framing my 60-inch flat screen TV--and settled in my chair for a stress-reducing read.

But reading didn't help, so I abandoned the den, slipped quietly out of the house and settled on our front porch swing. Idly shoving my feet at the brick porch floor gave me no consolation, despite the refreshingly cool nighttime air and endless sky bespangled with flickering stars. Of course I noticed that Mars and Venus occupied distant constellations in the night sky.

Moments later, I deserted Mother Nature for the comforts of my king-sized Sleep Number bed, where both firmness remotes had been set on 65 for the past three years. The gentle humming sound of the overhead fan bundled me off to sleep after reading several pages of Hans Delbruk's masterpiece on Hannibal's strategies in the Second Punic War.

****

The dream began as it always did. Will, Beth and I are riding a train through the muddle of low hanging clouds. Oddly, Anna Grace is not in the dream. We're seated by a large window in the public section, peering out at a moonless evening sky pocked with distant, dimly lit stars blinking through the scattered clouds. Seated next to Beth with Will in my lap, I'm drifting off to sleep, seduced by the train's humming sound as it hurtles down the track at breakneck speed, destination unknown.

Beth's head rests softly on my shoulder; Will's face lies buried in my chest, his arms dangling by his sides. He's dead asleep, his breathing slow and steady.

Then we hear them. People screaming, the conductor scrambling past us toward the rear compartments. No, not scrambling... fleeing. From what?

I rise to see what's happening, with Will tightly wrapped in my arms. Suddenly, we're all at the front of the train, standing on a railed platform above the tracks we're speeding over. Darkness owns everything around us.

Then we see it—a large fiery maw; an opening in space and time, its light blinding, its heat palpable but not searing. We're going to hit it in seconds.

I only have time to leap off the platform into the darkness with Will in my arms; no time to reach for Beth standing several feet away from us.

I leap. As we're falling through space I spin around to see Beth's eyes widen, her lips part to make way for a scream that never has time to sound.

I roll over in the air and see the ground coming fast. I clutch Will tighter and—

I woke soaked in sweat, Will clinging desperately to me, his fingernails digging into my shoulder blades. Although I couldn't make out his features in the darkness, there was no missing his terrified voice shouting, "Daddy, Daddy!"

My flannel nightshirt was sweat-soaked like a used dishrag.

"It's all right, Will. Everything's all right."

He clung to me with one hand, soothingly patting my back with the other in the exact same way I patted his back with mine. "It's all right, Daddy."

I suddenly remembered that, during the night and before the dream, he had stumbled into my room and climbed into my bed.

"What's happening in here?" Anna Grace said, flicking on the light.

She spied us clinging to each other, patting each other's backs.

"Another nightmare, dad?"

"Yes…I suppose so. Did I shout out loud?"

"Yes!" they shouted in unison.

"Everything's all right now," I said, glancing at the bedside clock. "It's three o'clock. Let's go back to sleep."

"May I sleep with y'all?" she asked

"Sure!"

"Yes," Will chirped, suddenly grinning ear to ear.

I took the middle portion of the king-sized bed, happy to have a child on each arm. Young and resilient, they quickly fell asleep.

I was not so lucky. Their presence helped, but a nagging thought wouldn't let me be. There was something different about the dream. What was it?

Or rather, what was my subconscious trying to tell me?

But the dream faded as they often do, and the only thing I knew was that I needed more sleep before the Ghost's preliminary hearing later that morning.

The last thing my conscious mind realized before drifting off to sleep was Will's arm tightening around my neck and Anna Grace rolling over on her side, slipping away from me toward the far edge of the bed.

CHAPTER SEVEN

Ryan Finn awoke in his hotel room bed with the sound of his buzzing cell phone and answered it, noting the lateness of the hour. "Yes?"

"Your hook is set," deadpanned a familiar female voice.

"You mean *your* hook, don't you Garrott?"

"Go back to sleep, Ryan."

"I'd sleep better with you here beside me."

"I wouldn't."

"So true."

She imagined his grinning into the phone at his own double entendre. "Ryan, you just can't help yourself can you? Let's keep this on a strictly business relationship, okay?"

"As you wish. Nothing but plans, blood and destruction. That's your preferred approach now, is it?"

"Goodbye. Just do your part and let's get this over with as soon as possible."

Finn shook off the rather loud hang up click with a bemused smile, rolled over on his side and was sound asleep within almost no time at all.

*** * ****

After a restless night with little sleep I took Will to the day care in my federal office building at 8:30 AM. The sun shone brightly in an azure sky nettled with cumulonimbus puffs, while a crisp winter's frost lay heavily on the ground. A cool breezed buffeted us and sent those clouds scudding across a radiant sky as we strolled from my reserved parking space to the employee's entrance of our new federal building, erected last year at a cost of $150 million dollars. December Mississippi days often reach 72 degrees by noon, but Old Man Winter, like government spending, won't be delayed forever. We reveled in paradise for the moment, but there was no forestalling winter's inevitable approach.

Marshall Josh Reed met me in the reception room of the U.S. Attorney's Office. Never had a man been blessed with less personality than Joshua Cade Reed. Anyone confused about the meaning of the word, 'nonplussed,' need only meet Reed once and hear that his personality was the polar opposite of that word would forever recall its meaning. A broad shouldered, heavy man with short dark hair balding in the back and a well-trimmed, bushy mustache drooping over his upper lip, he was far too phlegmatic to start a skirmish with anyone, much less assault in innocent victim. That he was capable of an energetic response to violence surprised anyone who had ever met him.

Even when defendants acted out in the courtroom and forced him to whip them back into line, his bland expression never changed, much less reflected the anger he surely must have felt when they cursed and punched him during their fruitless protests. More often than not, his intimidating size and the .45 caliber pistol strapped to his side usually kept the most cantankerous miscreants cemented in their place.

The Ghost had proved a rare exception.

"How's the world treating you, Josh?" I asked, motioning for him to take a seat on my cordovan office couch. He waited dispassionately for me to pour a cup of coffee and camp behind my large mahogany desk before answering.

"Fine."

"So," I said distractedly, "I hear you whipped this guy's ass so bad we're playing hell keeping the ACLU from making you their new poster boy for police brutality."

His face remained emotionless. "That's funny. You ready to go this morning?"

"Sure. Anything I need to know that's not in the file?"

"Nope," he gestured toward the file on my desk. "It's all there,"

"Any idea yet who the Ghost is? That's our nickname for him, by the way…The Ghost."

He sniffed at the fanciful sobriquet and stoically plowed ahead with the facts. "We got nothing. What about the FBI?"

"Nothing yet. See you in a few, okay? Magistrate Judge Kelly Day's courtroom, second floor. We'll put this guy away, don't you worry."

"I won't."

No one thought you would.

Judge Day called the case at 9:15 in her small courtroom set aside for preliminary hearings with no jury box and only four long benches for witnesses and the public. The only others present were her court reporter and clerk seated on each side of her bench, the Ghost cuffed hand and foot, and his attorney Breeland Jones, seated at the counsel table beside him. Two marshals kept a wary eye on the Ghost from their perch near the room's only exit apart from the judge's chamber door.

I called Reed to the stand, and the Ghost sat impassively with a stupid grin plastered on his face while the marshal testified to the events that landed the defendant in federal custody. It was perfectly straightforward. Upon discovering he needed a $150 filing fee, or a pauper's affidavit, and the address of any government defendants upon whom he wished to serve his complaint, the Ghost had become "agitated." When the clerk refused him further assistance, the slightly built man suddenly flashed a bonfire-sized temper, littered the clerk's office with paper, cursed the clerk and refused to leave the room.

Called to the scene by a deputy clerk, Reed approached the Ghost and coolly said, "Chill out, buddy," whereupon the Ghost tossed papers at his chest, insulted his parentage and punched him in the nose. Reed brought his massive paws to bear on the Ghost's shoulders, crunched him to the floor, cuffed him, and dragged him kicking and screaming expletives to the federal lockup down the hall.

Warrants were issued, fingerprints and a photo taken, and the Ghost consigned to a holding cell pending transfer to the Hinds County Detention Center a few blocks away, home to federal prisoners awaiting arrangement or trial.

"Anything else?"

"The Hinds County jailer reported yesterday that, since his incarceration, the John Doe has sat quietly in his cell, like a monk in a monastery, saying nothing, doing nothing but eating his meals and whistling to himself."

Per usual procedure, Breeland asked no questions of Reed (why give a man of few words the chance to add anything else damning?) but requested reasonable bail from the court.

Judge Day nodded and said, "Your client's clearly a flight risk as no one knows his name or address, and he's a danger to the community for assaulting a federal officer."

"Five thousand?" Breeland urged in his usual polite manner.

"Fifty-thousand," the judge declared.

"My God," Breeland breathed, playing shock as well as any Oscar-winning actor or careless U.S. Congressman asked to explain the lurid photographs of himself and a stripper in the public fountain near the Capitol. "On a misdemeanor like this, where no one was harmed, no weapon was used, and no prior record on file? Fifty-thousand dollars? You may as well make it fifty-million dollars, your honor!"

"Don't tempt me Mr. Jones. Anything else?"

"Ten thousand, judge?" Breeland persisted, even more politely than before. "Precedent in these circumstances holds that…"

"Mr. Jones," Judge Day interjected bemusedly, "does your precedent, presumably concerning bail in a misdemeanor assault case, include facts such as a defendant having no name and address or any other conceivable ties to the community other than invading it with other similarly undistinguished and un-domiciled malcontents, then defecating upon it in a public place before striking a U.S. Marshal?"

"Not precisely, Judge, but…"

"Thank you, Mr. Jones. That's my ruling and I'm sticking to it. Bail is set at fifty-thousand dollars, cash bond only, as the defendant owns no property in this county. Should your client provide his identity to the court, I'll consider lowering his bail. Meanwhile, trial is set on the March docket, with non-dispositive motions to be filed by tomorrow and heard next Friday afternoon; dispositive motions filed by January 31, and discovery to be exchanged four days prior to trial. There being no further business before the court, the record is closed and the marshals will escort the prisoner back to the county jail."

"Your honor?"

"Yes, Mr. Jones?"

"Here's a copy," Breeland said confidently, handing a bundle of papers to the clerk, "of my motion for habeas corpus I filed earlier this morning." He handed me a copy, then said with an engaging smile, "I guess I'll see everyone Friday next."

****

A few minutes before noon I picked up a turkey and ham sandwich, bag of apple slices and cup of unsweet tea at the Capitol Street Subway restaurant and took lunch on my own in Smith Park behind the Governor's Mansion. On a wooden bench near the place the Ghost had used as his private restroom, I contemplated both his scatological crime against humanity and Breeland's choice of cases to resume his criminal practice.

I understood the Ghost relieving himself in the park with no place to call home and nature's demands being what they are. Breeland could cast that event as a sympathy plea on the Ghost's behalf. But going postal on an armed federal marshal for no apparent reason, then sitting quietly in jail as if his lifelong ambition had been to occupy a cell in Hinds County's fashionable hoosegow made no sense at all. In fact, it almost seemed as if the whole exercise had been orchestrated.

But by whom? Foresight and planning didn't seem the Ghost's forte. And how had he come up with Breeland's fee? Who paid it for him? And why hadn't his benefactor appeared at his hearing as he had promised Breeland he would?

Breeland's habeas corpus motion made even less sense than the rest. The excessive bail allegation I could certainly appreciate, although I was impressed/surprised/mystified that Breeland knew in advance that the Judge would set such a high bail. His allegation that the government had no eye witnesses against his client seemed disingenuous in the extreme, like something filed by one of those advertising attorneys with bad hair and crooked smiles who, when pressed to do something other than ask an insurance defense attorney, "how much?" offers a canned phrase gleaned from a form book that the offending governmental action "violates the law of the land." The operative word being "land," as in cloud-cuckoo-land, where the bar examiners lived when they gave law licenses to such dimwits.

But Breeland, inexperienced as he was, knew better than that. What dire plot was afoot, I wondered. What did my buddy have up his sleeve?

And then, as if on cue, another even deeper mystery presented itself through the technological miracle of 5G cell phones.

I didn't recognize the area code appearing on my screen, but it was a strange day already and I owed money to no one, so I answered it right away.

"Yes?"

"Is this how you answer your phone, John?"

I blinked a few times before my mind connected to the voice to the woman. *How the hell did she get my cell phone number?* Before I could inquire, she blurted, "Cat got your tongue? First time for everything, I suppose. It's Jenny, silly. Wanna' come by your old stomping grounds tonight and give me a lesson in fine wines and dancing to Renaissance music?"

****

Late that afternoon I phoned Domino's and ordered a large cheese pizza and cheesy bread for Anna Grace and Will. She promptly barricade herself in her room, her IPhone headphones clamped on her ears, the sounds of teeny bop music blaring through the wires. Will and I played a few rounds of Hi Ho Cherryos before I headed out on my big date.

"Can I have some candy?" he asked.

"May I... You say, may I have some candy."

"May I?"

"No, not before your dinner."

"Awww. Please! I'll love you forever."

Ahh, yes, I thought, he's not above manipulation, and he's just not as smooth about it as his sister. "No, buddy. Not until after you eat all your dinner."

"I hate you," he scowled.

Where does this come from, I wondered, then remembered that Anna Grace had said it a week ago when I refused to let her go out with her buddies on a weeknight with a big test coming on Friday.

With the admonition in mind that parents should pick their battles, I ignored Will's comment, greeted our nanny at the front door, and slipped quietly out the back door to the garage while Mariana challenged Will to another cherry picking game.

CHAPTER EIGHT

"I don't like it, Ryan," Aziz grumbled from the hotel room couch.
"Why not?"
"With respect, you know damn well why not. We've never done this before. We hit them from a distance, never putting ourselves in harm's way. Live to fight another day… That's always been our style."
"Jamahl…I'm getting the feeling you're not at all happy with my plan."
"Why go in? That's all I'm asking. Why risk our lives unnecessarily?"
"War is about risks, my friend."
"Yes, but…."
"You afraid of dying?"
"Hmph. You know better than that,"
"Then what's the problem?"
"Ryan…And I say this with all due respect…Quit toying with me and answer my question. Why go in at all?"
The tall, shaggy haired man rose from the table, strode to the hotel window, peered through the drapes, and then answered the man who had served him without complaint for the past eight years. "Okay, Jamahl. Okay. You want to understand why, very well, I'll tell you. Yes, we've hit a few courthouses, banks and military bases from afar. We've caused our share of trouble, to be sure. But what else has that

gotten us? Has anyone appreciated our work? What have they said about us, afterwards?"

After ruminating for a moment, Aziz replied, "that we're not an organization anyone wants to mess with. When *we* send a note, they evacuate right away. They know the UFF means business."

"And we do mean business, don't we? But what do they say about us in the press?"

"That's the man's mouthpiece, nothing more. We're freedom fighters and they paint us as terrorists. With the same brush they laud the industrial billionaires who run this county into the ground. The news corporations are *owned* by the same military-industrial complex CEOs who take the government's money to make war on children abroad, destroy poor American children by denying their parents jobs, education and health care. The American press is a soiled propaganda machine, nothing more."

"But propaganda wins wars, my friend. Not tactically, but strategically. You remember Vietnam, do you not?"

"I was there. And not of my own free will."

"Quite right. But the American press does more than paint us with the *terrorist* brush. Far worse, they label us cowards, Jamahl, questioning our commitment to our cause for striking our enemy from a distance. The *religious* freedom fighters on the other hand, the ones they call international terrorists, they don't call them cowards, do they? And why not, I ask? Because they either risk or give their lives for what they believe every time they strike."

"They hate them more than they hate us."

"Yes, but they fear them more, and nobody accuses them of lack of commitment, or having yellow streaks down their backs. By taking the same approach here, we show them our commitment to our beliefs. Demonstrate that we are not only unafraid of them, but contemptuous of their power."

Aziz breathed deeply and nodded his acquiescence. "I understand."

"We demonstrate that five Americans citizens, two of us home grown and three immigrants who came here for freedom, found that freedom to be a chimera, and took up the fight, made a total commitment for change. Made it here in Jackson, Mississippi, the very heart of rebellion from that monolithic abortion called the United States government."

"I understand, Ryan. But you do have a plan to get us out of there after we go in?"

"Oh, yes. I've a plan for that, as well. We'll need a few things first; things related to access and control. I've no doubt that you and Gitts will persuade a few federal employees to meet our needs."

"Was there a reason you chose this place?"

"I always have a reason. You know that, Jamahl. Jackson, Mississippi is one of the country's least populous state capitols, half the size of Oklahoma City. Security here, if not actually lax, is by no means as heightened as at courthouses in larger metropolitan areas. Easy in, easy out, you see. Every structure has its weak points, Jamahl, and I'm counting on you to find this one's. Perhaps a way in from underground, or weakness in the original construction plans to exploit. May I count on you for that?"

"Of course....But why choose this particular time?"

"Simple. With this Chinese virus headed our way, assuming it gets here in time, as my sources in Italy suggest that it might, we'll be going in facing minimum resistance, with government employees either working at home or ill with the virus. Of course if it doesn't arrive soon enough, no matter. I suspect the Christmas season will accomplish the same result, with everyone in a festive mood, on holiday, or at the very least, with their guard way down."

"But what if the authorities see us coming? We shouldn't underestimate them. What if they-- "

"You needn't worry about that," Ryan insisted smoothly. "I've got something planned on that account. Remember the immortal words of Sun Tzu- 'All warfare is based upon deception or distraction. The whole secret lies in confusing the enemy, so he can't fathom our real intent.'"

Aziz smiled. "Yes...'Mystify, mislead and surprise the enemy.' They taught The Art of War at Harvard, just as they did at Cambridge."

"But this is not a classroom, Jamahl. Here, we no longer study war, we make it. We'll hit them where they least expect it, because we'll be in there with them, and they won't expect us to risk our own people.

Then, when they think they've got us, we hit them again. 'In the midst of chaos, there is also opportunity.' They'll never see it coming, and in the end, they won't dare try to stop our escape."

"Not without taking down some of their own, I imagine."

"That's right," the tall man grinned, placing a large hand firmly on the other's shoulder. "Now you're back on track. Thinking with me, not against me."

"I'm never against you, Ryan. They're the enemy. They've always been the enemy, and they always will be, as far as I'm concerned."

"Well said."

"And about this chaos, as you call it. Do you have a decent IED man?"

"The best. Yurgev Gruzenko. He'll be here tomorrow from New Orleans."

"Gruzenko, huh? The silent but deadly type, for sure. Couldn't believe they granted him citizenship. You must be prescribing a rather large dose of chaos."

"By the way, Jamahl, I've always wanted to ask you... Your surname, Abdul Aziz. That's an Arabic name, an assumed one, no doubt, as you grew up in Chicago and matriculated at Harvard."

"I dropped my slave name early on."

"What does it mean, your name? You never do anything randomly. Nothing without due deliberation, eh? Tell me what it means."

"Abdul Aziz means 'servant of the powerful'."

"Outstanding! And your first name.... Jamahl?"

"A variation of Jamal, meaning handsome. That one was... suggested to me by another."

"A woman, I trust."

"Yes. Bonita, meaning..."

"Beautiful. I know. Where is she now?"

"No longer with us."

"Fatal disease?"

"Yes. One called the American government."

"I hope you made someone pay for that."

"I did. Payment in full."

"Well done. We've all lost loved ones. I'd imagine even Gitts had a mother. We use those losses to remind us of our duty. To remind us that we can never stop making them pay for what they've done, what they do every day. And mark my words, Jamahl, we will make them pay next week. But this time not just in monetary losses. This time, they'll pay in blood. Just as those we loved paid in blood. To paraphrase Jefferson, revolution doesn't occur in a feather bed."

"Then I'm with you, Ryan. With you all the way."

"Very good."

"Do you know what your given name means?"

"Why don't you tell me, Jamahl? I know your fondness for such things."

"Ryan means 'little ruler.' Your surname, Finn, is ancient Irish, the name of one of the High Irish Kings in the 7th century BCE."

"Americans hate royalty and kings above all things, don't they? How ironic that one of the forgers of their next revolution should be named for royalty and descended from a king."

"I only hope you're not underestimating our opponents."

"I thought you said our opponents were… how did you put it? Ignorant crackers?"

"Yes. But one hundred and eighty ignorant crackers held out against two thousand trained Mexican soldiers for thirteen days at the Alamo. Another gang of ignorant crackers inflicted over 2000 casualties on the greatest fighting force in the world, suffering a mere 13 killed, at the Battle of New Orleans. None of those were as well-trained or as blessed with the extraordinary weapons and technology as are the ignorant crackers we'll soon be inserting ourselves amongst in a federal courthouse."

"Yes, my friend, but your historical examples were of men defending a position; we're going on the attack, taking the fight to their unholy sanctuary. And you forget one other very important fact."

"Oh?"

"By your definition, I'm a cracker, too."

"But not an ignorant one," Jamahl smiled.

The tall man's eyes sparkled with amusement at this reply. "But a cracker, nonetheless. And it was the ultimate cracker, certainly an uneducated cracker cavalryman, who deceived, confused, harried, assaulted, slaughtered and defeated every Union opponent he faced in the Civil War, despite being outmanned and outgunned in every battle he waged. His success prompted General Sherman to post a $25,000 bounty on his head, saying this cracker must die if it cost 10,000 lives and bankrupted the national treasury. And they never defeated or even captured him during the entire four-year war."

"Are you likening yourself to Nathan Bedford Forrest?"

"Absolutely. If I cause this government half the misery Forrest did, I'll go to my grave a satisfied man."

"But not next week, I hope."

"Not next week. Are you with me, Jamahl?"

"Here I am."

"You'll make them bleed?"

"I always do."

"Yes, yes. Let your plans be dark and impenetrable as night," Ryan quoted as he strode toward the hotel room door, "and when you move, fall like a thunderbolt."

CHAPTER NINE

I had no difficulty finding Jenny's house on Greymont Avenue near the south-easternmost edge of the historic Belhaven subdivision. Beth and I had lived there for fifteen years, remodeled several rooms and made love in every one of them until Anna Grace arrived. We had shepherded Anna Grace through all the exquisite joys and anguished tears of childhood, and after Beth's belly had begun to swell, imagined what new joys the gods would grant us. Or so we thought until I drove her to University Hospital a dozen blocks from our home on a dreary December morning.

The old homestead looked rather worse for wear since the last time I had seen it. The couple who bought it had taken jobs in another city just as the market bottomed out and couldn't sell if for half its value, ultimately renting it to medical students from the University Med Center to avoid paying two notes. The students hadn't wrecked it, but neither had they kept it up, allowing the white paint to chip across the facade, kudzu to invade the back yard from a nearby wooded area, and the gutters to fill with leaves from the tall oaks guarding the front lawn.

But one of the renters did his part, because the red front door and green shutters glistened with fresh coats of paint, and the bushes running across the front were neatly trimmed and handsomely shaped.

Strolling up the front sidewalk I felt the strange sensation that someone had married my old flame and dressed her in red lipstick, a low cut blouse and tattered blue jeans.

Jenny met me at the front door with a bemused expression, almost as if she were embarrassed to have asked *me* out, or more likely because our first date took place at her house, rather than a restaurant or cinema. Or maybe that was just *my* imposing a Mississippi Delta-reared mindset upon this worldly wise woman from south Louisiana who sometimes spoke with a barely discernable hint of Midwestern accent.

"Come in," she said after I handed her a bottle of wine.

I should have greeted her before gaping at the living room from the foyer, but I couldn't help staring and then didn't know what to say.

"Brings back old memories," she asked, her voice a little off center. Was she as nervous as I? You could never tell with women, they so effortlessly hid their anxieties the first time they met you and the first time they bedded you.

"I don't know," I said. "With different furniture and rugs it looks like an old friend with a different haircut and brand new wardrobe."

She was casually attired in jeans, sandals, and a charcoal gray fitted Henley tee. Her barely discernable scent, whether conditioner or body lotion, proved so intoxicating I had to ask her to repeat her question.

"Pardon me?"

Her lustrous black eyes narrowed slightly as she repeated herself. "I said, do you approve of the décor?"

"The décor? Oh, yes. It's fine…I suppose."

"Something on your mind?"

Unsure how to answer that question, I changed the subject. "Do you know the wine?" I asked.

She perused the label. "Hmm, Volnay. Jefferson's favorite Burgundy red."

I couldn't hold back the wide grin. "So you did read my book!"

"Of course. Come in. Have a seat." She gestured toward a couch near a pastel-colored wall in a den sparsely populated with a narrow coffee table, two nondescript chairs, and a cabinet trimmed with objects d'art, candles of various sizes and, curiously, no photographs at all. "Are wine, cheese and fruit good for you?"

"Sure."

While she uncorked the wine and assembled the cheese tray in the kitchen, I settled back on her couch and considered my 'predicament.' Without pondering the consequences, I had accepted her invitation, forgetting that I would be entering the lair of a flesh and blood woman, replete with an inscrutable perspective, incomprehensible emotional makeup and, no doubt, an agenda entirely different from mine. For fifteen years, marriage had relieved me of the stresses associated with extemporaneously responding to different women's personas, just as it had educated me on the impossibility of converting the persona I had wedded into something more manageable or even comprehensible to my masculine mind, hopelessly and eternally foundering out of its depth.

She laid a tray of apple slices, red grapes, smoked Gouda cheese and Triscuits on the table before me and handed over a glass of Volnay, fortunately large enough that my first gulp didn't appear to drain it halfway.

"So," she said warmly, setting her glass on the table and delicately spreading cheese on a cracker, "Have you considered my suggestion about the subject of your next book?"

"You didn't care for the first one?"

"Oh, it was fine. Even enlightening as to some of the more arcane aspects of Jefferson's personality; tastes in wine, food and the like. But you offered little of his feelings for his friends, his lovers, or the people he met in his travels…"

"Lovers? What lovers?"

She regarded me like a college freshman who'd asked the biology professor where babies came from. "Really, John? Thomas Jefferson, in his forties, the prime of health, in romantic Paris, far from his peers, with amoral aristocratic ladies encircling him like lionesses stalking a wildebeest? He had a nubile slave girl in his quarters who resembled his beloved dead wife and attended him in his private chambers. Once outside his home, a beautiful, sexually and emotionally frustrated Maria Cosway, married to a twit she despised, swooned over him during long carriage rides across the countryside. And you ask me about lovers?"

Well, okay then.

I found her knowledge of Revolutionary-era history so comprehensive, her rarified interest in it so compelling, that I failed to abide by the prime directive of first dates, namely, to spin the conversation in *her* direction. To ask *her* questions about how *she* felt about things; let *her* talk about *herself* and whatever else *she* deigned to discuss. To never allow the conversation to focus on *my* thoughts or opinions—the surest roadmap to disaster, revealing my every blind prejudice, Neanderthal viewpoint, or deep-seated resentment against the things she treasured most. Thus convincing her that even soap operas and tenth-run Lifetime movies were preferable to conversations with a knucklehead like *me*.

More significantly, I entirely failed to notice that she was pumping me for information about my own likes, proclivities and opinions, but cleverly framing her questions in the context of a discussion about my Jefferson book. And like the masterful conversationalist she was, she used that information to puff my ego sufficiently to loosen my tongue on subjects I might ordinarily not discuss with a near-stranger. And there was always the wine.

"It really hasn't dawned on you, has it?" she asked, her luminescent eyes glowing in the lamplight, her body language and tone of voice exuding far more charm than I had been prepared to face so early in our relationship.

"What? What hasn't dawned on me?"

"Think of it this way," she said, pausing to sip her wine. I followed suit and inhaled the contents of my glass. "You enjoy travel, are devoted to your children, read from a book every night before you fall sleep, a book taken from an extensive library taking up two rooms of shelves in your house…"

Had I actually told her that the first night?

"…listen to Renaissance and Baroque music, practice several professions, and crave French wine…"

I refilled her glass.

"…seem a little shy and reserved around women…"

"I do?"

"...you haven't dated anyone seriously since your wife died four years ago, you abhor politics but nevertheless hold deeply entrenched views on every political subject, have a greater interest in history and architecture than almost anyone else you know and appear to be a host of contradictions to *everyone* you meet." She smiled triumphantly. "Am I right, John?"

'Well...I wouldn't exactly..."

"So, of whom does all that remind you?"

Her eyes caught mine for a moment, and even from across the couch, I felt an unexpected closeness to her that would have made me go weak in the knees had I been standing. Then I nodded to concede her point.

"You're absolutely right," I grinned, averting my eyes to a blank space on the wall. "In every way that doesn't matter, and except for the brilliant mind, the election to the presidency and penning the Declaration of Independence, I'm exactly like Thomas Jefferson!"

We shared a laugh at my expense, then I added, "And except of course, for the fact that I write about architecture and Jefferson designed the University of Virginia and Monticello. I listen to ancient music and he played it on the violin. And I drink wine and he planted vineyards. Speaking of which, I think I'll have another drink."

She refilled my glass then abruptly changed the subject and asked about my prosecution of the Occupy the Park defendant.

Rather than ruining the moment and acting the stuffy government functionary by declaring I couldn't discuss ongoing cases with strangers/dates/potential love interests, I attempted to navigate the choppy waters by saying, "it's going fine." Then, adopting her tactics- "but what about you? You like Jackson, so far? What brought you here from Louisiana?"

But she wouldn't have a bit of it. She deflected every question with lines like, "Oh it bores me to talk about myself," or "you needn't feel you should direct the conversation my way. We're not teenagers, after all."

Overwhelmed as much by her perspicuity as under the influence of the grape, I said nothing at all, doing my best to sit up straight without drooling on the carpet.

My non-strategy partially worked; she confessed to serving as a substitute teacher in the Baton Rouge public schools, and admitted a desire to play with the Jackson Symphony Orchestra. Then she abruptly shut off the faucet. I finally gave up plumbing the mystery that was Jenny, and after another extended moment of silence, used the opportunity of refilling her mostly full glass to slide closer to her on the couch.

"You don't give out much information about yourself, do you?" I asked.

Maybe it was our sudden physical closeness, my overly intrusive gaze, or the possibly indiscreet question, but she stiffened noticeably, uncrossed the leg aimed in my direction and crossed the other toward the opposite wall.

"Are you putting me on the stand now, counselor?"

I felt a slight dizziness that wasn't from the wine. I felt stranded in the middle of the street with traffic coming in both directions, unable to move to my left or right, pondering what the hell promoted me to cross the street in the first place.

Perhaps sensing my bewilderment, she placed her hand on my knee, softened her voice, and asked brightly, "want to dance?"

The only proper answer to such a question is 'yes', so of course I said, "To what?"

Undeterred by my reckless insipidity, she took my hand and guided me off the couch to the center of the room. Then she revealed a CD player inside a wide, oak wood cabinet, opened a drawer and produced two vaguely familiar CDs. "I own two Renaissance CDs," she beamed, "one with Michael Praetorius's Terpsichore dances, and another with the sacred songs by Josquin, Willaert and Thomas Tallis, in case you'd prefer a slow dance."

I finished my glass, set it down, and briefly stared off into space, wondering how she could possibly know the names of my favorite composers. "How did you…"

"Dance music then," she quipped, inserting a CD in the player. She placed one hand in mine, raising it higher than our heads, and snaked another around my waist as if she intended to lead. "I couldn't help hearing your music selection during our tour the other day. Your

IPod was turned up a little high. You're going to ruin your hearing, you know."

"Yes, but…"

"I suppose," she cooed with a wry smile as *Mistress Winter's Jump* filed the room with the sounds of recorders, crumhorns, sackbuts, fifes and cornets that moved my feet as if by magic, "you think you're the only one in this city who knows ancient music?"

"You really like it?"

"I played it with the Louisiana Philharmonic Orchestra when they performed *A Musical Night in Provence* years ago."

"Which instrument?"

"The recorder."

"You played Praetorius?"

"Are you going to dance with me, Mr. Jefferson, or discuss the finer points of music, books and architecture until the dawn's early light?"

****

I made it home a little after 10:30, expecting to find Will asleep and Anna Grace chatting up Malik on her cell phone.

I couldn't have been more wrong.

"Daddy, daddy," Will cried as he met me in the doorway, his terror-filled eyes brimming with tears.

"What's wrong," I blurted, hoping he'd tell me he had spilled his chocolate milk on the living room couch.

"Anna Grace has blood on her, daddy!" he panted, dragging me toward her room.

Panic always erupts in a rush from gut to head, but never with such force as when your children's lives are endangered. I dashed into her room and flipped on the light. She lay prostrate on her sheets, dressed in a t-shirt and underpants, her head on a pillow, her eyes half-closed, her breathing shallow. I grasped her shoulder to shake her out of it but froze dumfounded when I saw the blood smeared across her left leg. Narrow gashes crisscrossed her calf inches above the ankle, one larger cut snaked wickedly across her thigh.

I dropped beside the bed and shouted, "Anna Grace, wake up! Anna Grace!"

Will sobbed inconsolably, his breath catching every other moment before another howl fled his throat. Anna Grace's head rolled back and forth as she opened her eyes. I glanced at the bedside table and saw white, circular pills spread out on the surface, an empty glass resting on its side.

I held her to me, felt her labored breathing on my neck.

"Dad?" she mumbled.

"Hang in there, baby. Stay with me, Anna Grace." I started to slap her face but stopped short when I saw her staring wide-eyed at me.

"Did you take pills," I asked, grasping several of them off the nightstand.

"Yes."

"How many?"

"Ddd...Don't know."

"What are they?"

"Shleeping ppills."

"How many?"

She strained to focus. "Thwee, maybe more. I'm shorry."

"That's okay," I said, fishing desperately in my pocked for my cell phone. "You're going to be fine."

Will pressed himself against me, tears streaming down his cheeks as I dialed 911.

Fortunately my neighbor Wyatt was off call, answered the anxious knock at his door, and agreed to sit with Will while I followed Anna Grace's ambulance out of our neighborhood, sirens blazing and lights flashing to the consternation of our sleepy-eyed neighbors.

At the University Hospital ER in Jackson, emergency personnel spirited Anna Grace away and left me in the waiting room to contemplate my daughter's fate.

Emergency waiting rooms are cheerless repositories of human agony, peopled with weary friends and relatives, deep circles bracketing their eyes, haunted expressions masking their faces, the look of fear etched deeply into their furrowed brows.

After the longest forty minutes of my life, a nurse guided me to a small room where Anna Grace lay curled on a bed in the fetal position. When she saw me she bounced off the bed and rushed to my side.

"Daddy," she said, clutching me tightly. "I'm so sorry."

"The hell, you say," I babbled. "I'm just happy you're okay, baby girl."

We stood there, wordless, grasping each other as if any minute the Grim Reaper might whisk one of us away forever. A woman entered the room moments later—the ER physician on call, a youthful, thoroughly Americanized Indian named Dr. Sethi, a resident with narrow glasses and short black hair, wearing a crisp green scrub shirt and matching rumpled pants. Anna Grace seated herself in a chair while the doc and I spoke in hushed tones at the far corner of the room.

"I take it she's fine?" I asked.

"Absolutely. She's in no danger," the doc replied calmly, "and in fact, I don't think she ever was."

My face crinkled into a question mark. "How's that, doc?"

"Did she say anything to you before or after you found her?"

"Well…She phoned me while I was driving from Jackson to Madison, at about 10:15, and asked me if I was coming home soon. I told her I was."

"I see. Did you have much difficulty waking her when you found her?"

"No…Not really. Why? What did she take?"

"We ran the tests on her, and identified the pills you gave us in the ambulance."

"And?"

"We found nothing dangerous. Her system's clean. She was wide awake the whole time. By the way, you didn't find a note, did you?"

"You mean a suicide note?" I let that thought bang around inside my head for a moment. "No. I didn't."

"That's what I thought. Has she had a change of circumstances lately? New school? Broken romance? That sort of thing? Where's her mother?"

"Her mother died four years ago. I moved her to a different school, where she's had a hard time making friends. There's a boyfriend in the picture but I don't know where they stand."

"Uhm, hm," the doctor nodded, apparently confirming a theory in her head. "Did you know she's been cutting herself for the past several months?"

I shook my head in bewilderment. "I had no idea. She doesn't usually wear skirts, and never short ones. Almost always wears pants, jeans and the like. She never told me she was having emotional issues."

"They never do."

"So what's with the cutting? What the hell is that all about?"

"She told me it helped to take her mind off the pain."

"Physical pain?"

"No," she said, looking askance at me, perhaps wondering how I could possibly be so dense. "Mental pain. Emotional pain."

"Of course," I nodded. "But you didn't answer my question, doc."

"Oh?"

"What did she take, if there was nothing left in her system? She told me she took something and I brought the pills here for you to test. Why do you say she was never in danger?"

She glanced over my shoulder again, took my arm and pulled me closer to her so she could speak in a more conspiratorial manner. "If she had died, she would have been the first person on record to overdose on Melatonin, a completely natural substance that wouldn't kill you if you swallowed twenty pills."

CHAPTER TEN

Anna Grace fell asleep beside me on the front seat during our twenty-minute drive home from the ER at 2:45 A.M. After we arrived home and thanked neighbor Wyatt for putting Will to bed. Finally alone with her, I asked, "Why didn't you tell me you were depressed?"

"I don't know," she mumbled, clearly uncomfortable with the conversation she knew I expected to have.

"You don't know? You were in such pain you scrounged an old bottle of your mother's sleeping pills from God knows where, expecting to wake up dead, but you don't know why you were upset?"

"Can we talk about this later?"

"No we can't. I'll make you an appointment with a psychiatrist tomorrow but I need to know you're not going to swallow any more pills tonight. The doctor said you weren't in any real danger and that this was probably a cry for attention or help. Well, if that's the case, here's the attention. Let me help you if I can. Just don't shut me out, honey. I need to know you're going to be alright."

"I'll be fine," she pleaded intently, meeting my anguished glare with a resolute glower. "I promise. I just don't want to discuss it right now."

"Fine," I said, unable to disguise my frustration. Or perhaps more accurately, my shame for not noticing she had bottomed out and needed to cut herself and swallow pills to dull her pain and get my attention. Or that I had my head so far up my ass I hadn't even noticed she was down, much less quasi-suicidal.

I made a decision I knew she wouldn't appreciate. "But you're sleeping in my room tonight. And we're going to have a long talk when you get home from school tomorrow."

She shrugged her shoulders, too exhausted to argue.

As was I. "Just tell me one thing."

"What?"

"Has anybody hurt you? Touched you in a bad way? Anything I need to…"

"No!" she huffed. "No, dad! No! Do you think the brown boyfriend forced himself on me? Is that what you're thinking? The Muslim terrorist raped me in the back of the classroom?"

I returned her fierce look, then clamped down on my anger and simply shook my head "no." "You're right. We're both exhausted and would rather talk about this tomorrow."

"Right."

"If you swear to me you're going to be fine. Because if you're not we can admit you to the psychiatric unit until a doctor assures me you're really will be fine."

"I'm good, dad," she said patting my arm, her voice barely concealing the sarcasm she felt owing to anyone foolish enough to believe that a depressed teenager's promise not to commit suicide meant anything at all.

And she was right. All I could do was gamble she was telling the truth and her foolish act was nothing more than a cry for help. If so, time, a father's love, a little brother's guileless affections, and better circumstances would heal every wound she suffered now.

If.

But as I lay on my bed waiting for her to put on pajamas and join me, I asked myself how everything had spun so far out of control, and how much worse things would get before we saw any light in this hauntingly blackened tunnel?

I offered a prayer and a plea for heavenly aid, but as Kierkegaard often noted, God maintained his usual silence. John Steinbeck would have appreciated my turn on his phrase in stating the obvious understatement—our world was clearly not spinning in greased grooves.

CHAPTER ELEVEN

The next morning at 7:30 when I wandered into the driveway to retrieve the morning paper, I noticed an eight-by-ten brown manila envelope lying on our front porch. A freshly awakened Will met me on the porch, eager to hear how things turned out at the ER the night before. After assuring him Anna Grace was fine, I suddenly felt a strange sensation, as if we were being watched, or that something even stranger was in the air. Several of our neighbors heading off to work cast awkward glances our way in light of the late ambulance event several hours earllier, but I had more to be worried about than a nosy Gladys Kravitz or two.

I checked on Anna Grace again to be sure all was as fine as could be expected, then let the nanny in the front door. An hour later, I loaded Will into his car seat and drove him and a deathly silent, gloomy Anna Grace to her school. As she stepped onto the curb, I said, "We'll talk after school. I love you, girl."

"Okay, dad."

"Bye, Bye Anna!" Will shouted, happy to see her back in a recognizable pattern. *Way to go little buddy.*

"Bye Will," she said, smiling coyly at him before tramping slowly toward her school, her jam-packed book bag weighing heavily on her back and shoulders.

Watching her go, I wondered how this downtrodden, head-lowered, slumped-shouldered girl could be the frolicking little munchkin of two years before. The same girl who, as a two-year-old, squealed with delight when I crossed the threshold coming home from work. The same tyke who, during Mardi Gras four years ago, scrambled giddily onto the St. Charles Avenue neutral ground so she and her best friend could dance to the beat of marching bands invading Uptown New Orleans…

I couldn't connect the dots in my head, found myself unable to comprehend how someone with as much going for her as Anna Grace—beauty, charm, intelligence, a unique and delightful personality, a loving father and brother—could feel so low she needed to slash her skin to overcome the pain? To kiss it all goodbye, down some pills (not knowing they were harmless?) and check out of existence forever… To never know love, the carefree fun of college life, birthing her own children, taking her shot at making a difference in the world?

I simply couldn't wrap my mind around it, so I resolved not to try, and to hear what she had to say to me and a psychiatrist that afternoon after school.

Easier said than done, I realized halfway to the office.

Hadn't I noticed her grades dropping slightly at midterms this semester? But wasn't she happy with her new boyfriend? Playing with Will every night? Sure, things weren't the same with good ole dad—I was no longer her best pal, with her dogging my tracks wherever I went. And her mother was dead, I reminded myself with no small degree of chastisement. In the best of circumstances, that was always a bitter pill to swallow.

Or had this to do with something else entirely? Didn't teenaged girls discover boys and move on with their lives, go to sleep one night as little girls only to wake the next morning as young women? Was Malik somehow behind all this? Had they broken up? She wasn't pregnant at least; the hospital doctor had checked that first.

Better to give it a rest, Ferg, I chided myself. If they had wanted you to know all the answers they'd have reserved you a pedestal on Mount Olympus.

I had other fish to fry, and there was nothing I could do about Anna Grace until later in the day. Or so I told myself as I turned off I-55 onto Pearl Street a few blocks from my office.

****

Shortly after dropping Will at our federal building day care, I settled into my office and phoned Anna Grace's school principal, told her about our situation and asked her to keep an eye on my little girl. She assured me they would. But I couldn't help feeling blue, so I took the elevator to the first floor and Will's day care center.

I peered through the large plate glass window at my boy romping through the playground with his friends, John Mason, Susie and Christopher. A few minutes lifted my spirits considerably, and I began dialing Breeland's number for lunch at the Elite Restaurant on Capitol Street. Then I suddenly remembered his suggestion that I go to confession for putting Will ahead of Anna Grace and shut off the call.

Maybe confession *was* a good idea. Though I no longer believed in absolution, I had learned from experience that confession to anyone, but especially a priest schooled in the art of listening, was a worthy salve for a guilty conscience or an aching heart. Also, my regular therapist, Jones Seveer, had committed suicide a year ago and left my priest as the only real option.

I determined to see what mother church could do for a backsliding member of her flock. Hadn't Jesus offered solace for the poor in spirit rather than the high-flying, life-without-a-hitch crowd? I could no longer cite book and verse, but a drowning man needs no engraved invitation to reach for any life preserver hurled his way.

Then I suddenly remembered the large envelope I had found on my doorstep earlier that morning, and drew it from my briefcase. I set the envelope on my desk, opened it, and read the note attached by paper clip to the front page of a typed manuscript that read-- "Greetings! Hope you enjoy this old diary. It's a 1960's-era typewritten copy of the original handwritten diary by William Short, secretary to Ambassador Thomas Jefferson in Paris, before the latter returned to America to serve as George Washington's Secretary of State. Enjoy!"

If finding my 15-year old overdosed on pills with gashes on her leg had shaken me to my foundations, this note at least rattled my cage. I lifted the 'diary' off my desk and gazed dumbfounded at the first page.

My book research on Jefferson's sojourn in Paris had never revealed the slightest possibility that Short had penned a diary of those heady days spent in the City of Lights shortly before the French Revolution's Terror darkened it for decades.

I should have immediately phoned the U.S. Attorney and reported that a strange envelope, with a typed note and manuscript had been left on the doorstep of an Assistant U.S. Attorney. One currently prosecuting a man with possible terrorists connections, whose identity could have been discovered with the help of fingerprints and typewriter matching.

Was someone sending me another message? That they knew where my family lived? Or, on a very different hand, was the historical find of the century resting in my hands? But if so, why send it to me? Because I had penned a Jefferson book?

To be sure, I wasn't in the best frame of mind, and my failure to act responsibly could have been excused as the act of desperate man grasping for straws.

But none of that mattered at the time. The reality was that, if curiosity killed the cat, it was very well positioned to slay me too. And I couldn't have been happier about it.

I held the manuscript gingerly and began to read....

Excerpts from the Diary of William Short
Secretary to Ambassador Thomas Jefferson, Esq.
Hotel Landron
Paris, France
February 17, 1785
8:30 AM- Shrove Tuesday

I begin this private journal of our experiences in Paris now that the Congress has appointed Mr. Jefferson to replace Dr. Franklin as Minister Plenipotentiary to the Court of King Louis XVI. I do this not to report on official occurrences, but to provide a record of such social events as the forthcoming party later this day. I do so for posterity's sake and for the protection of Mr. Jefferson, should such a need arise.

This nation is embroiled in every kind of turmoil, political and social, and my employer may someday appreciate that I kept a record of matters apart from those I'm required to record.

Indeed, there could be no better day to launch this journal. Mr. and Mrs. John Adams have requested our attendance at their residence in Auteuil this afternoon for a Shrove Tuesday gathering. Although the stated basis for the reception is to honor Dr. Franklin for his lengthy service here, and to welcome Mr. Jefferson as replacement, I believe the true consideration to be that of Mrs. Adam's--her desire to lift Mr. Jefferson's spirits, owing to the loss of his daughter Lucy this past January, a martyr to the complicated evils of teething worms and whooping cough.

The child, aged 2, fondly called by Mr. Jefferson "his little Lu," was especially esteemed by her father due to her reputed resemblance to his deceased wife, who died giving her birth. My employer and my friend is a man of great sensibility and parental affection, despite the confident and serene demeanor he shows to the world. He has remained in a state of melancholy since her death, and has largely confined himself from the world, even from his friends, to their particular dismay. This news has also greatly affected his daughter, Martha, affectionately known by him as "Patsy", a tall, slim child with her father's red hair and exceptional sensitivity.

Patsy is currently enrolled in and residing at the Abbaye Royale de Penthemont, a Catholic convent school also receiving Protestants, sans religious instruction. During a recent visit to the Abbaye by Mrs. Adams and myself, Patsy related to us that, when discussing Lucy's passing, Mr. Jefferson declared that, his "sun of happiness had clouded over, never again to brighten."

Patsy also related the even more dreadful story, as painful for us to hear as it must have been for the 12-year old child to recount, of her mother's demise.... How her mother died in her father's arms, but not before extracting his promise to never remarry and saddle their children with a stepmother. Patsy recalled how she and her Aunt Eppes feared mightily for her father's life, finding him insensible to the world for several months, wed only to his all-encompassing grief.

Only the intervention of his friends, Mr. Madison and Mr. Monroe, rendered him once more amenable to rejoining the world. They induced him to accept the assignment Congress had twice offered him before, as ambassador to this country. The prospect of removing himself from Monticello and the recent unhappy memories there, and of serving alongside his old revolutionary compatriots, Doctor Franklin and Mr. Adams, and resuming society with his friend Mrs. Adams, proved sufficient to abstain him from mourning and return him to the service of his country. At any rate, a forty-six-year-old man in the prime of health must do more with his life than interminably endure the pangs of separation and loss.

However, the weekend visits from Patsy, weekly shopping trips at the Palais Royal with Mrs. Adams, and his almost daily horseback rides through the Bois de Boulogne, his strolls among the fruit trees of the Tuileries with his friend, Marguerite-Victoire, Madame de Corny, discussing politics and the latest gossip at court, have failed to completely reinvigorate him. Nor have his excursions to the Comedie Francai Theatres des Italies, and the Opera, nor have even his visits to the city's fashionable salons and gardens with his occasional companion, Adrienne-Catherine de Noailles, Contesse de Tesse', returned him to his former self.

He no longer walks about constantly singing and humming the baroque music he once played on his violin to his wife's harpsichord accompaniment. Most significantly, the bookstalls beside the Seine and the shining architecture decorating Paris offer little of the same attraction for the man they once held in thrall. He who once declared, "I cannot live without books, music and architecture," only shows good humour in the company of Dr. Franklin and Mr. and Mrs. Adams, with whom he has, fortunately, renewed his old acquaintance with some degree of success.

Nevertheless, this afternoon's event may yet be the salve to mend his heart's wounds. I have told Mr. Jefferson that the business at hand is a fete' of Doctor Franklin, although all but him know the true purpose of the afternoon's delight is to bring light to his dark days. Mrs. Adams promised to be at her wittiest and charming best, and Mr. Adams has foresworn any heated political debates with Mr.

Jefferson, even promising Abigail that he will forego the testiness he has recently evinced while in the company of Doctor Franklin, and the latter's "friend," Anne-Catherine de Lingiville d'Autricourt, Madame Helvetius.

Also expected in attendance are our friends, General Gilbert du Motier, Marquis de Lafayette, and his lady, Adrienne (also the aunt of Madame de Tesse'), and the preeminent French philosopher, mathematician and political scientist of our times, Marie Jean Antoine Nicolas de Caritat, marquis de Condorcet. Only the adults are invited; Miss Patsy, Doctor Franklin's grandson, Temple, and the Adams family children, Nabby and John Quincy, must enjoy a later regaling of these events.

I finalized these and all other arrangements yesterday, including an order for Spanish Madeira and French Burgundy wine, both Mr. Jefferson's favorites. Mrs. Adams assures me that the cheeses, chocolates and pastries for her guests will be worthy of the wine, and this most congenial and gracious hostess has never disappointed.

I am greatly looking forward to this afternoon. My only concern is what Madame Helvetius may say to Mr. Adams by way of provocation... At a previous dinner, I believe his first in Paris, she bade one of her friends (a much younger and undoubtedly more enticing lady) ask him whether she might conclude from his name that he was descended from the first man in the Garden of Eden, and if so, had he learned from family tradition a question that had always troubled her---how did the first couple learn the art of lying together?

Although his face flushed at the question, Mr. Adams calmly responded that he was in fact so descended and was pleased to answer her question. There is in us a physical quality resembling the power of electricity or the magnet, he declared, so that when men and women come within striking distance of each other, they fly together like objects in Dr. Franklin's electrical experiments. The lady, most pleased with this answer, exclaimed that she had never understood the reason for it, but knew it to be a very happy shock!

Suffice it to say, Mr. Adams remained ill-humored for the balance of the evening. I certainly hope Madame Helvitius will content herself to pass such repartee' only with Dr. Franklin, and leave Mr. Adams to his wife, who is even more likely than he to crack a fearful response to any such foolishness at her own residence.

And so it ended. "Where was the rest of it?" I wondered aloud. Why had someone teased me with these entries and left me so cruelly in the lurch, begging for more? Yet, if this was truly a tease, then perhaps the best was yet to come! Imagine...Jefferson and Short, Franklin and Helvetius, John and Abigail Adams, and a roomful of 18th Century French intellectuals fiddling while Paris burned at the advent of the French Revolution!

Although the historical record mentions several parties thrown by Jefferson, Adams and Franklin in Paris, scant information remains as to what occurred and what was said at any of them. At least not until New York congressman Gouvernor Morris arrived in Paris after Adams' and Franklin's departure, and recorded many such conversations in his own diary.

If this document were authentic, it could be the greatest gift ever bestowed upon a man seeking the mantle of historian since a farmer gave Heinrich Schliemann the directions to the buried city of Troy in 1871.

I spent the next few hours on the internet searching for any reference to the existence of a 1785 diary by William Short, or to a Shrove Tuesday party at the Adams residence in February of that year. But I found not a hint of either. Of course, parties were an almost daily occurrence that year, and ancient diaries and accounts of them surfaced every year, not unlike the Dead Sea Scrolls discovery that shed new light on Jesus and his times over fifty years ago.

I could barely sit still pondering the possibilities. Only the nagging thought that there might be a nefarious purpose to this gift finally prompted me to take the manuscript to the FBI fingerprint expert in the McCoy Federal Building on Capitol Street a few blocks from our courthouse.

But they found no fingerprints except mine on the manuscript or the envelope. They identified the type as made by an ancient typewriter rigged with the Hansen Writing Ball, developed a century earlier for the first commercial typewriters. Beyond that, they could tell me nothing I didn't already know, except that, to them, the *lack* of any fingerprints seemed suspicious in and of itself. I returned to my office curious as the proverbial cat.

At precisely 10:30 AM my secretary buzzed me with the news that a Miss Shexnayder was waiting on line one.

"Want to meet for lunch at Two Sisters?" she asked. "I hear you Mississippi guys love fried chicken."

"If you can hold out till noon," I said.

"Okay. Meet you at Two Sisters at 1:00?"

"You paying?"

"If that's what it takes."

"I'm that good of a dancer? Or was it the kiss?"

"See you there, John."

Her line went dead.

Suddenly the past *and* future offered possibilities I hadn't imagined minutes earlier. But despite the delirium, I hadn't lost all conception of reality. A few miles north of my meridian, a dejected, probably clinically depressed teenaged girl sat in the midst of classroom full of her peers, yet very likely, as alone as she had ever felt during her brief, difficult existence.

CHAPTER TWELVE

Shortly before 11:30 A.M., I traipsed five blocks in 60 degree December weather beneath a cloudless, blue velvet sky to offer my confession at the cathedral. Located at the corner of Amite and West Streets directly across from Smith Park, St. Peter's stood on the site of the original church burned by the heretic General Sherman in 1862. Designated as a cathedral in 1957 by Pope Pius XII, this lovely Neo-Gothic building shone brightly amidst the callow steel towers of downtown Jackson with its red brick façade, stained glass windows and soaring cross-topped steeple.

As home to the Jackson Diocese, St. Peter's offered a cornucopia of available priests for confession, so you rolled the dice every time you bared your soul to a man of the cloth. Some made the process merely bearable, others something to look forward to, while still others made it akin to a trip to a ham-handed dentist.

I lump our local Irish priests in the second category, since they enjoy heated golf matches and quaffing draft beer. These attributes, I felt, made them worthy of pardoning the most desperate, puerile and shabby venal sins anyone could offer. But their penchant for cutting rationalization and self-aggrandizement off at the knee in a manner quite shocking to any unaccustomed with the Irish way accorded them the *gravitas* essential to granting even carnal sinners a free pass.

St. Peters' pastor, Father Joe Blackston, one of the few non-Irish priests in residence, prompted parishioners to opine that with his sandy red hair, expanding middle-aged girth, penchant for black humor and sardonic witticisms accompanied by the warmest smile imaginable, he seemed more Irish than the Irish priests themselves.

And that's why we had remained close over the years, even after my attendance in his jurisdiction had slackened to one or two visits a year.

But my confessor this day was a visiting monk from Ireland by way of San Francisco, claiming membership in the Third Order of Franciscan friars, famed for their work with emigrants, education, foreign missions and agitation for social justice.

He had found me fifteen minutes before time for confession, sitting on a pew near the rear of the cathedral, relishing the solitude of an empty nave. When I instinctively felt a presence to my right, I turned to see a tall man dressed in a brown monk's habit.

I couldn't see his face for the monk's hood. "I'm Father O'Shaunessy, a visiting Franciscan friar from California. Are you here for confession?"

I followed him into the confessional, a small room with a dividing partition and a screen that allowed the penitent to see the vague outline of his confessor without gleaning any of his distinctive features. And vice versa.

After brief introductions, I said, "Forgive me father, for I have sinned, It's been a damned long time since my last confession."

"Welcome back to the fold," he announced cheerfully. "What can I do you for today?"

This unorthodox greeting fit well with my mood, already heightened by the unexpected appearance of the Short diary and the pending lunch date with Jenny. And now I was enjoying the exotic pleasure of confessing for the first time to a Third Order mon, whatever that was."Father...I confess to..."

"Yes?"

"I'm not entirely certain what I'm confessing to."

He waited.

"That is...Rather, I feel I've done wrong, I'm just not sure what I've done. Wrong, I mean."

"Perhaps you'd like to offer a little more detail."

"It's just this, Father. My daughter, as fine a girl as ever drew breath…Well…. She…"

"Are you confessing your sins or hers?"

"Sorry Father. It's just that…"

"Just get if off your chest. That's what I'm here for, eh?"

Cut *me some slack, paddy*, I almost growled. Then, upon reflection, I said, "My daughter tried to commit suicide. Well, not really. She took Melatonin, but maybe she thought it was sleeping pills…I mean it is a sleep inducer, but a natural one unable to cause death with the ingestion of a few pills…. "

The priest waited for more.

"What I mean to say is, she wasn't actually attempting to off herself, just making a cry for help, or attention, something like that. At least that's what her doctor and I figured. But she was also cutting herself, on her leg, for at least a month or two before that, with a pen knife from her crafts class, for God's sake. The point is, she wasn't doing very well from an emotional standpoint. You understand?"

"Yes, I believe I take your meaning. And the matter you seek to confess?"

"Well…Obviously the whole thing took me by surprise…I guess I'm not doing my job as a father if my daughter uses herself as a whittling tool and eats a bottle of pills while I'm thinking she's got nothing on her mind apart from texting her buddies and what songs to buy on ITunes."

After a protracted silence that left me feeling useless, he said, "It's not uncommon for an older generation to misapprehend the thought processes of the younger. Have you closed the door of communication between yourself and your daughter in any way?"

"I don't think so, no. I ask her everyday how things went at school, how she's getting along with her boyfriend, or if she needs help with her homework... No, I don't think I've shut her out at all. Well…" I hesitated, strumming my fingers nervously on the side panel of my chair. "Maybe I've been more focused upon her younger brother… He's four and she's sixteen."

"Ahhh," he mumbled annoyingly, then fell silent once more.

"Father?"

"Yes?"

"You still with me?"

"Are you saying you've devoted yourself more to the boy than to the teenaged girl? Because if that's what you're saying, I'd venture that's rather like fretting over forgetting to pay the milkman Saturday at noon because you were out on the golf course at nine."

I tried in vain to understand what he was saying. "Beg pardon?"

"Well...Everyone enjoys the little one, don't they? And they take up a lot of your time, after all. Needy little buggers, eh? And who can carry on a conversation with an American teenager for more than fifteen minutes and not want to toss himself off the nearest bridge?"

I groaned.

"I only took my vows a few months ago, you know. They offer us direction, as it were, but it's really no substitute for the real thing, eh?"

"I see."

"May I ask *you* a question?"

"Why not?"

"Well then...Where is the girl's mother in all of this?"

"She died four years ago giving birth to our son."

"I see. I'm very sorry for your loss."

"Thanks. So am I."

"Do you blame yourself for her demise?"

Lengthy pause. "*I beg your pardon?*"

"Or do you blame God, perhaps?"

I didn't speak for a moment, not so much to gather my thoughts, as to regain my equilibrium before wondering aloud who in God's green acre qualified this presumptuous ass to take anybody's confession.

"Father, I don't blame anyone for what happened. Women die in childbirth. Medical science is far from perfect....What more can I say?"

"Have you lost your faith?"

At last a question I had no difficulty comprehending. Or answering. "If by that you mean faith in our leaders, political and religious... Hmpf. I believe in the psychiatric benefit of confession, Father, God or no God. And I'd rather talk to a priest than some half-baked psychologist voodoo practitioner."

He laughed.

"Of course I believe in the teachings and living example of Jesus as something worthy of emulation in one's life."

"But you don't consider him divine?"

"No one knows the answer to that mystery, and anyone who says otherwise is either deluded or selling something."

"Ahh," he murmured triumphantly, "but it's hardly a question of *knowledge*, is it? Only a matter of faith, in which you either choose to believe or not, eh?"

I felt a sudden urge to take control of the meeting. "You friars probably devote a lot of time considering these issues; tucked away in a monastery with little else to do but contemplate heavy matters like the existence of the Trinity, why certain books were included in the Bible, the number of angels dancing the Charleston on a pin head, *ad nauseam*. But we wayward souls who muddle through the real world need to focus on more practical concerns that plague us throughout our lives-- making a living, raising our children and surviving the deaths of those we love.

"Of course we sometimes tremble at God's altar, despite the hurricanes and earthquakes that destroy our communities, plagues that slaughter us by the millions, like this one currently ravaging China and Italy, and the children born deaf, dumb and blind for no good reason we can discern."

"So you believe God is to blame for humanity's ills?" he replied softly.

"He's certainly got to take credit for hurricanes and natural plagues, some of the more egregious birth defects, and the like. I realize we create many of our own problems every day due to selfishness, greed, lust, pride and all the other deadly sins, but some of it we neither asked for nor brought about ourselves.

"Sure, our duly elected leaders wage unnecessary wars, waste the public's money and care nothing about the good of the nation. But I don't see a guiding hand from above helping us sort those things out either, do you, Father? Frankly, I've had enough of God's silence to last me several lifetimes."

"Perhaps He's turned from us as we have turned from Him, eh?"

"Time for another flood or the fire next time, you mean? No, I wouldn't drown or burn innocent children regardless of their parents' sins. I suppose, in that respect, I'm not very God-like."

"But who is innocent? Did not Yahweh drown almost every man, woman and child with his great flood? Did he not destroy everyone in Sodom, or order his people to cut the throats of every survivor after Jericho's walls collapsed?"

"I'm sure Zeus did his fair share of raping and murdering too, but what has mythology to do with what we're discussing today?"

"Very well. Did not America firebomb children and non-combatants of Dresden in World War II? Do you suppose that the nuclear bombs President Truman dropped on two Japanese cities magically spared the women and children?"

I paused upon hearing this, wondering confusedly what kind of 'confession' I had gotten myself into. "Father, would you be offended if I requested another priest?"

"I apologize, if I've offended you in any way. I thought we were discussing relevant points as to innocence and guilt."

"Relevant how, exactly?"

"To your confession, eh? Was it not guilt that brought you to my door? What I am attempting to tell you, however ineffectively, is that we often feel guilt for things we've done that are not evil, while not feeling guilty about other actions that we don't interpret as wrong, but about which others feel quite differently."

"Okay, Father. I'm with you. That is certainly true. And the moon is made of rock, not green cheese. But how does this tangent we've taken about guilt and innocence apply to me and my daughter?"

"Will you bear with me for a moment and let us talk through my point, after which time I will gladly answer your question."

"Why not," I shrugged, checking the time on my cell phone. "Go ahead with your point." I took another glance through the screen and thought I saw the glint of metal flashing from his lap. A crucifix, metal prayer beads. More likely a gun in this case, I mused.

"I'm asking you this... When evildoers such as fascists, imperialists, Communists, and even the government of this fine country betray everything they're supposed to be about, isn't it justifiable to remove them even if it means taking a few innocent lives in the process? And if so, why shouldn't God do the same?"

"I don't know. I believe Thomas Jefferson advocated burning the whole world if it meant leaving two people free, as opposed to the whole world living in tyranny. He was a lot smarter than I'll ever live to be."

"Wow. He was quite the anarchist, eh? And you may have a little of that in you, if I may be allowed to say."

"Not really, Father. I lack the commitment for anarchy, and if I had it, I wouldn't murder children, or allow my own children to be harmed, for any crimes or moral outrages any government committed. I realize your 'loving God' sees it differently. But, as it turns out, my old man had a saying I've never forgotten—"if my dog gets in your henhouse he's still my dog.' So I guess your God and I see things very differently. I can't blame anyone, not even the wrongdoers, sufficiently to destroy everyone in the world."

"Then you have answered your own question," he crowed.

"What question is that? We've gotten so far afield that I've forgotten what we were talking about in the first place."

"About your daughter," he said thoughtfully, his voice bereft of all vestiges of debate or repartee. "You seek what's best for your little girl, and regardless of what you may have done or not done in the past, you serve no purpose by blaming yourself, tearing yourself down. For if you do, you only bring more pain into your home than already exists. You must forgive yourself and begin today being the best father you can be. Abjure unnecessary guilt, and try to hold onto your faith. God has not abandoned humanity. He has always sent those who right the wrongs of which we speak. And I believe he will again.

"Tell me for truth, now, will you? Isn't your sin, for which you came to confession, and for which you suffer guilt, really one of abandonment, rather than aggressive evil? That you have, to some degree at least, abandoned or poorly served your little girl?"

"Forgive me, Father, but, isn't 'abandonment' a little strong?"

"Perhaps. Let's say, ignored…Or overlooked. Or better still, fallen out of touch with. Am I getting warmer?"

You damn sure are, friar, and if it were up to me, I'd consign you to a far warmer place than this. Then I took hold of my frustration, reflected upon his words, and said, "Perhaps you're right, Father. Yes, I suppose you are. I didn't intend to, or even realize I was doing so... But yes, I suppose I've fallen out of touch with Anna Grace. But then, she is a teenaged girl, after all. How I am supposed to stay in synch with that?"

"Do you stay in synch with everyone in your workplace? Everyone you meet on the street? And how much more valuable to you is she?"

This sucked the wind right out of my sails. My face flushed as I absorbed his words. I showed enormous concern for those I dealt with on a professional basis—the victims of crimes, my colleagues, my coworkers, yet spent far less time with my daughter, who meant infinitely more to me than all of the rest put together.

After a long pause, I said, "Maybe I will ask for a little absolution, Father."

"Very well. Consider Timothy 5:8- 'If anyone does not provide for his family, especially for his children, he has denied the faith and become worse than the unbeliever.' And Colossians 3:21, 'Fathers do not provoke your children, lest they become discouraged.'"

"I will consider them, Father," I said meekly.

"And spend some time with your daughter. She may resist at first, but if you show her you really care, if you take the time to hear what she has to say, to understand how she feels, even if those feelings appear totally irrational to you, she will come around."

"Yes, Father. I'll try."

"That's all anyone can ask of us. To make a sincere and unbridled effort to do what we know is right, even that means taking steps that the law condemns, as was the case when Abraham sought to sacrifice his son. And having a little faith in ourselves and others is a good place to start when heading down that long and winding road."

Long and winding road? Was he a John Lennon fan, or just a St. Augustine devotee, haranguing me about just wars, the fall of man and unoriginal sins?

But I only said, "Of course. Thank you, Father."

"Go with God... Your sins are absolved."

I could see him through the screen making the sign of the cross, so I crossed myself, rose and slipped out of the confessional booth with a greater degree of humility than I had known entering it.

I had let my little girl down, oblivious to what was happening until this friar brought it home to me with a vengeance. How could I have been so blind to the feelings of one so close to my heart?

CHAPTER THIRTEEN

The bright blue sky notched with distant cirrus clouds drifting over the cathedral made me wince and shield my eyes as I stepped outside. Perhaps confession is good for the soul, but it's a damned painful blow to the ego. I phoned Jenny and begged off our lunch meeting, alleging a work emergency as the reason. I simply couldn't attempt romance with her while thinking about my little girl in pain.

I swung by the Subway and grabbed a sandwich, bag of chips and a bottle of water and took a solo lunch in Smith Park. I resolved to spend more time with Anna Grace, whatever teenaged horrors that entailed.

Satisfied with this plan, I let my mind wander back to the events in Smith Park and the Occupy the Park invasion that had set the Ghost in my sights. I couldn't banish the suspicion that I was missing something important in his assault case. To be sure, we had no idea who he was and what if anything worse we were dealing with. The Ghost's unknown identity, his likely involvement with other protest groups, some possibly more dangerous than the Occupy the Park/ Black Lives Matter crowd, and the sudden strange appearance of the Short diary on my doorstep seemed more than a little coincidental. Was the Ghost and whomever gifted me the manuscript conspiring to distract me while they brought domestic terrorism to my hometown?

Why had Breeland allowed himself to be sucked into in this case, inexplicably returning to criminal law after a twenty year absence in the field? I certainly understood the money, but there had to be more to it than that. Or did there?

Where did the Short diary fit in to all this? Who would give such a priceless manuscript to me, albeit only a copy, if it was truly authentic? Were they seeking a sponsor for their discovery? And why leave it on my front porch, if not to announce that the sender knows where I and my family live?

Were my children's lives at risk?

And where did Jenny fit in to this messy picture? Had she sent the diary to prick my interest in writing something more substantial about Thomas Jefferson? Why would she do that? How could she do it?

And by the way, had she and I something more substantial going on than I realized? Could I afford to strap on a heavy relationship right now with a needy four-year-old and a teenaged daughter gone astray?

I had always prided myself on my ability to think or intuit my way through problems, but now I found myself floundering in a calamitous sea, unable to safely navigate those roiling waves without splattering on a craggy reef or descending beneath the waves. There was far too much at stake—my children's lives, our future together, innocent people's safety, my job—to take a careless misstep now.

Then I remembered a great Jeffersonian quote I had used in my book-- 'the best pilot is the one who steers clear of the rocks and shoals.' Somehow, he never managed to do it, either in politics, with his constant warfare with the Federalists, or in his home life, burying his wife Martha, an infant son and four daughters, one of whom lived into her twenties and died from a difficult labor as had his wife.

On that lovely note, I tossed my garbage into a metal trash can and plodded heavily back to the office. Looking back for a final glance at pulchritudinous Smith Park, I saw a large shaggy-haired man wearing a wide brimmed floppy hat and dark sunglasses skipping briskly down the cathedral's steps. He seemed tall enough to have been my confessor, but I couldn't make out his features before he hurried out of sight.

I raised my hand to wave at him, but if he saw me he never acknowledged my gesture.

Time to get to work, I told myself, and find answers to the questions bugging me about the Ghost, the diary and Jenny.

But answers proved scarce that afternoon. Not so for the questions, however, that multiplied exponentially upon my return to the office.

My secretary stopped me at her desk and handed over a familiar looking 8 by 10 envelope. Addressed to me at my office, it had been hand-delivered, not mailed. The older type font appeared identical to that of the manuscript left on my front porch earlier that morning, suggesting the same or similar typewriter.

"Who left this here, Jill?"

"A boy dropped it off, according to the marshals." She didn't look up from her primping, flipping her long blonde hair across her shoulder then dabbing makeup on her chin with her fingers in front of a portable mirror on her desk. "The mail guys did whatever they do and then brought it up here to me."

By "mail guys" she meant the federal protection officers who x-rayed and fingerprinted every envelope and letter we received before delivering them to us.

"A boy dropped it off?" I frowned. "Did the marshals describe him?"

She looked up for the first time. "Do you think it may be trouble? A threat? Or," she added, melodramatically, "Laced with a toxic substance? Should I call the marshals back?"

"Just answer my question," I said calmly. "Did they offer a description?"

She paused for a moment, a purple fingernail tentatively probing her lower lip, a purple eyelid fluttering like a punch drunk butterfly. "Yes... Mark said the boy was about 13 or 14, slim build, African-American, no outstanding features, just brown eyes and black hair."

"How was he dressed? How did he speak?"

"Just a normal teenager, he said. Nothing unusual or threatening. "

"Probably paid to make the delivery. Offered cash on the street, down the block, then brought it right up."

"That would be my guess," she said anxiously. "Should I call the marshals? The toxicology unit?"

"Waste of their time. If the sender is a crook, there won't be any latent fingerprints to discover, I assure you. On materials like paper they're invisible and require lasers or chemical processes we don't have around here, assuming they weren't smudged, distorted or overlapped by the delivery boy's prints. Sender probably wore gloves when he packaged the contents. Just forget about it, why don't you?"

She shot me a skeptical glance. "A package sent anonymously, with no return address, by someone who took the time to type out *your* name and address, with toxic packages and letters sent to law enforcement people every day, and you tell me to forget about it? Then you waltz into your office to open it right up without a care in the friggin' world?"

"Actually," I grinned, "I was thinking of having you open it for me."

"Forget it, John-boy," she huffed, returning to her purple-stained nails. "You're on your own this time. And don't call me if it's laced with ricin powder or blows up in your face."

I smiled, tucked the envelope under my arm, and whistled loudly as I closed the door behind me. Jill knew as well as I that all mail addressed to Justice Department employees was subjected to radiation that kills the deadly elements in powders and spores. But as was often the case with many long-serving bureaucrats, she resented my laid back attitude about government regulations, especially those pertaining to our safety. Having cut my teeth in private practice for ten years and only joined the fed afterwards, I tended to dispense with bureaucratic trifles in favor of doing the job they paid me to do.

As long as you got results, moved cases, won most of them and didn't anger any U.S. District Judges or Senators, they generally overlooked your failure to march in lockstep with Uncle Sam's petty rules that most attorneys from private practice considered little more than admonitions for blockheads, scoundrels and bureaucrats.

Trial work, the art of prosecution--penetrating cross-examination, astute brief writing, scintillating closing arguments-- these were my focus, not minding the bureaucratic twaddle by which so many government employees measured their contribution to the public weal. The expression, 'good enough for government work,' was not coined in a vacuum. But it had never been my motto and I hoped it never would be.

I opened the envelope and withdrew the manuscript, expecting more excerpts from the Short diary. My eyes bulged when I read its title, *Copy of the Letters of Sgt. John Ferguson, Mississippi Dragoons, 1814-1815.*

I stared in disbelief at the yellowed papers in my hands. As I had told Jenny, Breeland, and anyone else who would listen, my great, great grandfather, for whom I was named, served under Major Hinds in the Mississippi Dragoons during their scrap with the British at the Battle of New Orleans.

Had my forebear written a diary of his wartime exploits, and if so, how had my father, the amateur genealogist, never discovered it? If a genuine diary, why was I seeing it now thanks to an anonymous sender?

Yes, I *had* told Jenny about my forebear, and she was well aware of my interest in Thomas Jefferson, having read my book. But the same was true of Breeland and everyone who had read my Jefferson book and my articles about the Dragoons in the Mississippi History Archives newsletter.

Was Jenny sending these manuscripts? How could she come up with them so quickly? A millionaire could possibly accomplish that, but not a substitute high school teacher. Not by herself, at least.

It certainly wasn't Breeland. He did have the right contacts at the Millsaps history department, but he could no more keep such a thing secret during our lunches than he could...What? Handle a criminal case in federal court? Son-of-a-bitch!

Aw, forget it, I told myself. He took that case for the money, with insurance defense being far less profitable after tort reform, and to righteously gig me for fun and profit by prolonging the Ghost's inevitable conviction.

Breeland had everything he wanted from the Ghost's case. Why waste the energy required to play even the most elaborate ruse on me?

No, I simply couldn't accept Jenny or Breeland as possible sources of the manuscripts. Which left open the most unsettling possibility of all.

Every prosecutor knows that domestic terrorists resort to every conceivable means to confuse, frustrate and misdirect their enemies.

Their preferred method is the use of 'green hackers' to distract, disrupt, and embarrass people on their hit lists by placing their personally identifiable information on the web. Wealthy industrialists, neo-conservative politicians, greedy corporate CEOs, military leaders, federals judges and prosecutors and just about everyone that ever pissed off domestic terrorists eventually saw their personal information displayed on the net, often accompanied by instructions intent on disrupting or even ending their lives.

But, so far as I knew, no one had ever used historical manuscripts from the 18th and 19th centuries, whether genuine or not, to distract Assistant U.S. Attorneys during terrorist investigations. What would be the point if they did? If a person's ancestors owned slaves, stole public money, or molested chickens, their fellow Americans wouldn't give a hoot in Hades. Let the malcontents say what they will about us, but we law-abiding Americans judge our fellows on their accomplishments in this life, not what their forebears did centuries ago.

As a distraction, such manuscripts could certainly be expected to garner the attention of a history aficionado and would-be-author like me. But to what end? The Ghost's case is so open and shut a trained ape could win it. And we have no direct proof he's involved with domestic terrorists at all.

Was there a message in the manuscripts? Join us in our unholy war against the descendants of Alexander Hamilton who utilize the federal government to make the rich richer and reduce the poor and middle class to penury and voluntary servitude, as Jefferson declared? Be one with the pirates who saved our nation at the Battle of New Orleans? Sure thing guys; I'll dismiss the indictment and send the Ghost on his merry way.

Not very likely. So where did that leave me?

Painfully aware that these speculations were gaining me nothing but a headache, I yielded to the temptation to satisfy my overwhelming curiosity about the manuscript. Although any letters my forebear wrote were penned in his own hand, these purported to be typed copies, and like the Short diary, were accompanied by an explanation about how they were transcribed from the originals.

I brushed all concerns aside and did what I had wanted to do since my secretary handed me the manuscript. I opened it to the first page and traveled back in time to 19th Century New Orleans, Louisiana

CHAPTER FOURTEEN

THE LETTERS OF SGT. JOHN FERGUSON

December 21, 1814
Mrs. Jenny Ferguson
Ferguson Plantation
Natchez, Mississippi

I laid the manuscript on my desk. *Jenny Ferguson?* I swallowed hard. Coincidence, I wondered? Or something else entirely? I made a mental note to check the family tree my father prepared to see if John Ferguson's wife was truly named Jenny.

My eyes dropped back to the manuscript.

Dear Jenny:

In keeping with my promise, I'm sending this letter. We will engage the enemy soon, on a battlefield of his choosing, so your letters would never reach me as they did when we were stationed in Pensacola. But keep me in your prayers and your daily thoughts, as I know you will. Please ask little Betsy to remember me in her prayers, as I pray for our lovely little girl every night.

We arrived in New Orleans around noon today. Some fortunate few of the company returned to their homes once we crossed the

Mississippi line, owing to wounds suffered on campaign against the Creeks in Georgia. Near 70 of us from Jefferson, Adams, Amite and Wilkinson County, still serve, and we received volunteers from other counties far away as Pontotoc as we filed down the Natchez Trace, bringing our number to about 150.

Our new commander, Major Thomas Hinds, "Old Pine Knott," drove us over two-hundred miles, day and night through cold and rainy weather on muddy and hazardous roads to reach the city this night. We bivouacked in a park they call "Lafayette Square", after the French General who supported us in our first war against the British.

What your father said about the City of New Orleans is true; it can't hold a candle to Natchez though five times larger with almost 25,000 souls. A mere three thousands of those are Americans, most being Creoles, the descendants of the original French and Spanish settlers here. Slaves and a large contingent of free Negroes like our Natchez barber, known here as gens de couleur libre, are everywhere in abundance. These free Negroes walk about proudly, own slaves themselves, and as mulattos look down on the full-blood African Negroes, according to the local Creole militiamen we've met. Not one of them will brook an insult from any man, white or black. Many are fine duelists, we're told, with gun, knife and rifle, and we've been ordered to lay off them at all costs, or be prepared to meet them under The Oaks just outside the city.

The Creoles are as Catholic as we, yet different by a league. The men dress in hat, cane and gloves wherever they go, drink French wine instead of whiskey, smoke expensive cigars, gamble daily on cards and horses, and take mulatto mistresses for themselves, which they set up in houses on the ramparts near the Vieux Carre'. The men kiss each other on the cheeks like we shake hands, and from what little I've seen of their women, they are very attractive, immaculately dressed in white satin gowns, and are always polite to us strangers. We've been told to stay clear of them, too, as Old Pine Knot wants no trouble, and certainly no duels, between our militia and theirs.

The wealthier Creoles, we are told, generally stay to themselves and do not mix with Americans, whom they find boorish and uncivilized. They worship differently, dress differently, and abjure all labor except that as bankers, cotton merchants, lawyers, planters, and nowadays, as soldiers. They even frequent their own saloons, such as the Le Veau Qui Tete' (Suckling Calf) on St. Philip Street, while the Americans relax at Maspero's Exchange at the corner of St. Louis and Chartres streets, directly across from Mayor Girod's house, reputedly a refuge for Napoleon had they been able to spirit him away from his Corsican island prison.

The free Negroes associate at the Café des Refugees directly across from the new French Market on Decatur Street, which adjoins the Hotel de la Marine, owned by Jean Noel Destrehan, a member of Plauche's battalion. Plauche' and Destrehan gave our officers a quick tour of these taverns shortly after we arrived in the city. We found the food and drink as excellent as any in Natchez, perhaps even better at times.

The best establishments are all located a few blocks from the Place d'Armes, a large square near the levee where troops regularly parade to the pleasure of the entire city. I'm told this has happened regularly the past few weeks to put the citizens at ease after British naval vessels were spotted in the Gulf. Different as they are, the Creoles, Americans and free Negroes have one thing in common- we all detest the British.

The city has a few charming two-story brick houses on Royale Street with elegant ironwork balconies, lush courtyards and small gardens with sweet-smelling flowers. But the streets are muddier than our Natchez pig pens with only cypress planks for sidewalks. They stink to high heaven. I don't doubt the rumors we often hear of continual yellow fever plague in this city, which carries away residents by the thousand every year. What President Thomas Jefferson was thinking, after he purchased this city and declared it destined to become the greatest city in the world, I cannot begin to fathom.

But, despite all that, these people do have a high time, even in the mud. These Creoles certainly enjoy themselves, but so do the rest. Much in keeping with those frequenting saloons in our Natchez Under-the-Hill, the rogues down here enjoy grog houses and taverns on every street corner, with about three loose women roaming the streets for every man with a nickel in his pocket.

But why the high and mighty British want to own this swamp I couldn't say. The Major allows that if they take the city they will cut off our river trade and box us in between the Mississippi and the Atlantic, blockade our coasts, and sink our trade. I say to hell with that, and to the Devil with the British!

We whipped those boys once under General Washington, and cleared Georgia and much of the Florida Territory of Indians and Spanish under General Jackson. The Gen'l has promised the citizenry they've nothing to worry about while he has breath in his body. I believe him, too, and so does Major Hinds.

Not that we don't take the British seriously, as they bring the hardened veterans of the Napoleonic wars, and presumably outnumber our force by at least three to one. The locals here are terrified of them, likening them to the hurricane of 1812 that killed several hundred people, cost $60,000 in property damage, sank much of the Louisiana's naval fleet, and made a lake of the land surrounding this city for a distance of forty miles in every direction. Others liken them to the annual plague, the ultimate scourge of all New Orleanians, black or white.

However, I assure you our Mississippi Dragoons are prepared to do their duty no matter the odds we face.

Still, this will be the strangest army the United States has ever fielded. Bivouacking with us are the Feliciana Dragoons, a Louisiana cavalry like ours including the famous guerilla fighter, Reuben Kemper, who gave the Spanish hell raiding Mobile and Texas fifteen years ago; a battalion of colorfully attired New Orleans Volunteers- merchants and lawyers serving under Captain Thomas Beale, with dark red jackets, gold embroidered button holes, waistcoats and breeches lined in white, and epaulettes of gold braid and tassel; and a battalion of free blacks, many from Santo Domingo under Creole baker and Major Jean D'Aquin. They are not as finely attired as the Creoles but look quite military all the same. There are also eighteen Choctaw Indians under Creole Captain Pierre Jugeat, rumored to be one-fourth Choctaw himself. If they fight like the Creek and Chickasaw, we'll be glad they're on our side.

Major General John Coffee also arrived here today with about 800 Tennessee volunteers on horseback. These fellows fought with us in the Indian wars, and they bow to no man. They wear long, full coats, dark-colored woolen hunting shirts and dyed cloth pantaloons, all made by their wives, some with floppy wool hats and others wearing those of coon and fox skin, with tails hanging down their backs. They carry knives, long rifles (many with elaborate engravings in silver and gold), but also tomahawks they took off Indians they kilt in the wars, hanging from untanned deerskin belts. Coffee himself appears as manly and rugged as any of his men, tall, muscular and powerfully built, although the look in his eyes betrays an intelligence and education perhaps not shared by many of his long-haired, wild-eyed charges.

We look right smart next to the Tennesseans in our new blue uniforms faced with scarlet, our rifles and sabers hung with white belts. John Ross was named captain of our old Jefferson Troop unit, Isaac Dunbar his first lieutenant and John Irwin second lieutenant. They're all planters from Adams and Jefferson Counties. I'm one of four sergeants, including James Truly, whom you may recall as the fellow with the peculiar laugh. He keeps us in good spirits much of the time. Some other fellows here you've met are Corporal Michael Trimble, cousin Sam'l Ferguson, Henry Corky, Dan'l Elmore, Eli Scurry, George Hancock, John Truly, Richard Spain and James Cessna. Other fellows from different militias joining us in Wilkinson County are Jessie Bell, J.W. Prude, William High and John Grisham of the Pontotoc Dragoons. I'm proud Mississippi is so well represented here, even if our accommodations are a far cry from our Natchez plantations. We'll make the British pay for inconveniencing us so.

At least the locals are in high spirits, with wine flowing freely and bands playing Yankee Doodle, Chant du Depart and the Marseillaise on every corner. Our only problem is that neither General Thomas's volunteer Kentuckians nor General William Carroll's three thousand militia have arrived, and word is we're terribly low on guns and ammunition. Major Hinds says General Jackson is deeply concerned about this, especially since a Natchez boat carrying most of our ammunition has not arrived, and rumor has it she hasn't left Natchez. Captain Henry Shreve's steamboat, Enterprise, arrived yesterday with some powder, flints and shot, but we need a lot more to carry the fight we know is coming.

With a British landing expected either below the city from Lake Borgne, above it from Lake Pontchartrain, or from some other unexpected venue, we need provisions quick. Major Hinds says the infamous Gulf pirates, the Lafitte brothers, have offered their services as gunners and sharpshooters, with all the cannon, shot, flint and powder we need. Some, including Jackson, are against taking them on, and others for it.

Jenny, our little army couldn't get any stranger, so bring on the buccaneers, I say. With just a few thousand of us (assuming Gen. Carroll arrives in time), and the rumored 25,000 British headed our way, we need all the help we can get.

Will write more tomorrow. Kiss little Betsy for me. Take good care of yourselves, and seek assistance at the neighboring plantations if you feel the need. Our friends assured me they will see to your safety and comfort while I'm gone.

And most importantly, don't worry over me. My star has risen fast here thanks to Major Hinds, who appointed me his secretary in the field, thus granting me access to letters, reports, rosters and records drawn here in New Orleans. He says that owing to my speaking French (courtesy of my French grandmother, a descendant of the wealthy export monopoly Milhet family of Paris, who was determined I should speak her language in case I ever moved to France) he will often require my services as translator. This will keep me in close company with the officers, many of whom are French or Creole, and speak little English. He specifically asked me to remind you that the officers, and those near them, are always the last ones to die in any battle! He promises to "keep me safe to come home to my little one and my lovely wife." Even a Creole wouldn't bet against Major Hinds' word! They don't call him "Old Pine Knott" for nothing.

All my love,
John

December 22
Gen'l Jackson firmly established his presence in the city days ago by declaring martial law, but began preparing in earnest this morning after hearing the dreadful news from Lake Borgne. There, on the 13th,

former President Jefferson's five gunboats under the command of Lt. Thomas ap Catesby Jones were overwhelmed by a force of British barges in a hot fight between the Bay of St. Louis and Lake Borgne. We also heard the story of the loss of the tender, Sea Horse, which had braved British guns to sail into the Bay of St. Louis to destroy a powder magazine before its capture.

Supposedly, a woman viewing this scene from the shore asked her mayor whether anyone would lend a hand to defend their country, snatched the mayor's cigar from his mouth and touched off a cannon that sent the British barges scurrying from the Bay.

Nevertheless, the British navy won the day, clearing our ships from the entrance to Lake Borgne. A land invasion now seems imminent from that direction.

The British have spread the word among us that they plan to sack the city for 'Beauty and Booty', and we all recollect their atrocities after they burned Washington and Hampton. Major Hinds reminded us that more of our soldiers died in ghastly prison ships during the Revolution than were taken by British lead and shot in the field. On this account, Gen'l Jackson has issued orders to the New Orleanians exhorting them to "look to your liberties, your property, the chastity of your wives and daughters."

Jackson believes the citizens will surely rise in defense of their city, but should he be disappointed in this, he will "separate his enemies from his friends."

I do not believe anyone misunderstood his meaning; only the worst fool would betray the Gen'l's trust and side with the invader. We…

My desk phone's buzzer sounded, so I set down the manuscript, lifted the receiver and said, "Yes, Jill?"

"Still breathing in there?"

"Of course. We're all happy campers here. What's up?"

"Just wanted to remind you about the Robinson sentencing hearing this afternoon at 2:30 before Judge Alethea Rose."

"Thanks, Jill. Have a nice day."

"Hmpf," she muttered, ending the call.

.

I phoned a psychiatrist in Madison, and old college flame named Dr. Lucy Draughn. I told her about the late night ER trip with Anna Grace, and asked her advice on hiring a psychiatrist, psychologist or therapist for Anna Grace, and whom she recommended for the job.

"I can recommend plenty of capable people, John," she said warmly, "but I'll treat her myself if you'd like. I see children, adults and everyone in between, and I'd be glad to help you any way I can. Anna Grace is a lovely girl and I've enjoyed keeping up with her on Facebook. That is, if you trust me with your child."

We had dated for six months, explored every possibility of youthful desire, and parted friends when I graduated law school. She met her future husband, a first year law student, months later. Our children had become friends in the public schools, until I had moved to Madison after Beth's passing and we had allowed our friendship to falter if not lapse entirely.

She enjoyed a fine reputation as a psychiatrist and I saw no need to tarry. "I trust you all the way," I said. "Just one thing Lucy…"

"Yes?"

"I'm completely in the dark about this. I don't know what, how or why, okay? I need to know what's going on with my girl and what I need to do about it. And soon."

"Fair enough," she said, pausing to check her calendar. "Oh, good! We have a cancellation this afternoon at 3:30. Can you get her here then?"

"She'll be there. Thanks a million, doc."

Moments later I slackened in my chair as the full weight of exhaustion settled onto my shoulders. The vision of Anna Grace on her bed, her legs crisscrossed with penknife carvings, one thigh bleeding from an accidental cut deeper than she'd planned, seemed like Hieronymus Bosch's view of Hell; once you've seen it you're never able to shake it. Exhaustion had finally taken its toll.

To relieve it I went to my building's first floor day care, and peeked through a large plate glass window at Will dining on PBJ sandwiches, grapes and Capri Sun lemonade beside his best friend Christopher. I stood to the side of the window so he wouldn't see me, and watched him at play for fifteen wonderful minutes.

No matter your worries, your heart soars when you see your toddler laughing with his friends, as carefree as a turtle. You know then that nothing you've said or done has soiled his heart with bitterness, anger or fear.

Hang in there boy, I silently wished. Don't become like the rest of us; floundering haplessly in rough seas, some drowning in regret, others gasping for redemption.

CHAPTER FIFTEEN

My 2:30 sentencing hearing also failed to go as planned. When the clerk, a young man new to government insipidity, unceremoniously informed me that the hearing had been cancelled after I had cancelled other important matters to accommodate the hearing, I snapped at him, and immediately regretted it.

Was I overcompensating for my anxieties about Anna Grace? Or had I simply grown older and more cantankerous? As I considered that this second possibility ranked me with the likes of dinosaur politicians Donald Trump, Bernie Sanders and Nancy Pelosi, I decided that any other option would be preferable.

My mood improved substantially after work during a stroll across the office parking lot with Will. Perhaps sensing my need, he gave me a big kiss on the cheek as I lifted him into the car. "I love you, dad," he said.

"I love you the most, boy," I gushed while tickling him between his ribs.

We picked up Anna Grace at her school and drove her to Dr. Draughn's office in the Highland Colony shopping center at the corner of Highway 463 and Highland Colony Parkway, three miles from our subdivision. Anna Grace appeared copacetic with the arrangement and played games with Will on her IPhone while I filled out the insurance paperwork.

"What are y'all playing?" I asked.

"Fortnight!" Will exclaimed proudly.

With an understanding that the session would end an hour and a half later, we left Anna Grace in Dr. Draughn's capable hands and headed home.

As we pulled in our driveway, I saw a familiar package resting on my front doorstep. After settling Will in front of the television, where a cartoon cat named Gumball and a fish called Darwin generated inadvertent, slapstick mayhem in full view of their bubble-headed father, I retrieved the envelope off the porch and retired to my study to open it.

CHAPTER SIXTEEN

The next installment in the William Short diary picked up where the first left off, and I allowed the cares of the day to drift slowly from me as I devoured the manuscript like a starving man at a banquet.

2:00 PM.
The residence of Mr. and Mrs. John Adams
Auteuil, France
All is as expected! The Adams' grand fifty-room mansion set on five acres of elaborate lawns and gardens four miles distant from Paris is resplendent with beautiful collections of flowers in china vases, studded with the green, gold and purple colors of Carnival (where not natural, colors are painted on). Their elegant, if somewhat impractical, furnishings are perfectly exhibited upon the freshly waxed red tile floors as if the King and Queen themselves were expected. The most elegant first floor salon, to the left of the glass double-door entrance, and directly across from the dining room, is the setting for this event.

All seven servants, plus the charwoman and the footman, are maintaining their reputations for consideration and forethought, the former keeping everyone's wine glasses filled, while the latter, in concert with several of Madame Helvetius' servants, transported Dr. Franklin here from her estate, where he is her frequent guest. The

Doctor currently suffers such a terrible case of gout and stones that he cannot walk or ride any distance except on a six horse carriage that Madame has converted into a rolling couch with a velvet cover and silk pillows of various sizes.

All other guests are present (with exception of Madame de Corny, who sent her regrets on account of sickness) and were so when Dr. Franklin arrived, his head resting upon Madame Helvetius's lap. I was exceedingly proud of Mrs. Adams for restraining herself from demonstrating her little-concealed contempt for Madame, arriving as she latter did, with a married man's head lolling upon her lap.

As for her husband, Mr. Adams could not restrain himself from criticizing Mr. Jefferson's good friend, Dr. Franklin.

"No, sir," Mr. Adams complained after a second glass of wine, "I tell you that posterity will regard me far below Franklin, and below you as well, Mr. J. They will ascribe you the honor of penning our Declaration of Independency and celebrating that moment far beyond that of the infinitely more crucial vote for independence on July 2nd. They will declare that Franklin struck the ground with his lightning rod and out strode Washington with Victory riding his mighty shoulder."

Mr. Jefferson quickly changes the subject and compliments Abigail on her finery of French-style apparel, which does little to assuage Adams' ill humor.

But, try as he might, Mr. Jefferson cannot hide from "Mr. A" his keen affection for Dr. Franklin. He does not, for example, share the Adamses' view, owing to their New England puritan background, of Franklin's involvement with influential French ladies. Indeed, when he first observed the Doctor at his favorite brand of diplomacy, receiving kisses from several ladies and kissing those ladies upon their necks (a French custom to avoid melting their painted-on lead white makeup, fake beauty marks and dabbed circles of red rouge on their cheeks), he asked Dr. Franklin if the latter could arrange to transfer such privileges to him. Grinning, the Doctor replied, "You are too young a man." Many times Mr. Jefferson and I have heard Dr. Franklin say, with as much wistfulness as mirth, "Oh to be 70 again!"

Today, dressed in his beaver hat, long brown frock coat with deep collar and linen cravat, knee breeches with woolen stockings, wire buckle shoes, bifocals set low upon his nose, and abjuring a wig in favour of a few thin strands of hair falling loosely along his collar, Dr. Franklin is, to the French, the very romantic ideal of the American rustic, with a plain and firm demeanor, and the direct language of the manly backwoodsman. The French ladies declare that he has put the effeminate and servile refinement of their own men to shame. That he is also the pre-eminent diplomat and leading scientist of his age makes Dr. Franklin irresistible to everyone in France—the Adamses excepted.

The twenty-six-year-old General, Marquis de Lafayette, tall, sandy-haired, always unassuming yet offering an initial chilliness to strangers that so reminds of Mr. Jefferson, arrived smartly attired in a blue wool suit with red silk velvet trim, white linen shirt with ruffles, black satin breeches and silk stockings. He promptly inquired when we might expect Mr. Jefferson's arrival.

"He shall be here shortly," I replied, "on the arm of your wife's niece, Madame de Tesse'. This morning he attended one of her salon readings of Plutarch's Lives and his favorite novel, Tristram Shandy, and they are now strolling their way through the nearby woods and should..."

At that moment, the glass door from the gardens swung inward and the Ambassador and Madame made a dramatic appearance. Compared to all the other gentlemen, Mr. Jefferson, standing almost a foot higher than his lovely companion, was dressed quite plainly in a tightly curled powderless wig, black coat, silk stockings, silk cravat (purchased for him by Mrs. Adams), and low-heeled leather shoes more in resemblance to slippers than walking boots. Madame de Tesse' was attired in a fashion more adapted to strolling the park, a dark red riding coat (redingote here) of simply-trimmed woolen fabric, with full-length, tight sleeves and a broad collar with lapels, a rather modest wig and wide brimmed hat. She had small yet piercing eyes, and a very pretty face and fine mouth despite its slight imperfection owing to a nervous twitch that gives her the appearance of grimacing while conversing. But she is the very picture of grace, charm and, of greatest interest to Mr. Jefferson--wit, which she applies at all times in support of American liberty and to the detriment of those who would deprive us of it.

At first taken aback by the presence of so many guests and their effusive welcome, Mr. Jefferson quickly warmed to the occasion, greeting first General Lafayette, then Dr. Franklin and finally Mr. and Mrs. Adams. Our hostess was smartly attired in a robe a' la 'anglaise with closed bodice, natural make-up and mob cap. She had donned a gray, wool frock coat with turned-down collar and small round cuffs, ruffled linen shirt, breeches with wool stockings and shoes fastened with paste stone buckles. Perhaps the Adams's more simple country style of dress, versus the more formal styles of the French, helped set the even more plainly dressed ambassador at ease.

Sensing his initial reticence with the less familiar faces, Madame de Tesse' introduced him to the Marquis de Condorcet. "Monsieur Condorcet," said she, "May I present the new Minister Plenipotentiary to our king and country, Mr. Thomas Jefferson, the former Governor of Virginia and the author of his country's Declaration of Independence."

At this, Mr. Adams evinced a barely discernable grunt.

The Marquis de Condorcet, a tall, large framed man with powdered wig, sloping forehead, broad nose, and gentle eyes that masked the fiery soul within, was dressed in matching red coat, hip-length waistcoat and breeches with silk stockings and shoe buckles of polished silver cut into false stones. He bowed and said, "Then it is you, Sir, who are to replace Dr. Franklin?"

"No one can replace him, Monsieur, I am only his successor."

The Doctor, continuing his flirtations with Madame Helvetius in his chair, to which he was bound by gout, nevertheless listened intently to this conversation, and raised his cane in salute to the compliment.

"So," the Marquis continued, "you, Mr. Jefferson, are indeed the author of that estimable document, and not Mr. Dickinson, as some of us here have been lead to believe?"

At this point Mr. Adams bristled noticeably and injected the following: "Yes, sir, Monsieur, it was the privilege of Mr. Jefferson, myself and Dr. Franklin to attend the Committee appointed to draft a declaration in support of our position against the British king. Mr. Dickinson, who, like our companion, Dr. Franklin, hailed from

Pennsylvania, did all within his power to obstruct our unanimity in favor of independence!"

Mr. Jefferson smiled with that gentleness of visage that always increased in direct proportion to the heat demonstrated in any discourse in which he partook, said, "Yet Mr. Dickinson, upon ascertaining the will of Congress to revolt, immediately formed a company from his own finances and fought under our new banner as vigorously as Generals Washington and our beloved Lafayette."

"So, you admit authorship of the document?" the Marquis pressed.

"The Committee for drawing the declaration desired me to do it, and so it was done."

"Indeed," said Madame de Tesse', "I possess a copy of the document written in Thomas's own hand. I bequeath him to you, Marquis, as a man at once a musician; skilled in drawing; a geometrician, an astronomer, a natural philosopher, legislator and statesman. A Senator of America in the tradition of a Cicero at Rome, who sat in the famous Congress that launched a revolution; a governor of Virginia during the difficult invasions of Arnold, Tarleton and Cornwallis, and now a man with great fondness for our country, and I might add, Marquis, for your own inestimable work, the Progress and Rise of Man and the Perfectibility of Society."

"Then I am more than honored to make your acquaintance, Mr. Jefferson," Condorcet gushed warmly.

"The honor is mine," Jefferson quickly replied, blushing like a boy, as he often does when complimented or upon hearing the racy jokes told by all the French ladies. "We would do well in our country to adopt your method of tallying votes in run-off elections, and more significantly, your stance on a liberal economy with free trade among nations, free and equal public education and the adoption of a constitution guaranteeing individual liberties. However, it is not I that is the ornament of the age in my country, as you are in yours. It is Dr. Franklin, there, who is a scientist, statesman, author, newspaperman, philosopher and businessman par excellence, and the diplomat most responsible for inducing your country to aid us during the darkest hour of our revolution."

"Indeed," General Lafayette nodded vigorously, "it is well known among us that Dr. Franklin snatched the lightening from the heavens and the scepter from tyrants."

At this, Mr. Adams shot Mr. Jefferson a knowing glance, from which the latter turned immediately to Lafayette and smiled his approval.

At this, Madame Helvetius rose from Dr. Franklin's couch and addressed Mrs. Adams directly. "And how do you find us, Mrs. Adams," she asked coyly.

"You are," Abigail replied somewhat coolly but entirely without rancor, "easy in your manners, eloquent in your speech, your voices soft and musical and your attitude generally pleasing. I fancy French women must possess the power of persuasion and insinuation beyond any other females on earth."

"And yet... You have some objection to them?" Madame asked, standing almost toe-to-toe, looking Abigail full in the eye. For all her easy manners and pleasing attitude, Madame Helvetius never lacks for directness.

"I do find it scandalous that the women here casually take lovers, as their husbands do mistresses, as the English take their tea. Did you know, Madame, that the Hospital des Enfant-Trouves receives over six thousand abandoned infants a year, and that half the children born in Paris are illegitimate, prompting the placement of boxes at certain sites throughout the city to receive these for collection? I must say I find this quite distressing."

Out of the corner of my eye, I thought I spied Marquis Condorcet appraising Mrs. Adams with an approving eye, as if he had not expected an American woman to speak her mind as freely as do the French.

Ever seeking to avoid any confrontation, Mr. Jefferson interjected, "While it is true that the great mass of people are suffering under physical and moral oppression here in Europe, and conjugal love and domestic happiness do not appear to enjoy the same existence here as they do in America. I do nevertheless love these people, and wish my countrymen would adopt European politeness and temperance. Here it seems one might pass a lifetime without encountering a single occurrence of rudeness or drunkenness. In the pleasures of the table the French are far before us in good taste and temperance, and do not terminate the most social of meals by transforming themselves into brutes, even among the lowest of the people. And yet, they have as much happiness in one year as an Englishman in ten."

"So you are quite fond of us, Mr. Jefferson?"

"Yes, Madame Helvetius, I am. Were I to tell you how much I enjoy your architecture, sculpture, painting and music I should want words."

Turning to Mr. Adams, Madame Helvetius prodded, "And what, Sir, do you think of us? I'm sure the 'le fameux Adams' does not want for words."

This was a clever dig by Madame, as the Doctor had apparently informed her that many Frenchmen confused John with his more "famous" cousin, Samuel, arch-revolutionary and purveyor of a most exceptional beer.

"Why Madame Helvetius," Adams replied with a graciousness he rarely exhibited in contradictory company, "if human nature may be made happy with anything that can please the eye, the ear, the taste or any other sense, France would be a region for happiness. But I must admit," he added with a wink (Yes! An undisguised wink) to Abigail, "I would exchange all the elegance in dress, the magnificence in architecture, even the handsome and well educated women for the simplicity of my home and hearth in Massachusetts."

"Ahh," Madame exclaimed, "you and Mr. Jefferson are the best of friends, I am told, yet you are as different in tastes and you are in appearance. One tall and thin, the other short and round, no? The charging bull and the graceful horse, I think?"

Once more Mr. Jefferson stepped into the breach. "That is owing, Madame, to the distinctions between those residing in the northern and southern parts of our country. Those in the North, like Mr. Adams and Dr. Franklin, are cool, sober, laborious, jealous of their own liberties and just to those of others, chicaning, and superstitious in their religion."

"That is so," Adams laughed, "just as those in the South, like Mr. Jefferson and Mr. Short, are fiery, voluptuary, indolent, unsteady, zealous for their own liberties but trampling on those of others, generous, candid, and without attachment of pretensions to any religion but that of the heart."

To this the entire gathering cheered and applauded, everyone appreciating the spontaneous wit shared by old revolutionary friends, and all prospects of conflict were dimmed beyond view.

In this mood, Condorcet asked Abigail what she thought of the English press, and the unkind comments it often made about her husband, Mr. Jefferson, and Dr. Franklin.

"All they write are lies," she declared forcefully. "That story about Dr. Franklin being abducted by the Algerian pirates was propagated by the English newspapers as a dish cooked up to the simpering palate of their readers."

"Indeed," Mr. Jefferson agreed, "they reported a recent attempt by Americans to assassinate King George III. A pure fantasy I assure you. No man upon this earth has my sincere prayers for his continuance in life than him. He is truly the American Messiah."

"Of course the account was false," Mrs. Adams huffed, "if it is not too rough a term for a lady to use, I will say false as Hell, or substitute one not less expressive and say false as English."

General Lafayette raised his glass and saluted his American friends. Seizing the moment, Condorcet raised his glass and shouted, "To liberty, freedom and equality."

"To France," exclaimed Mr. Jefferson. "May she share in the glories of liberty and equality as does the country to which she helped give birth."

"Well said, gentlemen," Adams said. "Shall we have our music now?"

After receiving a chorus of "yes's" in two languages, he turned to Madame Brillon, who, along with Monsieur Pagin, began preparing for their presentation.

Adams then said, "Madam Brillon, will you and Monsieur Pagin please honor us with your arts?"

After sifting through their music sheets, they produced a most fitting piece, a selection from Vivaldi's *Contest between Harmony and Invention*, of which their performance greatly delighted Mr. Jefferson. The company saluted the performers, then formed their own smaller groups to discuss the issues of the day.

It was then that Madame Helvetius turned to Mr. Jefferson with another of her infamous inquiries.

"Have you, Sir, little religion like my Frankling, or are you a zealot like Mr. Adams?"

I thought to intercede on behalf of my employer, knowing he was loathe to discuss his or any other's religious beliefs, believing that to be between a man and his Creator. But he surprised me by answering, "Madame, I am member of a Christian sect of one. Believing as I do that the people who do my religion the most harm are the practitioners of it, not those who deny it, I practice a religion with no sophisms or mysticism, believing in only three maxims in relation to it. First, that there is a God who created this universe, as it is impossible to believe that it arose by chance, and since he did, we should never leave off thanking him for that accomplishment...

"Second, the morals of Jesus are the most sublime, benevolent and rational which have ever been offered to man. And third, that I should love God with my whole heart and my neighbor as myself. This, Madame, I believe to be the sum total of religion."

Madame bowed gracefully and returned to the good Doctor's side. Franklin then proceeded to laboriously rise from his couch with the aid of Madame and General Lafayette. "Well said, Thomas," he urged, "but you'd better be careful espousing your religion around some of the European priests of every sectarian persuasion. The pope and the sword is the sum of their religion."

"Well said, Dr. Franklin," Adams nodded.

"Nevertheless," interjected Madame de Tesse, "I should very much like to thank my friend, Thomas, for his Act for Establishing Religious Freedom passed by the Virginia congress. Hopefully, it will find support in our country some day."

"Indeed, Madame," Franklin agreed heartily, raising a glass of champagne. "Indeed."

Then he turned to Adams and said, "Although you and I have disagreed on occasion, I have always counted upon your directness and honesty in our labors, Mr. Adams, without which I would have been much distressed in my own humble efforts. However, I hope you will take one last word of advice from an older collaborator...

"One rule that I always followed in diplomacy as well as conversation-- never to contradict anyone, except upon repeated entreaties, and then only by asking questions, as if for information, suggesting doubts in the process. And after all, another man's error does me no injury, and I have no desire to become a Don Quixote to bring all men by force of argument to one opinion. If another's fact be misstated, it is probable that he is gratified by a belief of it, and I have no right to deprive him of the gratification."

Before Adams could respond, no doubt joking that "Frankling" rarely deprived himself of gratification of any kind, the older man turned to Mr. Jefferson and said, "Do your best to reconcile our loyal friends here with those at home, and do what you can for our Yankee trade in whale oil and the South's in tobacco. I know you and Mr. Adams will serve us well. For my part, I return to America to help inform Mr. Madison's constitution, if only to assure that it be written so posterity may understand it. We must form a government so excellent and so clearly understood that it cannot be corrupted for at least another three hundred years, by which time the people shall undoubtedly become so corrupted as to need a despotic government, being incapable of any other. You have your Republic, gentlemen. I pray you may keep it."

"I wish you all the best, Sir," Jefferson replied. "All good things end, but we must invest our experiment with longevity, if we can. The rate of corruption being exponential, I doubt America will remain a republic no more than two or three centuries."

"I would take that one step further, Tom," Adams interjected. "We must craft a stronger central government if we wish it to las another decade.."

"I shall take your words to Congress with me, Mr. Adams, but at present, I have a date with Madame Helvetius to view balloons rising over the palace at Versailles."

"Ah, doctor, of what practical use is a balloon? What good is it, after all?"

"Why, Mr. Adams, what good is a newborn baby?"

The three old friends laughed and offered their goodbyes, promising to meet again before Franklin left France. With that, he *and Madame Helvetius took their leave of us, as did Madame Brillon and Monsieur Pagin.*

Madame de Tesse' then engaged the Adamses in conversation, while Mr. Jefferson fell in with Condorcet and Lafayette. Accordingly, I attached myself to the latter group…

"Daddy!"

I turned to see Will framed in my doorway, chicken nugget in one hand and sippy cup in the other.

"You gonna' eat? I'm hungry."

"You got it, son. Is that chicken nugget as tasty as it looks?"

"Yeah. Miss Marianna says I can't have candy 'till I finish my nuggets."

"Good for her," I said, lifting him over my head and dropping him into my arms. "Dinner before dessert, every day."

"Then we can have Miss Marianna's homemade fudge?"

"That's right, boy. After we go get Anna Grace, we can slaughter a whole batch of Mariana's homemade fudge!"

CHAPTER SEVENTEEN

Ryan Finn's eyes, ablaze with the polluted intensity of a vampire's, so unnerved the woman she averted her eyes, rose abruptly from her chair and approached the Russian working at the far end of their hotel suite. "You want anything to drink?" she asked.

Gruzenko more than ignored her; he didn't acknowledge her presence. His hands continued gliding back and forth across the device spread out on the table before him.

With the air conditioning running on high since she entered the suite, she couldn't complain about the heat. It was the company she found, if not objectionable, certainly unsavory.

Finn poured himself of glass of Jamison Irish whiskey from the wet bar in the cabinet beneath the large, flat screen television. "Drink, Garrott?"

"Sure," she said resignedly. *Nothing else to do.*

"Here...Come join me on the couch."

Their roomy 12th floor Hilton suite near the interstate on the northern edge of Jackson seemed ideal for a temporary command post, Finn realized, but their appearance, activities, and accents were certain to draw attention sooner rather than later. This part of his plan concerned him most, the momentary vulnerability of their proximity to the public. But they wouldn't be there long; Gitt was securing new accommodations for them, likely at that very moment.

"I missed you," said Finn, after stalking her across the room.

"Did you?"

"Yes. But you knew that."

"And you know as well as I do," she replied, treading firmly but lightly, "that what we had ended decades ago."

"So you remind me on occasion. Just like Gitts keeps telling me his name is Gitt, while we both know the truth is otherwise."

"His name is what he chooses to call himself, and no other. Do you always go by Finn?"

"Good point," he nodded, his expression cold and hard as granite.

"Let's don't talk about it, Ryan."

"Might things have been different if our daughter hadn't...?"

She shifted almost imperceptibly in her seat, desperately trying to avoid being drawn into whatever web he was spinning, while scrupulously avoiding the dangerous misstep of giving offense.

"You didn't object," he continued impassively, "when I suggested striking Lloyd's of London. As I recall, you were quite angry with the bank at the time."

"I don't blame you for our daughter's death, if that's what you mean. It's not that at all."

"What then?"

"I went along with you voluntarily. I don't blame you or anyone else."

"You did more than go along. You placed the IED."

"As I said, I'm not blaming you, and I've told you so many times."

They both glanced across the room to see if Gruzenko was listening, but found him totally absorbed in his task.

"Then... Why so distant? Anyone hearing your voice or noting your closed body language might wonder if my breath had turned toxic or my deodorant grown corrosive."

She glared at him in disbelief. "How can you say that? The CTC chased us across two continents, and our child died in a fire fight in France. I wanted out. I got out."

"Or so you thought."

"Yes," she replied bitterly. "Or so I thought."

"That's the way you want it, then?" he said coolly, sipping from the whisky glass he had nursed in his lap throughout their conversation.

"You know that's how I want it. I do this job, this last job, and you let me go. Forever. That's our arrangement." She paused for a moment, then added tentatively, "Right?"

Finn lowered his head, his eyes narrow slits, his brow deeply furrowed beneath his perpetually unkempt hair. "She was lovely, though, wasn't she? Brave, proud and beautiful, our little girl. At least we accomplished that."

Don't let him draw you in, she told herself. *He only uses people, like he's using all of us now.*

"Did you know I became a priest in America, in San Francisco… After we split?"

"No. I didn't know that." *But you'll use that, too, if it serves your purposes.*

"That's all? No other response?"

"Nothing else to say."

"Gruzenko," he shouted. "Is it ready?"

"One minute and it will be."

"Good," Finn said, reaching for his cell phone. "When you're done, pack it all up. We're leaving. It's time to see our new abode."

As she stood to go, he grasped her by the arm, firmly but not angrily. His eyes, bright and lively during the discussion about their daughter, were dead now, two iniquitous hollow orbs.

"You know what to do, Garrott?"

"Yes." *You taught me well.*

"Good. Have fun," he said causally, as if she were his daughter, and he her father, sending her off to play with little pigtailed companions. "Everyone should enjoy their work, and as I recall, you always considered these 'assignments' more pleasure than work."

She ignored his jibe.

Finn bounced off the couch and stood beside Gruzenko, whistling "Row, Row, Row Your Boat," as he admired the former Russian's work,

Everything in life's nothing but a dream to you, now, she thought. But this was not a dream, she knew, although he would force this last nightmare on her before releasing her from his 'influence.'

When Ryan Finn entered anyone's life, she told herself for what seemed the thousandth time, whatever dreams they formerly held were forever soiled with suffering, regret and loss.

****

I left Will with Mariana and drove to Dr. Draughn's office to collect my daughter. Along the way I pondered my two latest obsessions— the manuscript excerpts I'd been receiving, and the woman who'd recently entered my life.

No less mysterious than the manuscripts, and offering little more information on her origins, Jenny appeared to have it all-- intelligence, beauty, and Deep South charm, as well as a *joie de vivre* and smoldering sensuality that made my blood boil.

The manuscripts were almost as exciting, albeit in an entirely different way.

The Short diary presented Jefferson, Franklin and the rest just as history knew them, with their unique 18th Century perspectives and gentlemanly manner of speaking. Sure, a few of Jefferson's comments were nearly identical to words he penned after returning to America, but who's to say he wasn't formulating those ideas in Paris before writing them down later?

The New Orleans letters smacked of even greater originality. They accurately described the city in 1814, and gave names and descriptions of soldiers, generals and even pirates that rang true to anyone remotely familiar with that era.

But what was the point of sending me these manuscripts, I wondered. The answer kept coming up *message.*

Was there a connection between Jefferson's more radical beliefs and those of the Occupy the Park crowd? Their message of fairness to taxpayers and ending political corruption seemed right down our third president's alley. Was that the message being sent my way?

But what about the New Orleans letters? Where was the message there apart from fulfilling Jefferson's dream of 1776 by finally putting the British in their place? There were certainly no revolutionaries in Jackson's army. Well....There were pirates, to be sure. The domestic and international terrorists of their day. Yet they saved our bacon in that fight. Patriotic heroes or flagrant opportunists? History might never answer that question.

Or perhaps that *was* the point, I mused. At certain times, anarchy, like revolution, heroically brings oppressive governments to heel. Was I expected to associate that fine sentiment with Occupy the Park knuckleheads like the Ghost, whose sole involvement in any radical movement was the loosing of his bowels in Smith Park?

Or was the message far darker-- 'we know where you live as well as where you work'? I tried to suppress that thought and take note of my surroundings.

Dr. Draughn's office was decorated in pastel colors, with happy family photographs dotting the bookshelves and lively impressionist paintings decorating her walls. A hopeful beginning if ever there was one.

Although congenial as always, she promptly ushered me into her office past the waiting room couch where Anna Grace offered a surprisingly pleasant expression as we passed by.

Once settled in her office, Dr. Draughn said, "I know you're tired of being left in the dark about her situation."

"That's putting it lightly," I said, eschewing the offered seat, swaying nervously back and forth before Lucy's desk. When she didn't reply, I blurted, "What's wrong with my little girl, doc?"

"Nothing's wrong with her, John. She's the same lovely person she's always been. But she's no longer anyone's little girl."

"I know that. What else?"

"Look, John, I can't tell you what she told me, as you well know. Those are the rules. So take a seat and let me ask you a few questions."

"Fine," I groused. As she sat beside me, I noticed for the first time that her hair hadn't changed since college, a lovely shade of auburn, the tips hanging just below her shoulders, curling up at the ends. Her forehead bore a few wrinkles, but apart from that, and her more staid professional manner, this was the same woman I fell deeply in love with during my second year at Ole Miss law school.

"John, how much time do you spend with Anna Grace?"

"Well….Not so much, I suppose. Not like before, at least. I've a rather heavy caseload…Had a recent book signing tour in the Delta, and of course, there's Will, a time-eating monster extraordinaire. Besides," I rationalized, "she no longer seeks my company as she did before. She has her friends, and her boyfriend. The debate team and the band, volleyball last year, and the damned internet of course…"

She lowered her head, choosing her words carefully. "Do you not think that the combination of the loss of her mother, a more distant father--."

"Now that's not---."

"Let me finish, John. A more distant father than before, the sudden presence of this superstar younger brother--the apple of his father's eye; a devastating rush of hormones, a new school where she's the new girl on the block, the estrangement of her best friend since kindergarten, the innate meanness and viciousness of many girls at that age, as well as the impact of the ADHD diagnosis she carries, and the sometimes odd behaviors resulting from medication side effects…. Would you not expect all of this to take its toll on a teenager in her circumstances?"

My eyes dropped to my shoe strings, an enveloping sense of shame and helplessness weighing me down like three-hundred pound steel anchor attached to a foot-long balsam wood boat.

Lucy gave her words time to sink in, waiting patiently for me to respond. But I found it difficult to look her in the eye.

"I guess you're right, Lucy," I finally uttered. "What do you think I should do?"

"Spend some time with her, John. Take her to a movie, help her with her homework. Listen to her. Tell her you love her."

"But," I sputtered helplessly, "what if she doesn't want to spend time with me?"

She placed a consoling hand on my arm and waited for me, the drowning man, to surface. "John, how do you deal with an evasive witness in a trial?"

"Stay on the attack till I get the answer I need."

"Inelegant phrasing for this circumstance, perhaps, but that's the general idea with Anna Grace, too. Keep plugging, big fellah. Isn't she at least as important to you as your job?"

"Of course, but…Does she resent me, Lucy? What the hell is this cutting business all about?"

"Sometimes it's about dealing with stress, distracting oneself from emotional pain or anxious thoughts. Stressful circumstances, loss of family members or friends, peer pressure, negative self-image, lack of coping skills, getting behind in school, underlying diseases or conditions like ADHD, however slight the condition may still be at her age. These are all reasons why teens cut themselves. Teen suicide attempts, both the cry for help variety and the sincere efforts, are often grounded in the same reasons. But it's often little more than no one to confide in during difficult times."

"You're saying she feels abandoned by her father?"

"Could be," she nodded. "I don't know that it's really come to that yet. I know she thinks you don't have any idea about what she's going through, or what she needs at this time."

"Lucy," I said, a wan smile tripping across my lips, "I certainly hope I'm not paying you $150 an hour to tell me that my teenaged daughter thinks I'm a dumbass."

On the way home I regretted my glib response to Lucy's efforts to guide me in the right direction. How was I ever going to set things right with Anna Grace? Then it struck me how much I missed Beth's counsel dealing with our girl.

How I missed Beth.

But this was not the time to revel in my own sorrow. Or guilt. It was past time to get it together and make my family whole again.

CHAPTER EIGHTEEN

On the ride home from Dr. Draught's office, Anna Grace sat quietly, arms and legs tightly crossed, gazing out the window at the moon.

"Do you know what author Walker Percy says about times like these?"

"What?" she jumped, as if stung by a bee.

"He said, 'On those days when you feel the worst, when you think that everything is hopeless—sometimes the best things happen'."

She frowned, glaring straight ahead. "I don't feel hopeless, dad."

Maybe you don't, but I damn sure do, I wanted to say, but before I could convey something equally daft, she murmured, "But thanks anyhow."

After we turned off Highland Colony Parkway into our subdivision, I reached across the seat and placed my hand over hers. Taken by surprise, she instinctively withdrew her hand, then placed it back inside mine, but not with any warmth. It lay inert in my grasp, like a dead fish you wrangle off a trot line that hadn't been checked in a week.

"I love you," I said softly.

"I know," she replied blandly.

"No, Anna Grace. I love you with all my heart. I'm sorry I haven't been there for you lately"

A tear trickled down her cheek. "Me, too."

The words to the song playing on the radio at that moment couldn't have been
more apropos: 'If you're lost and alone, or you're sinking like a stone, carry on. May your path beat a sound of your feet on the ground, carry on.'

Later that evening, I sent Mariana home early and we feasted on grapes, a large Domino's cheese pizza and Will's favorite desert, a half can of Pirolines. Then Anna Grace retired to her room for a FaceTime chat with her boyfriend, while Will and I settled into my king-sized bed for our nightly routine of book reading, storytelling and song singing, the same routine I had enjoyed with Anna Grace years before.

She had demonstrated an amazing capacity for memorization at age three, and Will's capacity was no less impressive, "reading" his favorite books in tandem with me. "I'll help you read this one," he would say with obvious pride.

"In the great green room," I would begin; "there was a red balloon," he would continue. Or, "dinosaurs happy," I would say, "and dinosaurs sad," he would finish.

But tonight he was too restless to read. "Let's play a game," he said.
"It's too late for that, Will."
"No, not that kind of game. A word game."
"Oh?"
"Sure. You read something and I tell you what it means. That game."

Of Will's many accomplishments, his capacity to fathom the meaning of phrases that should be well beyond his years amazed me more than his capacity for 'reading.' Quotes by Jesus, Jefferson, John Kennedy or Martin Luther King, Jr., promoted interpretations rarely far from the mark. So recently, I had decided to stump my four-year-old by reading philosophical sayings that were beyond his ken.

Or so I thought.

"Okay, Will, you've successfully interpreted the words of a Greek, Socrates; a Roman, Marcus Aurelius; a Jew, Jesus of Nazareth; and a Chinese, Confucius. Let's try a German god this time." I opened the century-old wooden lawyer's bookcase I had inherited from my maternal grandfather and produced a leather bound tome.

"Okay!"

"Good boy," I said. "I'll read the quote, and you tell me what it means."

"Fine," he beamed, ready for the challenge.

"Odin says, 'Time will surely kill us, even if spears do not.' What did he mean by that?"

He propped an elbow on the bed, cradling his chin in his hands, striving with all his might to grasp the meaning. But the answer eluded him, as I suspected it would. But unlike the other times when he didn't grasp the concept, he didn't ask the quotation's meaning.

"Daddy, who is Odin?"

"You know Odin... Thor's father. Remember the movie?"

"The old man with one eye?"

"Yes. Do you know how he lost that eye?"

"Sure. The Frost Giant hit him."

"In the movie, yes. But in Norse mythology, Odin offered his eye to Mimir, the wizard, so he might gain the Wisdom of the Ages. With that wisdom, he gave poetry to mankind."

"For real?"

"Yes, in real mythology, at least."

"Is Odin God?"

"Yes, son. He's just God as envisioned by the Vikings, just as Zeus was God as interpreted by the Greeks, and Allah is God as viewed by Muslims like Malik, Anna Grace's boyfriend. The Bible says God made us in his own image, but in reality, people of every time and place remake him in theirs."

'Uh, huh," he mumbled, apparently deep in thought. "Daddy?"

"Yes?"

"May I have ice cream?"

"Only if you can dip into Odin's Well of Wisdom and tell me what his saying means."

After hearing the quote again, Will opined, "Spears kill us, but if they don't, Time does."

"That's right son. But what does it *really* mean?"

"I don't know."

"We're all going to die sooner or later, Will, so we may as well fight the good fight before we go."

"Fight 'gainst what?"

"Evil, son. The bad guys who hurt other people."

"Like monsters?"

"What did I tell you about monsters, boy?"

"That the only monsters were the dinosaurs that died millions of years ago."

"And?"

"And bad people who hurt little boys and girls."

"That's right. And how does daddy deal with those?"

"Puts them in jail," he crowed.

"You got it, boy."

"Daddy?"

"Yes, son?"

"Do you miss mommy?"

Pause.

"Yes, of course, Will. And so does Anna Grace."

"I wish…."

"You wish…what?"

"I could see her."

"You did the day you were born. She held you in her arms and kissed you. I know you don't remember that, but you will see her again."

"In Heaven?"

"Yes. She really loved you, Will. Did everything she could to bring you into the world."

"How could she love me if she never got to see me?"

"She felt you moving in her belly for six wonderful months. She felt you kicking her from inside. And she spoke to you, just as I did."

"Did I talk back?"

"You were too young to talk, but you waved to us with your tiny hands. We could see the outline of them pressed against her belly."

He grew silent for a moment, then threw his arms around me, clutching me so tightly I almost gasped. Before I could pat him on the back I realized that he was patting mine. Had he seen the moisture forming in the corner of my eye?

"Don't be sad, Daddy. Anna Grace and I love you very much."

CHAPTER NINETEEN

The next morning at the office found me waiting restlessly at my desk for the clock to register 9:00 AM, when the diocese office opened for business. When I finally got their secretary on the line, I made an appointment to meet Father Joe shortly before lunch. I spent the next few minutes rehearsing my explanation to my old friend about Anna Grace's difficulties and my part in causing them. As I had found my first meeting with an oddball priest somewhat satisfying, I thought I'd give it another go with and old, and completely stable friend.

A loud rap on my door interrupted those musings.

"Come in."

"Morning John," said the U.S. Attorney, peeking around my door. "Got a minute?"

"For you, Jack, I've got two minutes."

"You're a prince."

He seated himself across from my desk and greeted me with a furrowed brow and a deeply concerned expression. Oh, boy, I told myself. What have I done now?

"John," he mumbled after a moment of silence intended to demonstrate the heavy burden of leadership he felt at that moment. "Did you know a recent study shows that since 2010, groups of white nationalists, neo-Confederates, skinheads, neo-Nazis, Antifa groups, armed militias, border vigilantes, and other so-called patriotic shitheads have more than doubled? Hell, they grew from about 800 identified groups in 2008 to over 1700 in 2012!"

When I responded with a blank expression, he produced a photograph from an envelope and laid it on my desk. The 8x10 black and white jailhouse photo showed the Ghost grinning wickedly at the camera, his face blackened with bruises, one eye partially closed and a Band-Aid pasted to his forehead.

"Jailhouse scrape?" I asked unsympathetically.

"Not exactly," he answered, gazing somberly out my window. "We weren't making any headway getting him to talk, and the F.B.I. guys apparently grew weary of his sarcastic attitude, so somebody arranged for him to share a cell with Bobo Dardy."

"Somebody arranged?" I said bolting upright in my chair. "With the worst bad-ass in the Hinds County jail?" Dardy was charged with beating three men to death with his bare hands in a bar fight in the roughest ghetto in south Jackson. By the time he finished rearranging their faces, their noses were split and their eyeballs crushed, more a part of the floor than their heads. "*Somebody* arranged?"

"Yeah, can you believe it? Anyhow, when the guards got there, they heard your Ghost shouting something about how Dardy couldn't hide in the jail, that even Dardy wasn't safe from the Dullahan.' As if the Dullahan was a name that meant something to anyone in the county jail."

"The only horror Dardy knows is soap."

"Well, apparently Dardy had heard of the Dullahan, and he backed off fast."

"Dardy backed off? Bullshit. He might get distracted from a rape or murder in progress by the sound of an ice cream truck cruising by, but he's not afraid of any half-assed goblin. What the hell is a 'Dullahan', anyhow? What was the Ghost babbling about this time?"

"That's what we wanted to know. We ran the name through the NCIC, and our computers lit up."

"Well, who the hell is the Dullahan?"

He handed me a faded color photograph. It showed a large man, with a full head of brown unkempt hair, a sneer on his thin lips, and a small, barely discernable scar on his left cheek. What caught my attention, though, were his iridescent blue eyes, the deepest blue found in waters off Florida's east coast, yet dispensing menace in a way that made me imagine Saturn's frigid volcanoes spewing icy glaciers down their slopes.

"This is the Dullahan?" I asked, the thought occurring to me that the man in the photo resembled the large fellow I had seen at my recent book signing, the night I met Jenny. I couldn't be certain; the man in the photo was large enough with the same color hair, but I hadn't seen his eyes concealed behind tinted shades.

"Uhm hm," Jack nodded gravely. "According to ancient myth, the Dullahan is a Celtic demon, a sort of headless horseman, also known as the 'dark man', who throws buckets of blood at onlookers as he gallops by, and whenever his horse stops, someone dies."

"Lovely. And this guy?" I asked, holding up the photo.

"A former IRA terrorist nicknamed 'The Dullahan' by the local Boston constabulary. He immigrated to this country in the 1980's, disappeared for a few years, then suddenly reappeared in the company of friends owning membership in the United Freedom Front, or 'UFF', a terrorist group of that era responsible for over a dozen bombings of big corporations like IBM and Mobile, a few federal courthouses and some naval and army bases. Your secretary is inputting that info in a computer file right now. Seems he was a suspect in several subsequent bank robberies and bombings after the UFF went out of business or underground, but all with their same MO. He's known by many aliases, but they think his real name, or at least the earliest version of his name they could find, is Finnerin. Patrick Finnerin."

"Taking the fight to the man, huh?"

"Yep. No convictions, though. Witnesses always disappeared, prosecutors dropped charges, jailhouse snitches wound up dead with their heads shoved in toilets and their short arm stuffed up their butts, no doubt to distinguish their MO from that of mob hitters who shove victim's dicks in their mouths. The police in Golden Meadow, Louisiana thought they had him on a jailhouse murder beef last year, but he iced a couple of guards and escaped their jail before our guys even knew he was in custody. This guy has the moral velocity of a petrified snail. Had some help with that jailbreak, too."

I leaned back in my chair, cradling my chin between thumb and forefinger, my feet wiggling nervously under my desk. "What's his connection to the Ghost?"

"Not sure," Jack shrugged. "The Ghost gave us a lengthy statement but it's not worth the paper it was written on—filled with tense hopping, non-committal expressions, abrupt changes of topics, and all the other indicators of lies and half-truths. After Dardy demanded to be moved from his cell there's not a snitch in heaven or hell that would take a run at the Ghost now. So we got nothing on that account.

"But a guy with Finnerin's description, or should I say vaguely matching his description, was seen hanging out in Smith Park with the Ghost and some woman a few nights ago, according to a witness's statement we took when interviewing all the bums in the park during the Ghost's assault investigation."

"Let's talk to that witness," I said.

"We tried late yesterday afternoon, but he's no longer hanging out in the park and has no other known address. He hasn't been seen the past few days at the Harbor House where he takes his meals, nor at St. Peter's Cathedral where he shows up for the communion wine when he's really desperate."

"I see."

"Yep," Jack mumbled, moving sluggishly toward my door. "Looks like you may have more on your hands than a simple misdemeanor assault on an LEO, John."

"So it seems."

"You up to this, John?"

I turned to meet his gaze. "What do you mean, up to it?"

"John, I would say you've seemed a little distracted of late, but you've seemed distracted since I hired you three years ago."

"I have?"

"Compared to the fire in your eyes when you fought us tooth and nail on every case as a defense attorney before I hired you, absolutely distracted. Everyone tells me you walk around in a stupor these days, those damn headphones over your ears, and a faraway look in your eyes, like a stockbroker whose investments just went south for the winter."

"That's the way people around here see me?" I asked more squeamishly than I intended. Beth had said something similar, but I took it as a gentle ribbing, not a slight as Jack intended it.

"What's eating you, John?"

"Nothing," I declared forcefully.

He studied me closely for a moment, as if deciding whether or not to ask a sensitive question. Then he shrugged as if he didn't want to know the answer, and said, "Why do you think you've been handling more arraignment hearings, more sentencing hearings, more DUI cases on the Natchez Trace, and not major trials like you handled your first year in this office?"

"The cases you give a kid just out of law school," I mumbled, shaken in the realization that he *had* been assigning me those cases of late. Or was it a lot longer than that?

I settled an elbow on my chair arm, rubbed my eyes and said, "You worried I'll screw up the Ghost's case?"

He leaned over my desk, eyeing the large manila envelope atop a stack of files. "Been receiving any anonymous deliveries lately, John?"

My face flushed with embarrassment. "Yes."

"Jill told me the day you received that one. And then another from some jerk on the street."

"Yeah?"

"We checked both for prints, and you were right. Yours and the delivery boys were the only ones on one of them, just yours on the other. We got nothing on the typed print either. An old typewriter, antique they tell me, but not otherwise traceable since they sell 'em at auctions and garage sales everywhere. Nobody keeps track of model and serial numbers of typewriters, so we can't even tell where the damn thing was last sold or auctioned. If he's a green hacker, he's a damned circumspect one, at that."

"I don't know what to say, Jack."

"Don't say anything," he barked, rising from his seat and striding toward the door. "Just pull your head out of your ass and get to work. Nail this bastard to the wall and keep your eyes out for anybody meeting this terrorist's description. And watch out for your family. If that manuscript is in any way related to the Ghost and his pals, you may get a nighttime visit from the headless horseman. "

I looked up in disbelief. "You think someone might harm my family?"

"That's not Finnerin's MO as far as we can tell, and the UFF only hit big outfits, never family members related to their targets. But this guy seems to slip off the hook in a myriad of ways, and we don't know how. Just keep a sharp eye out and phone the cops or the FBI if you sense anything out of the ordinary. You live in a gated community don't you?"

"Yes. Why?"

"We'll ask the Madison police to keep an eye on your neighborhood. We'll order an FBI stake out if anything suspicious happens. If this terrorist is responsible for your anonymous home deliveries, he may keep them coming. Keep reading them and let me know if he leaves any clues to what he's up to or where he's sending them from. And John?"

"Yeah?"

"Snap out of it, podnuh. We need the old gung ho Ferguson on this case."

"Right."

"Say," he said, lightening his tone to a more friendly banter. "You're fond of quoting famous personages to your juries aren't you?"

"Yes, I suppose so. Why?"

"Here's a quote for you, something to keep in mind during the days ahead."

"Yeah?"

"Liberty is fleeting. Terrorism is eternal."

"Very profound. Who said that?"

"Me. Just now. Get your ass to work."

"Right."

"And by the way," he said, framed by my doorway, "you ever hear of terrorists taking advantage of natural disasters to do their dirty business?"

"You mean like hurricanes?"

"No. Pandemics. Like this thing we're hearing about in China."

I blinked a few times, trying to switch horses in a very muddy stream. "It's in China, Jack. That's a little out of our jurisdiction, wouldn't you say?"

"Funny, John. It's in China *now*. Some deep reports from the CIA are suggesting that it may be here in a month or two."

"So? Wait...You're suggesting that...What?"

He frowned like a grade school teacher wondering if he was the only one in the room who could figure 2+2. "Suppose we do have a batch of terrorists on our hands. If this virus is acting up a month from now and we've got a skeleton crew guarding whatever they're after..."

"A good time to strike," I finally caught up.

"You bet. Just something to think about. Like I said, get your ass to work!"

"Right."

After he left I phoned our nanny and reminded her to keep our doors locked 24/7 (something no one would ever think to do in crime-free Madison), and not to let Will out of her sight for a moment. "And phone me whenever you see any strangers in the neighborhood, or anything unusual going on around the house."

"Oh," she said offhandedly, having heard all this before when I'd handled Homeland Security prosecutions my first year in the office, "I forgot to tell you that I picked up your mail yesterday, stuck it in my bag and forgot to leave it on the table where I always do."

"Anything important?" I said, more testily than I intended.

"Perhaps. There's a big manila envelope addressed to you that may be important."

Speak of the devil, I thought to myself. It never rains but it pours.

CHAPTER TWENTY

Just before 11:00 AM I turned right by the Governor's Mansion and strolled north on the West Street sidewalk abutting Smith Park toward St. Peter's Cathedral. The sun had earlier borne down with its usual tropical vigilance until a cold front had slid across the state line following a short-lived late morning rain, bringing weather more reminiscent of winter than the usual Mississippi heat wave. In other words, a perfect December day of 68 degrees, a slight breeze tickling every fancy, and the scent of magnolia hanging lightly in the air. Christmas decorations hung from Capitol Street utility poles and festooned the iron fence surrounding the Governor's Mansion grounds in holiday red, green and gold.

I met Father Joe Blackston in St. Peter's foyer at the door of the confessional. He stood six feet-three with barrel chest and broad shoulders, meticulously clean shaven with neatly trimmed hair and brown puppy dog eyes, the kind that prompted women in his parish to wonder aloud what his mother was thinking when she consigned him to the priesthood.

Although I hadn't confessed twice in a single year in the past four years, I had consumed the sacrament every December to the amusement of Father Joe, who took a perverse pleasure in castigating me for my backsliding ways. Yet he always made time to take my confession, though I often left the experience feeling a little less soiled than before I entered the box; my soul scrubbed cleaner than a pick-up truck emerging from a superblast car wash after a month's sojourn on Mississippi's dusty country roads.

But even though my present sins were more egregious than my usual slate of pathetic venalities, I would soon discover their relative insignificance compared to that of the malevolent specter enshrouding me and my family.

"Hello, Father Joe," I said as we entered the box. "It's always good to see you, but I was hoping to see your visiting monk again today. Not that you don't do a fine job of confession, but he—"

"What visiting monk?" he interrupted, rather testily I thought, as if I were taking forbidden liberties with the sacrament.

"What do you mean?" I asked confusedly. "I came to confession yesterday and your visiting Franciscan friar administered a sacramental spanking to me. I think he said his name was O'Shaunessy, visiting from San Francisco. He did a right smart job of it, I must say."

Although I couldn't see his ruddy face and thick shock of close cropped black hair through the confessional screen, I detected the motion of his head vigorously nodding 'no.' "We don't have a visiting friar, here, John. We never have. And certainly no one but Fathers Flannery, O'Brian and I have permission to take confession this week."

He may as well have said the pope had converted to Islam. "You're....You're not putting me on are you, Father?"

"No, John," he said with urgent sincerity. "I'm not. Did you confess to someone else yesterday? A Father O'Shaunessey, you say? That's the name of the priest who dedicated this cathedral in 1900."

My mouth suddenly went dry, my stomach churned like a sailboat tossed about on a rampaging rogue wave. A tempest in a toilet would be a more accurate description.

"John?"

"I...I don't know what to say...."

"Are you alright, John?"

"No Franciscan friars here?" I mumbled, barely able to force the words. "He said he was Third Order, Joe."

"Third Order friars do not take confession in this diocese, John, not without express permission of the bishop and the local parish priest, which would be me, by the way. And we've never entertained visiting clergy from San Francisco."

Although I had never been assaulted, sexually or otherwise, many victims of those crimes had told me through agonized tears about the sense of violation they felt at the hands of violent perpetrators. Even burglary victims felt befouled upon finding their home ransacked by strangers.

Now I fancied I knew how they felt.

"John?"

"I'm sorry, Father. Looks like I confessed to the wrong guy, yesterday."

"No, John, I'm the one who should be sorry. I don't know how he got the key…In fact I'm sure he never did. It's in a drawer in my desk. He couldn't possibly have—"

"Don't sweat it, Father. If he's who I think he is, he surely knows how to pick any lock."

"Who do you think he is?"

"You don't want to know."

"Try me."

"Well, he may be a former IRA bomber, now a known domestic terrorist, lately associated with one of the Occupy the Whatever protesters we arrested last week. Whoever he is, he knows a heckuva lot more about me than I do about him."

"But how would he have known you were coming here?"

"He's seen me coming for a long time now."

"So it seems."

Obsessed with ferreting out this latest conundrum, I decided to skip the usual byplay and get the whole thing over as quickly as possible.

I told him of Anna Grace's self-mutilations, her failed suicide attempt in a desperate plea for help, and Dr. Draughn's perspective.

He weighed his words very carefully before responding. "I'm sorry for your and Anna Grace's troubles, John. And for our contribution to them, allowing a terrorist to blaspheme the sacrament when you came to us in need."

I stared at the screen separating us, having never before heard him speak with such heat.

"Even so," he said, his anger dissipating slowly, "I'd like to ask you an important question."

"Why not?" I said resignedly. "Everybody else is."

"Have your recent troubles…I don't mean just these events of the past two days…"

"You mean the death of my wife?"

"Ah, yes. That also. That especially. Have these circumstances caused you to lose your faith?"

Damn, Padre…Don't take any prisoners while you're at it, huh? "I suppose so, Joe."

"Why is that? I've always recognized a strong sense of spirituality in you. Why would you give up on God now, when you, your daughter and your young son need Him the most?"

"I don't know, Father. Maybe I'm blinded by all the injustice and lack of mercy in the world that Yahweh seems content to allow."

"Injustice," he mused. "Isn't that on us, John?"

"I'm not talking about that kind of injustice, Father. I was referring to the cosmic injustice of some being born in perfect health, with good minds, strong bodies, ideal parents and comfortable lives, while others are born blind or disfigured to abusive, drug addicted parents who rape and abuse them. Where is God's justice for those unfortunate souls?"

"And lack of mercy, you say? Isn't that also on us?"

"Again, Father," I said with mounting impatience, "I meant the lack of mercy your God shows to those living in the path of hurricanes, tsunami, tornadoes, floods, flaming asteroids and His other acts that force me to admit that your supposedly loving God doesn't know the meaning of the word. At least the ancient pagan gods never claimed to be merciful."

"That's a difficult concept, I know," he said softly. Then changing tack, he asked, "Do you give your time and money to hurricane and tornado victims, John?"

"No Father," I growled. "I admit I fall far short of the mark. That's why I'm here in the first place. But while I'm here, may I ask you a question?"

"Surely."

"Wouldn't you... By that I mean the church as 'you'... Wouldn't you be happy if we all lived according to Jesus's moral example, without all the mysticism and the inquisitions, the holy wars and unholy acts perpetrated in the God's name, and especially by men of the cloth? Couldn't you be satisfied if we flushed all that, loved our neighbor and occasionally turned the other cheek? Why isn't that good enough?"

"Let me put it this way, John. You love architecture don't you? That's the impression I got from the book you wrote last summer."

"What in the world has that got to do with—"

"Bear with me, John. And tell me, how long any building would stand, with a lovely façade designed by the world's greatest architect ... If it had no foundation at all? How long would any such structure last?"

I considered his analogy for a moment. "Good point, Joe. Mark one up for Rome. My response is that instead of conventional architecture and a conventional foundation, why not just start over, with a more creative foundation, something less harsh than the slaughter of the Canaanites, something more rational than transubstantiation and the three-gods-in-one?"

"But sometimes, John, the heart requires more than reason alone can offer. You may not know precisely what it needs, but in moments of quietude or contemplation the heart's needs make themselves known to everyone with the openness to hear them."

"And my daughter, Joe? What about her needs? And my failure to fill them?"

"What is done is done, John. Your contrition is all you can offer for those failures. I can see you're truly contrite, and through the power invested in my by the Holy Spirit, I absolve you of your sins."

"That's all well and good Father, but what do I do now?"

"Face up to it, John. Listen to her. Show her you love her, don't just say it. Remind her how wonderful she is and what she means to you. Take her to a movie. To a concert. To Mass. You worry you're not the parent you were when Beth was here, but now use *your* creativity and be the parent you may never have been before."

"And if she rejects this offer of parental affection?"

"She won't, John. You're her dad, the only person on Earth other than Will who loves her the way she needs to be loved right now. Of course she wants to spend time with you. You only have to convince her that *you* do to, and be there for her when she's ready to receive you."

I heaved a capitulating sigh. "I'll do my best, Father. Thank you."

"That's why we're here, John."

"And my problem with the terrorists? Any suggestions on that account? I know that's not your specialty, but I could use some words of advice."

"Hmm. I can offer you a reading, a joke or both on that account. What will you have?"

"Father," I grinned, "that's such a spectacular offer I've no choice but to take both."

"Tell me, John, what can a man say to make God laugh?"

"I give up."

"Tell him your plans."

Pause. "We're not entirely in control…That's your point?"

"And nor are these terrorists, no matter their beliefs to the contrary. God has his ways, John. We must wait for Him to reveal them. Your concern that it's all up to you to heal your daughter or save the world from terrorists is an illusion. It's all in God's hands, and he'll lighten your burdens if you'll only bring them to him."

"That's what I thought I was doing, Joe, through his self-appointed representative on Earth. But since I don't have time to wait for God to reveal his cosmic plan, would you mind sharing the reading you mentioned?"

He brushed off my sarcasm and said, "Read Psalm 59 and offer yours prayers in accordance with those words. That may offer you some solace where these terrorists are concerned. And…."

"Yes?"

"I know people who do these terrible things think they're doing justice, and most of them were victimized by others in their youth, often by their own parents or someone else they trusted. We can only pray they eventually realize that hurting others will not heal their own wounds, and come to understand that God will grant them the patience to await justice in His own time."

"That's it?"

"That's all anyone can ask of themselves. Go in peace, my friend."

I rose to leave, but he accosted me outside the confessional.

"John, I've a favor to ask of you."

"Oh?"

"I would certainly understand if you declined, after we put you in harm's way, so to speak, but you've helped us in similar circumstances before...."

"How may I help, Joe?"

"We're giving a service for Catholic Charities here in a few weeks, their annual Christmas cheer for the underprivileged children. The usual fare: music by the choir, presents for the children, a fine holiday meal for their families."

"Yes?"

"A few of our donators didn't come through this year, with the bad economy I suppose, and we're short about $1500 for the party. I was wondering if you could..."

"I'll send you a check this afternoon, Joe."

"Are you sure it's not an imposition?"

"Not if you would grant me a small consideration."

His eyes sparkled as he regarded me closely. "And what might that be?"

"Ask the choir to include a few requests in their repertoire."

"Such as?"

"Three songs appropriate for the season. They've sung them all before, or so have the kids performing with the Madrigal Singers at their schools."

"Which songs do you request?"

"*Ave Maria*, by Josquin des Prez, and not the maudlin modern version always played today; Josquin's version of *Inviolata, Integara Et Casta*; and *Missa Papae Marchelli* by Giovani Palestrina. Or if things go poorly for me between now and then, *Missa Pro Defunctis*, the requiem for the dead, by Jacob Clemens."

"Speaking of maudlin," he chuckled, "do you think that last song appropriate for the occasion?"

"The kiddies won't notice, Father, if the presents are plentiful and the victuals to their liking. But I would greatly appreciate hearing any one of the first three if the choir isn't up to learning them all."

"And don't think," he grinned, "that I don't get your point about the terrorists, to whom you feel we gave aid and comfort."

"You were always quick on the uptake, Joe."

"But why these particular pieces, John?"

"They all end well, a very important quality in people, life and music. These songs finish with the most beautiful musical phrases of the Renaissance. And the words, especially those of *Ave Maria*, are as moving as the music. But when combined with the music, they soothe the soul in ways little else can."

"Which words are you referring to?"

"Josquin's ending couplet, one of the most poignant ever written. In a time of rampant plague, devastating wars, infant mortality, ubiquitous filth, poverty and drudgery the likes of which we've not seen in the West for five hundred years, Josquin writes, "*Mary, Mother of God, please...Remember me!*"

"Ah, yes. As relevant today as then. Especially with this plague from China descending upon us."

"I think so. What do you say?"

"I'll put in your request with the choir."

"And use your influence to get them performed?"

"I'll do the best I can, John."

"Well, as a somewhat portly but well-intended wise man once told me, that's all anyone can ask of themselves."

"May I ask one more thing of you?"

"Why not?"

"John, I'd like you to bring your family to that service, and bring a present for one of the children. Will and Anna Grace can help you pick it out. I'll get you the information on the child later today. What do you say?"

I nodded 'yes', knowing resistance was futile; he would never give up, and my intransigence would only make him try all the harder. He was, I told myself, Irish in all but nationality.

****

Back at the office, I mailed a check to Father Joe, then pulled a Bible off my shelf often mined for appropriate sentiments during closing arguments. To my pleasant surprise, Psalm 59 offered the words of another of my favorite Renaissance songs, *Deliver me from Mine Enemies*, surely, apropos of my current situation. Mark another one up for Rome, I mused, remembering why, years earlier, I had once sworn off fencing words with the all-seeing, all wise Father Joe.

Then I summoned the courage to march down the hall to Jack Ashton's office and tell him about my "confession" to a man I presumed to be the Dullahan in priest's clothing.

He gazed somberly out his fourth floor window for a full minute before responding. "So you think he's shadowing you now, sending you untraceable manuscripts, taking your confessions, and watching you day and night?"

"That seems likely. This really gives me the creeps."

"You want off the case?"

"Hell, no! These sons-of-bitches are going down, Jack. And I'm going to be the one to nail them, the Ghost at the very least."

"I'm glad to hear you say that. Maybe this case is what you needed to snap you out of your malaise and get you back on the first team."

"But….What about my family?"

"That's a problem, to be sure, if your faux priest is who we think he is. Still, neither he nor any of the UFF ever harmed family members of prosecutors or judges. Unlike other terrorists at home and abroad, they've only attacked government facilities and taken the fight directly to those they hold responsible for the wrongs they claim to oppose. At least that's been their MO so far."

"I suppose so….."

"Nevertheless, under the Anti-Terror Act, we've got the authority to guard your family 24/7, and keep an eye on your children at home and school. Of course we'll step up security here at this building, at our day care, and in the courthouse in general. But…"

"But, what?"

"You son's four-years-old, right?"

"Yes. Why?"

"Well, our day care is well guarded, but these people certainly do hit courthouses, and I don't think I need to mention Oklahoma City to tell you what I think you should do, if only for your own peace of mind. Is there anywhere he could stay for the next week, at least until after the Ghost's habeas corpus hearing? A relative perhaps? Preferably out of town?"

"Wouldn't Will have tighter security at our home, under guard, closer to the marshals and the F.B.I.'s main office?"

"Perhaps. But none of those can prevent a detonation in a truck just outside our building or your home. If he were my child, I'd take him out of here right now. Certainly on the day of the hearing, if nothing else."

"Thanks, Jack. You're right. I'll call my sister in Laurel. She'll be glad to take him for a day or two."

"Good enough. You ready for the hearing?"

"What's to be ready for? We have a federal marshal as victim and several eye-witnesses. If I can't win a case with the testimony of Matt Dillon, I may as well quit and hang out a shingle on State Street."

"My sentiments exactly. Meanwhile, since we may be dealing with more than crackpot protesters in the park, I want you to go see Dagney right now."

"Who?"

"The forensic psychologist we use in cases involving psychopaths, murderers and terrorists. She's here in the courthouse right now, at the second floor lockup, interviewing a defendant in one of my cases. I'll buzz her on my cell phone and have her come to your office right now."

CHAPTER TWENTY ONE

Dr. Dagney Criss was not at all what I expected. I hadn't met her before, and I know it's a stereotype, but the forensic psychiatrists I *had* met in sexual assault and molestation cases always proved odd, socially-challenged birds, if indeed 'odd' adequately expressed it. Even when they didn't *look* strange, their perspectives often seemed more bizarre or macabre than their attire, so I always figured that went with the territory.

By contrast, Criss, a large African-American woman wearing pressed khaki pants and white button-down shirt, greeted me very cordially in my office with a firm but gentle handshake, even apologizing for delaying me fifteen minutes longer than she'd expected. "My interview went on longer than I thought," she said, seating herself on my office couch. "This one had more childhood issues than most."

"Not at all," I said, seating myself beside her, "thank you for seeing me so quickly."

"Jack said it was important," she replied, businesslike. "So, what are we dealing with here?"

I explained our situation with the Ghost and his possible connection to a presumed domestic terrorist that may have attended my book signing, substituted himself for a priest and taken my confession, and was likely sending a putative diary and 19th century correspondence to my home and office like any green hacker worth his salt might do.

By the way she jumped right in, I'd have thought she'd been dealing with my exact circumstance for years.

"John, when most people of think of terrorists, they picture Muslims with bombs under their turbans, but that's not the usual profile here. Most domestic terrorists in this country are white Anglo-Saxon locals with little religious affiliation at all, or immigrants who claim to be all about salvaging our American way of life, thank you so very little. They often have no family ties, suffer from personality disorders such as a grandiose sense of self and entitlement, not unlike three quarters of Hollywood celebrities and every inch of the `Reverend' Al Sharpton."

"They're not psychopaths?"

"Not usually. Their profiles are more likely that of the pathological narcissist, like a Dick Cheney or Kim Kardashian."

"You're serious?"

"Not entirely. I'm just giving you easily recognizable examples of the disorder."

"But those people you mentioned don't blow up banks, military bases and courthouses. At least not in this country and then not contrary to our laws. What makes some of them, like, presumably, O.J Simpson and Ted Bundy, go that extra mile?"

She clicked her upper teeth with her right middle finger, scanning the ceiling.

Ahh, I mused. Here we go.

"O.J. and Teddy surely meet the super narcissist profile," she nodded, then suddenly snapped her fingers as if static electricity had struck her from deep inside my Naugahyde couch. "But, that's not your suspect's profile. Think… Lee Harvey Oswald--politically motivated in an absurd way. Idealistic, probably. Not entirely unhappy, perhaps. Poor social skills, likely. And beyond a shadow of a doubt, hates authority with a passion. May have had alcoholic or abusive parents, but, and especially in this case, is probably very well-educated, from a middle class or higher background. As likely as not, he's blessed with a touch of Messianism, not unlike a few of our recent presidents," she opined with a large grin, obviously pleased with her talent for deduction. "Except that your boy chose a different path than standing for election to cure our country's ills."

"What are our chances of catching him before he makes us pay through the nose for letting him slip through our fingers?"

"Almost nil, John. Better chance of winning the Publisher's Clearinghouse sweepstakes or Louisiana Lottery than catching him in the act of planning or perpetrating a terrorist act. They lay very low right up 'til the big boom, by which time they're usually miles away."

"Then how…"

"Simple. We nail them during their involvement in other criminal activities from sexual assault to traffic violations…DUIs mostly. Lately they've all started riding bikes and taking cabs to keep stupid from landing them in the slam. Aside from that, it's usually suspicious documents inadvertently coming to light, monitored phone calls, internet surveillance, or their incredible inability to stop themselves from joining paramilitary groups we're already eyeing closely."

"This one played a very good Irish priest. And got away with it clean."

"Probably is one. Or was."

"How's that?"

"Did he say where he was from? What kind of priest he claimed to be?"

"Well, yes, now you mention it. Claimed he was a Third Order priest, ordained in San Francisco. Ever heard of that, before?"

"Sure. Check with Saint Mary Province in Nashville, Tennessee. It's the original community of the Order of Franciscan Servants. They accept Mass intentions and prayer requests all the time. My brother's a member. In fact our whole family's Catholic, and has been since the first mackerel snappers poled their way up the Mississippi from the coast to settle these parts. Of course, *my* ancestors didn't originally come to America voluntarily," she quipped with a wry grin. "Tell you what, I'll check with him and see if he knows anything about your unholy Father."

"Thanks. I'm impressed you cast such a wide net."

"No prob," she grinned, hooking both thumbs through her side belt loops. "Give me a description and I'll get right on it."

But my elation over the first break in the case eroded shortly after I left my office an hour before dusk. Dagney got nowhere with her brother the Third Order Nashville priest, and the prospect of terrorists striking my family weighed me down like a bowling ball in my gut.

The terrorists on our radar had only bombed federal facilities so far, and those only after causing citizens to evacuate first. But life is nothing if not change, and terrorists, like Asian viruses, tend to mutate in all the worst possible ways the longer we give them free reign.

Would Will or Anna Grace be any safer out of town than they would be at home or anywhere else if unknown terrorists determined to strike at me through them? Fatigue suddenly claimed my soul. I rubbed my eyes, but that didn't stop my mind's eye from seeing terrorists around every corner like a vision of shadows in a narcissist's nightmare.

And then there was Jenny. What was her connection, if any, to all of this? Either Finnerin took the prize as the best pseudo-historian on the planet, or someone was feeding him inside information. I shuddered at the possibility that this someone might be Jenny or, inadvertently, Breeland.

Although it seemed little consolation, the thought occurred to me that if Finnerin was watching me closely, he had sufficient time to follow me to the cathedral and don priest's robes while I meditated on my troubles in the nave. And he did read my book, and possibly my article about my 1814 forebear. Maybe he got there on his own.

Much of what happened could be explained in other ways. My penchant for history, specifically my interest in the Battle of New Orleans and Thomas Jefferson in Paris, was well known in these parts. My book about Jefferson in France was certainly no best-seller, but anyone researching my name would nail all that information on the first Google entry. Perhaps I had no Benedict Arnold in my corner after all.

Phoning Breeland and asking him to betray client confidences would be a pointless exercise, I decided, but driving by Jenny's house on the way home might not be. I phoned the federal protection service and arranged for a car outside our residence on a 24/7 basis, plucked Will from our federal building's day care, and headed up I-55 toward the Greymont Avenue exit.

But when I gained her driveway, I found no lights burning in any windows. Ringing the doorbell proved fruitless, so I gave it up and headed for the friendly confines of Madison County.

A black, unmarked government car sat parked on the curb in front of our house, and the driver's seat agent acknowledged me with a 'thumbs up' as I wheeled into our driveway. Give Uncle Sam credit; he protects his own with alacrity and thoroughness.

Anna Grace met me at the back door, asking about the unmarked car. "Ole dad handles difficult cases sometimes, baby," I said with a studied casual tone. "So while I'm prosecuting a dangerous criminal, they sometimes place agents at my house to watch over us, just in case. Nobody's made any threats, no one's tried to hurt anybody, but sometimes it's better to play it safe. Better too safe than too sorry, huh?"

"Okay," she said, watching me like a hawk, seeking even the slightest sign something more was afoot. "If you're sure…"

"Yes, I'm sure, honey," I smiled. "Let's just keep the door locked at night, the alarm activated, and stay inside after dark. Just ordinary precautions that…"

"Ordinary? I don't know what planet you live on dad, but here on earth no one considers this ordinary."

"Look, Anna Grace, we live in a gated neighborhood inside a gated community, in the most crime free city in the state, and we've got two government agents parked in front of our house. We're safe, okay? Just keep an eye out and avoid strangers like the plague is all you need do. Now go do your homework and leave the security to me."

"Sure thing!" she barked, turning on her heels, diving into her room and closing the door a little too loudly for my comfort.

I'm sorry, baby, I thought. I know this is not what you need right now.

"Daddy, daddy," shouted Will as he rushed from Marianna's embrace and leapt into mine.

Ah, yes… There was always Will.

After feeding the kids, checking Anna Grace's homework progress, and playing several rounds of Angry Birds on Will's mini IPad, I left him in the den with Marianna, now in semi-permanent residence at our home.

A plate of cheese and crackers in one hand and a glass of wine in the other, I retired to the bedroom to take up my latest addiction. I hadn't mentioned the anonymous manuscripts to Anna Grace; no reason to worry her about that. But I had alerted Mariana to watch for any more deliveries, although they'd probably be coming in the mail with the agents parked out front.

So, with the kids settled, our doors locked and the alarm activated, I nestled down on my king-sized bed and held a typed manuscript in my hands.

After Dr. Franklin and Madam Helvetius left the Adams' Mardi Gras party, the following conversation took place, one that I believe to be as significant for my country's future as I found it entertaining and profound at the time. In order to keep it straight in my mind, I set it down with as little extraneous material as possible, hoping to do better justice to the words I did hear—

Condorcet: My good Mr. Jefferson, I note you are the plainest dressed man in the room, the most destitute of ribbons, crosses and other insignias of rank or pomp so favored by General Lafayette and myself. Is this part and parcel of your predilection for republican simplicity?

Jefferson: My predilection, sir, is for more than mere appearance. Like yourself, and General Lafayette, I support a republican form of government in my country, and I hope someday, in yours as well.

Condorcet: As do we, sir. But I wonder, how shall you obtain one? You must form a sufficiently strong government to resist European aggression, yet not so strong as to suffocate the liberties of your people. This is rather like taming a lion for the circus without making it wearisome to the public.

Jefferson: As you say, composing the piece remains our greatest difficulty. Our Congress agreed on independence, but we only succeeded by a hair's breadth. And that was after American blood had already been shed by a merciless invader at Lexington and Concord.

Lafayette: And our forces prevailed only after eight years of struggle, as much against the American Tories as the British Army.

Condorcet: And yet, your work, Mr. Jefferson, which you call your 'Declaration of Independency', is such a simple and sublime exposition of human rights! You Americans have based your peace and happiness on a small number of maxims, the simplest expression of what good sense could have dictated to all men centuries earlier.

Jefferson: And you sir, said much the same in your edition of the Encyclopedie, boldly terming yourself 'republican' before our own revolution began.

Lafayette: But with not such a small number of maxims, I believe.

Condorcet (laughing): Ah, but the question is not how many words, but which are the right ones, hmm? So I ask you, Mr. Jefferson, what was your meaning when you declared, just as boldly, that 'we hold the truths to be self-evident, that all men are created equal?'

Jefferson: I believe all men possess an innate moral sense, and that sense makes all men equal.

Condorcet: And do you believe they are also perfectible?

Jefferson: Once again sir, we play in perfect harmony. Man is naturally sociable, over time and change in circumstances his nature evolves, and under the right circumstances, evolution may lead to human progress and perfectibility. Unfortunately, his progress is made more difficult by his penchant for erecting and populating great cities. These add as much to the support of pure manhood or pure government as do sores to the human body. Nevertheless, the city dweller possesses the same innate moral sense as the yeoman farmer, even if his surroundings limit his capacity to divine it.

Condorcet: And does your Virginia Negro slave possess this equality of moral sense?

Jefferson: Indeed he does. Unfortunately, their current circumstance of generations of degradation and enslavement does not allow for equal talents or abilities. But whatever their degree of talent or ability, that is no measure of their rights.

Condorcet: And yet, Mr. Jefferson, you Americans have not freed your slaves, as have we, and even the English. Have you not, good sir, undertaken this holy cause?

{Before Mr. Jefferson could answer, Madame de Tesse', who was keeping an ear turned toward this conversation even as she carried on another with the Adamses, moved swiftly to Mr. Jefferson's defense}

Tesse': Monsieur Condorcet, I possess a copy of Mr. Jefferson's original draft of the Declaration, and there he makes an impassioned argument against the slave trade and those who perpetrated it.

Jefferson: An argument that was struck out by the Committee before presentation to the Congress.

Lafayette: But...why?

Jefferson: In consideration of the gentlemen of South Carolina and Georgia, who would not countenance it and remain with us, and also of the feelings of some of our Northern brethren, who, though having little interest in owning slaves themselves, were considerable carriers of them to others.

Condorcet: But surely there exists a sufficient degree of justice and reason in your countrymen to abolish this egregious blight upon mankind!

Jefferson: Sir, the abolition of slavery will be a long and painful process, requiring an abundance of patience and determination, and will not be accomplished by the artful use of a few maxims, no matter how just and rational they may be. My proposal in the Virginia legislature to abolish the slave trade and provide for gradual emancipation for all slaves was rejected by men as devoted to justice and reason as I. These have not changed their opinions to this day, nor do I expect them to in the recognizable future.

Condorcet: But to reduce a man to slavery, to buy him and sell him, these are crimes worse than stealing. Even if the human race unanimously voted approval, the crime would remain a crime.

Jefferson: You have no need, sir, of persuading me of that point. However, the problem in our country is far more complex than you believe. If they were all freed tomorrow, how would their owners be compensated so our economy would not crumble and our liberties dissipate with it? And what of our former bondsmen? What could they do, where could they go? Could we bear seeing our former servants, some of whom have labored in our households alongside our own families, banished from our farms, penniless, uneducated, cast out upon an unfeeling world? Do you believe for one minute that those in our northern states who agitate strongest for their freedom will allow them entry into their schools, workplaces, churches and places of voting? I assure you that will not occur for many generations, if ever at all. No Monsieur, I'm afraid we have the wolf by the ear, and we can neither morally hold him nor safely let him go.

Condorcet: Could you not, upon first abolishing the infernal slave trade, grant emancipation to those aged under five with a government stipend, and gradually free the older slaves, compensating their owners fairly at the same time, while making the former bondsmen tenant farmers on the lands upon which they now labor?

Jefferson: Perhaps, but how would we educate them? Money alone does not aid the man who knows not how to use it for his benefit. My efforts in those regards have convinced me that my countrymen simply do not agree with us, Monsieur Condorcet, and further agitation on my part will only prevent other good that I might otherwise accomplish. Nothing is more certain that these people are to be free, but in such slow degree, as the evil will wear off insensibly, rather than by force, a prospect at which human nature must shudder.

Condorcet: Then I weep for you and your delaying countrymen, Sir, and the future millions upon whom you persist in bequeathing this ongoing injustice and moral outrage.

Jefferson: Yes, but also weep for your own countrymen, Monsieur. For there are nineteen millions of your countrymen more wretched, more accursed in every circumstance of human existence, than the most conspicuously wretched individual of the whole United States. I believe many of our slaves are better treated than the majority of Frenchmen. Here, the truth of Voltaire's observation offers itself perpetually, that every man here must be either the hammer or the anvil.

{I hasten to add, that since the tenor of these conversations does not admit itself on paper, I note they took place without any rancor, and with more gentlemanly discourse than one usually finds with legislators who fully agree with each other on every point. Even Mr. Adams spoke congenially when he interjected himself into the conversation.}

Adams: Indeed, sir, your country's great disease at present, as well as England's, is the numerous and enormous emoluments granted by kings to private citizens. Avarice and ambition are strong passions, but when united and gratified in the same object, their violence is almost irresistible and they hurry men along into factions and contentions destructive of good government. Thus your public councils are destined for stormy seas when confounded by private interests.

Condorcet: What you say is true, my friends, and no one agrees with you more than I. Which brings us back to my original question...What is to be done about this sorry state of human affairs in your country and mine? Are we to be content with the perpetual continuation of your slavery and the total degradation of my people?

Jefferson: I pray I do not shock you, but I would rather see the entire earth razed, so long as one Adam and Eve remained and lived free, than see a continuation of slavery for some and degrading monarchy for the rest.

Condorcet: Then let us never cease our efforts to establish a new world order, no matter the cost to us. A world where all sentient beings, capable of acquiring moral ideas, and of reasoning those ideas, share in equal rights. Regardless of race, nationality, wealth and of no less importance, sex.

{Upon hearing this, Mrs. Adams joined the conversation, and, I might add, with exceptional gusto}

Abigail: I appreciate your sentiments, Monsieur Condorcet. I have asked my husband to remember the ladies in his legislation, and be more generous and favorable to them in education and equality than his ancestors were. To very little avail, I fear.

Adams: I confess as great a terror of learned ladies as does Mr. Jefferson. I already have such a consciousness of inferiority to them that mortifies my self-love to such a degree that I can barely speak in their presence. I consider that offering them equal education and rights would merely be to lower their position in society.

Abigail: It is far more mortifying, my dearest friend, when a woman possessed of a common share of understanding considers the difference of education between the male and female sex, even in those families, such as Thomas's and ours, where education is attended to.

Why should your sex wish for such a disparity in those whom they one day intend for companions and associates? Pardon me if I cannot help sometimes suspecting that this neglect arises from an ungenerous jealousy of rivals near the throne.

Condorcet: Well said, my lady.

Abigail: If particular care is not paid to the education and rights of the ladies, we are determined to foment a rebellion, and will not hold ourselves bound by any laws in which we have no voice or representation.

Condorcet: How do you respond to that, Mr. Ambassador?

Jefferson: I must confess that I am no foe of rebellion. A little rebellion now and then is the surest way to preserve our liberties by reminding our leaders that they have much to fear from oppressing the people. However, I must wonder how men such as John and I may have the time to foment such revolutions, if women, determined to possess equal rights, abandon their duties at home? What reason do we then have to foment rebellion at all if our children have already been abandoned by their mothers who have forsaken them for the legislatures and marketplaces?

Condorcet: Surely, Mr. Jefferson, an enlightened, educated woman exercising her political rights would be better equipped to raise children as free citizens?

Jefferson: You may be correct, sir...

Abigail: May be? Hmpf.

Jefferson: Yet, the ground of liberty and equality of any kind is to be gained by inches, and we must be content to get what we can from time to time, and eternally press forward for what we've yet to get. It takes time to persuade men to do even that which is clearly for their own good.

Condorcet: And tyrants, Mr. Jefferson? I mean those with absolute power over all their countrymen, who have not yet succumbed to rebellion? What shall we do about them?

Jefferson: Again, I do not wish to distress you, but where such tyrants are concerned, we are not expected to be translated from despotism to liberty in a featherbed.

Condorcet: If not in a featherbed, then where? How?

Jefferson: Let the people take arms to gain their liberties.

Lafayette: Blood will flow in that case, Thomas. Perhaps a great deal of blood. Perhaps far more of patriots than of tyrants.

Jefferson: What signify a few lives lost in a century or two? The tree of liberty must be refreshed from time to time with the blood of patriots and tyrants. This is its natural manure.

{Unable to remain silent at length, Mr. Adams joined in with his usual unrestrained vigor}

Adams: Speaking of manure, what then, Thomas? When you have loosed the masses from the leadership of the aristocracy? What then? Shall we endure a mob rule that is infinitely worse than what we have now? Mobs are just as tyrannical as kings and emperors, and there are a great deal more of them.

Jefferson: There is no other solution than this, John....That we form a constitution consistent with the spirit of 1776, giving our government the power to raise revenue for defensive wars, regulate trade, and maintain order within our borders. And to that constitution we must append a bill of rights guaranteeing, without the aid of sophisms, freedom of religion for all--protestants, Catholics, Jews, Muslims and atheists alike; freedom of the press, as I would prefer newspapers without government to the reverse; protection against large standing armies; the eternal and unremitting force of the habeas corpus laws; and trials by jury in all significant matters.

Adams: What need of a written bill of rights have a free people who elect their own leaders? Such a bill would suggest that those rights were not already inherent in our Republican form of government. And even if you had your bill, how would you expect the people to understand their 'rights' after laboring for centuries under tyrannical rule and the domination of priests, absolved like the British and French from thinking for themselves?

Jefferson: I have sworn upon the altar of God eternal hostility against every form of tyranny over the minds of men. Whether that tyranny comes in the form of priest, king or aristocrat, I say we must abjure it. There is only one aristocracy, John—the aristocracy of talent and virtue. Any other is mere "pseudo-aristocracy," founded on wealth and birth, lacking talents or virtue.

Adams: Thomas, you will never entirely dispense with aristocracy, or the reality of the few and the many. Aristocracy, like the waterfowl, dives for ages and rises again with brighter plumage. Inequalities of mind and body are so established by God Almighty in his constitution of human nature that no art or policy can ever level them. Philosophers and politicians may nibble and quibble 'till doomsday, but they will never get rid of it.

Jefferson: Perhaps not in Europe, where the people are crowded in great cities and steeped in vices that such cities generate. But in America, where feudal privileges are outlawed, there is sufficient land for everyone, and an educational system rewarding talent accessible to all, should we be so wise as to establish one. This should be sufficient to guard against the artificial aristocracy we both disdain.

Adams: I predict that power in the hands of the "people," as you call them, the mob, I say, will result in abuses worse than tyranny, both in America and here in France.

Jefferson: The people are the only safe depositories of ultimate power, and if we think them not enlightened enough to exercise their control with a wholesome discretion, the remedy is, not to take it from them, but to inform their discretion by education. This is the true corrective of abuses of constitutional power. If any nation expects to be ignorant and free, in a state of civilization, it expects what never was and never will be.

Condorcet: I hope you are right, Mr. Jefferson. Because I foresee the day, not too distant from this one, when the people of France, like your countrymen, will take the reins of power for themselves, whether by reason, force or terror. But I am wondering, sir, about your nation. What hopes do you entertain that your countrymen will avoid our present circumstances?

Jefferson: I pray I am correct in saying that we will never have a monarchy in America. It is inconvenient to have a weak government; on the other hand, a strong government with its king holding a pistol to the peoples' heads must be admitted to have its inconveniences too.

Condorcet: Ah, but what about a monocracy, Sir? And by that, of course, I mean a Republican form of government that, like a monarchy, provides, shall we say, "bonuses" from a national bank to certain favored corporations, keeping them afloat and competition free, in return for political support? A government that uses the people's taxes, gained at ever-increasing rates, to support war, by which the republic becomes an empire and from which the favored corporations profit? A government which quells the voices of all who oppose its policies? Mercantilist policies such as abolishing free international trade in favor of blasphemous tariffs to support favored businesses destroy competition at home and raise prices of goods at the expense of the small businessman and hard-working farmer. What assurances do you have that, once enthroned, or shall I say, once elected and seated, that your congressmen, presidents and national judges will not bring about the same vices that every other monarchy or republic has henceforth sated themselves?

Lafayette: Indeed, Thomas, in my meetings with fellow aristocrats who have expressed an interest in passing fairer laws to avoid revolution, many of them, including my friend, Jean Milhet, the owner of a large export concession, wonder aloud if they will retain the same concessions they previously received from the King.

Condorcet: Men are men, my idealistic friend. To what magic will you resort to alter their natures? What reason can compel the human heart to abjure greed, self-interest and an unquenchable lust for preferential treatment? They change their sky, but not their souls, those who cross the ocean, hmm?

Jefferson: I swear to you, my friends... So long as I live, we will not take the bread from the mouth of those who labor for it and lay it at the feet of dishonest politicians who use it for their own self-aggrandizement and for the destruction of peace throughout the world.

Adams: With magic, Mr. J?

Jefferson: By whatever means may become necessary, Mr. A.

{To which the Marquis gave a most engaging smile}

Condorcet: Ah, very good, Minister Plenipotentiary. I believe you will see such methods here very soon, and judge for yourself how well you like them. But... I see the hour is late, and I must thank my hosts, Mr. and Mrs. Adams, for a delightful afternoon, as satisfying to the mind as to the palette...

The manuscript ended abruptly, leaving me to wonder once more at the intended message, if any, offered by the anonymous sender. Jefferson's and Condorcet's philosophies were quite radical, even in radical times. Did they really expect to take the reins of a corrupt government by force, instituting rebellion, razing the earth if necessary, causing blood to flow in the streets? Or was that just posturing and hyperbole, Jefferson's habit whenever Madison wasn't around to temper his comments? Certainly, Condorcet's predictions about a grasping, war-mongering mercantilist government had come true on our shores, just as it had in every monarchic, republican or even democratic government since the beginning of time.

Truth to tell, the Jean Milhet of whom Lafayette spoke was a forebear of mine, as my other forebear, Dragoon Sgt. John Ferguson's French grandmother was a Milhet. At least the (pseudo?) diary entries got that right. Almost every American has tyrants or terrorists sprouting from the branches of his family tree.

Suffice it to say, any terrorist with an agenda of striking against just such a government by blowing up a courthouse might justify his or her actions with Jefferson's and Condorcet's revolutionary words. Was that the message I was meant to hear? The purpose of the Ferguson letters and Short diary was to convince me that the terrorists infesting our city had a legitimate basis to carry out violent acts? And how could they expect that these materials, however intriguing and related to me personally, would persuade an assistant U.S. Attorney to…

"Anna Grace is crying, daddy," said Will from the doorway.

"Honey," I shouted outside her door, "what's wrong?"

"What's wrong?" she said bitterly, "What's wrong? Everything's wrong."

I sat on the corner of her bed. "Tell me, baby."

"I'm not a baby," she glowered, then resumed weeping, her head buried in her hands.

"I know that," I said, then waited for her to speak. That much, at least, I had learned from Dr. Lucy and Father Joe.

But when she ceased crying, and still said nothing, I finally asked, "What can I do, Anna Grace?"

"Nothing. I'll be fine."

"Hey, the new Spiderman movie is opening this weekend? Want to see it with me and Will?"

She looked up at me, weighing her options. "No, but how about the Lord of the Rings movie?"

How to beg off and not bug out, I fretted. "Would you like me to take you and...And Malik to the movie?" *And you could watch it with him instead of me?*

"Malik's on probation with his parents. He can't go anywhere this weekend."

"What did he do," I asked, imagining cherry bombs exploding in school restroom toilets, marijuana smoke seeping out from his closet at home, or....

"He didn't do anything, dad. He made a 'C'."

He what? Pause to recover and douse flames on burning bridge. "Of course he did nothing wrong. I'm sorry, Anna Grace. Yes, I'd love to take you and Will to see the dwarves and elves kick dragon butt. How about Saturday afternoon?"

"Sure."

"Well, okay then," I said and beat a hasty retreat. Before closing her door, I said, "I love you, Anna Grace."

"I know," she uttered in monotone.

The end of a sorry day proved better than I deserved, with Will snuggled up to me in bed for stories, songs and big plans for the weekend. But I was restless all night, burdened with the thought that, even with a guard outside and a nanny within, like Holden Caulfield, I couldn't protect my children from anyone determined to harm them. The prospect of Anna Grace's possibly deteriorating mental state was even more troubling.

Recently, the only respite from those problems apart from Will's innocent smile was a vision of Jenny on her couch, her deeply tanned legs, the scent of her hair, the sensation of her lips pressed to mine. I loved my children dearly, but no one snuggles better than a new girlfriend. But even that image offered little solace, and if anything, only frustrated my efforts to find a toehold in dreamland.

An hour later, asleep yet beset by restless legs and beads of sweat on my brow and chest, I dreamed of the smell of cordite, horrific flashes of blinding light; shattered wood and concrete airborne all around me, and the demented screams of innocent victims.

※ ※ ※ ※

"Don't you think it's time to get back to work?"

"Whatever you say, Ryan."

"Why the reluctance? Don't you like him?"

Garrott shot him a rare steely-eyed glance. "I once *loved* you, but that ended too."

Ryan Finn suppressed a smile. "Fickle as ever, I see."

"At least he's human. And that's more than I can say for you."

"Oh, Jen, you cut me to the quick. I concede the point, but it's a little late for you to be claiming a connection to anything approximating humanity?"

The hotel room suddenly seemed as confining as it had felt frigid the minute he had entered it. *Oh, God, when will it end? Will it ever end?*

"No witty retort? You finding it harder to spew wit than the relative ease with which you tossed Molotov cocktails through bank windows?"

Yes, she had loved him. Had joined him in their fight against oppression and injustice. Until she had seen the change overtake him. An overwhelming desire for revenge against the world, abetted by a perverse obsession for causing pain. Either leave or become a part of it. This was her choice, and she made it. Her first decision of any kind since the death of their child during the shootout in Dublin.

But now…

"Cat got your tongue?"

But she wouldn't be baited. Not today, or ever again if she could help it. Just finish this job and move on. That wasn't much to hold onto, but it was all she had.

"Very well. We'll speak when you're in a more loquacious mood."

Finn rose from the couch and slipped out the door just as Gitts entered through it.

"Want a drink, Garrott?"

"Fuck off Gitts."

That was as far as the conversation went that unpleasant afternoon.

CHAPTER TWENTY TWO

Monday morning at the office I phoned Dr. Lucy Draughn and told her of Anna Grace's late night woes. She agreed to rearrange her schedule and see Anna Grace that afternoon in addition to a planned session on Wednesday.

Then my secretary zipped through my doorway clutching a raised manila envelope in one hand and a note in the other. "Father Joe left a message for you, here's the slip; and your anonymous fan hand-delivered another package for you late yesterday afternoon."

December 23
Dearest Jenny:
Oh, my! To have waged this fight and return unscathed, I cannot tell you how many times I have thanked God for my deliverance from battle this day. Let me tell you how this rag-tag army fought hand-to-hand with His Majesty's finest soldiers. My God, what a fight it was! And without the flint, powder and shot Jean Lafitte and his pirates gave us, we would have been lost, for sure. Imagine, men known the world over as terrorists saved our country today. How mysterious the ways of Providence!

Early this morning Major Hinds woke me and bade me accompany him to General Jackson's headquarters at 6 Rue Royal, a three-

story building with second story gallery where the generals were coordinating their defense. He brought me to interpret the words of the French commanders, so as not to rely solely upon the versions related by General Jackson's interpreter, the Creole banker, Major Dussau de la Croix.

Then about mid-morning, several of us met the renowned buccaneer Jean Lafitte at his blacksmith shop and part-time residence at the corner of Bourbon and Dumaine Streets, where we also met his older brothers, Pierre and the one calling himself Dominique You. Their home away from Barataria is of a porous brick-between-hand-hewn cypress post construction, quite popular here in this city, covered with a coat of lime plaster. A fire raged in a large hearth set between the two front rooms, tempering the frigid winter air.

Comfortable as their residence appeared, filled with important European furniture and stocked with the best French wines (pirate plunder no doubt), we'd heard rumors that it was occasionally used as a blacksmith shop, or more likely, as a bartering house for slaves and goods taken from Spanish ships and maintained at their pirate stronghold on Lake Barataria. But if our new indispensable allies wished to call it a residence or blacksmith shop, so would we.

Ah, but you should have seen them, Jenny, as they were not at all what you might expect, considering their reputations as the scourge of Barataria and floating terrorists of the Gulf. Jean, although the youngest is apparently their leader, and there is no wonder about that. He stood six feet tall, with dark hair and complexion, a thin but impressive mustache; and dressed most elegantly in a long, double-breasted black jacket with silk shirt and decorous cravat, walking cane and black wide brimmed hat. He seemed as much the gentleman as Jackson or any of his generals, with a decorous manner to match his attire.

We had all heard the rumor that, when Governor W.C.C. Claiborne issued a $500 reward for Jean, he had walked about the city unmolested, nay, well received by the populace who paid the lowest prices for his contraband goods. He brashly posted notices offering $1500 for the delivery of Governor Claiborne at Grand Terre, just west of Cat Island! This man's natural grace and confidence is such *that the romantic legends surrounding him are more believable upon meeting him in his element.*

Lafitte had risked his life to betray the British, who offered him a pension and his own ship of the British navy to assist them in their liberation of Americans "from a faithless, imbecile government" by allowing them to use Barataria as their launching point for an invasion. Lafitte brought the offer to Governor Claiborne, thereby alerting the Louisianans to the British presence in the Gulf. Without this information, the British would surely have taken the city by surprise.

However, Pierre was not cut of the same cloth as Jean. He was rather slovenly and unconcerned about his appearance, dressed in a soiled green shirt and baggy pants. And yet, nothing about him gave the impression that he was the bloodthirsty pirate of legend. Now, Dominique You, on the other hand, fit that mold perfectly. About five-feet four, he had a swarthier complexion than his younger brothers, was considerably stockier, and blessed with an unforgettable hook-nose, raven-colored hair, thin black mustache, muscular arms and the blackest of eyes, surely witness to the many horrors of piratical depredations on Gulf Spanish shipping. His red shirt, open across the chest, and multi-colored bandana, left no doubt of his status as a first class buccaneer.

In the next room waited other less savory characters of the Lafitte gang, debauched rogues by the name of Renato Beluche', Gambi, and Nat Chigazola, none of whom I would turn my back on for a second were we not to be comrades at arms against an even more dangerous and infinitely more numerous hoard of barbarians.

During that meeting they renewed their promise to Gen'l Jackson to provide five hundred muskets, seventy-five hundred flints, powder, shot and various cannon, and about 80 men at arms, in return for full and free pardons for all their past misdeeds.

This agreement proved to be a timely one, as at about noon a rider galloped up Royale to Gen'l Jackson's headquarters with news that the British had landed south of the city. This fellow, one Rousseau, heatedly blathered to the General (in French) that he had been sent by Latour, who was reconnoitering below the city, to warn that the British had landed at Bayou Bienvenue from Lake Borgne and had taken over General Villere's plantation, and taken prisoner both General Villere' and a Creole financier-turned colonel, Denis de la Ronde, of a neighboring plantation! Moments later, none other than Villere's son, Major Gabriel Villere', and Colonel De la Ronde himself, burst into the room, mud-stained and quite out of breath, shouting (in French) that the British occupied their properties, from which they had made a daring escape!

Under Gen'l Jackson's questioning (and interpretation by de la Croix), they related that the British had landed with a force of over two-thousand, with five times more expected within the hour. They planned to march up the river road near the levee and take New Orleans from the south.

Jenny, the British had landed unopposed, and had situated themselves eight miles south of the city, gathering their forces for an overwhelming assault. And we had been caught entirely unawares!

Jackson's face grew red as he slammed his fist on a table, declaring, "By the Eternal, they shall not sleep on our soil." Then he gathered himself, poured everyone a glass of Tennessee whiskey, and said with surprising élan, "Gentlemen, the British are below, and we must fight them tonight."

He immediately ordered the alarm gun fired and the cathedral bells rung. He ordered Major Hinds to bring his cavalry from the edge of town and to send them to divine the exact locations of the enemy below the city, his strength, number of heavy guns, and as best as could be determined, his intentions.

Hinds set me a'horse to retrieve my comrades outside the city, which I did with great dispatch. Before I left, I heard Gen'l Jackson shout with great anger, "We'll smash them, by God!"

The Jefferson Troop galloped back into the city, rode down Royale Street, past several militia battalions, including two composed of over five hundred gens de color under the command of Major Pierre Lacoste, whose plantation also lay below the city, and the local baker, Major Louis D'Aquin, whose command included many recent arrivals from Santo Domingo.

Two Creole militia units followed, including Major Jean Baptiste Plauche's Batallion d'Orleans composed of Creole volunteers dressed in colorful uniforms and with flowers pinned to their shoulders by their wives and mothers, and Major Beale's Rifles, a unit of both Creole and American volunteers. Major Hinds said that Plauche's battalion included prominent merchants such as planter and legislator Jean Noel d'Estrehan, surgeon German Ducatel, and vintner Francois Seignouret, while Beale's volunteers included cotton merchant Vincent Nolte, shipping magnate John McDonogh, lawyer Edward Livingston, New Orleans District Attorney John R. Grymes, notary public John Lynd and U.S. Marshall Peter Duplessis. They had marched to meet us from their post at Bayou St. John.

Also joining our ranks were Captain Pierre Jugeat's eighteen Choctaws and Jackson's United States 44th and 7th Regiments, this last being supported by a 14-year-old mulatto drummer boy named Jordan Noble, whose vigorous rat-a-tat drum beats kept them marching at a lively pace.

We rode (and the militia and U.S. regiments marched) to the cheers of the Creole ladies waving lily-white handkerchiefs in salute on their second story balconies. What a heartening sight to see the ladies in their finery and hear the bands playing rousing versions of Yankee Doodle and the Marseilles, cheering us on to victory. Every one of us swore to defend these people with our lives.

In all, we numbered about 1500 men, set to square off against 2000 British soldiers. They were well-trained and battle-hardened troops, each capable of firing two or three aimed shots every second with their muskets, bringing with them large navy cannon from which they could deliver four rounds per minute. According to Latour, their guns had a long range of about thousand yards for firing iron balls (called shot) of various poundage, or shells filled with shrapnel that cut its victims to pieces. Up close, they fired canisters filled with iron musket balls that spread out and blew whole units to eternity. However, their naval guns could not swivel and adjust for windage, or be raised and lowered with ease as could American field pieces.

Unfortunately, we were largely untrained and entirely inexperienced in European-style warfare, and would have few cannon unless our

Baratarian allies came through as promised. Yet we were heartened by our commander's lack of fear and grim determination to wipe the invaders off our soil at all possible hazards. "We will fight them on the battlefield, before the city, in the city and beyond the city if necessary," Jackson declared, and we knew he meant every word.

We all met at 3:00 PM at the gates of Fort St. Charles on the Esplanade at the downriver edge of the View Carre.' Major Latour returned from his reconnoiter much to Gen'l Jackson's relief, and as Plauche's volunteers arrived, running at breakneck speed to keep up with our cavalry, Jackson shouted, "Ah, here come the brave Creoles!"

When Captain Jugeat's Choctaws arrived, their tomahawks held on high and their war whoop resounding through the cold night air, one Tennessean standing near Jackson questioned the wisdom of arming "damned Choctaws" in our defense. The Gen'l admonished him, not without some humor, to never again say "damned Choctaws," as they were "good fellows, every one of them."

We all knew better than to lay on about the free black troops, as Jackson had made his position clear back in Pensacola. When a paymaster had questioned the Gen'l's authority to use or pay them, Old Hickory's eyes flashed fire as he ordered the paymaster to keep his concerns to himself; his job was to pay the men "without asking whether they were black, white or tea."

After our forces gathered on the esplanade, Jackson addressed us from the second floor balcony rail of a large Spanish house.

"Men of Louisiana, Mississippi and Tennessee! Tonight the enemy camps on our soil. On American soil, by God! After burning our Capitol and President's House to the ground, raping and pillaging through Maryland, and boarding American ships in the Gulf, they seek to bring rapine, fire and the sword to our greatest southern city. They seek to command the Mississippi, and forever cut our nation off from its destiny of western expansion. Then they will blockade our east and gulf coasts and strangle our trade until we have no choice but to once again bend our knees to their wicked king and corrupt Parliament.

And do you know what I say to that?"

"What?" shouted a thousand voices in unison?

"We'll send them back to England or straight to Hell, whichever they prefer!"

"Hoorah for General Jackson! Give 'em Hell, Genr'l! We're with you, General!"

Then he drew his sword and brandished it on high. "Never again will our countrymen be ruled by a tainted aristocracy bent upon enriching the few by every means they can devise, at the expense of the many, where their god is enthroned in a worldly palace and their countrymen forced into back-breaking labor to provide wealth and privilege for those who neither toil nor sew.

"Will you have such a god and government, men?"

"Noooo, Genr'l! We will not!"

"Do you believe with Mr. Jefferson that all men are truly created equal according to the laws of nature and nature's God?"

"Yeah Genr'l, we do! By God, we do! Hell yeah! Let's go give 'em hell, Genr'l!"

At this point Major Hinds, standing with the rest of us on the cross street balcony, said to no one in particular, "I wonder if the General knows that the same Jefferson whom he quotes said in a letter that he believed Jackson to be a great warrior but unfit for American politics?"

"I think," General Carroll opined, "that Jackson would quote the devil himself if he thought it would do him and his cause any good."

"Are you with me, men?" Jackson thundered.

I tell you, Jenny, they were all with him, every mother's son of them, as much as their grandfathers had been with General Washington at Yorktown. I believe at that moment they would have swum the Gulf of Mexico to fight any British soldier they could find.

After a few hundred more 'hurrahs for General Jackson,' we reformed in our companies and headed for Montreuil's Plantation just east of the Mississippi River where it turns south toward the British Headquarters at the Villere' Plantation. Before that plantation stood the La Ronde and Lacoste plantations, several miles south of Montreuil's. Once at Montreuil's we rode in darkness abetted only by moonlight, but in total silence, as Jackson planned to surprise the enemy. Hinds declared that anyone allowing his saber to rattle would *answer directly to him. And as he is not called "Old Pine Knott" for nothing, we took special care to obey that order.*

We soon arrived near the Macarty Plantation, a two story affair with double galleries with large Greek columns, shaded by groves of orange trees and enhanced with fine, cultivated gardens, not unlike those at our finer residences in Natchez. It stood a few hundred yards from the riverbank and the river road upon which we were traveling.

Jackson lead a second force of over 800 men paralleling the levee road on our right, to strike directly at the main British camp dining by firelight in the distance before us, and to meet our forces moving from his left toward the levee. These included the 7th and 44th U.S. Regulars, Plauche's Battalion d'Orleans, and D'Aquin's volunteer gens de coulour from St. Domingo. A detachment of marines and artillerists set up two batteries on the levee to support our assault.

In those positions we sat in readiness until the third prong of the Gen'l's plan floated into position. As expected, at about 7:00 PM, the U.S. schooner Carolina, a two-mast ship, about ninety-feet long and displacing 230 tons, slipped down the Mississippi, dropped anchor and furled her sails directly across from the main British camp just beyond the levee on the northwest section of Villere's plantation. There she rested silently, motionlessly, in the dark. We heard the enemy hailing her, and upon gaining no response, firing a few rifle shots across her bow. With still no response, they apparently assumed she was a commercial vessel and returned to their supper.

At precisely 7:30, three rockets, red, white and blue, rose from the ship's deck, and we heard Carolina's Commodore Daniel Patterson say, in a clear, manly voice, "Give them this for the honor of America!"

Then she opened up on them broadside with grape and round shot from five six-pounders and her two swivel cannon on bow and stern. These raked the British lines and sent many of their shell-shocked men to hell. The rest stumbled around in the dark yelling, cursing and scrambling for their weapons, or hiding behind the levee from that terrible fire that was like so many thunderbolts, knocking kettles off fires, scattering blazing beams of wood about, maiming some soldiers, blowing others apart, turning well-organized troops into a panicked mob. To their credit, they quickly found their units amid the chaos and destruction, and readied themselves for the attack they now realized was coming.

After the Carolina softened up the enemy for an hour, her guns fell silent and we launched our assault. We dragoons expected to drive ahead of the infantry and turn the British left flank, but Gen'l Coffee held us in reserve owing to the ditches, canals and fences that would have lamed our horses and sent us flying over their heads toward the enemy's bayonets. Although deeply frustrated to have come all this way and not be allowed to fight, we nevertheless enjoyed an excellent view of the field of battle and the carnage thereon.

And of that, Jenny, I can say without fear of contradiction, that no soldier has ever seen the like of this night battle in Europe or America. I dare say there is little precedent in the annals of modern warfare for the actions taken on those fields just below the river levee.

Our forces met with initial success, driving the British back into the heart of their own camp. But then a heavy fog descended upon the field, likely hailing from both the river and swamp, and the gun smoke hanging over the field, and we were immersed in total darkness for want of any further moonlight. Consequently, our planned pincer attack was blunted by the darkness, fog, smoke and ensuing confusion they caused.

All communications broke down in the darkness, fog and gunsmoke. The struggle degenerated into a vicious melee', with individuals dueling with individuals, and groups of men attacking opposing groups, fighting hand-to-hand, to great effect and with unparalleled effusion of blood.

Early the next morning Jackson led us back to the Macarty Plantation headquarters, where he set a detachment of troops and a contingent of about 100 slaves from nearby plantations to raising an embankment on the Rodriquez Canal. To reinforce the mud walls the men used stakes, planks, fence rails and any materials they could scrounge. When some of the men objected to laboring beside slaves, Jackson scheduled the work on a rotating basis, one unit, another, then slaves, and so on.

He ordered us Dragoons to stay behind on La Ronde's plantation to keep an eye on the enemy and report any further advance on his part. We also enjoyed the sport of picking off the odd sentry when Providence offered the opportunity.

I am writing you now by candlelight under a blanket on the levee. Although you'll be gratified to know that I am yet safe and in high spirits, and was held out of the worst action so far, I and the men intend to play our part in this affair, and do what we can to win this battle. But I promise I will not be careless with my life.

I love you, Jenny, and miss you and the little one very much. Kiss Betsy for me and hold her close to your breast, and think of me as I now think only of you. Do not fear for my safety, and remember you are a Christian and place your faith in the Almighty to give us victory and bring us all home safe to the felicity of our firesides and the arms of our loved ones.

December 25. Christmas Day

Merry Christmas to you and Betsy! I know you said a prayer for me during Christmastide service at the Cathedral, as I said one for you here. Did you cook a fat turkey for dinner? I left instructions with Old Nate to see that you were well provisioned for a fine Christmas feast. I hope your holiday proved a delight, and far less eventful than mine.

On a lighter note, the highest-ranking prisoner taken was one Major Samuel Mitchell, as haughty an Englishman as you could find. When Jackson asked him whether he required anything for his comfort, he thanked the General for the courtesy, but declared that, "my army will be bringing up my luggage in the morning." As you might expect, Jackson quickly tired of this gentleman's company and sent him on to a prisoner camp in the deep woods near Montrieul plantation.

I once read that Thomas Jefferson, the namesake of our troop, said, 'we must keep the light of liberty burning, for if the British or other monarchy-favoring Europeans extinguish it, it may never shine upon this earth again.' We must finish the job our forefathers began in 1776, and never be the cause of the extinguishment of that holy flame of freedom.

But all was not so serious today, and I include these two occurrences for you and Betsy as a little Christmas story-telling treat

While visiting the men working on the breastworks, I observed Vincent Nolte, a German cotton merchant and a member of Beale's Rifles, standing near Jackson while the Gen'l inspected several wagonloads of two-hundred cotton bales commandeered from a merchant ship to fortify our artillery redoubts near the levee. Nolte noticed from their revenue stamps that the bales were his, and not the cheap seven cent per pound cotton Jackson had ordered. Nolte's cotton was of the long-staple variety, which as you know, is valued thrice that of the shorter staples. Nolte complained to the Gen'l's secretary, Mr. Edward Livingston, that his cotton was worth near $100,000 and to take it without recompense was unreasonable.

"Well, Mr. Nolte," Livingston quipped impatiently, "if this is your cotton, you, at least, will take pains to defend it."

Livingston and Jackson continued down the line where the men labored, the Gen'l addressing them by name after his familiar and democratic fashion, exhorting them to strive their mightiest in defense of their country. He soon happened upon the pirate, Dominque You, who with his brother Jean and Renato Beluche', were preparing their battery for the rising ramparts. You was brewing that buccaneer coffee that's as black as tar and so strong it introduces itself to the nose at twenty paces.

"That smells like much better coffee than we can get," Jackson allowed. "Where do you get such coffee? Smuggling it, perhaps?"

"Mebbe so, Zheneral," You mumbled in his nigh-incomprehensible English, offering Jackson a cup. "Much like we smuggled zeez guns and shot here to you."

As Jackson walked off he commented to one of his aids, "I wish we had fifty such guns as theirs to place on our line, with five hundred devils such as those fellows there. I could storm the gates of hell with Dominique You as my lieutenant."

But I have gone on too long, and you are surely celebrating Christmas with our families in high style. I miss you dearly and wish I could be there with you.

Even so, all is well here, so I will go to bed and wish you and Betsy a Merry Christmas. I pray I can be with you to celebrate the New Year, if it be God's will that we celebrate it according to our own wishes, and not those of our would-be masters.

Sgt. Ferguson's manuscript ended and I set it aside. What I couldn't put aside, or out of my mind, was who had sent it and why.

The Short diary offered Jefferson's words supporting violent resistance to government, a notion that appealed to terrorists of every stripe, however confused they were about the actual beliefs and intentions of our 19th Century revolutionaries. But what in God's green earth did the Ferguson letters have to offer along those lines? Why send it to me?

Drawing me in because of my forebear's involvement, sure... Mission accomplished. I'd have read those letters if the building were burning down around me. But what was the intended message? The pirate angle? That even violent acts by pirates were justified under extreme circumstances when an evil government (England's) sought to deny Americans their freedom?

Getting nowhere fast, I flushed those thoughts, clicked on my cell phone and dialed a familiar number.

"This is Breeland Jones."

"This is John Ferguson. You available for lunch tomorrow?"

"John! Good to hear from you. Is it lunch you have in mind, or an impromptu plea bargaining session replete with an offer to dismiss all charges against my client?"

"Sure thing, Breeland. And we'll give him an apology and government benefits for life."

"I rather doubt the apology, but I know you're sincere about the benefits—three hots and a cot for six months to a year."

"There's no slipping anything by you, pal. Mayflower at 11:30? I've got some discovery info about your client and his 'friends' from terrorist headquarters."

"Sounds interesting, John. I'll see you there."

The crucial matter of lunch handled, I returned to the task of giving Uncle Sam a hundred and ten percent for the rest of the day.

But my mind wandered like a blind man in a desert, and I couldn't focus on mundane matters like preliminary hearings for trespass on federal property and DUI arrests on the Natchez Trace.

I shuffled those files to a far corner of my desk, slapped on my headphones and headed for the elevator and a downtown stroll.

But as I strode by my secretary's desk, Jill cried, "You got a woman on line one."

"Oh?"

"Seems eager to talk to you, lover boy."

"Oh, don't you start."

"Shall I connect you?"

"What do you think?"

I never knew what to expect from this mystery woman dropping in and out of my life like a kangaroo on steroids. But that didn't stop me from hurrying to the phone.

"Hello?"

"Hey John. Miss me?"

"What's up, Jenny? Where you been?"

"I'll take that as a 'yes'. Wanna' come over to my house tonight?"

"Sure. What've you got in mind?"

"I thought I'd serve you a Louisiana dinner. What'd'ya say?"

"What can I bring?"

"Nothing but yourself. I even found the perfect wine."

"What's that?"

"It's Monthelie, a Burgundy wine like Volnay but less expensive, more flavorful and just as smooth. You up for it?"

"Absolutely. What about dessert? May I bring…"

"Just bring yourself, John. I have something in mind for dessert, too."

CHAPTER TWENTY THREE

Breeland offered a cryptic smile as I seated myself across from him in our favorite Mayflower booth underneath the large spear-snouted marlin stuffed and mounted on the west wall. "What's new, John?"

"Not a thing, pal. You're still a rich big firm lawyer, I'm still a humble government functionary, and your client is certain to receive a savory taste of southern justice come Friday morning's hearing."

"What a fine greeting that is," he said, signaling our waitress. "I wouldn't bet the farm on that if I were you."

"Breeland, did you know your client is connected to a world-class domestic terrorist? Or that this terrorist, called Finnerin, may be sending me manuscripts purporting to be renditions of my forebear's letters written during the Battle of New Orleans, and William Short's diary penned during Thomas Jefferson's French ambassadorship?"

He gave a perplexed look then turned to our waitress, whose name I suddenly recalled was Brandy. "I'll have vegetable plate surprise, and another for my friend."

"You got it."

Breeland whipped his napkin in the air and laid it on his lap. "I'm sure I don't know what you're talking about, John. But if there's an offer of leniency in return for a plea I'll gladly relate it to my client. Not that he's authorized me to make any deals at this time."

"Breeland, are you taking this case as seriously as you should? By now you should have him leaping at any deal we offered that didn't involve serving the maximum one-year sentence."

"You're full of good spirits and holiday cheer, aren't you?" he laughed good-naturedly. "Let me guess....You've got a new girlfriend, haven't you?"

"What?"

"Ahh, I'll bet you've got a date with her tonight. Congratulations, John. Is this the one you met at the booksigning?"

My mind reeled, too flummoxed to respond. How did he know I had a date with Jenny tonight? Who was feeding him the information?

"John? If your mouth hangs any more open you'll empty this place of flies for a week."

"What makes you think I've got a new....Friend?"

"Your reaction to my question, for one. Your sudden defensiveness for another. So....You gonna tell me about her or should we just chew our food and speculate on whether this Chinese virus will put an end to Jackson's imbecilic city government we all know and loathe?"

"Okay, Breeland, okay. Yes, I had a date with someone the other night, and we're going out tonight. Her name's Jenny."

I watched his reaction closely, but if he was hiding something from me, he certainly didn't show it.

Later, when we parted, he wished me good luck with my new 'friend' and headed up Capitol Street toward his office. Had he noted the nervous edge in my voice? Was I anxious about possibly being betrayed, or for having an important rendezvous with Jenny that evening?

Chiding myself for feeling like a pimpled teenager sweating a first date with the neighborhood beauty, I hastened my stride toward the Mayflower parking lot.

CHAPTER TWENTY FOUR

That afternoon I took Anna Grace to Dr. Draughn's office for her appointment, and afterwards, took her and Will to an early dinner at her favorite Madison restaurant, Local 463, where they feasted on a wood grilled filet and redfish topped with sautéed crabmeat on a candle-lit-table.

"Why aren't you eating dinner, dad?" she asked with more interest in my affairs than she'd shown in two years.

"Well…. I've got a… (Why was it so hard to say it?) Kinduva date. At seven."

"Kind of?"

"Well…I just met her. But sure, it's a date."

She smiled broadly for the first time in weeks, and said, "Your first date since Mom died, Dad. Big deal, huh?"

Yes, it was a rather large deal, one that I hadn't yet considered in that context. Now, I felt a wave of guilt rush over me, as if I were cheating on Beth and admitting it to the children. Jenny was the first woman that had engendered feelings in me of the sort I once held for their mother.

Ever the good listener, and always with his finger wrapped tightly round the pulse of any conversation we felt certain he wouldn't comprehend, Will grinned and stuck a fist in my side. "Daddy's got a date. Daddy's got a date!"

Anna Grace glared at him as if he had puked on the table. "Do you even know what a date is, Will?"

He pursed his lips, fishing for the right answer. "Uh...no. What's a 'date,' daddy?"

"Well, Will, it's like this. You know how Thor likes Jane Foster, and how Spider Man likes Mary Jane?"

"Sure. They kiss and make funny faces at each other."

"So daddy is going to go make funny faces with a very nice lady tonight."

"And kiss?"

"The only kisses I need come from you and Anna Grace."

I puckered up and leaned toward him until he planted a quick kiss on my lips. I peered across the table at Anna Grace, who raised her hands palms outward and said, with a sparkle in her eyes I was very glad to see, "Don't even think about it, Dad."

"Once upon a time you kissed me every day."

"Ancient history. That's what dates are for, old man."

"Are your kisses reserved for Malik, now?"

"Anna Gwace kisses Malik. Anna Gwace kisses Malik."

"Shut up, Will!"

"Anna Grace!"

"Sorry." She leaned over the table and patted Will on the head.

"Are you okay with me having a date?" I asked on the way home.

She screwed up her nose, causing the skin at the corner of her eyes to wrinkle the way it often had on Christmas mornings when she tried to guess the gifts inside the packages stacked under the tree.

"Of course, dad. It's about time you got it together and had a date or two. Just don't bring home some skank that makes me pull my hair out."

"Don't you worry about that, girl. I'm going to her house tonight."

And just when I thought I had it all under control, Will shouted, "Daddy's got a date with a skank! Daddy's got a date with a skaaaank!"

****

At 7:00 on the nose, Jenny Shexnayder greeted me at her front door with two wine glasses in one hand and a bottle of red in the other.

"Where you been, stranger?" she asked, her dark eyes shimmering with anticipation.

"I could ask the same of you," I replied warmly, taking the bottle in hand. "Yep, that's Monthelie," I nodded approvingly, perusing the label. "It doesn't get much better than this."

"We'll see," she murmured.

As she passed by me into her den, I caught the scent of strawberry shampoo in her hair and vanilla lotion on her body. The vision of her lovely olive skin in a shoulder-less black mini, her tight, sun-burnished thighs and perfectly sculpted derriere moving gracefully away from me gave full vent to feelings I had largely submerged for the past few years, my neighborhood fling notwithstanding.

She settled on a white slip-cover sofa near a coffee table laden with an assortment of cheese and crackers, crossing her legs in a way that intoxicated me before the wine had even been opened.

"Close the door and come sit down," she said, her voice softer than I had noticed before, an inviting smile dancing across her lips.

I sat beside her and opened the bottle with an old fashioned corkscrew she handed me. I filled the glasses and tried the wine. All was perfect except my nagging inner struggle about whether to ask where she had been the past few days, what she knew of the manuscripts, or to just go with the flow. I may well have saved myself the trouble. Experience had taught me that, like most people, I was quite capable of disciplining myself to pursue the truth while refraining from any and all temptations...Until temptation settled squarely upon my doorstep.

"You look lovely in your little black dress," was all I could manage. I raised my glass, leaned towards her, hooked my arm around hers in the Russian manner of toasting, and said (far too presumptuously), "to us."

Our eyes locked as we drank, her dark irises turning to discs-- tiny loving cups filled with liquid Eros. I felt myself sliding down a slippery slope from which I had neither the strength nor the wish to emerge. I leaned in for a kiss.

We kissed gently at first, then deeper for several minutes. She suddenly pulled back and said, "I forgot about the oysters!"

"Who needs oysters," I garbled, pressing myself against her, kissing her hard on the mouth.

But this time she escaped my grasp, offering a "good idea, wrong time" smile.

"Would you care for some French music to go with the French wine? How is it by the way?" she asked, gliding on bare feet toward her CD player on the far wall. "The wine, I mean."

"Perfect," I cooed. Yes, it was excellent, but infinitely tastier on her lips than in my glass.

One of Josquin's six-voice French chansons suddenly filled the room with exquisitely melodic plainchant, and I recognized it as *Faulte d'argent,* a song about a man who wakes with a prostitute and no money to pay her!

A pleasant touch of sensuous overload enveloped me as she sat beside me and tucked a shoeless foot under a lightly muscled thigh. Three years ago, on a work trip to DC, I had visited the arts museum; after viewing paintings by Dali, J.M.W. Turner, Van Gogh and Leonardo for several hours, I had turned and seen a lovely, dark haired woman in a fashionable sweater dress that fit her like a pair of $500 gloves, and was suddenly overwhelmed with a sensuous overload that I didn't recover from for an hour.

But this moment with Jenny, my sudden inescapable need, my favorite red wine, the sound of her voice, emanating from those painfully luscious lips, the rich polyphonic texture of the music, and the infinitely deep pools of sensuality that passed for her eyes threatened to overload my senses to the point of nuclear implosion.

"So, John, what shall we discuss tonight? Politics, religion, history? Or did we cover those sufficiently the last time?"

The question prompted me to formulate my first rational thought since I met her in the doorway. "Well…I thought perhaps I had said something wrong when I didn't hear from you for so long."

"So long?" she laughed incredulously. "A day or two constitutes a long time here in central Mississippi?"

In my mind's eye I saw Anna Grace shaking her head and muttering, 'not cool, dad.' I shook off that vision and ventured, "When a woman as lovely as you pours such excellent wine and plays music that's the envy of the gods, a few moments separation can seem a lifetime."

"Really," she said, one eyebrow arched, Spock-like, head bent slightly, the toneless inflection in her voice giving no hint of how she read my words.

Sensing that I was somehow dampening the mood, I shut my trap and waited for the expected mocking reply.

But that wasn't what happened.

Ten minutes later, when we came up for air, she reached down to the table, handed me a cracker spread with cheese, and said, "Appetizer?"

I thought of slapping it out of her hand, throwing her back on the couch and assailing her alluring lips, but she stuffed the cracker in my mouth, and the bitter taste of brie dulled the edge of my rising aggression.

"Appetizer?" I mumbled, my mouth stuffed with cheese. "You mean there's more?"

"You bet. Did you think I'd short you on the meal? The oysters are on ice and the gumbo's hot and ready."

"You should have told me to bring some champagne."

"Nonsense," she grinned. "I've got a bottle of Montrachet in the fridge."

Rationality told me the season was too young for love, but as I teetered on the verge of that most peculiar brand of insanity, all things suddenly seemed possible where Jenny with the dark eyes was concerned.

To my consternation, she soon resumed her usual mode of conversation—asking me about myself and diverting the conversation every time I turned it toward her. This time, though, I determined to wreck her tactics.

"I'm a substitute teacher in the Hinds, Rankin and Madison public schools," she finally offered. "Reading, bike riding and going to movies are my hobbies. I was married once before, have no children and am a Scorpio on the cusp of Libra. Anything else you want to know?"

I nodded and raised my hands in surrender. "No, thank you. What would *you* like to talk about? Or," I continued, with a surreptitious agenda in mind, "would you rather go to a movie after we dine? I think *Argo* is showing at the Fondren art theater if you like films about launching revolutions and fighting terrorism abroad."

I watched her closely for any reaction to my question, but if she was hiding something, she responded like a riverboat gambler holding a royal straight flush. "No thanks," she said absent-mindedly.

"I hear it's a great movie. Don't you like it when we put one over on the terrorists for a change?"

"I'm good here, thanks. Why the sudden interest in revolutions and terrorism?"

"I don't know," I lied. "I suppose that shooting at the Rankin County elementary school earlier this week somehow piqued my interest."

"I understand. A terrible tragedy. But hey, we're both drinking and shouldn't be driving. Besides, we're having a wonderful time here. So tell me, what would *you* like to do tonight?"

"Not let the gumbo get cold, for starters," I said.

"White wine with your oysters?" she asked on her way to the kitchen.

"Sounds great, Jen. May I help you with anything?"

"Not at all," she beamed, pouring seafood gumbo into a bowl and setting it on a plate atop a granite island. Then she drew a platter of raw oysters on ice from the fridge, set it on the island, and gestured for me to join her there. We sat on kitchen stools, and devoured her feast de resistance--raw oysters, seafood gumbo and white Burgundy wine, that disappeared faster than revelers at a party when the doctors started talking shop.

As we made our way back to the den, my head began spinning like the proverbial top.

"Are you okay?" she asked.

"Sure I am. Guess I'd better slow down on the wine. Got to drive home to Madison and the cops out there don't take DUI prisoners."

"Oh, I think you'll be fine on that account."

"Huh? Why's that?"

At that precise moment, the Ballet des Bacchanales, one of my Praetorius favorites, flooded the room with a riot of tabors, viols, trumpets and drums.

"Wanna dance?" she breathed in my ear. Her closeness, magnifying the scent of her skin, made my head spin as I guided her onto the carpeted den floor.

Moments later I twirled her around and laid her back in my arms. Before I could raise her she righted herself, pulled me to her, and kissed me with such heat my knees almost buckled.

The next thing I knew, we were standing in a bedroom just off the den, the one where Anna Grace spent her childhood and Will his first few weeks of life.

She removed my shirt and guided me toward the bed. I was gazing dizzily at her feet when her skirt landed on the floor around them. Looking up, I beheld near perfection in the human form, a worthy subject for Michelangelo had he sculpted her instead of David.

I kissed her lips again, then her neck, shoulders and breasts. As my hand moved slowly down her body I thought I felt a warm pulse of electricity dancing beneath my fingers. I slipped off her underwear, touched her firmly but gently in a circular motion until she moaned in my ear. I squeezed her nipples tightly as I knelt before her, then cupped my hands on her hips and pressed my lips to her sex.

Several moments later she guided me to my feet, lay me back on the bed, stripped off my pants, and fixed her eyes on mine as she took me in her mouth.

Oddly, the last thought I had before passing out was, "aren't the blinds still open?"

I woke in her bed, our nude bodies pressed closely together in the 'spoons' position, with her as the outer spoon. I had no idea how long I had slept. When I swiveled around and touched the side of her face, she opened her eyes. Through the alcoholic haze clouding my eyes I saw in *hers* a fleeting sense of... What? Embarrassment? Regret? Then in the blink of her eye the sparkle returned along with an inviting grin.

"You fell asleep," she murmured softly.

"What time is it?"

She glanced at the digital clock on the bedside table. "2:30. You okay?"

"Has my cell phone been ringing?"

"No. Why?"

"My kids. Thought they'd be worried."

"They must know you're in good hands." Moments later, I was. "Oh," she grinned, "You're all awake now!"

Although I couldn't read her expression, what she was doing brought perfect clarity to her purpose.

"Last night…Did we…?"

"Not exactly."

My eyes framed the question.

"I was….attempting to interest you….When you passed out."

Suddenly I remembered.

"I'm sorry. I must have drunk too much too quickly."

"Never mind. You're plenty alert now."

She hefted herself over me and placed me inside her. She moved with ravenous intensity, as if she were making up for a long dry season. When I lowered my hand from her breast to what the Germans call her 'tickler', she shuddered and moaned so intensely I wondered if she hadn't known an intimate touch for a very long time.

An hour later, I left her sleeping soundly on her side, slipped quietly from her embrace, and gathered my clothes in the near darkness, aided by a familiar streetlight shining through the bedroom window.

After a serene fifteen-minute drive to Madison, then a terribly anxious moment tiptoeing through our house to the master bedroom, I collapsed on my bed. My head smacked against something on the pillow. In the darkness I could feel an 8 by 10 manila envelope nestled atop my pillow, likely left there by Marianna after I left for my big date. More exhausted than I realized, I tossed it aside and slept more soundly than I had since the night I had found Anna Grace bleeding on her bedroom floor.

CHAPTER TWENTY FIVE

The next morning around 10:30, after cooking breakfast for Marianna, Anna Grace and Will, I slipped out of the house while they were absorbed in an episode of *Regular Show* and made a mid-morning dash for the office. I didn't ordinarily work on Saturdays, but I wasn't up to explaining my late-ending date with Jenny to the kids before I decided what to say.

Truthfully, I had no idea what to tell them. What could I say? We'd been more about action than words last night and early this morning.

My secretary's eyes flashed question marks at me when I rushed by her without speaking and collapsed in my office chair.

No pressing business awaited me so I opened the envelope our nanny had left on my pillow the night before and read the latest 'entry' in William Short's purported diary.

September 17, 1789
Ambassador Jefferson's Residence
Hotel de Langeac
Paris, France
3:00 PM

This day Mr. Jefferson had four guests for dinner at his residence, the Hotel de Langeac, at the corner of 92 Avenue de Champs-Elysees and the Rue de Berri. Three are Parisians, good friends and kindred spirits all--the Marquis de Condorcet, Marquis de Lafayette, and the gentleman farmer, Louis-Alexandre, duke de La Rochefoucauld, author of the estimable work, Maxims. The fourth is the New York congressman, lawyer and financier, Gouverneur Morris. As a direct consequence of his drafting the United States Constitution, and his favorable letters of introduction from George Washington and Benjamin Franklin, Morris was quickly accepted into Mr. Jefferson's coterie of philosophes, intellectuals, would-be revolutionists and bon vivants.

Morris, more than any of the others, seems the living example of Mr. Jefferson's own self-appraisal, that he was bred to the law, which gave him a good view of the dark side of humanity, then took up poetry to see the brighter side of life.

All consider Morris uniquely qualified in the bon vivant respect, as his congenial personality and preference for the society of ladies stands him in good stead with those of like mind. As to the revolutionary aspect, although Morris supports the idea of republics in lieu of monarchies, he does not share the other gentlemen's' optimism for a favorable outcome to France's political situation, nor does he concede their republican beliefs in the equality of man or of man's presumed moral and intellectual progress.

Morris is a tall (about six-four, two inches taller than Mr. Jefferson), powerfully built man with intelligent eyes and a high-bridged aristocratic nose. He is so similar in frame to General Washington that the famous French sculptor Houdon asked Morris to pose for the life-sized statue of our President to be sculpted for the Virginia legislature at Mr. Jefferson's behest. The physical similarity ends, however, as a consequence of the wooden leg Morris has sported since his youth.

One might presume that a wooden leg would dull the ladies' interest in Morris as prospective lover, but nothing could be further from the truth. The ladies here, like those in America, find him well-nigh irresistible. And the confirmed bachelor has never denied them the pleasure of his company.

Madame de Corny opines that Morris owes his success with women less to his manly appearance and gift for witty conversation that to his capacity for listening to his lovers and appreciating their many intellectual gifts along with their physical delights.

I suspect that Morris's penchant for the ladies is one of the matters Mr. Jefferson intends to discuss with him, in preparation for the former's succession to the ambassadorship to France.

Mr. Jefferson has ordered a fine repast to be delivered from his favorite restaurant, and has reserved several bottles of his best French wines for this occasion. I pray it will keep the participants in good spirits so they don't quarrel unnecessarily.

The diary entries ended, leaving me wondering about the significance of the forthcoming meeting between Jefferson and Morris, and how it applied to anything relevant to the Ghost's case, my life, or anything in particular. However, I had no doubt that each entry had a particular private message for me. Then the thought struck me…Was all this business about Morris's affairs a nod to my recent intimacy with Jenny? Was it possible that--

A forceful knock on my door cut my musings short. Jack Ashton strode into my office and plopped in a chair across from me. He held a familiar-looking manila envelope.

"You ready for this habeas hearing Friday?"

"Ready as I'll ever be." Try as I might, I couldn't stop staring at the envelope he held, my name and address clearly emblazoned across it in black magic marker.

"That tells me nothing, John. I'm worried about your handling of this case."

"Why?" I asked with affected calm.

"These letters from your forebear at the Battle of New Orleans, the Jefferson diary…"

"Short diary," I corrected gently.

"Damnit, John. I give two shits worth whose diary it purports to be. You and I both know who it's really from."

"Who?" I asked innocently. I didn't know for sure and neither did he.

He glared menacingly at me for a full five seconds before he spoke. "Who it's likely from. That damned terrorist Finnerin. The son-of-a-bitch who heard your blasted confession, knows where you live, forcing us to put a car 24/7 at your house at the G's expense, and who's sending this crap to your office, distracting you from your responsibilities and laughing in our faces all the while."

"Did you get any fingerprints off...?"

"You know damn well we didn't. Other than yours and mine, that is. Hell, this is the first time I've ever found fingerprints on potential material evidence that belong only to me and a lawyer on my own goddamned staff."

"Material evidence of what? A conspiracy to provide the most interesting reading material since the Federal Anti-Terrorist Act, our government's latest incarnation of the Alien and Sedition Acts?"

He glowered at me in disbelief. "Whose side are you on, John? Now you're talking like one of them."

"Actually, Jack, Thomas Jefferson did say that we should never surrender our Constitutional rights in the face of threats from home or abroad...."

"Screw Thomas Jefferson, John. And you'd better believe that you're just as screwed if you somehow blow this case and piss off Judge Wyngait and the entire marshal corps."

"I've got it, Jack. It's an open and shut case. Three eye-witnesses, one of whom is a marshal and..."

"One eye witness, John. The other two who witnessed the struggle in the hallway were served with subpoena but are nowhere to be found and probably won't appear in court Friday. This is the way it happened in Boston and other places, where these terrorists got off the hook because witnesses disappeared at the last minute or showed up and changed their stories."

"Are you suggesting that Marshal Reed can be intimidated by these geeks? Is he going somewhere, changing his story, or am I entirely missing the point? He's the only witness I need, Jack."

As he stood, I believed I could see heat rising off his head, both hands death-gripping his belt. "Just win the fucking thing, John."

"Jack, it'll all work out, I promise you. The great Oscar Wilde once said that 'success is a science; if you have the conditions you get the results.' Well, we got the right conditions, so we'll get the right result."

"What the...? You're quoting Oscar-fucking-Wilde to me now?"

"You didn't care for Jefferson, so I took another direction. You got a problem with the truth?"

"Damn the truth, John. And to hell with Oscar Wilde. You know the main difference between you and me, John?"

I chose the better part of discretion and remained silent.

"It's that I know when to keep my damn mouth shut, and you don't. Got to make the witty comment, cite the funny quote, the hell with the consequences. Well let me tell you this, wise ass. Win this case Friday or you may find yourself handling nothing but traffic citations on the Natchez Trace in Judge Day's court."

It would be superfluous to say he slammed the door loud enough to be heard in East St. Louis. "I guess literary quotes just aren't good enough for government work," I muttered to myself.

CHAPTER TWENTY SIX

Still lacking Jenny's phone number, I drove by her house on the way home from the office. She wasn't home, and the house seemed somehow more deserted than the last time I found her absent. As deserted as the first time I drove by it after I had moved the kids to Madison. Or maybe that was just my imagination. It was certainly my direst fear.

God help me, I missed her terribly. I hadn't felt connected to another woman for a good long time. Not really. But there was something different about Jenny, and I was hooked, line and sinker.

Hadn't I seen something in her eyes, heard something in her voice as we danced, as we made love? Or was that also just my imagination? I felt foolish sitting in her driveway, staring at a red door and green window shades I had painted five years ago.

Then I suddenly realized that all the front window shades were closed, not open with curtains drawn. Around the side I saw that only her bedroom window had shades hanging open. Hadn't I noticed that the night before?

I rang the doorbell several times, but got no response. My cheeks flushed with an unwelcome sensation as I backed out her driveway and headed for suburbia.

A hard case of the blues hit me during my drive home, but holding Will in my lap as we snacked on popcorn and during an episode of animated *Marvel's Avengers Christmas* greatly heightened my mood. Anna Grace sharing dinner with us proved another bonus until she shut herself in her room with a bag of Twizzlers and cell phone.

Although Dr. Draughn and I agreed the worst part of her depression had passed, her occasionally disconsolate demeanor remained a source of concern for me and bafflement for Will, who felt his best friend's sudden change of mood.

So when she had asked me during desert if I'd like her to come see me try a case, I leaped at the opportunity. "You bet I would, sweetheart."

But she grew sullen shortly thereafter, saying not another word, picking at her food before excusing herself and slinking back to her cave. That I could hear her chatting happily with Malik on her phone gave me reason to hope things were better than they appeared.

Will and I bathed in the master bathroom Jacuzzi tub, playing the 'guess which are numbers and which are letters' game with his tub-friendly, foam rubber figures.

After he fell asleep in his bed during our nighttime reading session, I padded quietly to the den and poured myself a glass of wine. Then I remembered the envelope on my kitchen counter that Jack had dumped on my desk during his extemporaneous temper tantrum.

I settled in a den chair and opened the envelope.

December 28
Dear Jenny:
We concluded another terrible battle with a glorious victory today! The attack we were expecting finally came .....

****

From their vantage in the shadow of the Chevy van, the tall man and his much shorter companion waited patiently for their intended victim to quit making small talk with his colleague and walk towards that Chevy van in the federal courthouse parking lot.

They had secreted themselves into the lot, clamoring quietly out of their Buick's trunk and slipping by the guardhouse while Garrott had sweet-talked the guard from the car's front seat. Her low cut blouse and affected air-headed southern girl accent had given them the free pass they sought.

"Here he comes," Gitt whispered in a in low conspiratorial tone.

"When you hear him opening the door, hit him from behind, hand over his mouth so he makes no noise. I'll grab his keys, throw him in the back, and we go. Clear?"

"Yes. You sure he's the right one, with the codes we need?"

Finn responded only with a raised eyebrow.

"Sorry. Of course he is. Garrott does good work, just like before, doesn't she?"

"Gitts, try not to speak again until you have something to say that's not as redundant as it is insipid."

The German immigrant complied, saying nothing at all. He knew he had no one to blame but himself for this slap down.

But he consoled himself with the pleasures to come once he had this man, the young couple and the others under his control. Finn expected no dumb questions and a job well done, but he was fairly generous when it came to indulging Gitt's and Gruzenko's desires for "entertainment" at the expense of their victims.

"Focus. Here we go...."

********* *********************

After a long bout with the Ferguson diary in the den and another struggle remembering the words to poems by William Blake and Robert Louis Stevenson for Will's benefit at nighty night time, I left him slumbering peacefully and slogged down the hall to my bedroom. Sleep finally overtook me. I dreamed of rockets exploding over the Mississippi, of French peasants clamoring for aristocratic blood in Paris streets, and of Chandra, the Hindu goddess of fertility, spreading herself across a wide four poster bed with feather mattress top, silk sheets and satin-covered pillows, opening herself to me and swallowing me whole.

CHAPTER TWENTY SEVEN

Anna Grace, Will and I spent a lazy Sunday watching Drew Brees and the New Orleans Saints demolish the Atlanta Falcons while we put the finishing touches on our holiday decorations. Having hung the tree lights days earlier and trimmed the tree with Mickey Mouse picture frames filled with photos of Anna Grace and Will, we finally got around to adding my mother's forty-year-old glass ornaments.

No matter your troubles, there's nothing like the anticipation of Santa's arrival to put the kiddies at ease, on their best behavior and filled with the holiday spirit. Yet something else about the season, something ancient and unknowable, always lifted my spirits this time of year. Perhaps I was intuitively harkening back to the season's mirth-filled pagan roots or merely enjoying the Renaissance carols reverberating through our house every night. Whatever the cause, I welcomed the season and gave thanks that I wasn't forced to spend it entirely alone.

Say what you will about Mardi Gras parades, summer at the beach, or Halloween festivities; nothing says family fun like a Deep South festive holiday season. Whether enjoying a Delta Christmas parade, harkening to the singing Christmas Tree at Belhaven College in our former Jackson neighborhood, or viewing the lighted trees in the lobby of the Roosevelt Hotel in the Crescent City (with a side trip into the Sazerac Bar), Christmas in Dixie was a joy to behold for pagans and Christians alike.

I drove to the office early Monday morning to finalize preparations for the Ghost's Friday habeas hearing. My secretary copied several pages of the file and phoned the Ghost's lawyer, Breeland Jones, and arranged for him to meet me at the Mayflower for lunch and an impromptu discovery conference.

We met at 11:30 and seated ourselves in the booth beneath a stuffed sailfish hung on a stucco-covered wall. After greeting Frank and placing our orders with Brandy, I came straight to the point.

"Here's your discovery, Breeland," I said congenially, handing him a thin manila envelope.

"Thanks," he said, scanning the pages while sipping his tea. "I thought discovery wasn't due for another month."

"It's an open and shut case, and we're pals, so why not," I replied confidently.

"Good enough," he said, setting the papers aside. "You want to hit the links next Saturday after we put all this behind us?"

"Wait a minute, there, partner. First things first. Got anything for me?"

"Like what?" he grinned. "If my client didn't confess I'm certainly not going to do it for him!"

"I meant, what about your defense? You're required to give me notice of alibi, self-defense or any number of other affirmative defenses you probably don't know anything about, Mr. Insurance Defense Lawyer."

"Hmm," he pondered, "does that rule include constitutional defenses?"

"What do you mean, constitutional defenses?" I scoffed. "Are you suggesting that we violated his constitutional rights by arresting him for committing assault?"

"That's precisely what I'm saying. Your marshal violated his right to freedom of expression...."

"And that freedom includes assaulting a federal marshal?"

"As I was saying, his freedom of expression in filing a complaint against an abusive, Neanderthal cop, who had already violated my client's freedom of expression in the park."

"My God," I muttered, shaking my head in disbelief, "you know less about criminal defense law than I dared imagine."

He shot me a bemused look. "John, surely even you must admit that one of our most fundamental rights is that of protesting bad government, and to do so without having a modern day Sedition Act crammed down our throats?"

"Breeland," I replied, mimicking his pseudo-serious tone, "protesting is one thing; mashing your fist into a law officer's face in reply to his command to 'move on' is something else entirely."

"Yes, and British soldiers in colonial Massachusetts whacking tax protesters with the butts of their muskets is no different from federal marshals thwacking tax protesters in modern-day Mississippi with their automatic pistols."

"You're saying 'British soldiers' to me, now? Really? Has Frank slipped a little LSD in your sweet tea? If so, I'm thankful I ordered unsweet."

"No one accuses heartless prosecutors of excessive sweetness, John. As the esteemed political pundit Gore Vidal once said, 'we are the United States of Amnesia, as we learn nothing because we remember nothing.'"

I stared at him blankly, then, determined not to forfeit the point, I cocked an eyebrow, steepled my fingers, and replied, "And as that wiser political pundit, William F. Buckley, Jr., once decreed, 'idealism is fine, but as it approaches reality, the cost becomes prohibitive'."

"Excuse me, John, but is this the same Buckley who, in the 1960's, and on national television, foamed at the mouth and threatened Vidal, saying something like, 'I'll hit you in the mouth, you damned queer'?"

"That's a fine *ad hominem* debating point, Breeland, but these people you've involved yourself with, the Ghost and his terrorist pals, are dangerous. Not just for innocent bystanders, but also for idealistic lawyers who fail to appreciate the danger they pose to him once he loses their case."

"According to you, his was a lost cause from square one. Why should they blame me if they never had a chance to prevail?"

"Breeland, since when do terrorists give a fat rat's ass about reason? Do you think these jackasses that bomb courthouses and blow up marathon races care that they had no prospects of ever successfully launching a revolution on our shores? Hell, no, they don't. They just enjoy hurting people. You're my friend, Breeland, and I'm afraid you don't realize what you've gotten yourself into."

He grew pensive for moment, took another sip of tea, and said, "You're right, John. When you're right, you're right. I'll advise the Ghost to enter a guilty plea Friday morning."

Taken in by his serious expression and tone of voice, I blurted, "You will?"

"Yes, John, I will," he said, finally evincing the broad grin he had been saving for just this moment. "And I'll have my client's apology drafted in large letters, framed in glass, notarized by my secretary and hand delivered to your office to be shoved up your lily white ass."

There are days when you can't kick yourself hard enough for foolishly answering the alarm clock's toll and dragging yourself out of an otherwise comfy bed to face another round of human, all too human ludicrosities, served raw as dead fish on the half shell.

CHAPTER TWENTY EIGHT

Although the bound man struggled to remain upright on his knees, the other would have towered over him even if they'd both been standing.

"Tell me the code," Finn urged, "and this will end quickly and relatively painlessly. Deny me what I need, and, well... You now know what I'm capable of."

The bound man glanced across the room at the gutted remains of a bloody corpse.

"Why'd you do it, man?" Sweat rolled down the bound man's cheeks, tears puddled in his eyes. "You weren't even asking him for anything. You just... You just killed him."

"Oh, no, my friend. I didn't just kill him. Had I intended merely that, I would have done so hours ago. No, I plucked him off the street to sate Gitts' appetite for personal mayhem, and to make a point to you. I suppose you could say that he died for you. No, that's not accurate either. He suffered for you and died for me."

At the sound of the tall man's soulless laughter, the bound man's chest heaved, his throat closed tighter, and the last glimmer of hope faded within him.

"Even with the code, you won't succeed. You can't. They prepare for that every day."

"I'm sure they do, so you have nothing to worry about by giving me what I want. Now," Finn said, brandishing a fish filleting knife under the bound man's nose, "prepare to suffer a long time, or die quickly if you will. The choice is yours. Make it now."

******

The week passed quickly, with little happening at the office and a fevered anticipation building at our house for Santa's arrival and our annual Christmas feast of a fourteen pound turkey and the kids' favorite pies, cakes and pastries courtesy of their aunt Martha from Laurel. Anna Grace embraced the season with more abandon than she had since our last Christmas on Greymont Avenue four years ago, teasing Will about the presents under the tree and offering us kisses on the cheek every time she caught us under the mistletoe sprig I had hung between our living room and den. With a week to go, I was hoping for one of our greatest family Christmases yet. Even a weekend trip to New Orleans with dinner at Arnaud's and walk through the Christmas tree wonderland at the Roosevelt Hotel seemed likely, with the time I would have off for the looming Christmas holiday. If I could set it up, we might even head Uptown to Upperline Restaurant, where I could perhaps coax owner and celebrated *bon vivant*, Joanne Clevenger, into revealing more enjoyable anecdotes about her beloved Thomas Jefferson to include in my next book, while the kids sated themselves on Louisiana Pecan pie and Thomas Jefferson's Crème Brulee.

Tuesday Will and I enjoyed a Victorian Christmas in nearby Canton, where we rode the horse-drawn carriage and the miniature train around the courthouse square, made several trips around the carousel, and posed for a picture in the lap of a plump, white-bearded Santa. Say what you will about the Deep South, but the convivial populace, the old-timey fun with the entire town decked out in red, gold and elves, and the lack of any serious problems besides the heat make for a delightful holiday in which everyone generously remembers Dicken's admonition that, despite everything that pulls us apart, we are all "fellow travelers to the grave," seeking the true heart and soul of Christmas. Christmas, Hanukkah, Twelfth Night, Kwanzaa, Yule, or for hard core would-be Juvenalian pagans like me- Saturnalia.

I had heard nothing from Jenny in days, the only blot on an otherwise perfect holiday week.

Wednesday morning at the office went swiftly with little to do, and after putting the finishing touches on my preparation for the Ghost's habeas hearing, I left work early and beat the I-55 traffic to Madison by an hour and a half. When I arrived home I found another manila envelope in the day's mail, and felt absurdly glad that at least someone hadn't forgotten me.

I found Anna Grace and Will playing a game of *Racko* on the den floor, an episode of *The Muppets Christmas Carol* blaring on the large flat screen TV high above their heads.

After suffering the indignity of having them both ignore my declaration of "Daddy's home," I went straight to the kitchen cabinet for a wine glass, filled it with my new favorite French wine, Monthelie, and settled in the living room with manuscript in hand.

3:30 PM
Ambassador Jefferson's Residence
Gouverneur Morris, attired in collarless dress coat and matching gray waistcoat with covered buttons, silk shirt with pleated frill at the opening, silk stockings and silver buckled shoes, arrived this afternoon in very high spirits. He appears quite the dandy, although no less manly in his bearing for that, and moves rather gracefully despite his wooden leg.

Mr. Jefferson met us in the oval salon, dressed in his best black suit, the very picture of health; sinewy and alert, standing straight upright, his red hair and freckled skin more vibrant than I had seen them in years; his prominent cheekbones and heavy chin set to a glowing smile for the occasion. When the gentlemen clasped hands, I could not help noticing what large and powerful hands they both possessed. One normally associates both men with their searing intellects and love of the finer things, and forgets they both spent their childhoods in the back country, chopping trees, tilling the soil and riding horses from dawn to dusk.

We seated ourselves in chairs upholstered in blue silk set before damask draperies, where a servant immediately presented us with glasses of wine.

"What do you think of the wine," Jefferson asked before sampling it.

Morris tasted it, and asked, "Burgundy?"

"Yes. Volnay 1785, my favorite red from the Cote d'Or. We'll also serve a white from Cote de Beanne, a 1784 Montrachet, and I have one bottle of Meursault and one of Chambertin unpacked, if you prefer either vintage..."

Here there appeared to be a break in the manuscript. When it resumed, Short noted that he had been called away on an 'emergency' by a servant, and picked up where he had left off.

"How do you find the king and queen?" Morris queried. "Are they easily approachable? I hear he tortures cats."

"The king is a decent man, albeit a rather dull one. But however well he may support his people's interests in change, I believe he is insensible to his queen's extravagance, and the ill effect this has upon the people. You are undoubtedly aware that her close confidant, Cardinal de Rohan, was recently arrested for complicity in a scheme to sell her a diamond necklace for a ludicrously exorbitant sum. The people are starving in the streets while their queen bathes in untold luxuries, and the king seeks only to satisfy her appetite for excess. However, I believe the rumors about their sexual perversities to be unfounded, although the constant repetition of these rumors to the people does little to increase a fondness for their rulers."

"Surely the people do not begrudge them a few perversities," Morris replied flippantly. "Especially where their king or his ministers are concerned. A Frenchman loves his king, as he loves his mistress to madness, because he thinks it is noble to be mad. Furthermore, here in the madness of the Paris whirlwind, the people know a wit only by his snuff box, a man of taste by his bow, and a statesman by the cut of his coat."

"Then," Jefferson replied, "They must think very little of us, in our black suits bereft of ornamentation, and our penchant for republican simplicity of dress and manners."

"Not so. The French pique themselves on possessing the social graces, and readily excuse in others the lack of them. To be unique among them, as with Dr. Franklin, covers a multitude of sins. On the whole I think an American Minister at this Court gains more than he loses by preserving his originality."

"Then perhaps they will take our example to heart and give their country a bill of rights to preserve their opportunity to seek originality in all things."

"Yes, Thomas, we have seen, in the space of five months, the calling of the Estates-General, the creation of a National Assembly, the fall of the Bastille and Lafayette's request to you to aid the Assembly in forming a Declaration of Rights for the people. But to expect any people to abolish a despotic government and rigorous social distinctions that have oppressed them for centuries is extremely problematical in any situation, but with respect to this country, I am sure it is wrong. To suddenly take upon themselves such power will undoubtedly confound the people. And to demand a bill of rights before erecting an ordered system of government will merely unleash the unpredictable energy of the people, with the likely result of either a tyranny of one or anarchy and terror for all."

At this, Mr. Jefferson bristled almost unnoticeably, yet restrained himself and allowed his companion to continue.

"They desire an American constitution without American citizens to support it. And as for the Assembly, there are able men there, yet the best heads among them would not be injured by experience. Unfortunately, there are many who have great imagination but little knowledge, judgment or reflection. Indeed, while people were cutting each other's throats for a loaf of bread and carrying the Bastille governor's head on a pike, it was reported that the delegates to the Estates General were deciding the details of the delegates' costumes. Gracious God, what a people!"

"During the taking of the Bastille I quietly slept through the whole event as ever I did in the most peaceable moments. Just think of it, Gouverneur, we have seen in these fourteen years two such revolutions that were never before seen in all the world! As for the few deaths this one has occasioned, when was the blood of those victims so pure?"

"And yet you do love the architecture here, do you not?"

Mr. Jefferson paused, unsure of his companion's point. *"Why...Yes, you know I do."*

"Indeed, you have never missed an opportunity to instruct me on all the important works of architecture here in this city. And yet, the splendor of Parisian architecture is owing entirely to despotism, and it will most certainly be diminished if not lost to desecration by the adoption of a better government."

"I would rather see the destruction of all the architecture I love," Jefferson urged, the fervor in his voice clear and unwavering, *"and the loss of a million lives, if these people who have suffered for so long under the despotism of kings, ministers and priests, might be carried into the arms of liberty as we have been in America."*

"Well," Morris sighed resignedly, *"I pray you may get your wish. From such crumbling matter as we find here the great edifice of freedom must be erected. Perhaps, like the stratum of rock spread under their country, it may hold firm when exposed to air; but it seems quite as likely that it will fall and crush the builders."*

"Then to that end, Gouverneur, we must do all we can to aid them in their transition from despotism to freedom. We must present to them, in our persons, and by our conduct, worthy examples of what may be accomplished by free men and women."

Hearing this, and taking his companion's meaning with the inclusion of "women" in his suggestion, Morris rose to the discussion he knew was coming with the coolness and nonchalance we had come to expect from him during the past two years.

"I suppose you are going to tell me that I am setting a bad example for a diplomat with my relationship to Adele, and that our mutual friend, Madame de Corny, has undoubtedly revealed the precise nature of that relationship to you."

Mr. Jefferson cleared his throat before replying. *"Your relationship with that lady is well known to everyone, Gouverneur. You have played it out to the surprise of many audiences on more than one occasion. In hotels drawing rooms, carriages, and now I hear, the environs of a country chapel."*

"I cannot help myself, Thomas," Morris pleaded. "When I look into those large brown eyes that are the liveliest in the world, whilst she expresses her love for me, her desire to marry me...I confess I am unable to resist her charms. I see the game, but yet appear the dupe."

"You enjoy the game, sir."

"Indeed I do. I have great relish for it. Adele shamelessly leads me on as she does her other lover, Bishop Tallyrand. She glows with satisfaction looking at the bishop and myself as we sit together agreeing in sentiment and supporting the opinions of each other. What triumph for a woman! Then I watch her go home with him and thus heroically risk the chance of cuckoldom."

"And yet, in this country, Gouverneur, love has a political resonance, whether in the throne room, where Marie Antoinette dominates the hapless King Louis, or in the salons, where the leading men defer on all matters social or political to their 'enlightened' hostesses. As a consequence, moral decay and political corruption advance unchecked."

"While I must agree that Adele is hardly a sworn enemy of intrigue," Morris replied soberly, "she has no more influence upon my political thought than she does upon Tallyrand's. And regardless of the queen's directives to the king, I've no doubt that the storming of the Bastille showed him that all is not perfectly quiet in this city."

"And yet, as future Minister Plenipotentiary, your involvement with this lady will suggest to others that she wields the same influence over you that the ladies here do over their men."

"Thomas, I believe the men in this government, all of whom have lovers, and whose wives also take lovers, understand, as I do, that there are two kinds of men, one made to head families and the other to give them children. Adele and I chose to take to heart our Lord's first commandment to Adam shortly after we met, and that is the sum total of our commitment."

"And your commitment to the other women with whom you share your gallantry; one the wife of a duke, the other an ambassador's bride? What are the French to make of those relationships?"

"Thomas, I confess that I enjoy their company to the utmost, and they appear to enjoy mine. The combination of tenderness and respect *for their intellectual talents, and the ardency and vigor with which I approach them, makes a great impression upon them. Yet I assure you I will never place my desire for their companionship before the good of my country."*

"Meanwhile, sir," Jefferson said, *"we must also hope that we do not allow our personal weaknesses to prevent us from aiding the French in their struggle for liberty, a struggle already made difficult enough by their own weaknesses and failures."*

"It appears, though," Morris said, obviously changing the subject, which he correctly perceived was not moving in the direction of his interests, *"that our people have yet to discover this "middle landscape." I presume you have heard the reports concerning the rebellion in western Massachusetts?"*

Jefferson rose and peered out a barred window, deeply lost in thought. Moments later, he turned and said, "Indeed I have heard. The farmers and debtors there, under the leadership of veteran soldier, Daniel Shays, have risen against the machinations of eastern merchants, who refuse them credit while encouraging the legislature to raise taxes. Consequently, these men, many of them former veterans of our revolution, cannot pay their debts or taxes, and are summarily deprived of their land—the sole source of their livelihoods and the anchor of all their domestic comforts. Accordingly, they rebelled, unhorsed the tax collectors and closed the courts."

Morris stood beside his host at the window. "But must we not, sir, honor the rule of law in our country, lest we devolve into anarchy and terrorism, as is occurring here on the very streets just outside your window?"

"Yes," Jefferson nodded, *"we require a country of laws for the preservation of our liberties. But you will recall that our own revolution violated every law of those who oppressed us. The spirit of resistance to government is a good thing, and as necessary in the political world as storms in the atmosphere. It is so valuable on certain occasions that I wish it always kept alive. It will often be exercised when wrong, but better than not to be exercised at all. What country can preserve its liberties if its rulers are not warned from time to time that the people preserve their spirit of resistance? I assure you sir, when the people*

become insensitive to public affairs and the memory of rebellion is forgotten, you and I and Congress, our national judges and state governors shall all become wolves."

"But surely, our new Constitution will make sufficient accommodation of these concerns to content the people in their liberties while preserving the right of men of business to seek their fortunes as they choose, both with the full protection of the laws."

"Mr. Madison sent me a copy of your Constitution, Mr. Morris, and I must compliment you on your elegant preamble, that begins, "We the people, in order to form a more perfect union...".

"Thank you, sir. Coming from the man who began another document with the words, "We hold these truths to be self-evident...," that is indeed high praise. But what do you think of the later document?"

"I agree with Dr. Franklin that we may expect no better constitution, and also because it may be the best we could achieve, considering the diversity of opinions strongly entertained by its framers. Yet I do not believe that it must bind the strivings of future generations as a carpenter nails a coffin. To the contrary, I set out on this ground, which I also suppose to be self-evident, that the earth belongs in usufruct to the living, and that the dead have neither powers nor rights over it."

Morris nodded accommodatingly, but without agreement.

"At any rate, I hope you and Mr. Madison have made an excellent constitution, for we are in dire need of the very best. From the moment you wrote it, our nation goes downhill. The leaders will come to forget the people, and the people will forget all except the sole pursuit of making money, and will never think of uniting to affect a due respect for their rights. Rights, I dare say, which, in a distant future, shall either revive or expire in another bloody convulsion."

Before Morris could reply, I said, "Gentlemen, I do not wish to intrude, but the hour is late, and the other gentlemen will be arriving shortly, and I must take my leave of you."

Mr. Jefferson and Mr. Morris then bade me farewell and removed themselves to the dining room to inspect the chef's delicacies in anticipation of the arrival of the other guests. I took my coat and hat, and left them in good spirits, but in no better than mine, as I *borrowed Mr. Jefferson's coachman en route to a rendezvous with my lovely Rosalie...*

CHAPTER TWENTY NINE

A pleasant breakfast with Will and Anna Grace, and a delightful drive to her school discussing her plans for the weekend with her boyfriend, Malik, left me in high spirits as I rolled into the office Thursday morning.

United States Attorney Jack Ashton promptly crushed my ebullient mood when he stormed into my office just past nine o'clock.

"John," he growled, eyes bulging, cheeks flushed, nostrils flaring like a rampaging bear's, "I need you to come with me. *Now!*"

I followed him to his office, wondering what I had done to cause this ordinarily stolid man to spew fire and brimstone like Vesuvius in eruption mode. He slammed his door, turned and handed me an 8 by 10 manila envelope identical to the one he had brought me yesterday containing the Jefferson manuscript. But this one was slimmer, lighter and addressed to him with no return address. I opened it cautiously as if a cloth-covered wire spring snake might leap out and stop my heart.

What I saw next surely broke it.

"What do you have to say about that, John?"

The photographs were of near-professional quality, obviously taken with an expensive camera aimed through the bedroom window of Jenny Shexnayder's Belhaven house. The photos were set in order of our carnal progress that evening, her undressing me, me on my knees before her, she attending me before I passed out. In the last explicit photo, taken some time after the first three, she sat atop me, her back arched, her head flung back and to the side so both our faces were clearly recognizable. My face radiated with a glow of unguarded ecstasy, a scene you never hope to share with your parents, your children or your boss.

"John?"

"Yes?"

He glared at me like a school principal eyeing the local hood-in-training, caught in the act of spray-painting profanities on the bathroom wall. "Who is that woman?"

"Well," I said, paraphrasing a resourceful Louisiana politician of yore, "Whoever she is, she's neither a dead girl nor a live boy."

"Are you fucking kidding me?" he bellowed, actually baring his canines at me. For the next few seconds, his immoderate use of the F-bomb stupefied everyone in the office within the sound of his booming voice.

"Can you tell me," he growled after regaining his self-control, "why those photos arrived in the exact same type of envelope, the address typed with the *exact* same font, all delivered in the *precise* way as your damned historical manuscripts, from a kid off the street, just like before?"

I didn't respond, cowed with the certainty that Jenny had not only used me, betrayed me, and played me like a fool, but was unquestionably involved with the terrorists backing the man I was set to prosecute in less than 24 hours.

"WELL?"

"Jack, you're making a lot of assumptions, and I'm not sure that...."

"Not sure," he exploded, springing out of his chair so hard he banged his knee on his desk. "God.....Bless America he howled. "That bitch is involved with...Oh, hell, I don't even need to say it, do I? Well, do I?"

"No," I said meekly.

"Are you still screwing her?"

"I haven't heard from her in days. Jack, I passed out before some of those photos were taken, and I hadn't had that much to drink. I believe she drugged me and set me up. Whoever took those photos must have been outside the bedroom window the whole time."

My explanation gave him enough time to corral his rampaging anger.

"You're probably right, John, but that hardly matters now. Do you realize the danger you've put yourself in, put your family in, if she's involved with these guys? Which we both know she is! Well do you?"

He gauged my answer from my crestfallen expression, and adopted a milder tone. Whatever his other limitations, Jack Ashton seemed a decent fellow at heart.

"Has she been to your house?" he said, staring into space.

"No."

"Then…Well… There's another picture I think you better see."

He handed me another 8 by 10 photo, this one depicting me hugging Will on my red brick front porch. The shot was taken from outside our neighborhood, by a camera with telephoto lens. Of course, I got the message that a scope on a sniper rifle would yield the same view. At least my senses weren't failing; I had sensed we were being watched at the time.

"Where is she John?"

I gave him Jenny's name and address, for all the good it would do him. Or the FBI.

"Anything else that might be helpful?"

"No," I said glumly. "It appears you've got as good a photographic description of her as you'll ever need."

"Okay, John. Good enough. I'm not going to pull you off the Ghost's case unless you request it. These haven't gone to the press yet, and we don't allow scum to intimidate or distract us as a matter of policy."

"I don't want off the case, Jack. Just keep the car parked in front of my house, okay?"

"Sure," he said, moving toward the door, the meeting mercifully ended.

"Thanks," I said, shuffling toward the door, my tail between my legs. "I won't let you down tomorrow."

"Good," he mumbled in the hallway, his tone of voice as far from the picture of confidence as that of Hollywood's version of Davy

Crocket's, peering over the Alamo's walls at five thousand crack Mexican troops, saying, "We're going to need more men."

CHAPTER THIRTY

I'm ashamed to admit it, but I drove by Jenny's house on the way home, hoping against hope to see lights shining through her windows, or any indication that the woman I thought I was falling in love with hadn't taken the midnight train to Chicago or wherever the hell she really came from.

I allowed Jenny, if that was even her real name, to make a fool of me, cut me to the quick, and maybe even endanger my children. But they remained unharmed, at least so far, and having taken all reasonable precautions to keep them safe, all I had lost on her account was my self-respect, not my children or my job. Which I would surely lose if I blew the Ghost's case.

I waved to the agents parked on our curb, then plucked a familiar-looking manila envelope from my mailbox. Finding Will asleep for his afternoon snooze and Anna Grace ensconced in a lively cell phone conversation with Malik, I violated my rule against pouring a drink before five and settled into my deeply cushioned den chair for another trip into early 19th century Chalmette, Louisiana. If that sounds foolish or inexplicable, my response by way of rationalization to myself is that the past, even perhaps a fake one, was the only place where I felt not so much an ass as I did in the present. With my children living under threat, my dreams of romance in ashes, and my prosecutorial career put at risk by my own shortsightedness, this manuscript was all I had to help me keep a tight grip on sanity.

January 1, 1815
Dear Jenny:
Hail Mary, full of Grace! I will never forget this day so long as I live! Though our Troop played no real part in today's fight other than dodging cannonballs flying over our ramparts, we saw the most amazing artillery duel ever fought on these shores! And thanks to our pirate gunners, we held our own against the mighty British batteries, despite being outgunned, out-manned and caught with our pants down around our ankles.

We should have known what was coming; our sentries had told us the enemy had moved up in the darkness to within five hundred yards of our ramparts. What's more, we heard them digging, hammering and pounding throughout the night, and we figured they were setting up batteries and redoubts. But when the noise grew silent just before dawn, we figured they returned to camp for shut-eye in preparation for an assault, perhaps later in the day.

As usual, a great fog rolled in with the dawn and we could see nothing of the field. As we heard nothing from the enemy, Gen'l Jackson decided to hold a grand review of his troops. You should have seen it, Jenny, 'grand' hardly describes the scene in our camp. We unfurled our regimental and company flags, put on clean uniforms, and marched and galloped about to the music, mostly Yankee Doodle, played by our regimental bands, and of course, the rat-a-tat of Jordan Noble's drum. Despite prisoners' comments that the British thought us 'bumpkins' entirely lacking in taste for favoring rustic tunes, we enjoyed them immensely, celebrating both the New Year and our rough handling of the enemy so far.

So I reckon Jackson decided to show them how we 'bumpkins' looked wearing our finest on parade. Many city folk came out around 8:30 to join us and toast our victorious army.

Around ten o'clock the fog lifted and treated those of us on the ramparts to a heart stopping vision.

Arrayed across the field were five thousand British troops, with two rows of three batteries on the field and several set upon the levee. Of the three batteries set closest to our lines, two were fitted with eight cannon, and the one nearest the levee with two, including, ten eighteen-pounders, and four twenty-four-pound carronades. They had erected the batteries during the night, with sugar barrels placed in the parapets to afford the gunners protection from our fire.

Then before we could react, a rocket exploded in the air above us and all their cannons fired in unison. They struck at the Macarty house first, knowing it was home to Jackson and his officers. Within the space of ten minutes, no less that one hundred balls, rockets and shells slammed into the house, sending shattered bricks, smashed furniture, ceiling beams and splintered wood flying in every direction. Through Providence alone Gen'l Jackson and his officers standing on the balcony watching our revolutions suffered little injury apart from their wounded pride.

The spectators from the city panicked and fled to our rear, but, to their everlasting credit, our men stood tall behind their five-foot high ramparts. At least they didn't panic for more than several minutes...

Around noon our gunners wrested the advantage from the enemy. British guns inflicted little serious damage on our ramparts, most balls burying themselves harmlessly in our precious Mississippi mud. But after our gunners began sighting on the enemy, he suffered greatly. We saw balls strike soldiers peeking above their ditches, ripping their heads from their shoulders. One ball knocked a prone soldier's pack clean off his back.

During the hottest part of the exchange, a Louisiana militiaman, whom we later discovered to be a Jew named Judah Touro, hazarded his life on many occasions carrying ammunition from the magazine to Captain Humphrey's battery near the levee, seemingly insensible of the bullets and balls whizzing about his head. Eventually, he received a twelve-pound shot in the thigh, which took a huge chunk of his flesh with it.

We took him to Dr. Ker, who pronounced him shortly to be with his Maker. Unwilling to accept the physician's judgment, Touro bade his friend, Pvt. Shephard, convey him to the city in a cart while he sampled brandy along the way. We since learned to our great pleasure that he survived.

But none proved more courageous than our pirate gunners, straddling their cannon and making sure of their aim before firing, the hazard of their lives leading directly to our victory over the enemy. Their expert marksmanship took down every cannon with which the British sought to soften our defenses. A glorious sight to see!

Before I close, allow me to say how much your love has meant to me, and how grateful I am that you consented to be my bride and my boon companion along life's hazardous journey. You are everything I ever dreamed that a wife should be, and little Betsy is the daughter I always desired. Words cannot express how much I cherish everything you and the little one mean to me.

May our Lord bless you and keep you, and may this business have a happy ending as soon as possible, so that I may return to the happiest homecoming any man ever knew.

And to think that, but for the flint, canon, shot and powder given us by our buccaneer allies, this wretched plan, hatched by a corrupt and greedy monarchical government, would have already succeeded. My God, Jenny, this piebald army, the oddest assortment of freedom fighters the world has ever known, may be the final bulwark between tyranny and liberty!

I'll write you again when as I know more. Fired by this new revelation, our troop are some busy harassing the enemy outposts helping our comrades prepare for the decisive attack we all know is coming...

CHAPTER THIRTY ONE

I set the manuscript down and brushed the wetness from my eye. My forebear was huddled in a frozen ditch awaiting the onslaught of the conquerors of Napoleon and thrashers of the U.S. Army in Canada and Washington. How could I ever give way to fear and self-pity under far more favorable circumstances than Sgt. Ferguson faced?

Buck up, Ferguson, I chided myself, as I lifted the manuscript and turned to the next page.

January 8

Thank God Almighty! The enemy made his final assault today, the likes of which I have never seen before, and never hope to see again. But Jenny, we smashed them as Gen'l Jackson predicted! No one can believe the slaughter we inflicted among their ranks. The British are broken and will never try our ramparts again!

Of course, when I say "we" smashed them, I mean our pirates, Choctaws, militia and U.S. Regulars. The Mississippi Dragoons were drawn up in reserve near the Macarty house, while I, lacking a horse, manned the rampart lines on our left, near the swamp, where our line was weakest, so I could signal for Hinds and our Dragoons to come forward should the enemy breach our line. I held my sword in one hand and my pistol in the other, but had little use for either during the attack.

Our Tennessee riflemen and Baratarian gunners laid waste to rows of advancing soldiers time and again. They used long rifles, shot and shell at a distance and pistols and canister at close range to devastating effect.

General Pakenham was cheering on his Highlanders when grapeshot struck him in the arm and kilt his horse. As he mounted another, holding his hat high in the air, a bullet struck him in the throat while another stuck him in the middle and knocked him to the ground, never to rise again. Colonel Joseph Savary of Lacoste's free Negro battalion later claimed he made the fatal shot, and none dared to dispute him.

As they carried Pakenham from the field, General Gibbs and Col. Rennie assaulted our levee redoubt and chased our 7th Regulars across a plank and back behind the ramparts, but our boys shot Gibbs off his horse. The gallant Rennie mounted our ramparts and urged his men on, but one Mr. Withers, a merchant in Beale's Rifles, shot him down, too. These things I heard about after the battle, as I occupied the far ramparts near the swamp.

About fifteen hundred of the enemy shared Rennie's fate, casualties in a brave but misguided effort to deprive us of our freedom. After our riflemen stopped firing at stragglers around 8:30 AM, our batteries kept the heat on the retreating enemy for two more hours.

But enough smoke cleared the field to give us a good view of the carnage. We could smell the stink of burnt flesh and the blood-soaked ground, but were unprepared for the sight we found covering Chalmette plantation. My God, Jenny, you could walk across the whole field and never step on the ground for all the dead bodies on it.

In fact, I did walk across the field after spotting a boy of no more than fourteen who had fallen beneath our ramparts. His drum lay beside him, his eyes staring straight ahead at the angel of death that came for him. Heaven help me, I struggled to fight back tears as I knelt beside him, thinking what a terrible way for a child to die; that he spent the last few moments of his young life in wretched agony from his gaping wounds, finally expiring in the knowledge he would see *no more of the world than what his travels had already shown him; never again behold his mother's face, or hold his own child in his arms, as I have been blessed to do. Oh, how my heart ached for that handsome boy....*

But the bloodbath all across the field seemed endless. Headless torsos, and those with heads but without arms and legs, were strewn everywhere, and the groans, shrieks and dying pleas of the wounded sickened us beyond human endurance. Other boys younger than many of our soldier's sons cried with agony, begging to be put out of their misery. One large dapple-gray horse lay silent among the slaughter, and a Creole told me this was Pakenham's horse.

Even Old Hickory was amazed at the "field of slaughter." He likened the scene to that of the final day of resurrection, with hundreds of Britons rising from heaps of their dead comrades, coming forward and surrendering as prisoners of war.

However, one of the enemy, a stout-looking fellow in a red coat, slowly trod back toward the British camp, making gestures toward us that I would describe as the opposite of complimentary. After fifty shots from our ranks failed to give him pause, one of the Kentuckians hollered, "Hurrah, Paleface...Load quick and give him a shot. The infernal rascal is patting his butt at us." He made the request owing to Paleface's reputation as a crack shot, even among his fellow Kentuckians. Taking careful aim, Paleface let off a round, and the man staggered a few steps then pitched forward, face down, still as a stone.

But Jenny, I have said all this to say to you that I am safe; our entire troop are victorious and safe! New Orleans is saved and the British are in full retreat. We did it, by God! May the saints and angels who interceded on our behalf be praised to high heaven! And thank God for the pirates Lafitte, who as much as Jackson, saved our bacon, and preserved our country against a great and merciless horde!

In honor of the God who spared us, and in consideration of the common humanity we shared with our enemy, we and the people of New Orleans gave tender care to the British wounded, and treated them like heroes for their courage under fire. We did so knowing they had promised to be far less charitable toward us had they carried the day.

Jenny, we lost only six men on our ramparts. Considering their fifteen hundred dead and about half that number severely wounded and likely to die, such a victory may be unprecedented in the annals of military warfare. And to think that a disorganized, inexperienced ragtag collection of militia, Creole merchants and lawyers, free Negroes, pirates, Choctaws, Tennessee, Mississippi and Kentucky frontiersmen could smash the greatest army the world has seen since Caesar's Tenth Legion....Well, it is almost beyond belief. Surely Providence has redeemed or Republic once again, as in the days of our glorious Revolution.

May God be praised!

Now, my love, sleep tonight knowing your husband will soon be holding you in his arms. Tell my little girl her daddy is coming home to hug her neck as he has never done before.

I will write you again when I know of our plans to return home.

P.S. Do not be alarmed at the rumors sure to reach you soon of plague affecting our glorious troops. Only two Tennesseans have succumbed to Yellow Fever and not another in our ranks is ill. We will escape Yellow Jack's clutches as surely as we did those of the British. I...

"Daddy..."

I looked up from the manuscript to see Will, rubbing his eyes from his nap, dragging the now one-eyed teddy bear of my youth into the den. He climbed into my lap, thrust my manuscript aside and curled his arms around my neck.

"Did you sleep well little man?" I beamed.

"No," he moaned, rubbing sleep from his eyes. "I had a nightmare."

I ran my fingers through the golden curls dangling behind his head. "About what?"

"I dreamed I saw your face all red, and then you died."

Pause. S*hake it off, John.*

"It was just a nightmare, son," I whispered, cradling him in my arms, his chin warm on my shoulder. "I'm right here, alive, and just about to bring you chocolate milk and brownies. How does that sound, big fellah?"

"Good," he said flatly.

"Just good?" I asked, kissing him on the cheek. "Not great? What would make my little man smile this fine Thursday afternoon?"

"Dad?"

I never liked it when he called me 'dad' at his tender age, something he had undoubtedly picked up from Anna Grace, and probably said to show how grown up he'd become. Why did children wish so fervently to grow up, when all the rest of us wanted so desperately to drop as many years off the ledger as we could coax from the unfeeling gods?

"Yes, Will?"

"Can you stay home tomorrow, and play games with me?"

"I wish I could, son, but Daddy's got a big court case tomorrow. You understand, don't you?"

"No," he said willfully. "Can I come watch you in court like I did the other time?"

'No' to a child is as unacceptable an answer as 'that dress makes you look fat,' is to your wife, but taking him to court was out of the question with the threat of a possible terror attack hanging over our heads.

"Daddy?"

Oh, no, I almost groaned out loud. Now it's 'daddy'; he's pulling out all the stops. This will surely end badly.

"Will, tomorrow's not a good day for you to come to court."

"But why not?" he whined.

"I'm trying to put a bad man in jail, but some other bad men are angry I'm prosecuting him, so I must take every precaution to assure that you and Anna Grace are safe from these miscreants."

"I'm not afraid, daddy."

"Nor was I, when I was your age, but you can't go to this hearing, Will.

I promised your mother I would take care of you and Anna Grace if it was the last thing I did. That's what I'm doing now, and after court is over tomorrow, I'll take you for ice cream, or to the park, or wherever you want to go. Deal?"

"Will you buy me a new book?"

Wow, I thought, what a negotiator you're gonna' be! Skip law school and go straight into hostage negotiating for the government.

"Sure, son. Soon as I get home tomorrow. But you can only have one book, okay?" Couldn't let a four-year-old completely out-negotiate me...

And then he said something that surprised and pleased me immensely. Out of the mouth of babes, they say, and *they* never said anything more profound in all their incessant babblings.

"Thanks for keeping me safe, daddy," he said warmly, kissing me on the cheek. "I only want more books so we can read 'em together. You're the best daddy in the world, and I love *you* too." He wrapped his arms around me so tightly I could barely breathe.

I wish this moment could last forever, I mused. With the problems facing our family and the potential danger facing everyone at the courthouse, the moment felt more precious for being all the more tenuous.

Will was everything I had ever hoped for in a son, just as Anna Grace was all I'd ever dreamed of in a daughter. No matter what the future held, the gods could never deny me that.

I made them turkey sandwiches, trimming the crust for Will and cutting his apple into slices. Will laughed as Anna Grace told us about pouring baking soda in her boyfriend's trumpet before band practice, and how the boy turned red in the face until he blew the white powder on the trombone player in the front row.

"Big day in court, tomorrow, Dad?" she asked.

"Yes, how did you know?"

"I know everything," she said with the bristling confidence of the 16-year-old teenager. "Or had you forgotten that?"

"You don't know everything," Will blurted, "Just everything you want to know."

"That's right, Will. Have another apple slice."

Looking back on it now, I can't help but wonder- was the angel of death watching us and laughing out loud?

CHAPTER THIRTY TWO

After dinner I sent Anna Grace to her room to finish her homework and gave Will a bath before putting him to bed. He nodded off quickly while I read him poems from my college English lit textbook, and I waited until his breathing slowed and reached a measured pace before I slipped out of his bed and padded into the den.

" Daddy?"

I looked up to see Will standing beside my chair, rubbing his eyes with one hand and scratching his leg with the other. I lifted him into my arms. Will, I'm having a happy Christmas vision, and not of sugarplums and candy.."

"What?"

"A vision of snuggling with you in my bed."

Moments later I slipped my arm under his neck and he laid his head on my shoulder, just as I had done with Anna Grace years earlier.

"I love you, dad," he mumbled, then drifted back to sleep with the unerring ease of the innocent.

And for the first time since the day I met Jenny at the bookstore, I slumbered like a baby and enjoyed pleasant dreams of wriggling my toes in the sand, and swimming in the Gulf of Mexico with Will on my back and Anna Grace gliding gracefully beside me.

But just before I nodded off, it had occurred to me that I should have asked Anna Grace why, after several years disinterest, she wanted to see my try a case *this* week.

Sleep took me before I resolved that mystery, and the thought didn't reoccur the next morning.

CHAPTER THIRTY THREE

At breakfast the next morning I reminded Marianna and the children to keep a watchful eye out until the day was over. "Thanks for protecting us, Daddy," Will said. And then, "Are we going to the bookstore later today?"

I suppressed a knowing smile. "You bet son. Right after my hearing in court."

"What about me, dad? You gonna' get me a book, too?"

"Absolutely, girl. Whatever you want."

"Good," she said, drowning her waffles in maple syrup. "I'll take the latest Harry Potter book."

"Fine," Will announced, energetically stabbing his scrambled eggs with a toddler-sized Cookie Monster fork. For no particular reason I stared at his utensil, wondering why Cookie Monster was red instead of blue, his actual color on *Sesame Street*. Or was that actually Grover cradled in my hungry son's fingers? Then it struck me that in a mere six hours I would be handling a case that, should it go wrong, might cost me a damn fine government job, set a possible terrorist on the street, and far worse, invite the very devil himself into our midst by demonstrating our ineffectiveness in terror control. And here I was, mentally debating Cookie Monster versus Grover.

Then, I took note of a far more bittersweet incongruity-- my beautiful teenaged daughter, her lovely brown hair hanging haphazardly over one eye like Veronica Lake, innocently preparing her waffles exactly as she liked them, her childlike expression belying the maturing soul that hatched covert schemes to sneak out of class to make out with her boyfriend in the band hall.

Across the table from my young Aphrodite, my four-("and a quarter')-year-old toe-headed Adonis with porcelain blue eyes and swirling curls impervious to comb or brush, cradled Grover tightly in his hand as he speared another maple-drenched morsel.

If only it could be like this forever, I mused. *If only...*

A half hour later I kissed Anna Grace goodbye as she shuffled out the door toward her carpool ride to school. She turned to me on the front porch, and with an odd grin, said, "I'll see you later, Dad. Good luck on your big case today."

Before I could answer, Will shouted for help getting dressed for school.

"You're not going to school today, son. Your aunt Martha will be here shortly to take you to Laurel for a few days."

"Aunt Marna's coming? Awright!"

As he gathered his favorite toys and books for a trip to south Mississippi, I wondered how Finnerin and his ilk could bring themselves to destroy such innocence for any cause they espoused. For that matter, why had every government on earth, including ours, perpetrated crimes against humanity comparable to the worst outrages imagined by the authors of the most blood drenched mythological tales?

Despite all the world's recorded wisdom, the teachings of the sages and prophets, the holy books and philosophical treatises, the divine work of satirists, and the small, quiet voice inside each of us that warns us against folly and wrongdoing, we never seemed to...

"Daddy?"

"Yes, son?"

"Are you talking to yourself?"

"Probably so," I chuckled, "it's nothing to be worried about boy, I'm just getting old, you see?"

"You are old," Will laughed a little too loudly to suit me. "Old as dirt."

"That's funny boy."
"Yeah," he laughed again, "it is!"
"You bet."
"You bet," he repeated, then laughed even louder.
"It's not that funny," I groused.

During the drive to work, I couldn't help feeling that I had overlooked something as ominous as it was obvious. Was it something about Anna Grace and the way she told me goodbye this morning? Whatever it was, it eluded me, and I ignored my instincts and brushed it off as a father's endless anxiety about his teen-aged daughter.

CHAPTER THIRTY FOUR

The Finnerin gang's temporary home base was a modest, pastel-colored two-bedroom house in the art-deco-styled Fondren neighborhood a few miles north of downtown Jackson. Finnerin, AKA Finn, had chosen the house because of its location, but nevertheless appreciated its two-car garage with automatic doors that hid a wealth of his comrades' sins.

Not that any of his confederates would have objected to settling there had they disapproved of his choice. Never had any one of the three voiced a hint of disagreement with his ideas, plans or tactics. From day one they had accepted him as their leader, but after their first strike against a London bank produced an uncomplicated getaway with a million in cash, not one of them had ever questioned Finn's commands before or after they immigrated to America.

It wasn't just a matter of his being the tallest man in the room, his almost herculean strength, or even the malignant, piercing look in his eyes that chilled the blood and stifled opposing views before they were even conceived. His leadership qualities spoke volumes for themselves.

Time and again he had proven supreme with strategic planning--setting opponents at each other's throats, devising schemes that resulted in a total incapacity of prosecutors to hold them accountable for their actions. His tactics had been no less impressive—setting off explosives with perfect results and making good their escape no matter what unexpected circumstances arose. Most importantly, using reason, guile, deception, bribery, distraction, inspiration or intimidation, he bent friends and enemies alike to his inexorable will like a professional potter molds his clay.

The shortest and stockiest of the three, the ex-Russian immigrant Gruzenko, could handle any cop, patrolman or federal agent in a scrap or shootout, but experience had taught him to bite his tongue whenever he differed with their leader. Aziz, the slender man with the dark complexion and darker eyes, and by far the most self-confident and educated of the gang, had never once found reason to doubt or debate the man he knew as Ryan Finn.

On the other hand, the wild-eyed, balding little ex-German immigrant calling himself Sier Gitt, had learned through the crucible of pain--several ass-whippings and one gunshot to the thigh, that the man he had known as Patrick Finnerin for several decades would suffer no disagreement, brook no argument, and enforce his will by any means necessary.

As with the woman they knew as Jennifer Garrott, who had once loved him and bourn him a child, they were his to command. But unlike the woman, they well knew, whether she did or not, that he associated with them only for their skills in war.

No matter. They had chosen their paths and gloried in the destruction they had wrought among the supporters of the debased and callous governments in Britain first, then later in their adopted nation, the United States.

Now, they were determined to finish this job at all hazards, in part because they believed in their cause, but also because they feared betraying or deserting Finnerin more than they feared capture by the authorities or death by any other means. There were worse fates than death, and all the proof they needed on that point lay prostrate on the floor in the corner of the basement where they now carried out Ryan Finn's plan.

"Time to go to work!"

Finn turned from the worktable in the heart of the dark basement of the house they had recently commandeered. Through the dim light afforded by a solitary bulb hanging from the ceiling, he saw the man and woman lying nude, bound hand and feet and gagged with industrial tape, on the damp, brick floor. Blood stains darkened their hips, buttocks and her genital area; tears had cut valleys on their faces. At the sound of the tall man's voice they cringed and inched closer together, perhaps seeking one more moment of closeness before the end they knew was coming.

Gitt had induced the man, an employee of the U.S. Clerk's office, to bring him papers needed to file a lawsuit in the U.S. District Court, claiming he was paralyzed and couldn't come to the federal building downtown. Once Gitt waylaid him at a deserted house, he had taken him to the man's own house, where Gitt quickly subdued his wife and made them both his prisoners. The hapless young man's identification tag was essential to their plans, just as his body proved necessary to satisfy Gitts' sexual gratification. The young woman had proved equally `useful' to the ex-Russian, or so he had quipped in his stilted English the first time he raped and sodomized her. In every way, the terrorists had turned their home in to a sinkhole of unearthly delights.

Finn faced his companions. "Are you ready," he blared, more order than question.

"What about them?" asked Aziz, eyeing the bound couple on the basement floor.

"That," said Gitts, warmly appraising the cast metal canisters, timers and electric firing cables sitting atop a dusty cabinet on the far wall, "is set to go off in two hours, simultaneously with its rather larger brother that will explode in the courthouse at about the same time," he said, patting the devices on which Gruzenko had been working furiously for the past three hours.

But Aziz remained focused on the smaller device. "Shrapnel?" he asked matter- of-factly.

"Yes, and incendiary too," Gruzenko announced.

"You all know what to do," Finn said. "After you get me in position by the creek, take your ID's and the building code and drive to the courthouse. If they're on alert and guarding the employee entrances too, take down those guards and wait for my....signal. Either way, remain hidden, by whatever means you require, until all hell breaks loose."

"Yes, sir," they said in unison.

"Oh, and Jamahl?"

"Yes?"

"Keep them all out of the west side of the building. I need all of you in one piece to finish this job."

Aziz almost asked Gitt if he was sure the first blast wouldn't take down the whole courthouse and them with it, but thought better of it. Even if it did, the result couldn't be any worse than suggesting, even by implication that their leader wasn't in full control of Gitts, the IED, and every aspect of their situation. Never give the devil an opportunity he reminded himself as he hurried out of basement several steps behind the rest.

CHAPTER THIRTY FIVE

At straight up nine o'clock in the morning of the Ghost's habeas corpus hearing, Jack Ashton banged on my office door, entered before I could respond, and strode single-mindedly toward my desk with Marshal Reed in tow. "Let's get this show on the road," he barked.

"As you wish," I replied calmly.

He turned to Reed. "You're people ready?"

"Yes, sir. Double guard at the main entrance, all other entrances are guarded, all cameras fully functional, and the JPD is providing additional support at all four street corners with roadblocks on Court and West Streets. You won't be disturbed during the hearing, I assure you."

Unable to contain myself, I ventured, "Marshall Reed, you don't suppose the good folks at those other courthouses that got blown up were thinking the same thing, do you?"

"You just do your job," Ashton snapped, "and let the marshals handle the security. *He* hasn't been compromised this month."

I ignored the jibe about Jenny and contented myself with the knowledge that at least I hadn't been bitch slapped by the Ghost, either.

Our stroll to third floor courtroom was brisk and accompanied by a near-deafening silence.

CHAPTER THIRTY SIX

Cutting an opening in the steel chain link fence guarding the entrance to the underground access to Town Creek had been the first, easiest step. Finn had done it several days before, at night, and left the fence hanging in place so that no one could see it had been cut without eyeballing it from inches away.

That would have required standing in five feet of water, because that was the creek's depth where it meandered from the southwestern edge of the city through several seedy neighborhoods and finally into the western edge of downtown Jackson. There, a stone's throw from the train station, located several miles from the federal courthouse, the stream disappeared under a concrete structure that might have passed for a train tunnel through a mountain at the dawn of railway travel. The structure vanished a few yards before reaching a large building just across Capitol Street from the Mayflower restaurant. From there, Town Creek, flowing underground and unobserved, turned southeast on a direct path toward the United States Courthouse at the corner of Court and West. It flowed under the courthouse toward the southernmost edge of downtown, where it resurfaced and made its way into the bowels of southern Hinds County.

Few Jacksonians ever gave a thought to the largely concealed Town Creek, apart from those homeless souls who ventured close enough to urinate or defecate in its putrid waters. Almost no one remembered that it flowed under the Mayflower, the Municipal Museum, or the federal courthouse. But a brief check of city records in the antebellum, Greek Revival style City Hall building a few blocks from the federal courthouse revealed everything to Aziz that Finn needed to know.

Now, Finn peeled back the severed fence section and laid it on the western creek bank, and continued poling his johnboat forward into the concrete tunnel. Having previously swum Town Creek as far as the courthouse, he knew he had about thirty minutes of poling or paddling until he reached his destination. The creek was unobstructed he knew, so there was no danger of upsetting the boat and sinking his explosive devices.

He had only to pole at a leisurely pace, arrive beneath the courthouse in thirty minutes or less, consult the plans Aziz had copied at city hall, place the devices and set the timers.

In the resulting terror and confusion after the first explosion, he would enter the courthouse, climb over rubble to the third floor courtroom, which, like the western outer wall, should still be intact despite the damage to its inner wall, the second story floor and first floor ceiling. There his companions would have already taken charge of the situation. The woman would have done her part, and all would be ready for his grand entrance onto the scene.

For the first time in almost a hundred and fifty years, the U.S. Government would finally find itself vanquished on its own soil, by its own citizens, and receive a lesson in humility long overdue.

CHAPTER THIRTY SEVEN

When Anna Grace's substitute teacher had suggested that Anna Grace and Malik take a field trip to the courthouse to surprise her father and watch him try a case for the first time in years, the teen had laughed out loud.

Although she had been fascinated with his trials at age seven, she had long since lost interest in such boring matters. After all, Facebooking, texting, surfing and blogging with Malik and her buddies were far more interesting than the goings on in her father's federal courthouse.

But this idea of surprising her father, and doing it with the boyfriend whose name he struggled to pronounce correctly, had soon appealed to her. Once adopted, it had been difficult to keep the secret from her dad and Will, who would surely have given the surprise away five seconds after learning it.

Anyway, she liked her substitute teacher, Miss Wilson, who had replaced the boring Civics teacher who had taken a sudden leave of absence from which she had never returned. Anna Grace also needed a good grade in that class to meet her father's expectations and keep her cell phone and IPad, and Miss Wilson offered an A+ pop quiz grade for taking the field trip.

What could be better, she pondered, surprising her dad, getting an A for sitting beside Malik for a few hours, and maybe even stealing a kiss in a restroom or empty courthouse room?

From the front seat of the older model green Buick beside Ms. Wilson, Anna Grace said, "I can't wait to see the look on dad's face when he sees me in the courtroom today."

"Cool," Malik announced from the back seat.

"Are you sure we won't get in trouble for this," Anna Grace asked. "A newspaper article said the marshals were planning to close the courtroom for dad's hearing."

"Are you kidding me?" Ms. Wilson said. "The public has an absolute right to see every hearing held in that courthouse. Besides, do you think we look like terrorists they should be worried about?"

"I don't know," Anna Grace said, smirking at Malik, who nodded his head, well aware of what was coming. "They may take Malik for one. He is quite brown and thoroughly Muslim, as you know."

"Death to the infidels," Malik shouted in mock anger, fist raised on high.

Anna Grace and Malik laughed and high-fived each other over the seat. Ms. Wilson merely checked her watch before turning off the interstate onto the street that would take them directly to Jackson's federal courthouse.

CHAPTER THIRTY EIGHT

Jack Ashton sat on the front row of the courtroom gallery directly behind my seat at the prosecution's counsel table to the right of the judge's bench. Otherwise, the courtroom seemed eerily bereft of onlookers apart from two women I recognized as members of the press. Most trials attract at least a few variously interested spectators: family or friends of the parties or their lawyers, throngs of school children, thrill seekers of the lowest order, and retired elderly men with little else to do.

Although the marshals had temporarily closed the courtroom to all but relatives of the defendant and the press, I doubted Judge Hank Wyngait would uphold that ban if anyone raised an objection on behalf of the defendant's right to a public trial or the public's right to view any trial, especially one laced with political implications.

Breeland Jones entered the courtroom with his mystery client, the Ghost, in tow. Manacled from shoulders to ankles, hands in front and feet far enough apart to shuffle slowly for a short distance, the Ghost sported the customary jailhouse orange. By contrast, his sartorial attorney impressed with his charcoal gray suit, blue bow tie dotted with red, starched white Kennedy collar shirt and black saddle oxford shoes. He carried a briefcase in one hand and several stapled documents in the other.

Broad shouldered, thick-bearded federal marshals stood two at every doorway, dressed in dark suits and black ties, their cheerless expressions conveying their readiness for all contingencies. No joshing with each other today; they were treating a defendant with no known criminal record charged with a misdemeanor as if he were a psychopathic killer thrice escaped from the federal pen.

Then again, he had assaulted one of their own.

As I expected, no sooner had Judge Wyngait entered the courtroom to the sound of the clerk bellowing three Oh Yezs and a ringing 'ALL RISE,' Breeland stood and said, "I have a motion, your honor."

"Proceed," the judge announced.

"Your honor, I've prepared a written motion…"

"Orally will suffice."

"I move the court to open the courtroom to the public. My client has a constitutional right to a public trial. Furthermore, the public has an absolute right to---."

"Correct me if I'm wrong, counsel, but aren't those two ladies seated a few rows behind you esteemed members of the press? What good are they if not capable of informing the public about our proceedings today?"

When Breeland paused to offer a response, the judge continued in his deep gravelly voice, "Don't answer that counsel. It's not relevant insofar as I have no choice but to grant your motion unless the U.S. Attorney's office has something interesting to offer. Well, Mr. Ferguson…?"

I rose to address the court, ignoring Jack's attempts to signal me from behind. "We have no proof that the claimant himself poses a danger to the court or the public, but we believe that he may be associated with a domestic terrorist organization linked to the bombings of several Massachusetts and New York federal courthouses, military bases and private businesses."

"Mr. Ferguson, you used two phrases that caused me to lose focus on your argument, including 'we believe' and 'in New York'. Anything else?"

"We're pursuing the presumed connection, your honor, but have nothing ironclad to report at this time."

"A most artful way of answering 'no', counsel. You always delight this court by offering a dozen words when one would suffice. Defense motion granted. Mr. Marshal, open the doors to the public. Mr. Ferguson, call your case."

"I call the case of United States versus John Doe, habeas corpus hearing."

"Are you and Mr. Doe ready to proceed, Mr. Jones?"

"We are, your honor."

"Very well. Call your witness, Mr. Ferguson."

Behind me a few men wandered inconspicuously into the gallery and seated themselves on various benches.

"I call Marshal Josh Reed."

The clerk stood to administer the oath, but the judge motioned him back to his seat. "I'll waive the oath," he said, in deference to his longtime courtroom enforcer.

"Mr. Reed, state your name and profession."

He complied.

"Did you have occasion to interact in any way with the defendant, there?"

"Objection, your honor," Breeland began, "this is--."

"Sit down," the judge shrugged, cutting him off in mid-sentence. "Let's don't drag this out, shall we? What would be the point of asking the witness to identify the defendant in a courtroom with only five other men and four women, none of whom look anything like him, most of whom are obviously spectators and none of whom are currently charged with a crime by this court."

"As you wish, your honor."

The judge's comment about four women in the gallery prompted me to see them for myself. What I saw chilled my heart and choked off my breath as if I had seen a pyroclastic flow rolling down a volcano toward us. The woman seated beside Anna Grace wore a doughty green dress, glasses and her dark hair in a bun atop her head, but I recognized her at first sight.

"May I indulge the court for a moment, your honor?"

"Yes?" he asked impatiently.

"I..."

"Mr. Ferguson? Cat got your tongue?"

"May we approach, your honor?"

"Be my guest."

Jack eyed me angrily, palms raised in WTF mode, but I ignored him and approached the judge alongside Breeland Jones.

"Your honor," I said, gesturing toward the rear of the gallery, that's my daughter, Anna Grace in the back of the courtroom."

The judge gaped toward the gallery and located Anna Grace, who, realizing what was happening, feebly raised her hand in salute.

"That's nice, Mr. Ferguson. I presume you mean the younger one."

"Yes, your honor. But it's the older one that concerns me. I don't know why they're sitting together...The young man seated on her right is her boyfriend..."

"Right handsome fellow. What in God's name is your point?"

"Judge, this is difficult for me to say, but we suspect that woman of being involved with the defendant, perhaps the link we were searching for in connection with a terrorist organization..."

Judge Wyngait greeted my comment with a quizzical frown. "Then what is your daughter doing with her?"

"That's what I'd like to know," I bleated, my voice betraying a fear that caught the judge's attention.

"Your daughter seems quite happy in her company, Mr. Ferguson. I can see no coercion from here. Make it plain for me, will you?"

"May I have a moment to speak with my daughter, judge?"

"Don't take all day," he sighed.

"Thanks, your honor. I won't."

As I hurried toward the gallery, I turned to Breeland and asked, "Did you know about this?"

"About what," he asked, genuinely confused.

"Forget it," I said, leaving him stewing in my wake as I hurried toward Anna Grace.

When I reached her bench, she hugged me and said in an uncharacteristically weak voice, "Surprise..."

"I'll say," I whispered, leading her away from the woman known to me as Jenny Shexnayder, who smiled serenely as if she had never seen me before, then leaned toward Malik as if to make small talk while

Anna Grace and I spoke. "What are you doing with that woman?" I breathed.

Anna Grace shot me a stern glance. "*That woman*, as you call her, is my Civics teacher, Ms. Wilson. We're on a field trip for extra credit."

"Just the three of you? What happened to Mrs. Brown? I thought she--."

"She's on leave of absence. Ms. Wilson is the substitute."

"Since when?"

"Since two weeks ago. What do you care?"

My God, I thought. They really saw me coming. They've been planning this...Planning something...For several weeks or longer. Then it hit me hard between the eyes--*my little girl is in danger! We are all in danger...*

I glanced around the courtroom and noticed two men watching us closely across the way, then saw another, a short, portly man with greasy white hair and an odd expression, sitting two rows behind Jenny and Malik. The thought occurred to me that he hadn't taken his eyes off me since I had rushed down the aisle to speak with Anna Grace.

My gut churned like a concrete mixer on overdrive. I grasped Anna Grace firmly by the arm and pulled her with me toward the counsel tables fifty feet away.

"Let go of me," she yelped. "You're hurting me!"

"Your honor," I shouted as I passed the bench where the two suspicious men eyed me like hawks focused on a sparrow, "I think we've got a--."

The first shots fired by the two men felled the two marshals standing before the large wooden doors at the main entrance, and their second volley knocked two more off their feet near the judge's courtroom entrance. Moving faster than I could have imagined, the short stocky man reached me before I could react, knocked me aside, grabbed Anna Grace by the neck and brandished an automatic pistol at her temple.

The first two marshals entering the main doorway took bullets to the head, as did the others rushing through the door beside the judge's bench. Judge Wyngait attempted to slip out his private doorway near his bench, but a shot fired over his head showered bits of sheet rock over him and stopped him in his tracks.

"Back away from that doorway and step down from the bench, judge," said the thin black man, aiming his pistol between the judge's eyes. To my surprise, Wyngait whirled and bolted for the door a few inches distant, but the back of his head exploded in a shower of blood and bone fragments before he took a second step. The court reporter screamed and the court clerk dove to the floor.

"If it wasn't obvious before," the black man shouted, "you should see we're all quite serious. Now, lawyers take a seat at this counsel table. You two at the other one."

As the clerk led the distraught court reporter to the far table, Breeland sat down immediately at mine, but I held back. "Give me my daughter," I said to the short, bald man leveling a pistol at her head. He looked toward the black man, who nodded 'yes.' He shoved Anna Grace toward me, but she turned to Malik, shouting his name twice.

"Go," Jenny said, and Malik sprinted unimpeded to Anna Grace's side. We seated ourselves beside Breeland.

"I'm sorry daddy," she said, clutching my left arm with her right and Malik's with her left. The short man stood an arm's length behind us, ready to use Anna Grace as a shield if anyone rushed the courtroom from either entrance. His companions shadowed us the same way. One took aim at the main doorway while the other pointed his pistol toward the judge's bench entrance.

Before I could answer Anna Grace, the third man, the one with crazy eyes and white hair, looked up from his watch, said, "Now!" and ducked to the ground, holding his hands over his ears. The other two followed suit.

I grabbed Anna Grace and forced her to the floor, but before I could cover her body with mine, a metallic-sounding explosion rocked the courtroom.

Years ago I had seen a lightning bolt strike the ground just off the highway in an open field several hundred feet from my car. The sound had been almost identical to the explosion that reduced a section of the wall to rubble behind the judge's bench, covering everyone with dust, asbestos and small chunks of drywall. Fortunately, the building's outer wall held up, the roof didn't cave in on us, and the floor didn't give way beneath us. But I doubted those in the offices between the courtroom and outer wall had been so fortunate.

The first thing I noticed after the explosion was the Ghost standing free of his shackles, a .38 revolver in his hand. He pressed the barrel under the court reporter's chin, while the court clerk, an inoffensive, diminutive man, cringed in his seat beside them, his trembling hands covering his head.

I finally located Breeland through the smoke and dust settling all around us. He lay on his back just beyond the counsel table where he sat when the bomb went off. I stumbled toward his inert body, and checked his pulse. He still lived, but his breathing was as weak as his pulse. A large red knot had formed on his forehead, and a chunk of wood from a door frame lay inches from his head.

Stay down, buddy. You may fare better asleep than the rest of us will awake.

I knew there were other marshals in the courthouse, at least five federal security guards at the first floor public entrance, and by this time, a gaggle of Jackson police officers gathering outside our courtroom should the order come to rush our assailants. But they knew civilians were inside, court personnel, and, as far as they knew, a still breathing federal judge. Only the highest level authorities could give that order if indeed it ever came at all.

Marshal Reed, who had removed his sidearm before entering the courtroom as a witness, stood as helpless as the rest of us. He quietly took a seat at the far counsel table, beside a substantially humbled Jack Ashton, who sat with his hands in his lap, undoubtedly expecting the worst.

I heard the court reporter sobbing, and turned to see the Ghost pressing the barrel of his pistol between her large breasts, stroking her long blonde hair with his other hand. He caressed her cheek with his tongue.

"Knock that shit off," growled the black man. "Keep yourself ready. They could charge us at any time."

"I don't think so," said a booming voice from the gaping hole in the courtroom's west wall. Through that hole stepped a tall, raggedy-haired man, as if entering our space from another dimension, making his way through the smoke and rubble to the other side of the counsel table from Anna Grace and me.

CHAPTER THIRTY NINE

"Hello one and all," Ryan Finn announced as if arriving fashionably late to a country club affair. "Well done, men," he nodded to his charges. He glared at me as he walked slowly around the table, stopping inches from me. At least six-feet-four, he towered over me, but his self-confidence and sense of purpose made him appear several feet taller.

"John Ferguson, I presume?"

Unable to avert my eyes from his, I composed myself sufficiently to say, "Have we met?"

"Not formally," he replied coolly. "Unless you consider flushing your sins down the confessional toilet a more formal occasion than I."

"Not that it matters now," I nodded, "but I how--"

"How did I do it? Years ago, before I came to my senses, I became a Third Order priest."

"We checked every Third Order organization in the country. No one ever heard of anyone matching your description."

Finn, Finnerin or whoever he really was, gave a broad grin and spoke with the quiet confidence of the master strategist in total control of his situation. "You checked with every Catholic Third Order, Mr. Ferguson. Ours was a Franciscan Order in the Anglican Communion."

"Anglican?"

"Such limited vision, Mr. Ferguson. Not all priests and monks are minions of the Pope, the living embodiment of the Biblical whore of Babylon. The Third Order Society of St. Francis, Anglican Communion, was headquartered in San Francisco, where I first settled after immigrating to this country. Our Order required neither poverty nor abstinence, eh? Only that we participate freely in Christ's message of reconciliation and love.

"Can you imagine that?" he gestured dramatically. "As a newly sworn American citizen I offered myself up to an organization whose business it was to make us malleable automatons, enslaved to the unholy government/corporate/industrialist megalith that runs this country. In so doing, I went as a sheep to the shearing, with the understanding that I was also to teach others to submit, to fall in line with the other worker ants who daily bent their knees to the ruling aristocracy.

"My role, Mr. Ferguson, was to set the example-- put love of my fellow man ahead of wealth and privilege, thus abetting our leaders' curious ritualized thievery by allotting them an even greater share than the ninety-three percent of wealth and property they already owned in this country. I played along so perfectly they never had the first idea that my motivations were far different than they suspected. Suffice it to say, I shed my priestly skin as soon as time and international anonymity allowed. But the experience gave me the time I needed to bury myself in America and throw all the British bloodhounds off my scent."

When I didn't respond, he turned to Anna Grace. "Speaking of growing up...This must be your daughter, Anna Grace. How lovely she is."

"Go to hell," she blurted, turning away from him to clutch Malik's hand.

"And such a mannerly child she is. I congratulate you, Mr. Ferguson. You're as capable a parent as you are at discerning the storm clouds blotting your horizon."

He peered over my shoulder at the woman I had known as Jenny Shexnayder. "My compliments, Garrott. I'd say you could leave right now, but we may need you as a 'hostage.'"

"My pleasure," she said, but not as if she meant it. Even so, I could see from her nonchalant comportment toward me that everything that had passed between us was nothing but an act. This woman had no more compassion for any of us than a spider had for a fly.

"Not a bad show, yourself," I said to the tall man.

"Oh?"

"So *you* planned all this, Finnerin, or whatever you're calling yourself now? And had it carried out by four other psychopaths who managed to hold it together long enough to pull it off. Joseph Stalin's got nothing on you."

Out of the corner of my eye, I saw the black man smirk at my characterization of him as a psychopath. The one who had spoken with a Russian accent gave no indication that I was even in the room, much less speaking of him. But the short man with the crazy eyes and strange hair glared at me as if I had insulted his mother.

"You're not a coward, John Ferguson," Finn said. "I'll give you that. A little dense, perhaps, and lacking a great deal of judgment right now, but certainly no coward."

"But you may be. You haven't given your name, or are *you* more comfortable with cowardly anonymity?"

He gave a stately bow and said, "I'm Ryan Finn, as you guessed, Mr. Ferguson. CEO and owner of the United Freedom Front. And this," he continued, gesturing toward the Russian, "is Yuregev Gruzenko, my IED expert. He contributed a great deal to that hole in the wall you see behind me. The dark gentleman there is Jamahl Abdul Aziz, a Harvard graduate, and of immense help to my strategic and tactical planning efforts."

"Another Erich von Manstein, I'm sure," I said, likening Aziz to Hitler's wartime strategist.

"My great great grandparents were slaves in Alabama," Aziz said coolly. "My grandmother was killed in a KKK church firebombing in Georgia. My father died in penury, an ally-wandering alcoholic who finally despaired of a decent opportunity to support his family of ten in a country that had nothing for him but a hard life and an early grave. But you can link me to Adolph Hitler if it makes you feel better. It certainly makes my job easier today."

"I'm sure it's very easy for you," I couldn't stop myself from uttering, "murdering innocent women and children. I bet that would have made your father proud."

"The other gentleman there," Finn continued blithely, "is Sieur Gitt, who assists me in, well…Other less definable and best left unmentionable matters."

"Other matters?" I asked almost involuntarily, my penchant for cross-examining psychopaths in courtrooms surfacing once more. "By that do you mean rape, torture and mass murder, or just general pandemonium?"

"Hmmm…Let's say he's quite versatile where his special talents are concerned."

"I don't doubt it. Perhaps his talents' run in his family. I seem to recall reading about a Gitt or Gitts, an actual Nazi," I said, returning Aziz's baleful glare, "who proved very versatile where his Dachau master's concentration camp extermination needs were concerned."

"My, my, mister Ferguson," Finn nodded, "you surprise me. Perhaps you're not quite as obtuse as I believed."

"He probably changed his name and dropped the 'S'," Anna Grace offered unexpectedly, "when he found out that GITTS is an internet acronym for 'Giving In To The Sphincter.' Hit too close to home, I bet."

"Ahh, yes," Finn gushed approvingly, "the apple never falls very far from the tree."

I glared at Anna Grace as if to say, 'how did you know that,' and 'refrain from offering threatening comments to this gang of killers and perverts'.

"But, be careful, young lady," Finn said menacingly with a sideways glance toward Gitt. "Gitts, as you and even I sometimes call him, is not one to take a joke, and I suspect that he is slightly less intimidated by you than he is by me."

Gitt lowered his head in a failed effort to disguise his disdain for Finn's highhandedness, or possibly, his inability to take revenge on me and my daughter. For now.

As if reading my mind, Finn added, "But let's not have any more unpleasantness than becomes absolutely necessary today. What we are about right now is finding a way out of our situation, having made our point by striking a blow at the United States of Voracity, Jackson, Mississippi branch."

"You've triggered a bomb in federal courthouse," I snapped, "killed no telling how many people, including a federal judge, and you think they're just going to let you walk out of here?"

"Walk? Not at all, sir. I expect them to fly us out of here, in a helicopter from the pad on the roof of this very building. One large enough to accommodate the five of us and however many hostages we're not required to shoot before they accede to the inevitable and send us on our way. If anyone in this ungodly backwater had taken the slowly but surely coming Asian plague more seriously there would have been less of you to terminate today, and made for a less dramatic occasion for us all, but we were ready to go before the pandemic could arrive, so here we are. Prepared for all contingencies and in complete control of every person still drawing breath in this courtroom."

At this revelation, Anna Grace pressed her free hand into mine, then released me and clung to Malik's arm.

Seeing this, Finn took several steps toward Malik. "Now, this is a nice-looking young man. A good choice for your daughter, no doubt. But I wonder about his religion," he said to no one in particular, then focused a malevolent gaze on Malik.

The boy held up better than I probably would have at his age, but I could tell he was squeezing my daughter's hand too tightly. She gave no hint of the pain, however, as they both stood their ground. Had I the opportunity to speak privately with them, I would have suggested that challenging psychopaths while *they* were in charge was tantamount to petting a frothing, snarling mad dog.

But Finn was enjoying himself too much to spoil the fun by setting the dogs loose on the teenagers. At least not yet.

"Could it be," he said, circling Malik like a ghoul preparing to dine, "that you believe that Allah is the only God and Mohammed his prophet?"

Beads of perspiration pooled on Malik's forehead, rivulets of sweat snaked down both his cheeks. "I do," he said quietly.

"How fortunate for you, then, that you may soon enter paradise, meet your prophet face to face, no longer suffering the disability of knowing only one virgin."

Finn then turned on his heels and glared at Marshal Reed, then smiled at Gitt, "I suppose we must shoot one of you in order to show whoever lurks outside those doors we do mean business."

"No!" Anna Grace shouted, interposing herself between Finn and Malik.

I cringed at the sight, a father's worst nightmare forming a few feet in front of me. *Mother of God, please, don't let her sacrifice herself for any of us!*

Finn nodded to Gitt, who whirled and fired a round between Marshal Reed's eyes. The big man's head exploded, then his body lurched forward, tumbling headlong out of his seat and crashed to the ground in a bloody, rumpled heap. The court reporter screamed again and buried her head in her hands, precisely as Finn had wished.

"You in the courtroom!" boomed a deep voice from the other side of the main courtroom door.

Finn's charges immediately swung into action. Each moved closer to one of us, their pistols trained on our heads. Finn moved a step closer to the large doors at the main courtroom entrance and answered in an equally impressive commanding voice. "What do you want?"

"If you shoot any more of the hostages, we *will* rush the courtroom."

"And you *will* find a room full of corpses to go with the men you'll lose in the effort."

"Understood. But we'll do what we must."

"I'm sure you will. After which you may explain to the parents of these school children that it was upon your responsibility their children were sacrificed to your 'duty'?"

The voice outside the courtroom grew silent for a long moment. "What do you want?"

"Rotorcraft, if you please."

"What?" Anna Grace asked aloud.

"Helicopter," I whispered in her ear.

"What kind of bird do you want?"

"A Mi-26 would be nice."

"Wouldn't it, though? What about one for this reality?"

"Give me a Sydney."

"We don't have Disneyland or Six Flags around here. Anything else?"

"There's a Sydney in Memphis, I understand, and at least two in New Orleans. But if you insist upon being a skinflint, any Medevac bird with a capacity for nine or ten will suffice. Before you ask, I believe there's one at University Hospital on State Street. It'll have sufficient capacity once you remove the medical equipment." He gave a satisfied wink to Aziz.

"We can have it here in two hours, with extra fuel and provisions for a long flight. But we require something from you in return."

"I'm all out of Christmas cards and candy canes."

"I'll get over it. Meanwhile, we want hostages. Give us the teenagers. We know you have at least two in there. Why bring the kids into this?"

"A fine time for you worry about involving kids, after doing all you can to deprive them of their future my making war on other countries, selling out their constitutional rights, bankrupting their country and taxing them into penury."

"I plead guilty on all counts. But I haven't murdered any children yet."

"You will if you persist in stalling me. No teenagers, Mr. Hostage Negotiator. You can have one of the adults…Your U.S. Attorney, his honor the judge, or a woman. Personally, I'd take the woman, but that's up to you. Back away from the doors and make up your mind within the next five minutes. I'll give you thirty minutes to land my helicopter on the roof, whereupon I'll send your hostage of choice through these doors, you and your men will evacuate the building, then we'll make our way to the roof, and be out of your hair."

"I don't think we can---."

"Thirty minutes. We shoot one hostage for every five minute delay on our bird. As for the teenagers, remember the words of the great statesman and soldier of Republican Rome, Marcus Furius Camillus, who said he would take a city by Roman courage and arms, not hiding behind hostage children. I will release them as soon as we land, and notify the local authorities of their presence. But be warned, as with the Etruscan cities that defied Camillus and were burned to the ground, so too will we show no mercy if our demands are not met in full. Is that clear?"

"Crystal."

"Now, one more word from you and we shoot a hostage. Get me my bird, remove yourselves from the third floor, and have a nice day."

Without another word they herded us into a circle in the middle of the room, between the gallery and the counsel tables, seating us on the floor. They placed 'Jenny' among us, as if she were also a hostage. I was thankful she had the good grace to sit as far from me and my daughter as the circle allowed. Aziz dragged Breeland into the circle and laid him, apparently comatose, beside me.

Finn's cohorts seated themselves at 2, 6 and 10 o'clock in our circle. Each produced a grenade, which they hooked to their belts placing a finger through the pins. With their other hands, they held their pistols at the ready in case the swat team (undoubtedly assembled by now) rushed the room.

"Now you see where you stand, my friends," Finn said, as coolly as a celebrity relaxing on a Mexican resort beach with a drink in hand.

I understood now why these members of the new UFF had never been caught. Their planning was precise, if not prescient, and their execution as clever as it was audacious. But, I wondered anxiously, why they had revealed themselves this time, and why they hadn't sent a warning to evacuate the courthouse prior to bombing it as the UFF had always done? Were they the new face of domestic terrorism? Or was this to be their final mission? And if not, why bomb the courthouse in person, trap themselves inside it, and take hostages to affect their escape, something neither the old UFF nor any of these perps had ever tried before?

"We are prepared," he continued, "to lay down our lives for our mission, and we don't intend to make the journey to Hades by ourselves. So let's all relax and bide our time like big boys and girls. It'll all be over within a matter of minutes, one way or the other."

"And what will you have accomplished," I wanted to know, rising from the floor to face Ryan Finn. To my right and left, I could feel his men training their weapons on me and looking to their leader for instruction. He waved them off with a shrug as I took several very slow steps toward him. As I did, I heard Jack Ashton groaning to himself across the circle from me.

"If they charge the courtroom and we all die," I continued, now inches from my antagonist, "or take you and your men down on the way to the roof, what will you have accomplished? No one will even know what you were fighting for, if you even know, yourselves."

"Ah," he smiled, supremely at peace with himself and whatever demons he managed by force of extraordinary will every day. "Just this morning, I mailed statements to every major newspaper in America. They will know what we did here today, and why."

"If they print them. But as you seem intent on dragging us all down to Hell with you, would you mind telling *us* what you're doing it for? I think we have a right to know."

He regarded me like a first grader asking, "Is the moon really made of green cheese? "Was I not clear in my most elaborate missives to you?"

"Missives?"

"Yes. The Ferguson letters, the Short diary…Did you bother to read a single word I wrote?"

"*You* wrote?"

"Yes, *I* wrote, with a great deal of help from a friend. Or did you think Gitts, over there, took a break from torture and rapine to invent centuries of history specifically relevant to you?"

"A friend?"

"Does it surprise you to know that I have friends in high places?"

"By high, I presume you mean an out of work historian, or radical Ivy League history professor?"

"Such egregious use of redundancy, Mr. Ferguson! I must protest. Are there any gainfully employed Ivy League history professors who are not left wing radicals? Can you think of any other reason why the brainwashed neo-conservative majority in this country knows less of its own history than it does of rocket science? Really, Mr. Ferguson…. In what cave have you been residing this past century?"

Perhaps I had been thinking like a caveman hoping the letters and diary were anything but frauds, no matter how true to history they were, even the history of my very own family. But I had no time to feel the fool; their author now held my daughter hostage at gun and grenade point.

Even worse, this man had used those manuscripts to distract me from his terrorist scheme, blinding me to events happening around me, and the danger to my family. Now my Anna Grace and other innocents were paying the price for my blindness.

"How, Finn? How did you find the materials, put them together and get it done so quickly?"

Beaming with satisfaction, he replied, "All it takes is access to information and money, both of which are readily available at the press of a computer key, or for the price of a long distance call."

"But the Ferguson letters were so...so personal."

"The names of the Jefferson Troop and their movements before and during the Battle of New Orleans were accessible on the Web. A perusal of the Ferguson family tree on Ancestry.com revealed your connection to the good sergeant and his bride. My friend in academia provided the battle details, company rosters, and the rest. The small details, personal, as you call them, I extrapolated from letters of that region and era, or simply crafted them from whole cloth.

"The Short diary was drawn from manuscripts in the Cambridge and Harvard archives. They made for a diverting and profitable sideline to the main event, planning this, my own historic event."

"More like half-witted cluster fuck, I'd say. What did you plan to accomplish by blowing up innocent civilians? At least the international religious terrorists took a shot at the Pentagon. Why don't you guys ever take on the military you claim to hate so much? By all means, tell it to the Marines. They'd have a good answer for you, I'd bet. Or if you've got a problem with Congress, why not devote all that energy and money you spend on firebombing children in their beds to throwing the corrupt Washington politicians out on their asses? I don't suppose that ever occurred to you?"

"Don't be a simpleton, Mr. Ferguson. You know as well as I that Jefferson's and Franklin's predictions have come true. When congressmen vote to hire one private corporation to supply the military with jets and missiles for $16 billion a year, and that company kicks back a few billion to keep those politicians in office, who has the resources to successfully oppose them? Certainly not the citizen who pays 40% of his income in taxes. And what does he get for his money? Good public schools? Affordable health care? No! The streets are littered with the homeless poor, and even middle class people can't find jobs or pay their medical bills. And the rich, who already own more than nine tenths of the wealth of this country, get richer every day. You can't tell me that I'm wrong, Mr. Ferguson. You know every word I've said is true."

"What of it? Did you think this cowardly attack on a small town courthouse would cause the American public to suddenly rise up and launch a second revolution to overthrow this government? Or hand you a crown as Savior of the Republic? Or just a starched white straitjacket at the federal funny farm until the shrinks bring you back to reality long enough for some government-funded executioner to put a potassium chloride spike in your arm?"

For the first time since he'd entered the courtroom, Finn's mirth-filled-eyes grew darker, more piercing, brimming with the homicidal rage that drove him to the extreme lengths he had taken leading up to this blasphemous denouement.

"Naïve Americans," he grumbled, "giving lip service to your constitutional rights and principles, all but worshiping your brilliant founders on July 4th, then allowing your jaded presidents, greedy congressmen, and imperious federal judges to rob you of every freedom your founders held dear, and funnel every dime of your exorbitant peace-time taxes into corporate welfare, imperialist forgers of war machines, and bank accounts of half-wit politicians. And why? I'll tell you why--to fuel the decadent pleasures of the most obscenely wealthy aristocracy and bloated bureaucracy since imperial Rome."

I shook my head in disgust. "What the hell does any of that matter to you, a foreigner?"

"I've made this country my own!" he thundered, "and I intend to save it from the destruction awaiting it; that awaits every republic that degenerates into imperialism."

"Destruction? You're the only one causing any destruction around here! You and your confederates are the only ones depriving people of their freedoms, to say nothing of their lives, with your homemade war machines and perverse pleasures taken at the expense of innocent victims wherever you and your kind go."

His eyes narrowed to tiny sparkling lights, like the nearest stars in an otherwise pitch black night sky. His nostrils flared like the gills of an on-rushing shark as he spoke. "Jamahl, what was that Confucian quote you claimed applied so perfectly to our favorite government stooge, here?"

Without a moment's hesitation, Aziz replied, "When a government is corrupt, it is shameful to take an office and receive a salary."

"That's the one. You say I'm a murderer, Mr. Ferguson, and so I am. At least I'm not a lapdog for a government so corrupt and vicious that it destroyed millions of lives, enslaved or exterminated millions more, bombed others out of existence and starved as many to death in countries refusing to bend their knees to the `American Way of Life'. I'd rather serve the god of war," he snorted derisively, "than the god of mammon. My only regret is that I can't live a thousand lives worshiping at that altar until tyranny is finally eclipsed."

"Hey, Jamahl," I said, turning my back to Finn. "Didn't Confucius also say something like-- `if you make a mistake and don't correct it, that is also a mistake?"

Before either could respond, a loud knock on the main entrance wooden door caused everyone in the circle to flinch. Finn's men, by contrast, remained as motionless as statues, their eyes fixed on him, awaiting his orders.

He took two steps toward the door. "Yes?"

"We're ready to take a hostage. Send out the woman."

"As you wish. She'll need a moment to compose herself."

"Understood."

Finn extended his hand toward Jenny, gesturing for her to stand beside him.

She gave me one final, cold-eyed appraisal before obeying his command. As she traipsed across the room, I happened to glance down at Breeland, who to my surprise, caught my eye and shot me a quick, hopefully unnoticed, wink.

Great! That's two of us still in the game.

"So, Jenny," Finn said, if not with tenderness, then with more humanity than I expected to hear in his voice. "This is goodbye."

She scanned his face, the question hanging between them she knew better than to ask out loud.

But he anticipated her thought. "Yes. Have you ever known me not to keep my word?"

"No."

Now he searched her face for any hint of emotion, but finding none there, simply turned away and said, "Go."

She opened one of the large double doors. We caught a brief glimpse of the negotiator, a large, muscular, black man with a hawk-like visage, his eyes apparently trained on Jenny, but undoubtedly taking in all he could with his peripheral vision. He held the door open until Jenny passed through, and as it swung closed in a great silent arc, he made deliberate eye contact with Finn.

I gave Anna Grace as reassuring a look as I could muster. She smiled as if to say I'm still with you, dad. Hang in there.

Finn stood beside me, his fingers loosely steepled, a pensive expression on his face.

I suppressed a smile, knowing as I did that Jack had sent Jenny's photos, driver's license info, and physical description from the NCIC, and a detailed statement of her involvement in this case to every law enforcement agency in America, including of course, the Jackson police department and the local FBI office. She wouldn't make it out of the building, much less the city. During the debriefing session sure to follow her courtroom exit, an agent would recognize her from Jack's report generated from the photos Finn had sent him, and hold her in the courthouse jail until our situation resolved. Then she'd be off to a federal pen of a federal judge's choice. A judge fully aware that her gang had gunned down one of his colleagues in that judge's own courtroom.

So long, Jenny. I thought I felt something for you. Something real. Now I *know exactly* how I feel. If Finn or his jackals harm my daughter, and I somehow survive this nightmare, I'll definitely see you again.

Finn shouted at the negotiator through the large double doors. "You still there?"

"You know it."

"Where's my bird?"

"On the way."

"In the air, or are you having it delivered by courier?"

"It's leaving the hospital now. It will refuel at Hawkins Field and be on the roof here in twenty. Right on time."

"Good. Before I hear it land, you and all your men exit the building. If I see any other living soul on my way toward the elevator to the roof, my men will start plugging hostages. Understand?"

"Affirmative. You'll have unimpeded access to the roof."

"Make sure we do."

"We've gotten a lot done in a short time for you. Couldn't you at least leave one more hostage on the helipad, one or more of the teenagers? It doesn't do your cause any good to put innocent children at risk."

"I'll consider it. No, I'll do more than that. If we make it to the roof in good order, with absolutely no interference, I'll leave both of them on the roof."

"Thank you."

"But if anyone follows us, in the air or on the ground, you'll start seeing the other hostages take their first flying lessons, as many as it takes for you to back off our tail. Are we clear?"

"Yes."

"I don't want to hear your voice again, Mr. Negotiator, or see even a hint of your presence, or that of your charges, ever again. Starting now."

A loud slap on the door, followed by the rumbling sound of dozens of feet shuffling hurriedly down the hallway told us we had been left to the tender mercies of our captors.

CHAPTER FORTY

Finn motioned for Gitt to check the hallway and confirm what our ears had told us. He quickly returned, flashing a thumbs-up signal before rejoining the circle and replacing his finger in the pin of the grenade hanging on his belt.

After Aziz signaled Finn to a mini-conference out of hearing of our group, I motioned for Anna Grace to join me in the gallery. She sprang to her feet but froze when Gitt and the Ghost swung around to face her.

Finn motioned for them to stand down. Like automatons receiving a telepathic signal, both men promptly faced forward and resumed their vigil over the circle.

"What is it, dad?" she said softly.

I held her to me, facing away from Finn with her chin on my shoulder, her eyes also blocked from his view.

"Listen very carefully," I whispered. "Keep calm and put your thinking cap on."

"Okay…" she said tentatively, uncertain whether she cared to hear what I said next.

"Keep your head on my shoulder, like we're hugging, and don't reveal what I'm about to tell you to anyone for any reason. Our lives may depend on it. Deal?"

"Deal," she breathed.

"Do you remember the game we played with Will? The one about the birds, and what to do when someone said the name of a particular water fowl?"

The game was Every Bird's a Duck, and we last played it at Orange Beach in July. Would she remember and make the right connection?

I needn't have worried. Young minds always connect the dots.

"Yes, I remember."

"Good. Be ready to comply when you hear that certain word, understand?"

"Yes."

We passed a few quiet moments holding onto each other, unaware of each other's thoughts, but nevertheless feeling more in sync than we had in years. "I love you, girl. With all my heart."

"I know," she said, raising her head to be sure I saw the grin, then squeezed me so tight I almost groaned. "Love you too, dad."

"So," Finn said, "what are we discussing over here?"

"I could ask the same of you," I said, gently pushing Anna Grace away.

"Yes you could, if you were armed like me," he grinned, striding resolutely toward us. "You, girl.... What were you discussing? Gitt," he barked, pointing to Malik. The odd little man with the even stranger name stepped into the circle of hostages and held his pistol barrel to Malik's temple.

"Tell me, girl, or I give the order and Gitt air conditions your Muslim boyfriend's brains. Do it now."

She took a step in Finn's direction.

I tried to remain calm, but if Finn had seen my face at that moment he would have read the fear in it as surely as a prison 'convert' reads a Bible the day before his parole hearing.

"I was asking my father..." she began, holding his steely gaze with unimaginable courage for a sixteen-year-old girl with guns and grenades hanging on her every word, "I asked him if he thought we would get out of this alive."

"And his response?"

"He said we would."

"Very good. Is that all? Don't lie to me girl. One less heathen in the world would suit me just fine."

"No, that's not all."

"Go ahead."

"He said you wouldn't make it."

This took even the professional terrorist by surprise. But not for long.

"Did he say why? Or how?"

"Yes."

"Well? Don't keep your lover boy in suspense. He's standing under the proverbial Damoclean sword as you tarry."

"He said no one, not even you, could defy heaven forever."

Hearing this, Gitt gave a nervous laugh, and for the first time, I thought I saw a hint of emotion shimmer across Aziz's face.

Well played, girl! You make your old man very proud.

"What an eloquent father you possess, young lady. It seems he and I have the same gods in common. Now please…Return to your seat."

She eyeballed him fiercely all the way across the room, waited for Gitt to resume his position across the circle, then seated herself by Malik, holding his hands in hers.

I silently prayed they'd both enjoy long lives, bargaining with God the way only the truly desperate do, that if they'd bring her through this, I'd even settle for a Muslim wedding, no matter how strange her eyes might appear garlanded with Arabian Kohl liner.

Possibly reading my mind, or at least the expression on my face, Finn closed the distance between us and said, "I hope for both your sakes she's telling the truth."

"She is."

"Oh?"

"Yes. You're not going to make it."

A wry grin trolled across his lips as he gave a knowing look, began to speak, then changed his mind, turned on his heels and rejoined the Ghost near the circle.

Did he know, I wondered? Did he have inside information about the new governmental policy about hostage takers on federal property?

As Finn walked away, the strangest thought struck me—in another life he might have been a likeable fellow; maybe even a real priest, or at least a patriot and good soldier for God and his country. He was, after all, an educated man apparently not incapable of entertaining recognizably human feelings.

But this was not another life. It was the only one any of us would ever know. And we were all in danger of losing what little of it we had left because of his particular brand of insanity.

CHAPTER FORTY ONE

Of everyone in the shattered courtroom, only Jack and I knew what would happen next. Or so we hoped. We didn't know the when, where or the how, but we both knew the government's recently adopted non-negotiation policy included all U.S. Attorney's offices and federal courthouses throughout the country.

The government simply would not negotiate. Not under any circumstances, at least not any that had presented themselves since the Justice Department invoked the policy. A gallery full of school children might warrant an exception; there *are* exceptions to every rule. But ours probably wasn't one of them.

The marshals, Jack and I knew the score when we took the oath, or when we stayed on after the word filtered down from on high. I would never have approved Anna Grace's 'field trip' to my hearing today had I been given the option, but, as is so often the case, the barbarous fates gave no hint of the threat Jenny posed to my daughter.

Still, our situation wasn't entirely hopeless...Anna Grace knew to hit the dirt when I gave the word. Jack and Breeland were, despite their appearances, ready to act when the need arose. I hoped Breeland and Jack had learned something useful in ROTC at Millsaps that they could put to good use when the time arose.

And for all their inside information, Finn and his miscreants didn't appear to be aware of this nine month-old untested, unpublicized government policy.

In short, it was three middle-aged lawyers, a terrified court reporter, an apoplectic clerk and two saxophone-playing teenagers against four battle hardened domestic terrorists with the blood of dozens already soaking their hands.

I silently prayed for the courage of the Spartan at Thermopylae who, in response to the Persian threat that their arrows would block out the sun, replied, "How pleasant then, that we will fight in the shade!"

The frapping of helicopter wings suddenly assaulted our ears. Whatever the good guys were planning would happen very soon.

"Gitt?"

The diminutive Nazi checked the hallway, and finding it empty, signaled his leader.

Finn turned to Aziz and nodded.

Aziz removed his finger from the grenade pin and withdrew an odd-looking device from his jacket pocket. He pressed a button, and listened intently for...what?

Moments later we heard the sound of metal clanging loudly against metal, as if someone had slammed our jailhouse door shut.

"Done," said Aziz.

"You locked them out, didn't you," I blathered to Finn in amazement. "You had the code. All the doors to the outside..."

"Are locked for the next hour," he said confidently.

"They'll break in."

"We'll be gone by that time, or you'll wish they hadn't. Let's move," he commanded, glancing at his watch as he hustled everyone through the double doors. "We don't have much time."

The three other terrorists herded the rest into the hallway, except for Breeland, whom they left lying on the floor.

Lucky you, pal.

As Anna Grace and I moved through the doorway, Finn placed a hand on each of our shoulders, holding us with him in the doorway. "Tarry with me a moment," he said.

I stood beside Finn while Anna Grace and Malik clung to each other.

Gitt lead the group down the hallway, followed in turn by the Ghost, Jack, the court reporter, the Russian, and the court clerk. Aziz brought up the rear.

They hurried toward the elevator at the end of the hall that would carry them to the roof. Once he reached it, Gitt pressed the 'up' button and everyone waited anxiously for the rooftop elevator to descend.

Moments later we heard three strange sounds our minds couldn't fathom -thwip, thwip, thwip, followed by glass tinkling on the hall floor beneath the third window from the elevator. Aziz, the Ghost and the Russian crumpled to the ground without a sound, blood spurting from their chests or temples.

"Snipers!" Finn said, shielding himself with Anna Grace, glaring out the shattered window toward the fourth-floor of the building directly across Court Street.

"Finn!" Gitt shouted.

The German had ducked beneath window level to avoid sniper fire, only to see the elevator door swing open revealing a swat team rifleman who fired three heavy automatic rounds into Gitt's face, splattering his brains against the wall.

"Move," Finn shouted, holding Anna Grace by the throat and backing through the double doors. Malik and I followed them inside. Jack, the court reporter and the court clerk tumbled through the courtroom's double doors just as the first grenade he had thrown went off, thrusting them headlong into the air falling hard on the tile courtroom floor. Two successive explosions followed, loud enough to deafen us momentarily. But the south courtroom wall, reinforced with steel beams for this very purpose, withstood the blast without giving way.

I felt Finn's eyes boring holes through the back of my neck. "You knew," he said, releasing his grip on Anna Grace. She moved quickly to my side. "I did. Don't say I didn't tell you so. Your men are dead."

He lowered his head, his face serene as the surface of a lake on a calm, windless day. "A quick and merciful death."

My smile collapsed. "What? You... You knew, too, didn't you? You knew about our non-negotiation policy."

"Of course."

"You set your own men up to die?"

"No. They lived with the prospect of death every day, and they knew no fear. The only thing they weren't prepared to accept was prison-- the total loss of their freedom at the hands of a corrupt government. Going in, it was success or death for all of us."

"They didn't know about the new policy, did they? You never told them."

"I told them what they needed to know. They died as courageous martyrs to a noble cause. Those swat team killers from the elevator didn't know about *our* grenade policy either. They're dead too. But I hoped you had potential they did not."

"Potential?" I sniffed. Potential for what?"

"You studied Jefferson. Wrote about him, understood his views on an aristocracy of wealth as opposed to merit. You know where that always leads. Your forebear actually fought tyranny at New Orleans. I fervently hoped you understood."

"Guess I'm as dense as you first thought."

"You know, John, we're really not that different. We both understand that it's either the few or the many. There's no other way, and there never has been throughout the course of human history."

"My father is nothing like you," Anna Grace blurted.

Finn ignored her, holding his eyes on mine.

I met his gaze. "What she said."

"Then you're just another half-witted adherent of a tyrannical and imperialist government that has betrayed every principle of its founding. You're content to go down with the ship, deprived of your liberties, denied your natural rights, drained of your financial resources by the privileged few who wouldn't throw you an anvil if you were drowning. You're no different from your demotic countrymen, just another sheep to be shorn."

"So you were going to save us by killing us, is that it?"

He lowered his head, stared at the floor for a moment. "Do you know where your country went wrong, John?"

"When we let you in?"

He gave a weak smile and said, "It doesn't matter anymore. Not now."

"Why not?"

"We have," he said, glancing at his watch, "less than a minute left. Your fellow stooges outside can't get in to help you, and you can't escape this locked building in time unless you smash a window and leap out a third floor window to the concrete sidewalk below."

I glanced at Anna Grace who had moved beside Malik near the doorway.

"Now why would I want to do that?"

He brushed off my question. "At least I can say I did something about it, Mr. Ferguson. I died setting an example for other courageous freedom fighters to follow. What have you ever done besides step and fetch it?"

"I never raped anybody, murdered anybody, or made war on children. I managed not to blow up any buildings jammed with people, aristocratic or otherwise, who never did me any harm. Why didn't you take your half-assed war to Washington where the bad guys live, according to you? Why lash out at the little guys in the boondocks, the ones who, according to you, are just as much victims of this tainted government as anyone?"

He shrugged his shoulders in exasperation, as if he were a math professor enduring a student's passionate exposition on how negative numbers couldn't possibly exist. "They have eyes but cannot see," he mumbled, then aimed his pistol between my eyes. "It's *you*, Ferguson," he said, pulling back the hammer with his thumb, "you and all the other sheep who are really to blame, happy as you are to be sheered so long as your government's bread and circuses satisfy your pathetic needs."

Breeland leapt up from behind a bench and struck Finn's arm causing the gun to fire wildly to my left. Unfazed by the surprise attack, Finn back-handed Breeland with the pistol and fired at him twice as he tumbled backwards across a bench.

I couldn't tell where the bullets struck him, but I saw Breeland react to the shock of the blows before disappearing behind a bench.

Anna Grace screamed as he fell, drawing Finn's attention to her and Malik. "I can't stop this government today, but I *can* send one Muslim to Jahannam."

Malik instinctively covered his face with his hands, but Anna Grace leaped past him, shifting her body between them.

As Finn raised his pistol I shouted "no!" and dove at him from behind. For a split second I thought I heard his pistol fire, but a deafening explosion drowned out the sound as the blast blew us off our feet, shattered the floor to pieces, and sent us all hurtling downward through space.

EPILOGUE

One year and a week later
December 22nd
Will's Birthday

"Are you ready to go, Will? I have it on good information that Santa Clause will be there. Not a bad start to your birthday, huh?"

"I don't wanna' go," he frowned, poking his lips out farther than I had thought possible without twenty Botox injections.

"You don't want to go to a party?"

"I don't wanna' give up my present," he squeaked, cradling the green and red- wrapped object like a drowning man clutching a life preserver in the bitterly cold North Atlantic.

I tried to suppress a smile but didn't quite succeed.

"It's not funny," he whined. "I don't wanna'..."

Father Joe had phoned minutes earlier, asking if we could bring a wrapped present to the needy children's Christmas party at St. Peter's nursery. They had come up one present short, he related, and I was the only invitee as yet unaccounted for.

"Hurry on down, now, John," he said. "Bring Will with you. He'll enjoy the festivities too. We open presents in thirty minutes. We don't want to disappoint the little ones, do we? He's Will's age, and he lost his parents last March to the Covid pandemic, so I don't want to disappoint him. Whatever you have on hand should do nicely. You wouldn't be able to beat the Christmas rush at the stores to make it here on time."

"Are the choir and brass quartet rocking the hall?"

"Yes. And we've got a little surprise worked up for you, John. They're going to play a few of your requests this year." *Something we failed to do last year after taking your donation*, he as well as said in a decidedly non-apologetic tone of voice.

"No problem, Joe. We'll see you soon."

"No we won't," Will bleated.

Who could blame him, I told myself. He'd lost a great deal the past year; in fact his life had been all about loss since the day he was born.

And so, for that matter, had mine.

But what is life if not a perverse mixture of joy and loss? The capricious gods rarely answer your most heartfelt prayers and almost never give you everything you want without a monkey's paw to go with it.

This makes cherishing what they do bestow upon you, if only for a cosmic wink of time, all the more imperative, their benevolence always being of the transient, fleeting variety.

Yes, I had probably lost more than most, but I still had my life, and something infinitely more valuable than that, my son Will. When Anna Grace and I had lost Beth bringing Will into the world, I thought fate had apportioned us our unavoidable share of gratuitous misery. But unlike those ancient Etruscan soothsayers who divined the gods' inscrutable will from sheep's entrails and the flight of birds, I soon discovered, like ill-fated Caesar, that I knew nothing of the gods' calamitous designs for me and mine.

We do our best, all we can, to deal with the hand life deals us. But nothing can prepare a parent for the loss of a child.

Not a day passes when I don't walk by Anna Grace's room, now spic and span as never before, and feel that sense of desolation that only a child's passing brings. Her empty chair at the dining room table, her favorite songs on the car radio, these are the fulsome gifts the gods grant me every day.

"If you're lost and alone, or you're sinking like a stone, carry on...."

I mostly listen to my homemade CDs now.

Will took it very hard, of course, losing his sister and best friend. But young children are more resilient than you expect, and he probably held me together at the funeral far more than I ever comforted him.

Yet, when Beth's former Episcopal priest, Father Brian Sledge, (Father Joe had an earlier commitment) offered words intended to give us solace, the full weight of our loss settled on my chest like a thousand pound weight. "We celebrate not only Anna Grace's life here with us, but also the life she's enjoying now..."

What life is that? I wondered bitterly. She had suffered the most terrible loss of all—her life, and all that it might have been if...

If only. Just when I thought I wasn't going to make it through the service, the priest offered communion in the customary Episcopal and Catholic manner, saying, "Alleluia, Christ our Passover is sacrificed for us."

The people responded, "Therefore let us keep the feast."

Will shook my sleeve and pulled me down toward him. "What's wrong with the priest?" he asked.

"Nothing," I whispered.

"So why is he leaving if everybody wants him to stay?"

"What do you mean?"

"Well," he said somberly, "they said let us keep the priest..."

Sometimes the law of physics doesn't allow you to hold them as tightly as you'd like.

Nowadays, whenever I feel the blues coming on, or see a tear forming in the corner of my eye in the mirror, or catch Will peering wistfully into his sister's room, I take heart from the incredible courage and self-sacrifice Anna Grace showed in her final hour, and thank the gods that they at least allowed me the privilege of knowing her for sixteen years, and to be with her when her time came around. And that before she was taken, she knew love, from her mother, her brother, me and Malik.

And Will? His spirit was far too great, his loving heart much too strong, to let even Anna Grace's passing damage it beyond repair.

"Daddy," he asked me just the other day, "will Anna Grace recognize me when I get to Heaven too?"

"How could she not?" I smiled. "No one in heaven will have such beautiful blue eyes and gorgeous blonde curls as you. She'll be very happy to see you, Will. I promise you, it'll be as if the two of you never parted at all."

"Wow," he said, envisioning the reunion in his mind. Then, after a slight pause, he wondered, "Will Jesus be there, too?"

His question was undoubtedly in reference to the story I had recently told him about Anna Grace reading a children's Bible I had given her at the age of seven. She had suddenly sat upright on the couch and asking aloud, "Jesus died?" Surely, demonstrating one of the benefits of a good optimistic Episcopalian upbringing.

I think of that moment from time to time, just as I did this morning, while reaching for the right inducement for Will to surrender his present to a boy he never met.

"Speaking of Santa Claus and Jesus," I began.

Will eyed me suspiciously. "Will they be there?"

"Well if they aren't, this won't be much of Christmas, will it, buddy boy? Let's go catch 'em in the act."

"But I don't wanna."

"Will, do you remember what you learned in Sunday School? About how Jesus asks you to share your abundance with those less fortunate than yourself?"

"What is…'bundance'?"

"Things we prize. My brand new golf bag. That present you're holding."

"But I don't wanna'," he glowered.

"I tell you what. Let's head down to St. Peter's and let you meet Santa and hear what Father Joe says Christmas is all about, and after that, if you don't want to surrender your present, you don't have to. Deal?"

Grasping the present tightly in his arms, he peered around it suspiciously, and said with the maximum degree of hesitation, "Okay…."

During the drive, I couldn't escape meditating further on the notion of loss. Anna Grace, Will and I had suffered incalculable losses, hers being the greatest, but we hadn't suffered them alone. Not in those harrowing hours at the federal courthouse a year ago, and the terrible week leading up to it. Judge Wyngait, Josh Reed and several other marshals were gunned down in the courtroom; ten court personnel died in the first explosion, three more in the second, including a janitor trapped in the building who happened to be hiding in a closet directly below the place where Finn's second bomb exploded. Four swat team members died from the grenades loosed on them by Gitt, Gruzenko, Aziz and the Ghost, whose real name we never learned.

But at least their deaths were mercifully quick. According the FBI and local police reports, a clerk's office employee and his wife, as well as two other federal employees whose fatal flaws were those of holding information Finn needed, endured unimaginable suffering before he or Gitt finally ended their lives.

Then, weeks after that tragic event, we found out about Wyatt, my next door neighbor. As best as investigators could figure, he discovered Finn or Gitt peering through my den window, and assumed it was an admiring schoolboy peeping on Anna Grace. Instead of phoning the police, he tried to deal with the peepers himself. The police found his body weeks later, battered, bloodied and sodomized, his skull crushed to a pulp, his face smashed beyond recognition.

My neighbor and friend, who had always been there when Anna Grace, Will and I needed him the months after Beth died, and anytime afterwards when I needed a baby sitter or a friendly ear to wrangle, endured those last terrible moments of his life because he cared more for his neighbors than he did for his own safety.

And to make matters far worse, the Corona virus pandemic finally arrived in Jackson with a vengeance three months after the courthouse tragedy, killing hundreds of people in Jackson, thousands in New Orleans, and hundreds of thousands in America and worldwide. As Finnerin had predicted, many failed to take it seriously, and lost their lives as a result. But so did many others who took every precaution. But that, I've found, is the way of the world. Not just wrongdoers and the negligent suffer; we all suffer, some more than others, and often the good more than the bad. But that's life. Either we come to grips with that reality and get on with worthwhile lives, or drown in self-pity till the day we die.

To many, no amount of philosophy or religion can serve as a consolation for that brand of loss, whether death by murder or plague. But when I hold Will in my arms and see the pure joy in his eyes whenever I can find it there, I realize that I'm still luckier than most. And I finally understand what my father, the still happily married former World War II top turret gunner on a B-24, said on his 95th birthday, when he told me that he was the last surviving member of his flight crew, but was still holding on to his parachute.

But through it all we weren't entirely denied the little miracles that give us hope that, despite it all, we haven't been abandoned by the fates to a gruesome end in an unfeeling universe. Breeland fell twenty feet from the third floor to the second, landing on a twin bed one of the elderly judges kept in his office for lunch hour naps. As luck would have it, a doctor called to that judge's courtroom for jury duty had stayed on during the terrorist strike in case his services were needed. His attention to Breeland's chest wounds undoubtedly saved my friend's life.

Suffice it to say, Breeland has sworn off felony criminal cases. His declaration to that effect during our first Mayflower lunch after the bombings, before I could even hint at 'I told you so,' gave me more satisfaction than I can say.

Ironically, Jack Ashton took the blame for our unpreparedness for the terrorist attack, and got the sack several weeks later. The community reached out to me in sympathy and prevailed upon our U.S. Senator to recommend that I serve as interim U.S. Attorney until a final appointment could be made.

When they made their selection, I tendered my resignation and returned to private practice with Breeland, who preferred renewing our old partnership to another twenty years of kissing the asses of pompous senior partners and insurance company claims representatives. As neither of us cared to spend another second in the courthouse where Finn and his gang entered our lives, we were thankful Uncle Sam spent $75 million dollars on a new state of the art courthouse where

Breeland and I could harass the new U.S. Attorney and his staff by trying Natchez Trace-spawned DUI cases.

Otherwise, we generally limit our practice to representing worker's comp, Social Security and 1983 Civil Rights action claimants. People who, but for quirks of unfeeling fate, might share the largely contented lives that Breeland and I now mostly enjoy.

Of course, one of the benefits of being a lapsed Catholic/part time Episcopalian pagan is that I feel no obligation to forgive or mourn the loss of those who brought terror into our lives; nor need I concern myself with the fate of their eternally damned souls. Do not pass Go, skip Purgatory entirely, and go straight to Hell, every last one of you. As I'm fond of saying, that's the pagan way. Or as Confucius said, "give those who love you love, and those who do not, justice."

That none of the terrorists survived their terror strike gave little solace to those whose lives they diminished or to the parents, sons and daughters they murdered. But it certainly didn't hurt. At least that was my view of the reaction by most family members who suffered losses similar to mine during those dark times. Perhaps I'm not entirely alone in my pagan tendencies after all.

For weeks after those terrible events I wondered what possibly motivated brilliant men like Finnerin and Aziz to kill innocent men, women and children in the name of abstract concepts, gloating over their victims like a pack of drooling jackals holding high carnival over the remains of their butchered prey. Did they ever wonder about the lives they ruined? Did they never realize that, however right they may have been about their principles, taking innocent lives never advanced their causes, and, if anything, gave the wrongdoers in government another soap box to stand on for more self-aggrandizement and curtailment of our liberties in the name of fighting terrorism? And always, ALWAYS, at the expense of the people upon whose liberties governments and terrorists daily infringed.

Perhaps. When they autopsied Finnerin's body they found cancer in every major organ. He knew he was dying and taking his last mission. Just as he said, either escape or a quick death was all he asked of the fates. He got his wish, I suppose, at the expense of his people and mine. Either way, he certainly proved the maxim, aimed at the likes of Finnerin and his compatriots, that those whom life does not cure, death does.

For months I wondered, did he ultimately come to believe that he and his misguided compatriots needed to go? That their cause was hopeless and their future was a spike in the arm or a life sentence at a federals penitentiary very different from the country club prisons white collar criminals such as wealthy celebrities, businessmen, lawyers and politicians temporarily inhabited?

Did he intend to shoot me before Breeland intervened, or did he hold out hope, in his bizarre and twisted way, that I would ultimately see things his way, and carry on his fight? Did he intend to harm Anna Grace so I might understand loss, the same loss we later discovered he and Jenny had suffered years before? Or was that a miscalculation, a mere quirk of fate, owing to his lack of appreciation for the courage of a young woman, willing to sacrifice herself for those she loved?

And why did he hand over to the authorities his former wife, Jennifer Garrott, the mother of his dead child? He undoubtedly knew, as did I, that his submission to the U.S. Attorney's office of photographs of Jenny and me, *in pare delicto,* during an ongoing terrorist conspiracy, would alert every law enforcement officer this side of perdition to her identity and guilt. I can almost hear him say, "She wanted out of the life, and that's exactly what I gave her."

She languishes now, for twenty-five years to life, in a federal lockup in Yazoo City, Mississippi. Does *she* ever think about the lives she helped destroy? Or is she, like so many of her fellow inmates, impervious to feelings of guilt or regret?

If I learned anything about her during our time together, however false most of it proved, it was that I believe twenty-five years to life is a long time to spend with regret, and I believe she suffers infinitely more today than Finn and the rest of his pond scum ever did.

Then, one Saturday last summer, Will wandered into our den and asked me when we were going fishing for speckled trout at Breeland's beachfront gulf coast summer house in Pass Christian. At that moment, I realized that questions about terrorists were a complete waste of my time, unworthy of another moment's consideration. All that really mattered was watching my boy toss jig heads baited with live shrimp into gulf coast honey holes on warm summer evenings with clouds wandering lazily across an azure sky, and a warm, gentle breeze fondling my skin like a lover's indolent caress, tossing Will's blonde curls about like lush goldenrods in a sprawling south Louisiana meadow.

And I'll enjoy those afternoons with him so long as time, fate and he will allow it.

I turned off the interstate onto Amite Street, prompting Will to mischievously ask, "Are we there yet?"

"Not yet."

"Then... are we there yet?"

We got there moments later. Shortly after we arrived at the cathedral nursery, a large unevenly wrapped present glued to Will's hands, Father Joe greeted us at the door.

"Ah, John, I thought you might not make it in time. They're about to open their presents and the choir is ready to perform." He knelt down and tousled Will's hair. "And how are you this beautiful morning, young man?"

"Fine," Will replied warily, unable to take his eyes off the children gathering near the finely appointed Santa Clause across the room. Dozens of presents wrapped in glittering red and green paper lay stacked by his chair.

"And I see you brought a present for little Jackie. What a thoughtful little boy you are, Will. You'll bring a big smile to his face today, you bet."

But Will wasn't so sure. He turned to me, the conflict dancing in his eyes.

"Daddy?"

"Yes?" I winked at the priest, who instinctively and unobtrusively made his way back to the stage where Santa played his big scene.

"I don't know what to do. What should I do?"

To my surprise and delight, the choir and brass ensemble launched into one of my year-old requests, a prayer to Mother Mary entitled, *Inviolata Integera et casta*, by my favorite composer, Josquin. Although the choir expertly rendered the piece in Latin, I knew the translation well—"May our souls and bodies be pure. Through your prayers' sweet sounds, grant us forgiveness for ever."

Such is the way of the faithful—forgiveness for all sin. Or so Father Joe reminds me every chance he gets. Well…I'd see about that in due time. More pressing concerns required my attention at the moment.

"I can't tell you what to do son," I said, holding Will's big-eyed gaze as I tussled his cotton-top curls. "I believe that, in your heart, you know the right thing to do. Is it better for you to open a big pile of presents on Christmas morning, and for little Jackie to go completely without? Or is there something you could do in, keeping with the Christmas spirit, to make Jackie's holiday a little better this year than he's ever known before?"

As if on cue, a little Asian-American boy of three stepped out from the crowd of expectant children, raised his hand and waved at Will.

Will turned and gave me a quizzical look. I nodded "yes" to his unspoken question.

He paused for moment, as if making a difficult decision, then shuffled across the room and handed the present to Jackie. "Merry Christmas, little boy," he said.

No matter how often you see it, there's nothing more wonderful than the way children express joy in those moments when they suddenly realize that life holds more surprises than they realized, even with all their extravagant powers of imagination.

Well, almost nothing.

To say that my heart swelled with pride at that moment would be to grotesquely understate my feelings. "Way to go, Will," I said, taking him in my arms. "You're mother and sister are smiling down on you right now, as proud as they could be."

Moments later, from the far corner of the room, we watched Father Joe and Santa Clause, the representatives of the holy and pagan spirits of the season, hand over presents to the grateful little toddlers.

"I love you, Daddy," Will murmured.

"I love you more," I barely managed to squeeze out past the gargantuan lump in my throat. If he later asked me if we could go by the toy store for a replacement, or drop by the bookstore to see if any new Christmas books had arrived, I never heard him say it.

To my mind, just as his sister had been, he was the very portrait of human perfection, and I saw no need to muddy that mental image with anything human, all too human.

Or perhaps it was the exultant blaring of the next song by the brass ensemble that drowned out every sound in the room. Although this one was unaccompanied by the choir, I knew the words of this very English Renaissance song by Robert Parsons-- *Deliver Me From Mine Enemies*.

Nor did I miss Father Joe's knowing glance in my direction.

I closed my eyes, held my boy close, and lost myself in the moment, silently recalling the all-too apropos words of the refrain--

"Deliver me from mine enemies. O my God:
Deliver me from them that rise up against me.
Deliver me from the workers of iniquity,
And save me from bloody men.

The End

www.ingramcontent.com/pod-product-compliance
Lightning Source LLC
LaVergne TN
LVHW091530060526
838200LV00036B/549